RAZOR'S EDGE

THE COWBOY AND THE DOM
BOOK 2

JODI PAYNE

BA TORTUGA

Razor's Edge: The Cowboy and the Dom, Book Two
Copyright © 2020 by Jodi Payne & BA Tortuga

Cover illustration by AJ Corza
http://www.seeingstatic.com/
Cover content is for illustrative purposes only and any person depicted on the cover is a model.

ISBN: 978-1-951011-28-4

Electronic edition published by Tygerseye Publishing, LLC, January 2020
Printed in the USA

CONTENTS

As always, to our wives.

1

"You want a ride home, little Sammy?" Angel looked tired and a tad grumpy.

Sam got it. It was four in the morning, and no one liked that time—just getting up or getting off work.

"You going that way? Toward Thomas's, I mean."

The big man looked over at him slowly, fingers combing his beard. "Thomas's? At this hour?"

"Yessir. We cleaned out James's place. It was time." Sam's late brother's apartment had been hanging over the two of them for too long. They'd cleaned it out; then he'd moved in with Thomas. Crawling into bed with his lover was amazing. A lot of things he was learning these days were pretty fucking amazing. Hell, he could feel Thomas with him, feel the sweet sting of his Dom's stripes right across his shoulders. It was proof they weren't alone, either of them.

"What, really? Thomas was really ready to do that? You need a place to stay, I got an extra room."

"That's kind as all get-out. Seriously. But I'm okay." Oh, maybe it was supposed to be a secret. Thomas had said it was important to him, to keep things where they belonged.

God, he needed to keep his fucking mouth shut. "I-I think I'm going to go take myself to breakfast, man, get some reading done, but thanks."

"Shut up, Sammy. It's not like I don't know he's your Master. Are you and Thomas a romantic thing now? Is this supposed to be some big secret because he's coming off a relationship with James? Don't be stupid. I'll give you a ride."

"Thanks. I appreciate it." He didn't know if it was a secret, if he was a secret. He hadn't even considered it. He'd been so caught up in everything, so proud to be with Thomas, that he hadn't been thinking.

In some ways he was always going to be a giant redneck.

"I'll tell you, it's a good thing you told me, because I was about to make a move myself. No lie. Leave it to Thomas to get two O'Reilly brothers. The little shit."

Angel led him out to that big Harley.

"There seems to be something about him, yessir."

About to make a move on *him*? Sleeping with Angel would be like sleeping with his big brother, Bowie. They were just alike, the two of them—huge. Angel was Thomas's good friend and Sam trusted him with his life, but the idea of...*whoa. No.*

He would let Thomas take him in every possible way. The idea of doing that with someone else made his butthole pucker.

"Hardly seems fair." Angel climbed on and offered him a hand, grinning wide. "Well, at least I can still get you to ride bitch."

"Absolutely. And you're on the top of my list for fixing me when I'm broke."

"If Thomas breaks you, I will break his head." Angel looked back at him. "Not joking." They took off down city streets that were much too bright for the darkest hour of the morning, and eerily deserted too. Angel didn't seem to care much for stoplights or speed limits or really anything that might be considered obeying traffic laws. He loved it, loved the adrenaline rush, the way Angel drove. It made him want to learn to drive a motorcycle.

Thomas lived on a more residential street, and Angel did back off the throttle a little so the Harley rumbled rather than roared, but Sam was still pretty sure they could be heard three blocks away. "You okay? You want me to walk you in?"

"Thomas will be sound asleep, I bet. I'd hate to wake him. Thank you, though." Angel had been a dream, driving him home, making sure everything was good.

"We won't. I won't come in. I just want to make sure you get in all the way."

He nodded. "Thank you. Y'all are all good to me."

They got into the building, and the elevator crawled up. He blinked slowly; now that he was close to home, he wanted a shower and a bowl of cereal and to curl up with Thomas. Possibly on his belly. Get the fabric off his sore shoulders.

When the elevator doors opened, he chuckled as Angel walked him to the apartment door. Sam fumbled his key out, dropped it, and picked it up, sighing at himself. "Ready for a long nap and a day off."

He put the key in the lock, grabbed the door handle, and bit out a "Fuck!" as a razor blade sliced into his palm.

"You okay? What the—shit, you're bleeding." Angel took the blade from Sam's hand and opened the door. "What the actual fuck?"

Sam stood there, staring at the razor, just stunned. *No. No way. No fucking way.*

He'd thought it was a prankster in James's building.

"Sammy? You okay, man? Go inside." Angel made him move, closed and locked the door behind them. "Hey. Sam."

"I don't understand." *God.* This wasn't a dipshit at the apartment. This wasn't a trickster. No. This was about him.

It was about him, and now he'd brought it to Thomas. The asshole followed him to Thomas's building.

Fuck. This was fucking about *him.*

His mind spun, and his heart pounded. "I need to see if Thomas is okay."

"If..." Angel started to question him but must have seen how serious he was. "Go. I'll be right behind you."

But before they made it halfway down the hall, Thomas called out for him. "Sam? Is that you? Everything okay?"

"We need you out here, Tommy."

"Angel?"

"Now, Tommy."

Sam just kept walking, his hand closed against his chest. He needed to see Thomas, to make sure he was...intact.

They met in the bedroom doorway, practically colliding in Thomas's hurry to join them. "Sam? Angel? What's going on? Sweetheart?"

Sam searched Thomas's eyes, which were sleepy and worried, but his lover was whole.

Angel held up the razor blade. "On your door. He wouldn't let me clean him up before he saw you."

Sam had brought this to Thomas's home. Him. *Goddammit.*

Thomas stared at it and sighed. "Fuck." Thomas looked back at him. "I'm fine. You need to let Angel look at that, boy. I'm calling Colletti."

"I'm sorry." He headed to the kitchen and stuck his hand

under the water, staring at nothing. He needed to...he ought to...he was...

Angel followed him, and he heard Thomas on his cell phone in the bedroom. "Who's Colletti? Sam. Hey." The water suddenly went ice cold.

His eyes flew open, his entire body jerking with the shocking chill. "I have to take a walk. I'll be back. I'll bring coffee."

What the fuck was wrong with him?

"Like hell you will. You're in shock, Sammy. You need to sit down." Angel took him by the arm. "Come on. You're going to sit and let me see that cut."

Angel sat him down, staring right into his eyes. This wasn't Angel his buddy talking now; this was Angel the EMT. Angel the retired Army combat medic. "Breathe, Sammy. In and out. Just relax. You're okay."

He wasn't okay. He wasn't okay at all.

"Hang on." Angel wrapped his hand up in a kitchen towel. "Sam? Do you know where you are?" He thought he felt fingers, pressure on his wrist.

"I need to get out of here. Somebody followed me." *Poor Thomas. God.*

"Detective Colletti is going to call me back in the morning."

Thomas.

"Is he okay?" Thomas knelt by his chair. "Sam, are you okay?"

"He's tachy, pulse is high. Not really focusing. I'm gonna guess he's altered. Special K probably, maybe on the blade. A little goes a long way."

"What? Are you kidding?"

"He keeps saying he has to go."

"Oh, Sam." A warm hand pressed into his cheek. "Sam, look here."

"I'm sorry." He forced himself to stay perfectly still, because this was going to hurt. "I brought this here somehow."

He was going to have to leave.

"Stop, Sam. He might just as easily have followed me. Or us. It was probably both of us when we were moving James's things and your things. This isn't on you. But we're going to catch him now. Colletti's on it. He'll call us in the morning."

"Shit, this is a thing?" Angel asked. "Like, it's happened before?"

"Sam cut his hand a bunch of times in the other building. Even I did once. And whoever mugged him took James's coat and nothing else. This is real, Angel. Really fucking real."

"Oh, fuck." Angel looked like thunderclouds were forming in his mind. "I can't fucking believe it. Let me see your hand, Sammy."

Sam looked to Thomas, frozen where he was. He'd known Thomas would agree that he should leave. That Thomas would say it wasn't worth it.

"Yeah. He's out of it." Angel just took his hand.

"Sweetheart, I'm right here. I've got you; you're safe, okay? Angel says there was something on that blade that's got you a little...stoned."

"I don't suppose you know when his last tetanus shot was?"

He heard Thomas snort.

"I'm going to call Gina. She's on tonight. He needs a tetanus shot and some stitches. Take some blood. It'll take a few. You keep him here and calm."

"I need to—I'm sorry." *And scared.* What if this was

punishment for falling in love with Thomas? What if this was all his fault?

"I've got him. I'm just going to take him to the couch. Hope Gina doesn't mind my boxer briefs. Come on, sweetheart. Come with me." Thomas pulled him out of the chair, but walking was hard, so he floated a little and landed on the couch in Thomas's arms. "You need to relax and stop saying you're sorry. There's nothing to be sorry for."

Sam took a couple of deep breaths, trying to clear his head, trying to focus.

Okay. Come on, Sam. Get with the program. Wake up. Focus. "I was going to take a shower." *A shower, a bowl of cereal, snuggling.* "I thought he'd gotten in, gotten to you."

"You were scared, huh? I'm okay, sweetheart. I'm fine. And you'll be fine once this...shit...wears off. Colletti thinks this is good. He thinks we'll catch him now."

Thomas just held him still and close. It wasn't snuggling, but it didn't suck.

"I vote we electrify the doorknob."

His words drew a harsh laugh from Angel. "I like it, Sammy. Fry the motherfucker."

"Security camera. There are some outside the building, a couple inside too. Maybe Colletti can get the recordings. We'll put one on the door." Thomas stroked his head, his back.

He felt the hint of ache, the buzz from where Thomas had marked him, and his body relaxed, his panicked thoughts slowing.

"Gina is on her way."

———

BETWEEN HIS DAY WITH THOMAS, work, the panic, the drugs —nobody was happier than Sam was when the EMTs quit poking at him and headed back out the door. Angel saw the paramedics out safe and promised to stop by the next day to check in.

Thomas locked the door, including securing a chain that he'd seen hanging but hadn't seen Thomas use before. "You want that shower, babe?"

"I do. I smell like beer." He stood up, telling himself he needed to act like a normal, functional human being, not a stoned, stitched-up, freaked-out asshole.

Thomas caught him under one arm with a smile. "You look a little like you've been drinking it." They headed down the hall together, that arm through his sturdy and warm. "You need help? Or can you manage with that hand? Or—is that a dumb question because you've broken every bone in your body and have somehow managed to shower on your own for twenty-five years?"

"Almost twenty-six." Did he need help? No. Did he want help? God, yes. There were terrors and guilt waiting in the back of his brain, and he didn't want to be alone with them.

"God, you're getting old. I better come help." He got a kiss and a smile, and Thomas started helping him undress. "You do smell like beer. Wow."

"It's Saturday night. I had four thrown at me. It was great."

Thomas just gave him a shake of the head.

He knew why his lover never said a word about the bar. It wasn't disapproval or a judgment on him. Thomas just didn't like it. He hadn't liked it from the start—since his initiation. But his lover seemed to understand that he needed the work and never asked him not to stay, never made a stink about his choices.

Thomas got the water hot and muscled him into the shower, then set his hand up on the tile to keep it dry.

He was already feeling less fuzzy—more tired and drained from the adrenaline rush, but those sensations he knew at least—and he just...well, he didn't understand. Why him? Why James? Why them? Was it someone from the building? Someone he worked with at Mike's? How could it be? James didn't go to Mike's, hadn't ever. Someone at Thomas's men's club? Why him, then? No one knew about them, and Angel had just found out tonight.

Oh. Angel knew. He needed to apologize to Thomas about telling their secret. He also needed to remind Thomas that he wasn't completely clear on all the rules and what was a secret and what wasn't and, shit, Angel was a friend. A real friend. But still, he needed to figure out what was between them and the bedpost and what wasn't.

Maybe he just needed a shot or twelve and a nap.

Was six thirty in the morning too late to start drinking?

"Earth to Sam. Give me your head. Where'd you go?" Thomas started scrubbing shampoo into his hair and massaging his scalp. Oh. Thomas was actually in the shower. Like, in it with him.

"I was caught in my brain." He hummed at the touch and leaned. He'd never done this—been with a lover in the shower. He didn't want to miss a second of it.

"Mm-hm. I've made it my personal mission to get you out of your brain. Or at least into the fun part." Thomas tipped his head back into the spray and scrubbed the soap out. "Like this. This is the fun part."

"Yes, Sir." He closed his eyes and let the world tighten to right here with Thomas. He should be worrying, but he was just wearing down.

"We are going to finish getting you cleaned up, and

you're going to go to bed. And you're going to stay there until this darkness under your eyes goes away and you have color back in your face. So tell me who I talk to at the bar, because you're not going in tonight."

"Daddy Mike." He answered without thought, without argument, because the idea of bed and Thomas and rest captured him.

"Good boy." Thomas spent some time with him, running gentle, soapy hands over his skin just because he needed it, not asking or expecting anything from him but that he stay present. They toweled off, and they both had a laugh as Thomas combed his hair. "This is a new one for me. Fun, but new."

"Me too. My first shower with a lover." He was living in a world of firsts.

"Really?" A kiss caught him by surprise, and Thomas winked. "You got ripped off. I'll make it much more fun next time."

"Sounds like a plan. I'm not feeling like Super Fun Boy right now." He tried for a smile. "Angel offered me a ride home; he does most nights. I told him I was staying here. He was shocked, and I didn't realize I maybe shouldn't have said anything. If I wasn't supposed to, I'm sorry."

"I appreciate that he gets you home safely, especially tonight. Why shouldn't you say anything? Are you worried about your job or something?"

"No. No, he just seemed like…" He closed his eyes as he tried to remember. "Like he was surprised. He offered me his spare room."

"Hey." Thomas took his hands, leading him back into the bedroom. "I'm proud of you as my sub, and I'm happy to show you off as my lover to anyone who is looking my way. Will some people be put off by it? Maybe, but it's really none of their affair. Angel probably seemed shocked because the last he knew we were still essentially negotiating. You and I have grown together very quickly, and I haven't spoken to him since you moved in. That's all. He didn't know because I hadn't had a chance to say anything, not because I don't want the whole world to know you're mine."

"Good." He leaned in, filling his senses with Thomas, letting it soothe the sore spots, let Thomas into the tender bits that needed loving on. "I felt you with me, all night."

Oh, Thomas liked that. That little growl deep in his lover's chest said it all. "Come to bed, sweetheart."

"Yes, Sir." He let Thomas settle him, prop him up and around with pillows and Thomas's body until he could melt into the comfort. A deep sigh escaped him.

"You sleep and trust that I've got this. I've got you." Thomas kissed him lightly. "Rest."

"Got me." He was gone before he could kiss Thomas back.

2

Over the years Thomas had called Angel for all kinds of assistance, though he'd never had to ask the man to babysit before.

But when Detective Colletti's "Hey, I'll call you tomorrow" turned into "We need you to come down to the precinct," accompanied by two uniforms at his door, he didn't have much choice. There was no way he was leaving Sam home alone.

He wasn't particularly worried about the cops. They wouldn't be able to tie him to any of this insanity because he hadn't had anything to do with it. He tried to be understanding that the cops had to clear people and that he had been James's lover, but after all this time, being their only potential suspect was starting to grate on his very last nerve.

He was worried about his boy, though. He'd spent so much time soothing Sam and making sure his boy felt safe; he was very concerned this could unravel all of that.

The little holding room he was in had not one but *two* cameras, and he glanced at them both, wondering which one was recording and which one was the live feed. He really wanted to get someone's attention; he'd been sitting here forever.

The door opened and Colletti stormed in, face like a thundercloud. "Your attorney is here."

He blinked at the detective. "My—"

"Don't say another word, Thomas."

Well, this was interesting. He hadn't retained an attorney and yet a gentleman in a sharp suit, whom he'd never set eyes on in his life, walked in behind Colletti and placed an expensive-looking leather briefcase on the table. From it, the man produced a business card and handed it to him.

"This would be your third interview with my client?"

"We have new evidence that suggests—"

"Do you? Were his fingerprints on the razor blade?"

"No, but—"

Oh, this was entertaining. Sort of like watching a lion getting ready to pounce.

"But? What's your new evidence, then? I dare you to tell me his prints were on the doorknob to his own apartment."

Where the hell had this guy come from? Had Angel called a friend? This man didn't seem like the type, but you never knew. Making assumptions was almost always a mistake.

"Mister...?"

"Blackwell."

"Mister Blackwell, I'd like to—"

"I'm sure you would, but you can't." Blackwell put another card on the table in front of Colletti and closed his briefcase. "If you wish to contact my client, you may do so through my office. Don't harass Mister Ward any further."

Blackwell gestured to the still-open door. Thomas stood, unable keep from grinning, put the card into his back pocket, and nodded to Colletti. "Nice to see you again, Detective."

"I'll be in touch."

Uh-huh.

Blackwell led him out, where he ran right into Clint, Angel, and a glaring Sam.

"We can go?" Sam asked Blackwell.

"We can."

"Excellent. Let's go. Now." Sam pointed toward Angel and Clint, then toward the door. "Y'all too. Move it. I promised to buy coffee."

Then Sam came to him. "You okay? I hurried as fast as I could to fix it."

"I...I'm fine?" Yes, that was a question, because for as long as he'd known Clint, he'd never once heard anyone tell the man to "move it." He was rather concerned that allowing his sub to do so might land him at the business end of Clint's bullwhip. "Am I...what am I missing here?"

Clint arched an eyebrow. "Mister O'Reilly was incredibly concerned about your well-being. He insisted that Angel and I assist him in finding you representation. Rather firmly, in fact."

"Damn straight. I am tired of this shit. They can't figure it out, so they mess with you? Fuck that. No more games, right, Blackwell?"

"Absolutely not."

Angel looked like he was about to bust out with laughter.

Fuck that, indeed. Every single fucking bite of Clint's whip would be worth it. Sam was fired up, and his lover was the hottest fucking thing he'd ever seen.

He couldn't recall the last time he'd found himself speechless, but he wasn't at a loss. He and Sam communicated just fine without words. He pulled his lover in hard with both hands and kissed him.

Sam didn't hold back a bit, giving him everything. When their lips parted, Sam took a deep breath. "Right. Better. I promised everyone coffee. I had to haze everybody a bit to get them moving in the direction I needed."

He laughed and winked at Sam. "Good boy. Make mine a triple."

He looked over Sam's head at everyone. Angel, grinning like a fiend, Clint, who looked a little like he'd eaten something bitter and was trying to decide exactly what he was going to wash it down with, and Mr. Blackwell, who in profile was suddenly quite familiar. It was the suit that had thrown him off; he'd only ever seen the boy half-naked at the club.

"I'm on it. Come on, y'all. Let's blow this popsicle stand." Sam grabbed the door and held it, herding them out. "Now, before they decide to take him back. All y'all did so good. I'm tickled shitless. Thank you."

He looked at Clint as they headed out the door, still grinning. "I'm tickled shitless as well. How about you?"

"Well, I'll be honest, I'd rather never have to spring you from the clink. But I will say your Mister O'Reilly is...determined."

"He is that." His boy was getting whatever he wanted later. "Did he tell you what's going on? That someone drugged him last night?" It was dusk and getting colder as they left the precinct, and they all pulled their collars up against the wind. Christmas was coming and the coldest part of the winter along with it.

"Angel did, yes. I want to speak with you about some extra security cameras. Something. This is insane."

"No shit on that. I'm going to start sitting outside the

door and zapping anyone that slows down with a cattle prod." Sam didn't sound like he was joking. "Coming to your goddamn house and taking you off like some motherfucking criminal. Asshats." Clint stared at Sam, and Sam stared right back and gave Clint a nod. "I appreciate your help, Sir. You're a good man. What do you want for your coffee?"

"Master Clint drinks it black, boy." Then his mentor would doctor it with who knew what. He'd never asked, and he didn't care. As far as he was concerned, it was Vitamin B. Clint was the best friend he'd ever had. "That would be great, Clint. We need a camera on our door at all times. Something sneaky that this guy can't see. And I'd like eyes on Sam."

"Yes." Clint chuckled softly. "He's committed to you. Totally. He threatened to beat Angel with his own arm, apparently. I might pay to see that."

"At this point, my friend, I would put absolutely nothing past him." He stopped outside the coffee shop, and this time he held the door for everyone. "We're committed to each other. You gave me excellent advice; we're creating a...a more integrated dynamic. It's heady. I'm so proud of him."

Angel ushered Sam and Blackwell through the door, then turned to smile at him, the look utterly wicked. "You should be. If you ever decided to let him go, I would snap him up in a second and turn him inside out."

Nothing riled Thomas up like a little competition. But where Sam was concerned, he was starting to love that rush. "Been there, done that, Gabriel. The boy has the welts to prove it."

Angel kissed his cheek, playful as hell. "Good for you, Tommy. Seriously. You found another great boy."

"Don't keep yourself off the market too long; someone deserves you."

"Yeah, yeah. Right now, I have my hands full with the two of you."

Sam and Blackwell came back with coffees and pastries, Sam's eyes on him like a hawk's. "Triple for you and a chocolate croissant. Do you need protein? I can get you a real sandwich or some cheese or something."

"Thank you, sweetheart, I'm fine." He was unaccustomed to having someone look out for him, but his boy did it so earnestly. Naturally.

Unconditionally.

If the boy's rewards added up any higher, he'd be the one on his knees.

"Y'all? I got black for Mister Clint and a caramel mocha for Angel. There's a bear claw, apple fritters, and a couple three random doughnuts. Y'all want anything else?"

Clint shook his head, "No, Mister O'Reilly. I'm fine."

"You did good, Sammy." Angel snagged the bear claw.

"Clint, are you closing Christmas week as usual?" The question was meant as small talk, but as soon as it was out of his mouth, he needed a deep breath. He was...going to miss the beach.

Clint offered him a half smile. "We are. No one wants to work over the holidays, hmm? We'll be open for the thirty-first, of course."

"Yes, of course. Some traditions have to hold."

A week ago, he hadn't thought he'd be going to the annual New Year's Eve party. Sam hadn't been ready, and he hadn't been interested in going alone. Now? Well. His newly integrated self thought maybe they'd talk about it, and he'd leave the final decision to Sam.

As for holiday plans, he didn't have any. He couldn't quite look at that yet. But something would have to give soon. At the very least, he had a boy that would be missing his family traditions.

"Are you going to stay home this year, then?" Angel took another doughnut. "I don't know that I've ever known you not to head out to the beach."

Thomas saw Sam's quick glance, but his boy didn't say a word.

He looked at Angel meaningfully. "Not this year. Sam's still getting settled at the apartment. The beach isn't going anywhere."

"Maybe we can share a meal together, then. It would be something else, to get together for a celebration." There wasn't a bit of guile in Angel's voice, just a hint of hope.

He reached out and cupped his hand over Angel's wrist. "I think that sounds lovely, Gabriel. I appreciate you thinking about us. Sam and I haven't discussed Christmas yet—can we talk more about it later in the week?" He hated to shut Angel down, but he just couldn't have this conversation right now. He wasn't ready.

"Of course. I'll be around." Angel leaned over to Sam. "How's the hand, Sammy?"

"What hand? It's fine." Sam had his hand mostly hidden in his coat. "You always nag, wingman. I'm good."

"Gentlemen, for the record, I just want to say thank you to each of you, but especially to my boy, who I am exceedingly proud of today. I feel he deserves the praise, out loud, in front of people whose opinions matter to me."

Sam blinked at him. "Well, you're more than welcome. I got your back, Mister. Always."

Thomas laughed softly and gave Sam a nod. "I appreciate that." He stood up, offering a hand around to shake. "I'm sure you will all understand that I'd like to get Sam home. It's been a day."

"Yessir." Sam shook Clint's hand, then Blackwell's. "Y'all rock. I swear to God. You saved me from getting my ass handed to me." Angel got a hard hug. "You're a good friend. I appreciate you."

"Sam's right, Angel. You just come through for me over and over again. Thank you so much." He gave Angel a bro-hug and a nice slap on the back.

"Clint." He and Clint exchanged nods. Clint's look made it clear they'd be talking seriously again soon. "And Mister Blackwell." He grinned. "Sam, you'll remember Mister Blackwell if you look carefully. The last time you saw him he was...a little tied up." That had been a kiss to remember. It's was almost hard to believe Sam was the same man.

Blackwell raised an eyebrow and didn't even so much as blush.

"Good on you, honey." Look at that smile—warm and friendly and not even the slightest bit sarcastic—even though it came with more than a bit of a blush. "I appreciate your help. I owe you. You call on me if you need me."

"I'll do that. You should be proud of the way you serve. It was a pleasure to meet you."

Thomas had to smile. Those were conventional words and he liked them, but he doubted that Sam would use those terms himself. Sam held out his arm. "Come on, Sir. Let me take you home. You've had a shit day."

"Goodnight, everyone." He smiled at Sam and took his arm. Once they got out on the sidewalk, he gave Sam's arm a squeeze. "It got a great deal better. You should have seen the look on Colletti's face. Blackwell just shut him down."

"I was going to be damned if they booked you. I know you. You didn't hurt James. You won't hurt me. I just started bellering until somebody listened and did what I needed them to do. You got good friends." Sam curled his lip. "I told

Angel that he didn't want me getting the boys from the bar in on this shit."

"Oh, no. No. That would have been...no." The idea was to stay out of jail, not be locked up with seven or eight of Sam's bar buddies. "I appreciate your faith in me. Your trust. I would never have hurt a hair on James's head. I loved him."

"I know. And you know that I would bring him back for you if I could, but I can't." Sam patted his arm. "You got me, though, and I got your back. You were the one he went with to the ocean, huh? He loved that. He always told the best stories when we got together for our shared birthday."

He nodded. "Usually somewhere in the Bahamas or the Caribbean. We loved the beach, the water. It was relaxing and fun and we just went...we just went as lovers. Just...us." Those were good memories, ones he used to remember even when James was alive. Tan skin, rested, happy smile, something cold and alcoholic in James's hand. Good times.

He looked at his boy. "I do have you. But you're not just the next best thing, Sam. I hope you don't feel that way, I try to make sure you don't."

Sam glanced over at him. "I don't. I'm not like James. James was a good man, a great teacher. If you'd hooked up with Bowie, I'd worry more that I was a replacement. I understand if you...if you want to go away for the holidays or if you want me to go away. Everyone grieves different. I haven't...well, I've had twenty-four Christmases in the same house. No matter what, this one will be new."

Oh, God. How had he given Sam that impression? Or had he? Was that just Sam, talking? Thinking out loud? "No, no. I want..." *Whoa.* His heart had started pounding. He took a breath. "I want you to do what you need to do, but if it were up to me I'd want you here. I need you with me. I...I don't know what Christmas looks like now, but it won't be what it was. It's going to have to be something else, and whatever that is has to have you in it."

"Oh, good. I just barely got home to you, and all this shit is happening—good and bad. We'll just figure it out together, you and me."

"That's right. It doesn't have to be ambitious this year, you know? What did you think about Angel's invitation? Do you think it should just be you and me? Or do you want to make him some dinner?"

He couldn't make a decision. Part of him would be perfectly happy to pretend Christmas wasn't happening this year, to just hide in bed and lose himself in Sam. Part of him felt like he shouldn't allow himself to disappear, that he should find something to celebrate, even if it was just thanking Angel for being a friend.

"We can order a pizza. I can't imagine how many boxes of cereal it would take to feed Angel."

"Frozen waffles?" He smiled. Thank God for Sam. "Queso."

They'd walked all the way home in the freezing cold, and he hadn't even noticed. He keyed into the building and steered Sam in through the door.

Sam watched everything as they got into the elevator. When the doors opened, Sam stayed close, then checked the door and the locks before opening the door and ushering him in.

He didn't interfere or try to help. It was what Sam needed to do to feel safe. "All good?" He pulled Sam away from the door and did up the locks.

"Yeah. I'll check the house real quick. You need anything? Coffee? Sandwich?"

"Wine. Shower. Then you—and whatever you want. I mean that."

"You got a preference to type? On the wine, I mean."

"Something in a glass will work."

"I'll grab it and bring it to you." Sam took his coat off, the nervous energy buzzing around him like static.

"Thanks." There was no reason to be concerned about a break-in, but this wasn't a rational thing for his boy; it was emotional. He knew he had to let Sam make the rounds of the apartment, put that worry aside before they could address whatever else might have the boy wound up, so he nodded and headed for the shower to wash the precinct off him. "I'll be in the bedroom, boy. I'm going to shower. I'll call you if I need you."

That might work, letting Sam know he'd ask for help if he needed it. The boy still seemed so worried about him, and there really was no reason to be. He was fine.

His shower was hot. He needed it hot enough to wake up his skin, hot enough to sharpen up his mind so he could see to his boy. He got himself clean and decided against shaving, going with his evening stubble. The bathroom mirror was fogged up anyway.

He left the bathroom with a towel around his waist, and his warm, damp skin instantly reacted to the cooler air in the bedroom, making him shiver. "Whoo. Chilly."

"Your wine's there by the bed, honey." It took him a second to find his boy, who was on the floor doing crunches, one after the other, like a machine. Sam was wearing a tiny pair of shorts and nothing else, and it was a vision.

"Thank you, boy." He pulled on his boxer briefs, went for his wine, then sat on the edge of the bed to sip it and admire.

But something about Sam's demeanor made him change his mind and set the wine back down untouched.

"Everything okay? Are these crunches something you just do, or something you do for a reason?"

"Three hundred a day, no matter what. Some days I do four hundred just to get the kinks out."

It did not escape his attention that Sam ignored his first question. He decided to push the point a bit.

"What do you mean by kinks, boy?"

"You know...sometimes you have to shut everything up for a second. Just"—Sam blew out a couple of breaths, then began to bring elbows to opposite knees—"fucking lats. Just be a body. Little like being high." Sam met his eyes for a second, smiled. "Sir."

"Thank you, boy." He returned the smile with a wink. "I do know. How many have you done so far?"

Sam needed to talk. Shutting things up was a legitimate temporary fix, but it wasn't good enough long term. He needed to get his boy talking one way or another.

"Three-fifty. Sometimes I wonder if I shouldn't have been born in the Old West, just another cowboy, just riding 'til I couldn't go another second."

Such a wise sub. That was exactly what he had in mind. "Very good idea, boy. Make it five hundred, and I want to hear the last twenty counted out loud."

Sam stopped, curled up halfway. "You got some faith in my belly."

Oh, dear boy. Sam hadn't quite figured him out yet. "You think you'll be able to do it?"

"I think so. We'll see. Muscle failure is muscle failure." Sam kept moving, doing twenty-five, breathing a minute, doing another set. By four hundred, he was panting, eyes closed.

"I suppose that's true." And if they didn't fail by five hundred, it would be on to push-ups. Possibly even if they did. Meanwhile, he was getting a lovely view; Sam's skin was shining in places, sweat starting to roll down between the ridges of his straining abs.

By four-fifty, Sam was slowing, reaching for the wall, the minute between sets closer to a minute and a half.

He sat down on the floor with his boy, watching Sam's face, watching his boy move. He didn't speak yet; he didn't want to interrupt Sam's concentration, but he wanted to be close.

The next set was ten. Sam huffed through each crunch, gritting his teeth, and when he rested, those abs were trembling. "Forty more."

Thomas didn't think Sam was talking to him.

"Sam. Boy. What is on your mind? What thought are you trying to quiet?" He didn't stop Sam yet, but he would if he thought the boy would continue past safety.

Sam's face tightened up, the look pained as he tried to—what? Hold something back? Speak?

Finally Sam shook his head with a frustrated sigh and started moving again, fast and hard, pumping out twenty.

He let himself smile a little. So Sam got it, or he was going to blow it out trying not to talk. Perhaps both. Either way, they were on the right track. Now was the time to really push.

"What is it, boy? Try to let the trust work for you, remember. What do you need to tell me?"

"Twenty. I—fuck. Nineteen. I'm fucking tired." Sam was moving slower now, rolling himself up, using his arms more than his stomach. "Eight-eighteen. Tired of..." Sam shook his head again.

"Tired of what?" He thought about the day he badgered Sam into using his safe word and asked again. "Tired of what, boy? Tell me. Tired of what?"

"Seventeen. Sixteen. Fuck. I'm fucking tired of—it's just been a long day, okay?" Sam huffed out air. "Back off me."

Sam managed two more before slamming down on the floor. "Thirteen more."

No way was he backing off now. But he took Sam's hand in his, giving him that connection at least. "Tell me."

"I don't know how. I don't know how to explain." Sam clung to him, gasping in air.

He took a deep breath and tried not to appear as indecisive as he felt. Should he push Sam off the edge again, hoping everything would feel *awake* for his boy like the last time? Or would Sam benefit more from struggling through this, finding the words together? He hated not knowing the answer. What kind of Dom didn't have the answers? Fuck, he wanted that rule book right now.

"Tell me how it feels, sweetheart. Start there."

"It feels...like I...I'm...just mixed up. Inside. I'm fucking tired of feeling like...it's stupid. Just let it go. I'm not making sense." Sam stared at him, eyes begging him for help.

God, those eyes. He knew this was on him now. He'd brought them to this point; he had to get his sub out the other side whole. There wasn't room for indecision. The only option was to take control and remind his boy that he'd earned trust, that his promise was to catch Sam when he fell, keep the boy safe.

"Up, boy." He stood up first and offered Sam a hand.

"I didn't finish. That's okay?"

"Good boy. It's fine with me, unless you think it's going to distract you. In that case, you should finish."

"I don't think I have thirteen more in me. I can build up to five, but not today." Sam took his hand, and he had to almost lift his boy's body weight on his own.

That worked fine; he let the boy's momentum carry

them both to the wall. "All right. Brace your hands on the wall any way that's comfortable. You won't be there long."

He waited—impatiently, but he waited—for Sam to sort out a comfortable position; then he moved up close to the boy's back in one long stride, bracing his own arms on either side of Sam's shoulders, surrounding the boy with his own body. "I will not let it go. We will make it make sense. Think. What haven't you said that you needed to? Give me something. One word if that's all you have. Breathe, boy. Tell me."

Sam pressed into him, entire body shuddering. "I'm tired. I'm scared that...it's different now, and I don't know how to..." Sam stopped himself, stopped the flow like he was stopping a faucet.

Was that what it was like in his boy's mind? No wonder Sam couldn't force things out.

"Boy," he said softly in Sam's ear. "Do you need my flogger?"

Sam gasped once, then ducked his chin. "I do. I'm sorry."

"No, boy. You can't have it if you're sorry. Our needs are not failures; they're truths. Try again."

Sam's eyes flew open, and his boy took a short, harsh breath like he was surprised. "I do. I need your help, Sir."

He moved quickly, retrieving the middle-weight flogger from where it was still sitting by the bed. "Can you stand, boy, or do you need a chair?"

"I-I need a chair, please. I feel like I took earthquake pills."

"Good boy. I appreciate that." He carefully moved his favorite tall black boots from in front of the chair and dragged the chair to the center of the room; then he went to his boy. "Come sit."

Sam held his eyes as he moved, gaze clinging to his. Sam believed in him, trusted in him. It shone from him.

Before he helped his boy sit, he gave Sam a smile. "My boy." But the fact was that he was as much Sam's as the boy was his.

"Yes." Sam nodded. "I'm trying. I swear to God."

"I know. I see it all the time. You're doing just fine. Sit, and let's get you what you need."

Sam sat, arms crossed over the top of the chair, eyes falling closed.

"I've gone straight for the middle one, boy. You're tired and you're already warm from your crunches." He was hoping to bring the boy down quickly, to find focus without the lengthy warm-up. Sam's shoulders were probably still tender, so a light touch should do, at least to start.

He rolled his wrist and offered Sam gentle falls while the boy found his breath. "Count, remember. Tell me when you're ready."

"I'll remember. I need your help. I'll remember." Sam was already breathing easier. "I'm ready, Sir."

Satisfied, he moved into place behind his boy, studying Sam's back and shoulders. He took a breath to focus; he was already feeling taller. "Very well, boy. We'll begin." His flogger landed twice, lower on the boy's shoulders than the day before.

Sam counted for him, voice steady, sure.

Excellent. "More, boy. Count, and breathe." He pulled his blows a bit, so they were slightly lighter and brought it down four times, high and lower on the left, mirrored on the right. Careful to not go so low as to lick Sam's scar.

"Six, Sir. Why does this work? How does this work?"

Was it working? A question like that left him wondering. Did that question mean that Sam was more in his head, or less? "You can answer that question for yourself, boy. Why do you seek out a fistfight?"

"Yes. I know that. I know that part."

"So, you want to know…" *Wait. Rhythm first, Thomas. Don't let questions throw you.* He raised his full arm, laying two strokes down for clarity.

Sam counted for him, breath actually slowing, deepening, Sam filling his lungs completely.

"Good boy. I believe you're asking me, then, why this dynamic works? You want to know how a relationship of this nature makes us…whole. Am I right?"

"I want to know why you make it so much *bigger*. I want to know why I'm not fighting back, and it still works." Sam's voice was loud, confused, but not angry.

"Because, my boy, this is done with respect." He tucked the flogger under his arm and took two steps forward, leaning over Sam's shoulders and placing his hands on his boy's arms. "This, Sam, is done with love."

Sam shook for him; then his boy went boneless, leaning toward him, not away. "Love."

He caught Sam, the flogger under his arm falling to the floor. He hadn't thought for a second about whether he was ready to say it—he'd understood the fear in Sam's confusion and his boy, his lover, needed the truth more than anything.

But he'd only just discovered that truth for himself and hadn't processed it at all.

He lifted Sam into his arms and took the few steps to the bed quickly before his own knees gave out. Sam opened his arms, begging him into an embrace. "Please, Sir."

He nodded and moved into Sam's arms, a raw sound escaping him as their lips met. It was oddly pitched and foreign to him, and it came from the last bit of him still torn open by grief and by guilt.

Sam took it in, took him in and wrapped around him, holding him tight and offering him anything he needed. Everything.

"It's true, Sam, I swear. But it…I have to…it hurts." He wanted to pull Sam inside him, let his lover fill all the cracks and the holes, smooth out the edges that still cut him so badly.

"I have you. I swear, honey. Love. I have you." Sam's kisses were soft, deep, almost drugging. "Just like you have me."

"Yes." He clung to those kisses, craved them, breathing in between and showing Sam the trust he'd asked for so often himself. "Love. Thank you."

"God, you make me happy." Sam kissed him again, slower this time, fingers sliding over his skin, comforting him.

"You're a wonder. I like the man you've made me." He found a smile for Sam and accepted another kiss as he pressed their hips together.

"Oh." The soft sound was sweet, and the look Sam gave him was dazed. "God, I love how that feels. How you feel."

He rocked a little, giving Sam more to feel and less to think about. "We fit, Sam. Don't we?"

"Yes." Sam held his gaze, and he was becoming addicted to this—to the clarity and sharpness, to the way Sam offered him this as much as the need. "Hand in glove."

Just like that. One made for the other. He looked into Sam's eyes, feeling that last little tear start to stitch itself back together. That quickly. And stronger than before.

3

Sam woke up on his belly, Thomas's arm heavy on his waist. He could feel Thomas on his skin, deep in his bones, and he caught himself smiling.

Because this was done with respect and love.

Love.

He hadn't understood how much he'd craved an answer from Thomas, how he'd needed to understand better. How he'd needed to understand that he could ask Thomas for what he needed, how he could crave all...*this* so fucking much.

He knew why.

Sam slid out from that heavy arm, left Thomas sleeping, and headed to the bathroom to shower. The spray ached in the best way as he stepped in, the sting and throb making his balls draw up a little.

He chuckled at himself. Lord have mercy, he was...

Happy.

Happy and in love and out of his mind and horny even after last night, which had been...lovemaking. Like slow and deep and easy and a promise.

Still, the spray on his back and the memory of last night —all of it, from the crunches to the flogger to the quiet orgasms—had him tugging on his cock, tickled as hell that his right hand had the stitches. Those would chafe.

"Good morning, lover." Thomas's voice sounded just-woke-up rough and playful. "I'm going to make some coffee and attempt scrambled eggs. Possibly bacon as well. Are you in?"

"Mornin', you." He chuckled softly, the sound husky. "I'll be there to help in two shakes of a dead lamb's tail."

Possibly three. You never knew.

"Dead...what? I'll just...go play with my eggs and try not to be jealous." Thomas laughed; then Sam heard the bathroom door open and close.

"Yeah, yeah. Your fault my morning wood didn't just decide to fade." He hummed, leaned against the tile, and arched—the cold and hot and sting made his eyes cross and his balls draw up so hard that he was halfway through his orgasm before he realized he was coming. "Damn."

"Mmm. That sounded nice, boy. I'll happily take the blame. Meet you in the kitchen."

He would have grumbled about peeping Thomases, but he felt too good—not to mention, he was tickled and still laughing by the time he got himself bundled up and ready to help with breakfast.

"Someone is in as good of a mood as I am this morning." Thomas looked up from chopping up some veggies. Ambitious. He definitely smelled bacon too.

"I am." He moved in for a kiss, enjoying the way Thomas slid one hand around his hip and held him close for a second. When their lips parted, he started making coffee for them both, humming low under his breath.

He heard the sizzle as Thomas threw everything into the

skillet and started eggs, then a low chuckle. "Really, you had to see the look on Colletti's face. I wish you'd been in there. He looked like he'd just swallowed nails."

"Good." He'd damn near lost his shit in a drastic way. "I've had enough of their bullshit. They need to hunt the bastard that's doing this to my people and leave us be."

He'd grabbed Angel by the ear and dragged him to Thomas's club and made Mr. Clint understand that he was neither patient nor willing to kowtow to anyone where his man was involved and that he would remind the entire fucking world that he was not from here.

It had worked out. He was pleased.

"You were magnificent yesterday. No one's ever done anything like that for me before. Just marched in and fucking fixed things. Not like that, rallying people and..." Thomas shrugged. "Sometimes I'm still surprised to find I have people around me to rally."

"No one?" What the hell? Not James? Surely James would have had Thomas's back. Surely so. "Well, I have you and I will move heaven and earth to make things right for you."

"I trust that. Implicitly. And you have to know I would do the same for you. I think what's shocking to me is how infrequently I've needed that before now, and how often you've had to catch me lately. It's not very...in character."

Thomas snorted and slipped the eggs out of the pan onto two plates, then pulled a tray of bacon from the oven. "I'm sure James would have stepped up if I'd ever needed him to, but I never did. Not one time. Clint certainly has my back, and Angel, but not...I haven't ever...I don't know. You're seeing me at my worst."

"We sorta met at a shit time for us both." What was he supposed to say? He didn't want to apologize, because that seemed weird and fucked up. Besides, he knew from worst. Thomas had seen him cry. No one had done that since he was five, and Bowie had explained the rules to him.

Bowie at twelve had been the scariest thing on earth. Worse than zombies.

He doctored Thomas's coffee and brought it to the little table, and it occurred to him: this was the first time they'd sat here, that they'd shared a meal like this.

Lord, he wondered if Thomas did stuff like a Christmas tree. Probably not. He didn't seem like the type.

Sam thought he'd buy himself one of the tiny USB ones. He could plug it in while he was doing freelance and Thomas was at work. That would do for him.

"Food looks good, honey. Thank you."

"I figured after all that energy we used up yesterday we deserved real food. Don't ask me to do anything other than breakfast—but this I got." Thomas put a hand on his arm. "It is what it is, you know? All I really mean to say is thank you."

"Any time." And Sam meant it. He did what he could to help ease Thomas's soul. That was what love was, right? He dug into his eggs, making sure to hum over them because they were just fine.

"I'm going back to work tomorrow. I have to be honest, I never use that office except to check my email, so you should feel free to just get comfortable in there."

"Thank you. I'll put my nose to the grindstone and see if anyone's got work for me." He'd put out his résumé for a virtual PA, a research assistant, answering emails—anything to add to what he had. Things would start happening.

He'd have to cut the stitches out of his hand tomorrow so he could type. He was sort of becoming Frankenstein's-monster-looking, at least in the hands. The ink covered the one on his leg...

Oh. Ink. Maybe for his birthday. He wasn't going to Vegas with James, for sure. Maybe he'd get more ink. Something about home, about Texas.

"I do have the week between Christmas and New Year's off so...I'll be home then. I guess they'll want you to work a lot that week, but maybe you can swing some time off. We need to talk about New Year's Eve at least."

Yeah, that wasn't going to happen. He'd get Christmas Eve and Christmas proper for sure. Besides that, he was going to be busting his hump and trying not to take a beer bottle to the eye socket. He'd seen that Wednesday last. Not pretty and he was short enough to be an easy target.

"I can talk to Daddy Mike, but I'm not holding my breath. They've got a huge-assed party planned. I may have to wear a suit of full-plate armor. Sucks, because I'd rather be with you."

"I'd much prefer...well. New Year's is the biggest party of the year at the club. Even with members only. And I'm not accustomed to spending New Year's Day with a boy broken to bits."

"Yeah, seems like a shit way to spend the first day of the year, huh? Torn to shit? I don't approve."

"I don't suppose anyone would believe you if you called out with the flu?" He got a big grin from Thomas, who couldn't seem to keep the straight face that really should have gone with that comment.

He mocked coughed, playfully. "Daddy Mike? It's Sam. I seem to have come down with a mild case of Ebola."

"You could tell him you're under orders from your Dom not to come in." Thomas looked at him over a hot mug of coffee. It was really hard to tell if his lover was serious.

"Wouldn't life be nice if it worked that way? Just, I'm sorry, I can't. I'm promised to someone that needs me."

"You never know. In some circles life does work that way."

"Really?" He got it, at home. Hell, even all the time. Thomas deserved his respect, his honor, his...submission. Lord, it was hard and strange and wonderful and exciting to think that. But with just folks? Really? He couldn't imagine that.

"Really." Thomas didn't offer him anything more than that. "Did you get enough to eat?"

"I did. It was delicious. Thank you." He stood up and gathered plates and took them to the dishwasher. "You want more coffee?"

"Yes, please." Thomas followed him, setting his empty mug down next to the coffeemaker. "So...did you have a good shower?"

Sam's cheeks went red-hot, but he didn't look away. In fact, he had to grin. "I did, thanks for asking."

"Sounded like it. I'm a little smug about that, if you're interested." Thomas watched him refill the mug. "I guess I'd better go clean up the bedroom. Oh. You're going to clean those floggers today. I'll show you where I keep everything."

"Okay. Is it much different than cleaning tack?" He didn't mind that. It was meditative. He got some of his best ideas working in saddle soap.

"Not really, you go much lighter on the soap, and there's a solution you'll spray on to disinfect them before you hang them to dry. But the concept is exactly the same. I might have you do my boots too, depending on how long it takes you. I don't need your whole day, after all."

Thomas sipped his coffee. "How was that chair? Was the back too high? I want you to be able to sit comfortably."

"It was just what I needed." He washed up the egg pan real quick, thinking as he scrubbed. "I have to admit, I'm dreading my crunches today. I was considering begging for mercy yesterday."

Those last few had taken everything he had to give.

"You could have; I might even have found some for you." Thomas looked at him more seriously. "That wasn't arbitrary, you know that, right? I was purposeful in my thinking."

"You were trying to shut up my brain by wearing out my body." How many coaches had him running laps? How many times had Daddy had him painting a barn or stripping a wood floor? It wasn't meanness. It was trying to get him to slow down a minute. "I will say, you're better at it than I am by myself. A lot better."

"That's good to hear, and it's how it should be. For each of us. You and I should be bigger together. Better. Our goals should be fairly lofty, right? Balance. Trust. You understood what I said about needs. This is the place where truth needs to be safe."

He loved how Thomas could do that, say things out loud that sounded so important, so fine. Sam did okay on his computer, where he could edit, where things could flow out, and he could delete the stupid parts. "I like how that sounds."

Thomas tipped his chin up and kissed him. "It's more than just words. I'm good at words. We need practice at what they mean, and that's okay."

"Practice I'm good at." He wrapped one arm around Thomas's waist, humming at the warmth they were building between them.

"All right, sweetheart. Let's get the house in order and get our chores done. Then maybe we can get takeout and put on a little King George again." Thomas winked at him. "Put those love songs to work."

"I'd love to. Dancing with you is one of the best things in the history of time." No lie. "Chores ahoy!"

He had his headphones, his cleaning and singing playlist, and a promise for a great night. He was all in.

4

Thomas stepped off the subway and climbed the stairs to the street level, footsteps echoing against the concrete. He had on his most beat-up, worn-in black boots —his favorite from over the years. They had a big buckle on the ankles and thick, heavy soles, and they made him feel like a badass.

Which was good because when it came down to brass tacks, he really wasn't.

He also had on a leather jacket that had been a gift from Angel years ago. It was the real deal, thick leather with a fair collection of zippers and buckles on it.

One way or another, he wanted Sam to be off work for New Year's Eve. Even if he decided the boy wasn't ready for the club party, he'd be damned if he was going to spend it alone when he had a lover he could be kissing at midnight.

So, he made his way to Sam's bar to talk with Daddy Mike. He wasn't nervous or worried—he wasn't an asshole, so he was fairly certain he wouldn't get his ass kicked. Otherwise he had no expectations for the evening. As the place got close he took a deep breath, went for as casual and relaxed as he could muster, and stepped up to talk with the bouncer, holding his arms out so the guy could check him for weapons.

"Good evening."

"Evening." The bouncer patted him down quickly, professionally, then waved him in. "Have a good night."

The bar was about half-full, way more leather and less denim than he had expected. Bob Seger was on the jukebox, the lights low, the dance floor holding a few slow-dancing bodies.

"Little Sammy, get your ass downstairs and see what's wrong with the Coors? It's all foam." From the description Sam had given him, that had to be Darla. Impressive.

"Yes, ma'am. I'm on it." His boy was in a tight T-shirt and eyeliner.

Whoa.

"Thanks, honey. Maybe we won't beat you."

"Tommy!" Angel stood up from one of the two-tops and waved him over with a huge grin. "I didn't expect to see you here. I just sent you a text."

He looked down at his phone, seeing a picture of Sam. The caption said, "He lost a bet."

"Ha!" He made his way over to Angel and shook his hand. "I don't know, he may have lost, but I think the rest of us won."

"No shit. What brings you out?" Angel looked him up and down, admiring. "I like it."

High praise from Angel. "Thanks. Been a while since I've worn your jacket, I was glad for an excuse. I need to have a conversation with Mike; can you set me up?"

"Can I listen in? I love to watch you work."

"Of course. You never know, I might need the backup." Thomas grinned.

"With Mike? He'll accuse you of fucking up for letting your boy get his ass handed to him; then he'll congratulate you on a beautiful boy."

He laughed. That sounded fine—just about what he'd expect. "I can handle that. I might respectfully disagree with the first assessment, but I see his point."

"It's how he works. What do you want to drink? I'll grab it and talk to Mike."

"Thanks. Something strong I can sip." He settled into a chair where he could see the bar with one eye and the door with the other.

"All fixed, lady."

"Good boy. Wipe down the bar for me and go take Will a bottle of water and spell him so he can pee."

"I'm on it."

Sam started wiping down the bar to a load of catcalls and whistles from men and women alike. Once he was done, Sam rolled his eyes dramatically and bowed. "My tip jar is the one with the Texas flag. Y'all know how to use it."

He tried to find the humor in that and ignore the possessive piece of him that wasn't pleased at all with the catcalls. It was Sam's game; he needed to stay out of it. He wondered if he should put a dollar in Sam's jar, but he didn't want to encourage...bad behavior.

Angel waved to him and he made his way to the bar as Sam headed for the door to relieve the bartender. Christ, his Sam was half the size of the man he was spelling.

Angel grinned at him. "Little Sammy's a beast. Will's all size and no ferocity. Come on. Mike's opening the good stuff."

All right then. That was a good sign. He glanced at Sam one more time and followed Angel toward the back of the house.

When Mike stood, Thomas could see how the guy might stretch out that damn silly sweat shirt. It was like looking at Andre the Giant standing up from behind a worn-out desk. His Sam was the bravest son of a bitch on earth.

He smiled...up...and offered his hand. "Thomas Ward. Thank you for seeing me."

"Of course. Mike Waterman. Call me Mike. Gabe here speaks highly of you. How do you take your whiskey?"

He gave Angel a nod and looked at Mike. "I could speak just as highly of Gabriel. Over ice, please. I appreciate the gentleman's welcome."

"Anytime. Your boy is one hell of a man." Mike poured out three drinks with a deft hand, the gold nugget ring on his pinkie the size of one that would fit on Thomas's thumb. "I'm sorry about his brother."

Thomas gave him a nod, not sure how much Mike knew. "Thank you. We're headed into the holidays, and it won't be an easy time. I appreciate how you've taken care of him."

"I wore your sweat shirt" just didn't seem like something he wanted to say, but he thought it.

"He's one of ours now. Took his licks better than anyone I've ever seen. Walked away. That doesn't happen often."

"I think you'll understand me when I say I would have preferred it not have happened at all. May I?" He reached for a glass but didn't pick it up. "But I had no right to interfere at that point. I do now."

Mike nodded and lifted his glass. "To Little Sammy."

Angel took his own glass. "To Sammy."

"To my boy." He took a sip, enjoying every hint of smooth heat as the whiskey practically melted into his tongue and slid down his throat. He took a second to let it burn. "Oh. That's lovely. Thank you."

Mike hummed and eased back into his chair. "You're welcome. So, you have a request for me?"

Angel chuckled. "Not a man for small talk, our Mike."

"We're men who know what we want; pussyfooting around things is a waste of time." Mike took another sip. "Let's get it said."

He took a seat now that Mike had. He'd been waiting to see how their initial few words played out to decide which approach would be the most effective, and it was fairly clear that Mike was a man who preferred straight talk. He did too —Angel picked a good night to listen in.

"Sam and I are at a critical moment in solidifying our relationship and clarifying our dynamic. As you may have observed, in addition to his brother, Sam has lost a great deal more in making the decision to stay here in New York rather than return to Texas." He took another sip of his drink before going on.

"I firmly believe that Sam is entitled to make his own employment decisions, and I have no intention of standing between him and his choices as long as I feel he is supported and respected. However, I need him whole over the holidays. I need as much time as possible with him, and I absolutely must have him with me New Year's Eve. I trust you and I can come to an understanding."

Mike leaned back, watching him with a shrewd gaze. "I believe that is not out of the realm of possibility. He's one hell of a worker, one hell of a fighter, but it would piss me off to have my girl come home bruised night after night."

"I believe he is learning that not all bruises are created equal. The ones he picks up here are helping me teach him the difference. My hope, though I can appreciate that it might not be yours, is that he'll grow tired of the ones that don't serve him and move on." He sniffed his glass. "What would upset me is if a job were to get in the way of his phenomenal progress in that regard."

Angel was sitting still, watching them with avid interest. Jesus, Clint needed to find the guy someone to work with. Now.

"You can have him from Christmas Eve to the first. Then we'll revisit." Mike's lips quirked. "I want some assurances. He's staying with you? He'll have food? Wi-Fi?"

His opinion of the big man rose even higher.

Thomas smiled, having secured what he needed, but also because he knew now, firsthand, that even if Sam stayed at this job for the foreseeable future, his boy would be as well looked after as one could be in a place like this.

"Sam and I cleaned out his brother's apartment last weekend, and he's moved in with me permanently. The boy is mine. You have my word he is being well looked after. He even uses my washing machine." He laughed into his glass and took a sip.

"Shit, Mike. Thomas here? Bought him a coat." Angel chuckled.

"I know. Little Sammy is proud of it." Mike nodded, the laugh sounding like it was pulled from a deep hole. "He speaks highly of you, man. So does Gabe. That's why I haven't paid you a visit before."

"As Sam would say, Mike, he appreciates the hell out of you. This isn't his dream job, but he knows what he's got going, and he likes being able to do what's expected of him. I appreciate your trust that I wouldn't ask a favor of this nature without good reason, and I'm grateful that you have his back. He needs people in his corner; it's been a lonely one for a long while."

"We'll always be his family. He knows that." Mike leaned forward, suddenly serious. "If you need protection—I saw

Little Sammy's hand, heard about the whole thing. I know people."

He returned Mike's look and nodded once. He hadn't wanted to play that card; he was trying to keep his own issues out of the discussion, but he'd been ready to pull it out if Mike had decided to be difficult about giving Sam time off.

Before the ordeal followed them to his building, he'd have laughed off Mike's offer as too extreme. But he wasn't sure where the line was at this point. "I'd like to make sure he gets to and from work safely. Angel has..." He looked at Angel and grinned. "Lived up to his name so far, but if the two of you could see that he doesn't head home alone, I would be grateful."

"He'll never be alone, Thomas. You have my word." Angel smiled at him. "And you can take him home tonight, can't he, Mike?"

"We're dead. You can have him when he's paid off his bet."

"He wears that eyeliner well." Thomas laughed. "Mike, when was the last time you were down at the club? Will you and your sub do me the honor of being my guests, perhaps after the holidays?"

"I'd love that. You're welcome here, anytime." Mike winked, dark eyes dancing. "I would suggest avoiding fight night. You can't hear yourself think."

He snorted. "Sound advice." Especially for someone that had no intention of throwing a punch. He sipped his whiskey, swallowing down the last of it with a sigh. That was worth the visit. "So, what was the bet?"

"Eyeliner, the shirt, fifty bucks in the tip jar. He's lucky he gave in when he did. The new bartender is training to do body piercing and is dying to do one of Little Sammy's nipples." Mike rolled his eyes while Angel rolled with laughter.

He shook his head and laughed along, but he felt like it was time for him to go before he heard something he truly didn't like. He set his glass down and stood up. "Mike, you're straight up and I appreciate it. Thank you again."

Mike stood and took his hand. "Best of luck. I appreciate the time you've let us get to know your boy."

"Look me up after the holidays, and we'll get you in at the club. Gabriel." He nodded to Angel. "Thanks again." He headed toward the door, wondering how much Sam had going in his jar.

Sam saw him as soon as he walked out from the back. His lined eyes went wide; then a huge smile broke out on his face. "Hey, you! I didn't see you come in. Let me buy you a beer. Y'all! This is my Thomas."

He'd been ready to ask Sam to check the tip jar, but that smile...and it sounded like Sam wanted him to sit for a minute. "Thank you, Sam. I'd like that." He pulled up a seat at the bar, nodding to everyone that welcomed him.

Sam made introductions, brought him a beer, and smiled at him like he was the moon itself. "This is the best surprise." Sam lowered his voice. "I love the jacket."

"Thank you. It was a gift from Angel years ago." He returned the low voice and smiled. "I love the eyeliner."

"I...yeah?" Look at that blush. "I feel a little silly, like I'm dressed up for Halloween."

"It's hot. Makes the green in your hazel eyes shine. Don't feel silly, own it." The boy's tips would triple if he looked like he knew how hot it was.

"Own it, huh?" Sam grinned and grabbed his hand, squeezed. "Do you need anything else before—"

"Little Sammy? Case of Bud Light, honey."

"On it. I'll be back. Y'all take care of him for me." Sam stood taller, was beaming. For him. Proud to introduce him around. *Damn.*

Angel sat beside him. "Do you think you can get him to wear the eyeliner at the club? It's a great look for him."

"It is but...never mind the eyeliner, Angel. I want him to wear that pride." He watched Sam disappear, feeling a little floored, then glanced at his friend. "That's a great deal sexier than the eyeliner."

It was everything. It was love and service, and it was the happiest Thomas had ever seen him.

Thomas sat and talked for half an hour or so before Darla came over, passing Sam the Texas flag tip jar. "Cash out, sweetie. Daddy says you're off the clock and can go home whenever."

Sam's eyes went wide. "No shit. Y'all sure?"

"Totally. You can make sure he gets home safe."

Thomas smiled at Darla. "Thank you, I will."

Sam chuckled softly but kissed Darla's cheek. "Let me go put real clothes on, and I'll come cash out."

"You want a beer, kiddo?"

"No, ma'am. Just a Coke, thanks."

"You want him to sit between us, Angel, so you can ogle him? I can slide over a seat." Thomas grinned wide, doing his best to fluster the man.

"He can just sit on my lap, man."

"I'd like to see that." It was possible that Angel was the only man in the world he wasn't jealous of when it came to Sam. Their trust ran deep—years deep. "Any bets whether he keeps the eyeliner on?"

"That depends if he looks in the mirror, huh?"

Privately Thomas thought Sam might leave it on anyway, for him, but he'd see.

Sam came out in a loose black button-up that he had seen on his boy a dozen times, that perfect, ripped belly hidden away. The eyeliner, though a little smudged, was still there. "Hey, y'all."

Something about a little smudged was hotter than not. He kind of liked the idea of seeing it blurred right down the boy's cheekbones. "Hey, Sam." He slid over a seat, giving Angel a wink. "Mike's a mensch, hm? Letting you off early."

"I'm a lucky man."

Darla brought over a Coke and a BLT. "Eat, Little Sammy. You're the size of a dime."

"Thank you, lady." Sam pulled a ten out of his tip jar and pushed it over. "So, did you just come out to visit? It was a great surprise."

He'd thought about this moment ahead of time, what he'd do when Sam asked him why he'd come. He certainly hadn't wanted to make a last-minute decision about how he'd handle things. He hadn't expected Angel to be listening in, but then again, what harm would it do? He'd decided to simply be honest. Sam should probably understand the universe he'd entered into.

He looked Sam in the eyes. "I came to discuss your holiday work schedule with Mike."

That earned him the patented Sam head-tilt, which he had come to understand was a sign of curiosity, of surprise, the beginning of that wonderful brain beginning to spin. Now he would either get the frown, which meant he had a struggle ahead of him, or the lifted eyebrow, which indicated that his boy was listening, willing to hear him, at least for now.

He got the eyebrow. "That's...a little weird."

"Angel, who is Mike's sub? Does she work here?" If his

friend was going to be part of this conversation, he might as well use Angel to his advantage.

"Darla."

Sam's eyes went wide. "No shit?"

"Ha!" He hadn't made that connection at all. "Oh, I do like him." He looked at Sam again. "Remember when I told you that saying you're promised to someone that needs you could work in certain circles?"

"Yes, Sir, I do. Darla? Damn." Sam leaned in, whispered low. "I would have pegged her as somebody that would beat you half to death."

And his boy was a fierce fighter and defended him like a pit bull.

"Take that as a lesson in never, ever, making assumptions." He leaned back on his stool, stretching. "You will not be on the schedule here from Christmas Eve through New Year's Day, after which Mike and I will discuss what he requires of you, and what will best serve us. You will be sure to thank him respectfully, and I expect that in the next week before the holiday you'll make your appreciation, and mine, evident."

And there was the frown, the flash of hurt that disappeared in a heartbeat. "I always work my ass off, and I got nothing but respect for Mike. He was good to me when I was in need of a hand up. You ask anybody. I earned my job here."

He lifted an eyebrow and let Sam sit with that emotion for a second before replying. He took a sip of his beer and set it down on the bar. "What cause would I have to question any of that? At any rate, I don't need to ask, boy. Mike told me himself."

"Then why did you question it? And before you fuss, I'm not being a bitch. I'm tickled shitless that you care enough to talk to Daddy Mike, even though that's...real different. But you don't ever have to tell me to be a decent man or to have a work ethic."

He thought about that. "I thought I was asking you, my sub as opposed to Mike's employee, to say thank you for the generous time off and to be extra vigilant this week. It wasn't meant to be an assessment of you or your work ethic. I apologize."

Angel was going to love that. Oh, well. They were who they were, and he owned his mistakes.

"Thank you, Sir." And just like that, the storm clouds were gone. No pouting, no drama. Just "Thank you, Sir," and Sam was relaxing. "And a whole week? No shit? I thought for sure I was going to have to pull doubles that whole time. That's amazing. Thank you." Sam grabbed his hand and squeezed it. "You want to share my sandwich? Did you eat supper?"

Angel caught his gaze, a warm, bittersweet smile on his face. He got an approving nod, a wink.

That look was meaningful and helped him relax. He still panicked inside when things became muddy between him and his boy, and the nod set him at ease. He didn't seem to be blessed with the ability to accept they'd worked things out and simply move on. The extent to which he had to rely on instinct as opposed to convention, despite all the positive reinforcement, was still disconcerting for him.

But damned if he wasn't catching on.

He patted Sam's hand and gave the boy his most approving smile. "A whole week. And thank you, I had something to eat before I came." Because negotiating with Mike on an empty stomach seemed like poor judgment.

"Good deal. Angel? You want some, or are you good too?"

"I'm cool, Sammy. Eat your sandwich before Darla pinches you."

Sam laughed and started eating, stealing admiring, heated little glances at him.

"Yes, boy. Eat up. You'll need your strength this evening." He'd be damned if he didn't take advantage of bringing his boy home early.

Sam gave him a burning look, head to toe, holding nothing back—not the admiration, the desire, the lust, the love. "Yes, Sir. I'm all over that."

5

"Did you get your packages, baby boy?"

"Yes, ma'am, today. Thank y'all so much." They'd sent warm socks and a knit cap, Wolf brand chili and Ranch Style beans. There were homemade pralines and Luzianne tea bags and some Longhorns pecan candies. He hadn't opened the wrapped boxes. Sam had set them aside for Christmas morning.

"We loved the ornaments. You remember to send something to your brother?" Momma was trying so hard—so hard—and it hurt him, knowing she was alone there with Daddy not right.

It hurt him, but not enough to go back home. He wasn't sure what that said about him. Probably nothing good. He didn't know.

"Yes, ma'am. I found him a real nice pocketknife online and had it shipped. He's talking about coming here on leave before he heads to y'all's."

"Oh? You have room for him?"

"He's getting a hotel room, Momma." They might kill each other in the same place for three whole days.

"For yours and..." She sighed softly.

"Yeah. Our birthday." He wasn't going to let James become a scary ghost. His brother had been real, and he'd loved the son of a bitch. "I really appreciate all the goodies. Seriously. Y'all spoil me."

"We love you. I miss your face. This is my first Christmas since I had babies that I won't have a boy here."

"I'm sorry, Momma. I love you too. I got to go, huh? Work." He wasn't going in, but damn. He couldn't take the disappointment, even if she tried not to show it.

"On Christmas Eve?"

Dammit. "Just a few emails."

"Y'all doing anything special? You and your...Thomas?"

He didn't think so. He worried about interfering in whatever holiday rituals Thomas had and, to be honest, he sort of thought Thomas just wished the whole thing didn't exist. So he'd figured they'd order enough pizza to eat for a couple days. He could watch football and be there for Thomas when he needed someone to hold.

"Just a quiet homey thing, Momma. Just peaceful and all."

"You get him something nice?"

Yeah, but the best thing wasn't for Momma's knowledge. "Yes, ma'am. I found him a belt buckle from a place in Santa Fe. It's real nice."

"Good on you. Call me tomorrow?"

"Of course." Like he'd forget. Ever. "Love you, Momma."

Sam sighed as they hung up. Christ on a crutch, he needed to move a little bit. He pushed away from his computer and stood, rolling his neck, his shoulders.

There was a light knock at the slightly open door. "Working hard or hardly working?" Thomas smiled and moved to him. Knowing fingers landed on his shoulders and dug in.

"Talking to Momma. I wanted to thank her for the goodies." *Oh, Christ.* That felt good.

"Mmm. I have my eye on the candy." Thomas chuckled and kept on working, finding a spot that sent a zing down his arm.

"Uhn." His eyes rolled back, and he stretched up tall.

"So, how's Momma?" Thomas's thumbs pressed into the muscles between his shoulder blades and his spine, working in long strokes all the way up to his neck and down again.

"Good. Momma...damn, that's good. Oh..." He hadn't even known he was tense. "She sent good chili."

"Sit." Thomas put a little pressure on his shoulders, and he folded into the chair. "Have any thoughts about tonight? Do you want to go out? Stay in?"

He wanted Thomas to be happy, but he knew that wasn't the right answer. "I haven't worried on it, honey."

"No?" Thomas pointed to the computer screen. "Is that work? I believe it's a holiday." He got a kiss on the temple. "We're just keeping busy today, huh? I just scrubbed the coffeemaker."

"Lord. Honey, we can surely find something more fun to do than that. We're smart dogs."

"It's just weird to be in town on Christmas." Thomas reached over and picked up his little USB Christmas tree that was lit up on the desk. "When did you put this here?"

"Couple days ago." He hadn't wanted to be a jackass, but he'd needed a little cheer, a little merry. He'd found a five-inch light-up USB tree that he plugged in while he worked.

Thomas turned the tree over and over in his fingers, looking at one side, then another, long enough that Sam got the feeling he wasn't really looking at it at all. Then he put it down suddenly.

"Get some pants on, stud. I'm taking you out."

"Sure." He could handle taking a walk with Thomas. It actually sounded fun. "Come keep me company?"

He went to the bedroom to find a pair of jeans and a heavier shirt. He stripped down to undershorts and started making himself presentable.

Thomas dressed too, finding a sweater instead of just a T-shirt and trading his sweats for jeans. They maneuvered around each other easily, and Thomas kept touching—his shoulder, a hand on his ass, a kiss on the cheek.

"About ready?"

"I am." He pushed in for a long, hard, happy kiss; then he tucked in and buckled up. "You?"

"Ready." Thomas took him by the hand and led him into the hall, where they pulled on their coats. "I can't stare at the walls anymore. We need to make some fun."

"I'm in." He wanted to walk around, see things. Do things. With his lover. His first Christmas Eve with a lover.

They left the building and went out into what he thought would be the cold, but it was surprisingly...not, considering it was December.

"Oh, it's going to be a beautiful night." Thomas put an arm around Sam's shoulders, and they started walking downtown. "So, what's the thing to do at holiday time in... what's closest? Austin?"

"Dallas, but I like Austin better—I drive down to the Armadillo Christmas Bazaar every year with some buddies." Amazing how they had just disappeared once he had come up here. By the time the funeral was over, no one had known what to say. "I love to go look at lights. There's a big old ranch in Hunt county that does a drive-through deal—

all sorts of huge characters and stuff. I guess we all just have that super-traditional thing—tree, lights, cookies, riding Maisey in the Christmas parade."

"Maisey?"

"My horse. She's a thoroughbred quarter horse mix. Pretty as all get out."

"You'll have to show me a picture sometime." Thomas gave his shoulders a squeeze. "When I was growing up we had a Christmas parade, but it was just for organizations like Boy Scouts and veterans, and the local gymnastic school or whatever. My dad was Santa for years and years. He'd ride on top of the ladder truck for the fire company, and all the volunteer firemen would throw us candy canes."

"Yeah? That's too cool. I love candy canes." He loved the idea of little Thomas watching his daddy be Santa.

Thomas looked at him. "You're used to celebrating. Sometimes I have a hard time believing that you and James were even related."

"I'm sorry, honey. I'm trying to"—To what? Keep his rejoicing on the down-low? Not interrupt Thomas's mourning? Figure out how to do this right?—"be respectful and all. So, it's usually colder, huh?"

"Hey. I miss James. But I'm with you."

"I know. I appreciate it. Same here." He missed James too. And home. But he was here. With Thomas.

Thomas smiled and kissed him, slowing their walk to barely a sway for a second. "Okay. Tell me what you love about Christmas, and let's see if we can find it in New York."

"I love the whole thing, from the lights to the silly cartoons to telling all the stories about the ornaments as you put them on the tree." He felt a little like a yokel. Oh, who was he kidding? He was a cowboy. It came with the territory.

He had to wonder which box James had buried his own cowboy in. If it had been easy.

"Let me guess. You were the little cowboy that would try to stay awake to see Santa."

"Are you kidding? My bedroom is upstairs with great big bay windows. They used to find me every Christmas morning in the window seat, wrapped up in the blankets, sound asleep, trying to see Santa."

"Got it in one." Thomas laughed, and it sounded light, genuine, like his lover was enjoying this. "Eggnog. Yes or no?"

"I don't mind it, but I prefer cocoa with a shot of whipped cream vodka. You?"

"Cocoa with peppermint schnapps. But I've never had whipped cream vodka. I bet I could be won over."

"Oh...that would totally work. Peppermint is one of my favorite flavors. I can suck on a peppermint stick for hours."

"Well. I know where to put my schnapps now." Thomas leered at him.

Oh, he had an answer to that. "It stings, honey. Bad."

"Ha!" Thomas laughed, letting go of Sam's shoulders and doubling over. "No. No way. You don't know that firsthand. I don't believe you."

"You can try it yourself, but remember—I had to occupy myself for a lot of time..." And he'd tried to get off in more than one way.

"Wow. No, I think I'll just trust you." But the man kept snickering, didn't he?

Thomas's fingers threaded through his. "Not long now."

"For what, honey?" He held on, finding himself laughing along.

Thomas grinned at him but didn't answer; he just gave a wink.

The streets were crowded. They were ducking around people carrying shopping bags, and the street they were on had Christmas lights running down it that were bright enough to be seen, even in the daylight.

"Hear the music?"

"I do." He grinned. Look at this. It was like...like a Christmas movie, almost. How much fun was this?

"Okay." Thomas tugged him close and covered his eyes with both hands. "We're going to turn right." Thomas steered him slowly, around to his right and carefully coaxed him up a small staircase. "A few more steps forward."

"Thomas?" Okay, this was fun. He couldn't stop smiling.

"Okay. Stop right...here. Ready?" Thomas moved his hands away. They were standing just above a big ice rink crowded with skaters, and at the far end there was an enormous Christmas tree, colorful lights twinkling and sparkling. Directly below it was a huge, golden statue of Prometheus.

"Oh." He had seen images of this a thousand times, but this was real. He was looking at it with his own eyes, and it was beautiful—real and alive and huge. He reached for Thomas's hand, holding on tight as he stared.

It was crowded around them, tourists and sightseers jostling them from one side or the other as they stood there watching people glide in circles and listening to the music that filled the plaza.

Thomas held on, standing close, shielding him from the crowd. "Now it's like Christmas, right?"

"Yeah..." He grinned like a newborn fool, eyes wide, taking everything in. "Look at this."

"I would take you skating, but I don't know how. I'd probably break my neck." Thomas snorted. "I wish you'd told me that a tree was so important to you."

"I didn't want to interfere in what you needed. I got my little tree."

"I don't know what I need; I don't think there's a right way to do things like this. God knows if there is, we've broken all the rules already, right? James and I didn't celebrate Christmas; we just went on vacation. I guess I just...don't know how to anymore."

"I swear, Christmas wasn't scary at our house. No one beat anyone, there were presents and Santa and good food, and James got a bike and a pony."

"Maybe that was how he wanted to leave it. Not make new memories. Or maybe he just liked the beach." Thomas shrugged. "I mean, he did really like the beach."

"Cool. I'm glad he was happy. Seriously. I'm glad y'all were happy." Sam nudged Thomas's arm. He didn't understand and, to be honest, he had this to look at. He wasn't James.

He didn't want to be a bunch of folks. He just wanted to be him and so far, it was working.

Thomas nudged him back. "So, what first? Spiked cocoa...or Lego?"

"Lego?" He grinned over. "Are you suggesting you want to play with me?"

"Play Lego with you? Yes." Thomas pointed almost directly to their right, where there was a two-story Lego store with a big, green Lego dragon running along the windows.

"Dude. Look at that!" Santa might have to get him something to do Christmas day.

"Come on." Thomas took his hand. "This place is fun. I used to come here when I first moved to the city. But the kits are kind of expensive, and I couldn't ever afford to buy the big sets I wanted. You know how college is."

The went inside and stood there a minute. "Where do you want to start?"

"Lord have mercy." He had a second of utter overload, just staring with wide eyes. "*Star Wars* or *Castlevania*?"

Thomas shook his head. "*Star Wars*. I'm too old for whatever that other thing is, clearly. Up the escalator."

"Castles and dragons are eternal, man. Knights were the original cowboys."

"Han Solo is a space cowboy. Doesn't that count?" Thomas hustled him, practically carrying him to the escalator.

"God, yes." He couldn't stop laughing, so tickled. He hadn't played in a long time.

The *Star Wars* section was easy to find; a life-sized Lego R2D2 stood sentry next to an entire wall of sets from the various movies. Thomas pointed up at the Death Star hanging from the ceiling.

"Oh, God. Look at that. Can you imagine how much that weighs? How many days it took to make that?"

"I always think about the engineers that design these things. How cool a job would that be?"

"Amazing. Science and art. I love it. Pop art and performance art at the same time." There were dozens of examples of this, going back until the dawn of art. "Like the Navajo—it's not the same, spiritual, not commercial. Unless of course you consider our religion pop culture and cash, right?"

Thomas blinked at him and grinned. "It is today. How about you build an X-Wing Fighter and I'll build a TIE Fighter?"

"Works for me. Let's do it!" He liked building shit. His fingers weren't stupid.

An hour later they'd built tiny little *Star Wars* fighters, made lots of friends with kids half their height, and Thomas bought him the little X-Wing set to take home for his desk.

They left the store and took a walk around the rink, weaving their way in and out of people going in all directions.

"Some of those kids have fast fingers. I am just not that creative."

"They're amazing, how they see things." That was a thing, wasn't it? How they perceived, versus how he perceived, compared to how someone saw things two hundred years ago.

"Right? I'm getting better at letting rules go, but I'll never be that good." Thomas pulled him close as they ducked around a group of tourists.

"Rules can be important. Everyone has the ones they follow." *And the ones they don't.*

He got another laugh. Thomas had done so much laughing in the last couple of hours, it sounded a little hoarse. "And the ones they make up. Or...create. Invent? Forge through compromise?" That grin was too cheesy to be believed.

"Negotiate. Lots of them are negotiated." He was smiling too. "Hell, some are just...made."

"Whatever it is, it's working." Thomas stopped right there, in the middle of a million tourists, and kissed him. In public.

Sam took a deep breath and kissed his lover right back.

Merry Christmas to him.

———

THEY SPENT the afternoon touring the holiday department store windows: Macy's and Saks, Lord & Taylor and

Bergdorf. They found cocoa and ate candy canes, had a casual but decent dinner, and went to see the tree lights one more time at night before heading home. Now, just a couple of hours before midnight, he was sipping tea and Sam was lying in his lap, listening to Christmas music and tracking Santa with the NORAD app.

He wanted to keep tonight low-key. His plan, assuming his boy didn't suddenly go off the rails, was to let Sam get the family phone calls and obligations finished in the morning; then he'd take his boy down deep for the rest of the day. He'd settle and find his headspace, and he'd do his best to take Sam away from those spinning thoughts, away from the stress, and into subspace.

That was the plan anyway. He knew all too well that his boy's chaotic mind might have other ideas, and even if Sam was able to comply to start with, it was going to be a long day and would require work to keep his sub down. He was fairly concerned it would take some work to keep himself focused as well.

With any luck, Christmas would be both good work and exhausting for them. Then they could sleep well and start their week, their discussion about New Year's Eve, and their prep for that evening with fresh eyes and clear heads.

Or, the day could veer off in any one of a number of unpredictable directions, and he'd have to improvise.

Again.

Someday it wouldn't cause him anxiety, right? Someday he'd have a broader arsenal of creative ideas, and he wouldn't worry about sending Sam into a tailspin by mistake every time they hit a crossroads. Right?

He laughed softly and ran his fingers through Sam's hair. *Probably not.*

"Mmm..." Sam stretched for him, nice and slow, letting

him admire that fine, tight little hard body. "Thank you. Today was perfect."

"You're welcome. I had a great time, you're a lot of fun. Comfy?"

"I am. You?" Sam put his phone down and smiled up at him.

"Yeah." He shifted so he could bend and give Sam a quick kiss. "Can we talk a little about tomorrow?"

"We can talk about anything you want to." Sam slid one hand under his shirt, the touch warm, connecting them.

He inhaled sharply, his abs shivered, and he covered Sam's hand with his. "Mmm. What do you need for tomorrow to be...right? Other than calling your parents?"

"Well, I have your presents. I'd like to watch you open them."

"Thank you, sweetheart. I have some for you as well." He smiled. "I'm asking because I'd like to work tomorrow. I'd like to spend most of the day exploring something new with you. Which means most of the day won't be your own."

"Exploring something new together sounds like a great way to spend Christmas. It sorta suits us, doesn't it?" Sam seemed relaxed, open to him, to his intention.

"I thought so, and also I was thinking...I was thinking that for most people, January first is the time for a fresh start, but we have this whole week open to us with time to relax a little and talk and learn. I feel like tomorrow is the perfect day to make our own fresh start. I want us both in a place where we can be really present with each other."

Sam tilted his head, nodding for him. "Okay. You'll have to help me learn what that means for you. 'Really present.' I think that a lot of when we get caught up is because we're speaking different languages."

"I agree. Which is why I was thinking we'd stay away

from too many words. What being present means to me..."
He stopped and took a breath and a second to find *their*
words. Not his, not Sam's, but ones that would speak to both
of them. "So, there's no yesterday; there's not even ten
minutes ago. You don't worry about an hour in the future.
Being present means what's happening right then.
Emotions, thoughts, sensations, worries, successes, the way
we're breathing. Impulses. Needs. A place where words can't
say nearly as much as a touch or a look."

"I would love that. For both of us." Sam watched him,
the expression easy, curious. There was a happiness in his
boy, a joy. "I have to tell you, I don't know how to do it, but
you know I will try."

"I don't know that I do either, yet. How to get you there, I
mean. There's a certain kind of floaty feeling, a totally open
headspace we're going for. We need to work a little and
stay...forgiving." He winked at Sam. "We'll figure it out
together. I think if we stay relaxed and honest, whatever we
come up with will be perfect."

"I'm better at honest than relaxed, but I'm in this with
you, honey. All the way."

"I'll take honest every time. Anyway, I don't want to talk
it to death or overthink it. The point of being present is just
letting the moment happen, whatever it is. Whatever it
means."

"Okay. I'm all yours." Sam hummed deep in his chest. "I
can't believe it's already Christmas. Today was so cool. I got
some amazing ideas for articles. I made a bunch of notes."

"Hey, that's fantastic. It's the strangest thing, being a
tourist in my own city, but I loved it. I'd never really thought
about braving the crowds and doing the iconic New York at
Christmas thing, but I'm glad we did. We definitely needed
to get out of here anyway. God." He might have started

cleaning baseboards or something. He'd been...restless. "Ready to turn in?"

"Into what?" Sam began to laugh, the sound completely merry, tickled. Free.

He chuckled, levered Sam up off the couch and got his arms around his lover. "Well, you want to be the moose or the unicorn?"

That earned him more laughter and a hard hug. "I'll just wear the reindeer pajama pants from home, thanks. God knows what they sent for you."

They sent something for him? "Shit, I didn't think to give you anything for them."

"You sent them ornaments from here. She loved them."

He blew a raspberry on the back of Sam's neck. "I could have been involved in that." He wasn't going to read anything into not being consulted. Sam was doing his best. It wasn't like he'd made Christmas seem the least bit festive before today.

"Yeah, I wasn't sure what to do, and I wasn't sure if I'd make it worse to ask you, so I just got them something they'd like." Sam leaned into him. "This is all so new."

"It is. For me too. It didn't even occur to me that...thank you for making me look so thoughtful." He hustled Sam down the hall, going after the boy's ass with grabby hands.

Sam let him chase, let them play on the way to their bed. Sam hadn't been joking—there were a pair of horrific reindeer pants with giant red noses. Scary.

He dropped his voice, making it gravelly. "Oh, those are hot. Very kinky, those large...red...noses."

He worried a bit now about what they'd gotten him.

Sam waggled his hips, which he had to admit, was actually impressive. Sam's flexibility always surprised him when compared to all the injuries.

"All right, Rudolph." Thomas scooped Sam right off his feet and dumped him onto the bed. "That never gets old."

"Come to bed and let me hold you, huh?" Sam scooted under the covers and snuggled in.

He undressed and climbed right into his boy's arms, which was as strange as it was perfect. "You take good care of me, Sam." He sighed and settled into Sam's warmth.

"It's my honor." Sam kissed his temple. "Merry Christmas."

6

S am decided, long before Thomas started to open his last gift, that opening presents while sitting in your lover's lap was sort of amazing.

The buckle had gone over well, and he was still running his fingers through the falls of the flogger Thomas had given him. They fascinated his hands.

"Hmm...long, thin box. Is it a tie?" Thomas pulled the rest of the paper from the box and gave it a shake.

Sam loved watching Thomas open presents. Next year he was going to fake the man out for every one. "Could be a tie..."

"Hmm. Okay." Thomas popped open the end of the box and Sam got a slow, sly smile, as his lover pulled the beautifully crafted leather crop from its box. "Oh. Very nice."

"Yeah? You like? I thought it was..." Hot. Erotic. Exciting. "...suitable."

"It's lovely." Thomas held it by the handle and gave it a couple of light swipes through the air. "It's got a very nice balance too. Beautiful. Thank you. I can't wait to try it out on my sub."

His cheeks started to burn, but what was he going to do? Argue? He gave it to Thomas for a reason. "You're more than welcome."

"Okay, one other for you." Thomas pulled a small, square box off the end table and handed it to him. "This wasn't the easiest decision, so be honest."

He tilted his head, curious as all get out. He opened the box, finding a thin, black leather necklace with a little silver ring attached. "Oh, that's fine."

He picked it up, the leather supple and soft, the ring simple and masculine. It was a piece he could wear.

Thomas smiled at him. "You like it? Jewelry is pretty personal. I wasn't sure."

"It's beautiful, honey. Truly. It's not like anything I've seen before."

Thomas was obviously pleased by that. "You want to see how it looks?"

"I do. Please." He held the box out to Thomas.

Thomas took the box and pulled the necklace out. "I thought about whether I should get you a proper collar. I even looked at several, but I decided I wanted you to be able to wear it around." The leather felt cool around his neck at first but warmed quickly. "Let me see."

He turned, fingers sliding over where the leather met his skin. Oh, that felt...it made him want to swallow.

Thomas reached out, looking awed, and touched the ring with warm fingers. "My boy."

He did swallow then, his world tightening to the two of them. It still stunned him, the way that felt. "Yours."

"Come see, boy." Thomas coaxed him up and took his hand. "I want you to see it."

They went to the bedroom, to the mirror above

Thomas's bureau, and...*oh*. The leather sat on his skin like it belonged there, the silver ring against his throat. "Lord, it's... it looks like it belongs, like it was meant for me to wear."

Thomas stood close over his shoulder, watching him in the mirror. "I knew I would be proud for you to wear it. I had no idea it would make you...make me feel...like this."

A rush of warmth hit him in a wave, his entire body flushing with a delicious heat. "Thank you, Sir."

Thomas grabbed him and spun him, then kissed him hard, bending him over the dresser with weight alone. He opened up, letting Thomas in even as he tasted his lover in return.

Thomas pulled back almost as suddenly and took a quick, deep breath. "Damn, boy. That was...heady." His lover's eyes were bright and tightly focused on him. "You're going to get us bottles of water, my lovely new crop, and your flogger if you'd like me to try it today. Don't rush; keep your mind on how that leather feels on your throat."

Sam reached up and touched Thomas's lips, still caught in that kiss for a heartbeat, and touched his throat. "Yes, Sir."

He wandered into the front room and gathered the flogger. His name was branded on the handle, and he had to admit that made his mouth a little dry. He traced the letters again, then grabbed Thomas's crop and stroked it. It had come in the box—he hadn't touched it yet and it was...flexible.

Okay. Water.

He pondered the water situation and went with four bottles instead of two.

Then he headed back to his Thomas.

At a glance, the room didn't appear any different to look at, but there was a new energy in the air he could actually feel, something electric that gave him goose bumps.

Thomas left him with the tools but took the water bottles and lined them up on the bureau.

"Thank you, boy. Strip down to your briefs and have a seat." Thomas gestured to the chair that had been moved into the middle of the room.

He chuckled softly as he slipped off his goofy holiday pajamas and sat, letting the flogger and crop come to rest in his lap. Thomas wore those ancient blue jeans like they were a second skin. Sam approved, all the way to his bones.

"Close your eyes, please." Thomas took the crop from his fingers but left the flogger in his lap. "Take a few breaths...let the weight of the instrument in your lap be meaningful, in whatever way that resonates with you. There's no right or wrong there. There will be no right or wrong in anything we do today. It will be impossible to fail; you can't disappoint me unless you're not honest. That's all."

He offered Thomas a smile before he closed his eyes. "Fair enough. Same here. We'll just be honest together."

"I appreciate that you expect that of me, and that you trust I will be. Hopefully we'll venture into some new territory for us today, and that will mean we have to rely on that trust. Give me your words, please."

"Yellow and revolver, Sir." That part was more natural every time.

"Yellow and revolver." There was something about the way Thomas said "revolver" that gave it this grave weight and reverence.

"When you're ready, I want three words that you believe describe you. Three words that describe Sam O'Reilly. Choose them carefully."

Okay, that was unexpected. Cowboy was easy and immediate. Texan. Son. Brother. Lover. Adrenaline junkie.

Fuckup. Historian. Researcher. He didn't know how to pick. "Cowboy. Texan. Rider."

Those worked for him because they talked about all the pieces at the same time.

Thomas put a hand on his shoulder and gave it a light squeeze. "Very good. Thank you." After the hand left him, he could hear Thomas moving around the room. Part of him knew instinctively that the light cough or quiet hum, those little sounds were meant to reassure him Thomas was still there.

"Your cuffs, boy. You seemed to like this set, so I didn't go looking for something new. Not for today." Thomas slowly and gently put them on his wrists. Sam felt them tighten, felt the buckles being fastened. "I'd like you to test those for me, boy. I'd like to know they're not too tight and don't hurt, and I need to know for sure you can't slip out of them."

He nodded and used the chance to stretch, pushing his arms out in front of him and spreading them as far as the chain would allow, letting his joints pull and the muscles lengthen before he relaxed and tried a short, sharp tug. They felt heavy, solid, and connected to Thomas in some way he didn't have words for.

"Thank you. And I appreciate that you took the opportunity to move a little. That's absolutely permitted, to the extent that you can, at any time. I don't need you to be still, and it's not good for you, personally, in any case." Thomas took his hands. "Now breathe, and concentrate, and again when you're ready, give me three words that describe you. Take your time."

He had to assume Thomas meant three different ones. "Son, brother, lover." Those were all true and good. All things he could own with his whole heart.

"Excellent. Thoughtful." Thomas laid hands on his

shoulders again, this time sliding them down across his chest, circling his nipples, then finally rolling them with knowing fingers.

He took a deep breath, the inhalation pushing his chest up into Thomas's touch, the sensation making him want to gasp, wiggle on the chair.

"Mmm. Good boy." Thomas hummed for him and walked away again. "How are you managing keeping your eyes closed? It's important that you don't open them now. Do you need a blindfold?"

He thought about it because it wasn't hard now, but if it was important...he nodded. "Please, Sir."

"Very good, boy. Thank you." The blindfold Thomas chose for him was soft and smelled like clean leather. When it was tied in place, Thomas took the flogger from his lap and put a hand under his elbow. "Turn around now, boy."

"Yes, Sir." He stood and turned, eyes opening as he tried to see the chair. He'd made the right decision with the blindfold.

Thomas guided him down again. "The cuffs might make the chair a bit awkward, but I wanted you seated and comfortable for now, concentrating on your state of mind, not struggling to keep your feet." Thomas put a hand between his shoulders. "The very light flogger, boy. To help settle your mind."

The tails of Thomas's gentlest flogger began to fall rhythmically on his back, over and over again, like rain. His thoughts would try to grab hold of something; then they'd be distracted by the brush of the leather against his skin.

"This time, boy, think about this moment." Thomas's flogger never let up, didn't change in rhythm or character. "Take in the room, the temperature, the sounds you're hearing, the chair, the cuffs, my flogger. The things you're feeling physically and emotionally. Take your time....Then give me three words that describe you *right now*."

Okay. The room smelled like them—not even like sex, but like them, together. He could hear Thomas breathing, hear the swoosh of the leather sliding on him. "Safe. Happy. Relaxed."

"Thank you, my own. I feel the same. I want you to stay present like you are now. Stay focused on all of those things you were just thinking about. If you find that difficult at any point, let me know, and we'll find a way to help you. Sometimes it will be easy. Sometimes it will be work. That's perfectly right and acceptable. We'll consider it a puzzle, not a problem."

He sensed Thomas adding to the distance between them. "A bit more of my arm now, boy. A bit more...thud."

A puzzle. Oh, he did love those. Something deep inside him whispered that they were starting to hear each other, find where they met.

Sam took a deep breath, letting it out so that he was ready. Clear.

The room went quiet aside from the fall of the flogger and their breathing, Thomas's a bit louder than his own. He was aware of the space between the blows growing, the longer silences.

Suddenly Sam wished there was music playing, something he could follow, something to grab hold of. What he found was Thomas, and he...was that okay? It had to be, right? Okay?

He lost his internal rhythm, his wrists turning in the cuffs. "Sir? I—"

Thomas's hand landed solidly on his shoulder. "Good boy. What's on your mind?"

"I don't know. There wasn't anything but you for a

second? I couldn't find anything else. Does that make sense?" Sam didn't want to fuck up, but Thomas had said he couldn't if he told the truth.

"Oh, my boy." Thomas huffed softly, sounding...pleased? "I am yours, and you are mine. I can't imagine anything more perfect. Did it worry you?"

"More that I didn't want it to be the wrong thing," he blurted out. He'd never been tied in to a person. A bull, a bronc—sure. For a few seconds. Not this.

"There is no wrong. Trust yourself. Trust the process. I think you'll know when something feels off. It's probable that in that moment there was only me because I was all you needed."

Respect and love. Thomas's words rang through him, and he nodded. "I can believe that. It just tilted me some."

"I'm glad you spoke up. Thank you. Those empty spaces can be difficult to navigate, and it helps me to understand when you might be struggling. Breathe and let me know when you're ready to continue."

This was another thing that was getting easier— believing he was giving what Thomas needed to take.

He took another couple three breaths, then stretched up tall before he settled. "I'm ready, Sir."

"Good boy. New flogger, now. Yours." He heard it swoop through the air several times, but it didn't make contact. "Mid-range like the one I've used with you before, but this one has fewer falls so I can place it more precisely. You'll have to tell me how you like it. Until I know how it hits, I'm going to go easy and we'll build up. All right? Be ready. Breathe. Use your words if you need them. I'm listening."

He understood what more precise meant from the first blow, as Thomas needed four to cover his right side instead of two.

Sam felt the edges more sharply on this one, like Thomas primed him and was painting lines on his skin. "It's different. Brighter."

"Brighter. That's an excellent word. I think I know just what that means. Thank you."

The next set fell on his left side, and it seemed like Thomas was laying down those lines a little harder. "Ah. Good. Yes, I see." He assumed Thomas was just thinking out loud.

After that they fell into a steady rhythm, Thomas creating a pattern on his back that Sam was able to follow. Right, left, lower, higher—it started to make sense to him. He'd even learned enough to know that Thomas wasn't anywhere near full swing. They were beginning to work, both of them breathing harder, the scent of them and the leather beginning to make him the barest bit high.

The stretches between blows got longer again, that silence settling over them, settling into him. When Thomas finally spoke, his voice was soft and his words drawn-out. "Three more words, boy."

Sam would swear there were no words to say, that he didn't have anything to give to Thomas, because he hadn't expected the question, but the words slipped out like oiled nickels. "Here. Lit-up. Ready."

A hand caught him under his elbow once more. "Stand up. We're moving to the wall for a bit."

He felt ungainly and clumsy as he stood, but Thomas had him, helped him move where he needed to be. His back tingled, and his knees took a second to remember how to function, but it was good work, not bad.

"Oh, I'm proud of you, boy. Look how relaxed you are. It might take a second until you feel steady. There's no rush, take your time. I'm going to see how this crop feels in my hand."

A second later, the crop he'd given Thomas sliced through the air and landed...somewhere. The chair maybe? The sound was solid and loud.

He was fixin' to have to remind Thomas that his hide wasn't as tough as a horse. Close, but not quite.

"This is a lovely instrument boy. Tell me, would you like your eyes back? Or are you more comfortable without vision for now?"

"I'm okay. It's starting to get hot, but I'm okay for now."

"Let me cool you off a little." Thomas was suddenly right behind him, fingers in the waistband of his briefs. "I'll just relieve you of these."

He sucked in to help, leaning instinctively to feel his lover, and Thomas chuckled softly, one finger tapping his belly.

"Oh, I need to touch you more, don't I?" Thomas lowered his briefs, sliding hands over his skin on the way down. He stepped out of them; then those hands landed on his ass. "Thank you for reminding me."

"I can't imagine not wanting your touch."

"There's wanting, sweetheart, and there's your brand of wanting. You crave touch; I know this about you now." One of Thomas's hands slid around his hip and settled low on his belly.

Sam's lips parted and he moaned, the sound rough, rattling his ribs. Oh fuck him, that was heaven on earth.

Thomas kissed his neck. "Apart from your blindfold, you're wearing nothing but my collar. You have no idea how that feels."

Oh. Now that Thomas mentioned it, that tiny strip of

leather felt like a part of him, the ring kissing his skin with every breath.

"All right." Thomas took a deep breath and exhaled, then stepped away from him again. "Since this is our first experience together with a crop, and since the instrument is brand new to me, we're going light and building. I'm going for your ass, which is a bit more forgiving than shoulders or limbs or chest. Remember your words; I expect you to use them if you need to."

"Yes, Sir. Yellow or revolver. I remember." He was a little nervous, a little tense, but he reminded himself that he'd taken a shit-ton of licks in his lifetime, and Thomas would stop if Sam needed him to.

"Yellow and revolver. Good boy. This was a thoughtful gift. I want you to get as much from it as I do. We'll figure out what that means together. Relax. These first few stripes won't be anything compared to what I can do with your flogger."

Right. Relax. Deep breath in, easy out. That made the ring at his throat move, and he smiled.

"Here we go."

Thomas gave him two stripes in quick succession. They were lightweight in comparison to the flogger. They stung up front and seemed to burn for a short couple of seconds before fading away. Thomas touched them right off, tracing a finger along each cheek. "How did that feel?"

"Fast. They went fast." The touches were actually worse? Better? More. Thomas's fingers made the sting linger, draw out. It fascinated him.

Thomas laughed softly. "They do that. These barely left a mark. Crops are meant to leave marks. Often, they break the skin. Deeper stripes last longer. You'll see. Two more."

He didn't have time to process any of that because the next two stripes came down instantly, lower on his ass.

He tensed, his jaw clenching. That was tender. Way more than higher up. Was it because of where or because they were harder?

"Hm. Talk to me, boy."

"Those were sharp. They burned."

"But you're completely intellectual about that response. It's not integrating for you the way the floggers do." Thomas moved around behind him, possibly pacing. "I would like to try your shoulders, and if that doesn't intrigue you...well. Let's see. Not every body is made for every instrument."

"It makes me want to pull away. Hide a little inside."

"Sam!" Thomas came up close behind him and tucked strong arms around his chest. "You're getting so good at articulating things like this. Thank you. That was just perfect. I'd sensed that, and it was exactly what I needed to hear." He got another kiss on the neck, and Thomas stepped away again.

Oh.

Oh, he felt ten feet tall and bulletproof, like a band of steel he'd lived with his whole life had loosened.

"So. We should keep working with this—I do think there's something for us to learn there. But I'd like to save it for a club session. I'll explain my reasoning for that later rather than taking the time now. For now, I want to make sure to reward you for that amazing work, boy. I'm setting the crop down, and I'm picking up your flogger again."

"Yes, Sir. You want me where I am still?" He wasn't sure what Thomas was thinking, but he could wait for explanations. He'd listened for a hint of disappointment in Thomas's tone, tickled shitless that he couldn't find any.

"If you are comfortable standing a bit longer, I would

love to leave you there. I can see your ink better and...it's inspiring."

"I'm just fine here." Fine and proud as a damn peacock.

"Full arm, boy. I'll keep them slow at first, and we'll see where we can go. Count, out loud. One, Sir. Two, Sir. Breathe. These belong to you."

Thomas didn't wait even a second, the first blow landing low on his left shoulder.

The blow rocked him, in the best way, lighting up his skin. "One, Sir."

"Indeed. Remarkable." The second time Thomas caught him high on the right. "Focus."

He sucked in a breath, trying to sink into the soles of his feet. "Two, Sir."

Thomas gave him three more, in a smooth rhythm, each one punctuated with his own words. "Here. Lit-up. Ready."

He nodded, counted, and muttered, "Yours."

"Mine." He felt Thomas close for a second, but Sir didn't touch, just breathed with him and stepped away again. "You're a joy to me."

That arm went to work, strike after strike, controlled and deliberate repetition at a moderate pace. Sir left enough time for him to count and breathe in between, but not to think.

His body felt heavy and light in the same breaths and he swayed with Thomas's arm, not trying to escape, but because he had to respond to his Sir.

He eventually lost count; then he thought maybe he forgot to count at all, but it didn't seem to matter. He was dimly aware that the blows had grown further apart— maybe lighter too, it was hard to know for sure. He had no sense of how much time had passed or was passing.

He was just there, his heartbeat and Thomas's breath the only thing in the world.

"Good boy." He heard Sir's voice in his ear and felt an arm around his waist. "Come sit. That's a good boy." Thomas smelled like sweat, felt hot as the sun, and the chair was cool relief.

He sucked in air, his hands in his lap, the cuffs the only things keeping him from floating away.

Thomas was close, footsteps and breathing somehow loud in his ears and blending with soft words. Loving words. "Beautiful boy. So proud, sweetheart. Such good work."

When Thomas touched him again, everything went quiet and still. "Three words, boy. Find me three words."

There weren't three words left in him.

Or maybe there were.

"Your boy, Sir."

7

The room was quiet. Thomas was awake but kept his eyes closed for a while, listening to Sam breathe and the faint, faraway sound of a Christmas party somewhere in the building. It had to be late, because when he finally opened his eyes the room was dark, with just a hint of light sneaking in around his bedroom curtains from the street below.

He would be going over that session in his mind for days. It had been more successful than he'd thought possible, and yet at the same time it hadn't gone entirely as planned. That was the beauty of it, he decided, that it had evolved into exactly what they needed it to be. He'd told his boy to trust the process, and he was glad he'd been able to take his own advice.

Sam was stunning. Clearheaded with the word games, thoughtful in his questions, insightful in the way that he was able to describe how that crop made him feel. Present and thoughtful. Generous with his reactions, validating, appreciative.

High as a kite, floating on success.

Perfect.

Perfect, really. He could throw out fancy adjectives all day long, and they all said the same thing in the end.

He let himself take a little credit; he'd thought a long while about working with Sam, his approach, about the way they would best connect. But he also understood the ways his sub had driven that scene even if Sam didn't.

Merry Christmas.

He couldn't imagine a better gift. As far as he was concerned, the last two days with Sam had completely turned the holiday around for him. He wasn't sure if they had a new tradition, but Sam had given him a new outlook. This would be a Christmas to beat.

He lay there with Sam heavy on his chest and couldn't help but chuckle at how his boy was calm and settled and still, and he was the one lying awake with his mind racing.

"Mmm. Love that sound." Sam kissed his collarbone, nuzzling him with soft lips.

"Oh, you're awake." He combed his fingers through Sam's hair and over one shoulder, careful not to graze sensitive, raw skin. He'd spent a long time on aftercare, talking and soothing; he didn't want to undo any of it.

"Uh-huh. So are you." Sam chuckled softly, the sound making it impossible not to smile.

"More or less. It seemed wrong to sleep through feeling as incredible as I do."

"I like that. Incredible. I'm still crystal clear."

Hearing that Sam felt that way, but also knowing that his boy really understood what it meant made him feel proud and strong. It made him feel powerful and accomplished. He'd left himself open, he'd relied on his instinct instead of routine, he'd listened in the moment, and they'd both come out the other side elated.

"I feel like a giant."

"Mmm…" That was a satisfied sound, and Sam tilted his head, kissing the bottom of his rough chin. "Gonna have to shave you in the morning."

He felt his chin reflexively. He usually had a pretty good shadow by late afternoon. He'd let Sam shave him—that could be fun. "Yes. I scruff up fast. How does your back feel?" It looked beautiful a little while ago. That new flogger let him pick his placement nicely and Sam's skin was a lovely, even, symmetrical work of art. It was hard to see in the shadows, but he could just make out a few of the darker lines.

"Like I'm wearing you. It pulls some." Sam often found it difficult to express himself, and yet…there were times the boy was so eloquent, his words touched Thomas's soul.

"You know, when you say things like that, I get this irresistible urge to kiss you."

"I'm right here." Sam slid up, dragging them together, rubbing every inch. "Bring it on."

Thomas grinned and slid a hand down Sam's side to get a grip on his boy's tight ass cheek. "Anything you want, love."

Every time he kissed Sam felt like a question. Like he was offering rather than taking, hoping like hell for Sam's dizzying brand of unconditional surrender, but never expecting it. Sam hummed for him, drawing him in and promising not to let him drown. His own personal cowboy siren.

He was so all over that.

He knew they needed to talk, and they would. Sam would need to debrief a little, he'd need to ask some questions. But not right now, not while they were reaping the rewards of their day. Not while Sam was this close. Not when he wanted his boy this badly.

Carefully, gently, he laid a hand on Sam's back, testing and waiting to see if the heat would interest the boy or pull him out of the moment.

Sam arched into his touch, rocking with a slow, sibilant motion that begged for more.

Every nerve ending from his toes, to his scalp, to his dick suddenly woke up, screaming *Fuck, yeah*. Sam made him shiver, made him groan.

Thomas spread his fingers wider and let go of being gentle, giving Sam what he wanted, and rocking his hips up off the bed.

"Love." The soft words belied the friction Sam gave him, as he straddled Thomas and leaned down toward his cock and up into his hand.

He nodded, the contact enough to make his vision cloudy. "There's nothing like this, Sam. Nothing like you." He found a raised line on Sam's shoulder and followed it with a finger, pressing down just hard enough to burn.

"Fuck..." Sam stared at him, eyes wide, the hunger in them palpable. "Need you like breathing."

"Want you, love." He stared right back, that connection between them easy, freely shared. "You want to ride, cowboy?" He rolled his hips and his cock slid along Sam's ass.

"I was made for it." Sam kissed him hard enough that his world swung wildly, and when his cowboy started teasing him, ass nudging his prick in a steady, driving rhythm, Thomas wanted to scream.

"Fuck. Christ, Sam. Just...God." He reached up and gave one of Sam's nipples a good tweak, hoping to slow his lover down for a second so he could think.

"Uh-huh. I hear you. We're fixin' to ride." Sam leaned over and grabbed the condom, the lube. "Get me ready while I do you." Then he was pegged with a look. "I ain't gonna break either, you get me?"

His throat went so tight it was hard to swallow, so he nodded and fumbled with the lube until he got it open. "Got it," he managed to croak. *Got it. Hear you. Want you so bad it hurts.* "Got you." Fuck if he was waiting one more second. He reached over Sam's hip and gave him two slippery fingers to think about.

Sam groaned, taking him with a couple of restless thrusts before grabbing the condom and opening the packet. It was gratifying to see Sam's hand shake as he worked the rubber out, but the fingers that smoothed it down his aching prick were steady as a rock.

Damn. He'd better get it together before Sam burned him to ashes. It was all he could do not to buck into his lover's grip, but he held still, his eyes steady on Sam's. He reached deeper with his fingers just to tease, and that bought him a second to get a breath, made him feel like he was back in the game.

Waiting for that beautiful fucking gate to open.

Sam's movements were natural and easy, and Thomas found himself staring. No one else on earth had ever been privy to this sight. No one had been where he was, right now.

Then Sam grabbed his cock in a firm grip, rubbing the tip over his hole. "Let's do this."

The heat and pressure as Sam drove down onto him, took him in, was sheer perfection.

He grunted and his hands flew to Sam's narrow hips, holding tight as he pressed his lover down farther, even as he planted his heels in the mattress and rolled up, pinning

Sam in place. "*Now*, let's do this." He bucked up, shoving Sam into his hands.

Sam's body tightened, the look on his boy's face pure bliss. It took no time at all for Sam to find his pace, to well and truly start riding him, meeting Thomas's thrusts, rocking above him.

His boy had taken off like the wind, and he was amused at how catching up seemed to require more concentration than he'd needed for his flogger.

It only took a few breaths, though, and once he was there he poured everything he had into this, finding their moment with mind and body, soul-deep desire driving into Sam with every thrust.

"I ain't gonna break" was the hottest thing he'd ever heard, and he let himself believe it as he lost himself in his boy. Sam held nothing back, offering him deep cries and low moans, ripped abs and tight nipples, his sweet ass like a fist around him.

He shifted one hand to the nape of Sam's neck and the other he wrapped nice and snug around Sam's cock, watching Sam's face, letting their rhythm do the work for now.

"Oh." Sam's jaw twitched as his hands landed on Thomas's chest. "Please. You make me ache."

"You make me burn." There wasn't any stopping them now. No way to slow the train down. His own need raged inside him and he pressed up, lifting Sam with his hips. Sam moved just so, and his boy went stiff, a look of pure hunger on his face before hot seed spread over Thomas's fingers.

"Sam!" The waves of his boy's climax strangled his cock, and he fought it for a few more shallow thrusts before he let out a rough cry, his knees tucking up and his body twisting as he came.

He soared, the world gone white-hot and distant. When he settled, he found himself with an armful of cowboy, Sam heavy and still against his chest, his cock still held tight.

Once again it was down to their breathing. He listened to his lover as he shifted himself free, groaning with even that little bit of effort. He held Sam, kissed the top of his boy's head—because that was about all he had the energy to reach—and made himself find control, breathing in deep and out slowly.

"Mmm...good ride, cowboy." Sam sounded like the cat that had gotten the cream.

"Mmm. Yeah. I think I earned that buckle." He grinned, the cowboy jokes making him happy.

"Yessir." Sam began to shake with laughter. "But I got me the belt."

"Ha! I suppose you did." He laughed also, the two of them vibrating against one another. "I'd smack your ass, boy, but you wore me out. Damn. I'm not sure what I did to deserve you."

"You were wicked in another life. I'm your punishment." Sam's laughter was warm, fond.

"Yeah? If you're punishment, I'll make sure to stay wicked in this one too." He was starting to recover, the laughter and joking hauling his brain out of the fog. He rolled them, settling Sam on one side. "Hey. Thank you."

"You're more than welcome. That was one hell of a ride." Sam's grin could light the whole room.

"It was." He kissed Sam and smiled. "I was talking about more than that, though. I swear, I'd stopped believing in Christmas. And after I lost James, I stopped believing in a lot of other things. You're helping me get it all back. I wouldn't trade these last few days for anything."

Sam stared at him, so serious, and when he spoke, his voice was husky with emotion. "You deserve that. I love you, Mister. All the way."

He nodded. He believed in Sam. He believed in what they shared together. He knew his lover accepted everything he was. "I love you. Every second. Every bit of me is yours, Sam."

Sam's answer was a kiss—one to his forehead, one to the tip of his nose, one to his lips.

Yeah, all those bits and others too. He shook his head and snorted. "So, we'll just stay in bed all week, then?"

"Sounds like a plan. A week-long nap. Maybe I'll order food halfway through."

"That works. You can feed it to me with your fingers, wearing nothing but my collar." The last two words came out with a bit of a growl and he grinned. "I could say that all day long. My collar. My boy, my collar. Mmm."

Sam touched the collar, traced it. "I would do that for you."

That was fairly low down on the list of things he'd like to ask Sam to do for him, but the offer was so earnest, it made him melt a little inside. "Thank you, boy. You're good to me." He touched the little silver ring, then Sam's cheek. "But if we stay in bed all week, we'll miss all kinds of other things we could be doing. Like Scrabble. And dancing." Talking, touching on a few things that might still be tender.

"Mmhmm. We'll wing it. We're good at that, you and me."

"That's for sure." It was still a little terrifying, but he was getting used to it. "You want to go wing a shower, stud? We're a little ripe."

"Sounds like heaven. You thirsty? I'll grab us something on the way?"

"I am. I've been working hard." He laughed and helped Sam sit up, knowing his boy's back would be getting a little tight. He'd massage something wonderful and healing into Sam's skin after they got cleaned up.

They climbed out of bed, and he turned on a lamp so they didn't kill themselves, getting a lovely view of his boy looking used hard and disheveled. He might have to make it his life's work to recreate this, again and again.

"You want water? Orange juice? Wine?" Sam looked him up and down, admiring him.

"Just water, please." He laughed and tried not to feel self-conscious. It didn't matter what he thought, really; he knew Sam thought he looked pretty good.

"Good deal. I'll be there in two shakes. I'm going to get an orange juice." Sam headed off, whistling and happy.

He headed for their bathroom, turned on lights, and started the water.

Amazing that all that time, inside an anxious, grieving, son and brother that had arrived in New York thinking it might as well be Mars, there was a happy, subby little cowboy just dying to get out. Maybe literally dying in there under all that pressure. He might have had a little something to do with coaxing that happy cowboy out. A little something to be very proud of. And he hadn't made out too badly himself.

8

There was a perfect spot in the hallway for headstands. Thomas was watching some documentary through his eyelids, and Sam had a new column idea about pop art compared with western art compared with indigenous art. So, he grabbed a pillow from the bed, leaned over, and kicked up. Then he closed his eyes and started pondering.

The last thing he wanted was to cause offense, so he needed to work out his comparisons very carefully.

"Sweetheart? Sam? Where'd you go?" Thomas's voice floated down the hall. He heard it, but it barely registered. "This thing on TV was fascinating. I didn't even have to watch it. I just kind of absorbed it and it gave me the weirdest...what the hell are you doing?"

"Thinking about a column. Did you have dreams?"

"It's possible I still am. Is this a performance art sort of thing? Are you trying to *be* the column? Don't you need ethereal...doodley music for that?"

"Haven't you ever done yoga? I did it for two years." He

slowly lowered his legs, one after the other, back still against the wall.

"No. I center just fine with a flogger and a punching bag." Thomas leaned against the opposite wall. "You did yoga? How did you shut your brain up long enough?"

"Huh? I just needed to stretch my hamstrings, and I wanted to learn how to stand on my head."

Thomas laughed and held a hand down to haul him up. "Okay, sweetheart. It looks like it worked for you."

"Yep." He liked how headstands helped him think. "I didn't wake you up, did I?"

"Doing a handstand? That would be a trick. No, I had this weird dream about..." Thomas scratched his forehead. "Something. With pollution. I forget now. Have you got a minute?"

"I have many minutes in a row, even." He grinned over, grabbed up the pillow, and tossed it on the bed. "Whatcha need?"

"Well, I wanted to invite you, officially, to the New Year's Eve party at the club." Thomas walked backward down the hall, watching him follow.

"I'd love to. I want to kiss you at midnight." He'd follow this beautiful man anywhere.

"Me too. But..." Thomas reached forward and took one of his hands. "It's...well, it's not like Thanksgiving."

Oh. He went back and replayed what Thomas said.

I wanted to invite you.

Not *I'm* inviting you. Okay, that was awkward as all get out.

Shit. What did he say? How did he give Thomas the out without pretending that he didn't want to be there? Thomas had been so determined that he have the thirty-first off. Had

Sam done something to make Thomas feel like he would embarrass him? *Shit.*

"No worries, honey."

There. That was a nonanswer answer for him to buy a little time.

Thomas sighed and pulled him over to the couch. "Well, maybe you should hear what I mean; then we can figure out what to do."

"Sure. Honey, are you okay?" He didn't want to be the reason Thomas stressed going somewhere he loved.

Thomas raised an eyebrow at him, which usually meant he'd said something off-the-wall. What was wrong with "Are you okay?"

"I'm...fine. All right. Let me start this over." Thomas chuckled. "The New Year's Party at the club is a formalized, full-out, kinky, leather, BDSM event."

"All right." Huh. He leaned back, still holding Thomas's hand, and waited for Thomas to talk to him and tell him what was required from him. He just needed to reserve judgment and listen. He could be all butthurt later.

Thomas watched him; he could feel the way those eyes studied his face. "So that means Doms in full gear, subs in very little at all...lots of kneeling and leashes and...rules."

"Ah." He didn't even know what to say because he didn't know...well, what to say. He wanted to go, but he wasn't the world's best rules guy, and he'd kneel for Thomas, but he'd done something during that whole thing he was never going to understand in a million years, and... "Well, why don't you say what you want from me, and I'll tell you if I can give it to you."

Thomas smiled. "That's the easy part. I want you to go with me...or, no. I want...to go together. The hard part is how." His Sir stopped looking directly at him, and those eyes focused inward, thoughtful. "That whole thing isn't us. I could do it; I did with James every year. He loved it. But you can't. Or—wait. You could, but you shouldn't. It's not you. And if it's not you, then it's not us."

Thomas glanced up at him again. "Did that make any sense at all? I can't find a direct way to say what I mean to say."

"Can't we just go together? I mean, can't we just go and be us? Is that against y'all's rules?" He wouldn't embarrass Thomas for love or money. He wouldn't gawk; he could just keep his mouth shut and make sure Thomas's wineglass stayed full and that they got home safe.

"I don't know. I think part of the point is to be seen as Dom and sub, you know? Not just a couple of guys. I think it would be disrespectful not to participate somehow."

He held his hands open. "You know what's most important to me is to be with you. It would...well, it'd hurt some to have the night off and be apart."

He'd been waiting for a kiss at midnight his whole life, he thought.

Thomas shook his head. "That's not on the table. Wherever we are, we're together. I got you that night off for a reason. That first midnight kiss is mine."

"Okay, then. I'm getting everything I want. Let's get you some of what you want." He leaned a little harder, breathing easier. "I'm at a little bit of a disadvantage, honey, because I'm not sure how to help you figure this. I'm willing to, but I don't know where to start."

Puzzles. These were puzzles. He needed something to start working on.

"Tell me what your favorite parts are, at the party?"

Thomas's forehead wrinkled, and he leaned back on the couch pillows. After a minute, he grinned a little. "All right. I like having a sub with me, and I like to show him off a little. I like it when the guys get why I'm proud. I do like some leather, but I don't need to be a dungeon master." Thomas laughed. "I guess I like the show—does that sound awful?"

"Shit, no. I mean, I rode rodeo for the show. I sure as shit didn't do it for the money. I did it to strap on my chaps, get my rocks off, and hear the applause."

"Do you want to wear them to the party?" Thomas leaned in again. "Your chaps?"

He blinked. That was unexpected. Unexpected, but he could strap them on. He wasn't stupid. He knew that buckling on the leather made him stand taller, made him cock-proud. Turned him from a cowboy to a roughstock rider. "Surely. I'll have to make them pretty, but they look good."

"Would you be willing to show some skin? Maybe...just my collar and some cuffs?" Thomas was definitely putting something together in his head.

His cheeks lit up with heat, but he didn't work so hard on his belly to be ashamed of it, right? "You gonna let me wear my hat?"

"Yes. I'm thinking I might wear mine too. And I won't ask you to go naked under the chaps; you can wear your Wranglers."

"I'd blister if you asked for that. They're not for show. Those buckles would tear me up." If he had his hat, he'd be a little hidden away, a little in the shadow. "I love how you wear your hat."

"You do?" He thought maybe Thomas sat up a little straighter at that. "Thanks. I think we'd look great together. What do you think for me? Maybe a vest and cuffs? Or do you think I should wear a shirt?"

Sam looked at Thomas, imagining both outfits,

imagining them together. "I guess that depends. I love you in leather, I love the way it makes you smell. But if you're going for the look, the...visual between us? We'll dress you like a high-dollar cowboy." It would be...

His cock filled, and he reached down, gave himself a little rub.

Yeah.

Thomas watched him, shameless, eyes on his crotch. "You like that, huh?"

"What's not to like? I'm going to have to pack my whole self in ice not to embarrass us both with you cowboying up with me."

"All right. You'll dress me, I'm in. I guess that means we need to go shopping." Thomas rocked a little on the couch —looked like somebody liked that idea.

"I would love to. You in a bright white starched shirt and Wranglers is one hell of a fantasy." He dared to scoot over and straddle Thomas's thighs. "This okay? We can keep talking..."

"I can't say anything coherent with you on my lap."

"Are you sure?" He chuckled softly and leaned in to kiss the corner of Thomas's lips. "I know not to call you by your name. What else do you want me to know?"

"Don't...uh." Thomas turned and kissed him. "Don't look anyone with authority in the eye. Doms, bartenders, DJs, security, or anyone Clint has with him." A hand slid up his shirt and pressed into his abs.

"Lord, that's going to be hard to remember. It's so damn impolite. I'll do my dead-level best and keep the hat down super low." He flexed, tempting more of those touches.

"If it's hard, just don't look at anyone at all. Hm. Stay a little behind my shoulder; that way I won't have to ask you to kneel. If I sit, they'll expect you to kneel or stand behind my chair...but since standing for a long time is damaging to you, we can claim any kind of accommodation I want. I'll just tell you to get a chair." A second hand joined the first and ran up his sides.

"You know if it saves your pride, I would kneel for you, don't you? *Only* for you, but I'd do it." He stretched up into those hot hands.

Thomas looked at him seriously. "You will see some subs crawling instead of walking, some will have fully covered faces or their Masters will be leading them, literally, by the balls. Humiliation is a legitimate tool, and some subs actually crave it. It's never been part of my ethic; I won't ask you to kneel just to save my pride. I can't say I won't ever ask for what I consider a legitimate reason, but I'm not interested in humiliating you."

"I appreciate that. I'll give you what you ask, if I can. I want you to know that I'm yours. I will be polite and all, and you know Angel is a dear friend, but I'm not..." He tried to figure out how to explain himself. "I'm not looking to play chess to play chess. I'm looking to be across the table from you."

"Then I guess it's a damn good thing I'm neurotically possessive and jealous." Thomas slid those hands around him, spreading fingers across his shoulders.

Sam leaned back, his eyelids going heavy. "I love your hands."

"I love the way you're always moving. Leaning into me. Tracking me." Thomas was quiet for a second, then added, "You know, if it makes you feel better, the only reason anyone in that club would ever touch you without my permission is if you weren't safe. Otherwise, security would see them out, and they wouldn't be allowed in again."

He stretched back with a grin, knowing Thomas would

hold him, his spine cracking. "Is that your way of saying no bashing anyone in the nose, and trust in the bouncers?"

Thomas chuckled. "Pretty much. You know we're going to be the subject of a lot of conversation. This isn't a BDSM club in Austin."

"I don't think that's legal in Texas. I know sex toys aren't." People seemed to talk, no matter what. Didn't Thomas say there were lots of folks with lots of ways to find how they joined together? If he had to respect them, then they damn well could respect him and Thomas. "Is that bad or good? I'm proud to be with you."

"Oh, I'm going to be very proud to be with you too, sweetheart. We're going to look fantastic together, and I did say I wanted to show you off, didn't I? We're going to stand out. People always talk about the ones that stand out." Thomas laughed softly and reassuring hands shifted to hug his hips. "Remember, I only see a lot of these guys a few times a year. At the last New Year's party, I was in full black leather, and James was mostly naked and on a leash attached to some ferocious nipple clamps. This is a far cry from that. They'll be curious."

He so did not want to think about naked James, and he couldn't imagine there being enough nipple on his chest to put a clamp on, so he dismissed that image out of hand. "I like your leather, but this will make a statement. A 'Your ass is fine in jeans' statement."

"As long as it makes a statement to you, I'm happy. I love that you're into this. Thank you. It's a fun party, it's crazy busy, and there's music and dancing, and friends, and when you need a break, there's a sub's lounge so you can regroup. Then midnight is a thing to see. Really."

He was just tickled shitless that he'd managed to help

Thomas figure this out without Sam losing his mind or Thomas getting all huffy and hurt.

"I'll just stick close and admire your butt."

"Trust me, there will be a lot of admiring going on, hot stud in chaps." Thomas pressed a hand against his fly and traced his bulge with a thumb.

He arched a little, rolling his hips. He knew how good he looked in the chaps. If you earned them, you knew it, and you could see it.

"We'll go shopping tomorrow morning, and I'll try to trust you on what best suits my backside." Thomas grinned at him. "I guess we could take a nap before dinner. Not watch another documentary while you stand on your head some more. We've got nothing better to do, right? Such a *slow* afternoon." Thomas drew out the word "slow" like it was a promise.

"We could." Sam leaned in, let his lips brush Thomas's ear. "Or I could spend some quality time loving on you. Your choice."

"Hm, tough choice. Let's go with that." Thomas tugged on his hips, sliding him about as close as they could get. "Why does that sound so much hotter when it's your idea?"

"Because it's good to know you're wanted, and I do. Want you. Bad." That was an easy one. He took a kiss that liked to burn them both up.

Enough chatting. He wanted to play.

9

If you wanted to go shopping for serious cowboy gear, the best person to have along with you was a serious cowboy.

Their shopping trip hadn't taken that long, considering they'd been all over Manhattan on the subway. Sam had a plan, apparently, and dressed him up in minutes. The hard part—and the expensive part—had been the boots. He was completely in love with the pair his boy had picked out for him, though. Maybe even more than his hat. Maybe. Maybe not. His boots said "cowboy," but his hat said "hot."

They put all the bags down and Sam hung up his shirt, mumbling something baffling about having to press his jeans.

He stood in the bedroom doorway, watching Sam fuss and marveling at how happy his boy looked. It was a little like the last time Sam cleaned all the floggers; just give Sam something to keep his hands busy, and the boy was happy as a clam.

"I'm looking forward to wearing the buckle you gave me."

"You'll look like a cowboy's dream, honey. I love the white button-down on you, although the gray is fine too." Sam smiled at him, those eyes so warm, focused on him. The lines at the corners were fewer, and the dark circles were gone.

Thomas had known Sam was tense, tired, and worried before, but he'd had no idea how bad it had been. Now that he had a comparison, now that he knew what Sam looked like when he was at peace? He didn't want to let that escape.

"You can send a picture to your mom." Thomas winked at him.

"She'll think you're handsome. James looked like her, you know?" Sam pulled out his wallet and opened it up to show him. There was an old photo of three stair-step young men framed by their parents. He would know James anywhere, standing there in the middle of his brothers. Bowie was massive, standing in his uniform with his equally beefy father. Sam was tiny—easily half the size of Bowie, a tiny, fierce-looking little cowboy with a cast on his arm. Their mother did look like James, and he could see where the hazel eyes came from. "This was Bowie's Basic training graduation. It's the last time we were all together. I was eleven."

"The last time you were all together was fourteen years ago?" He didn't know why that seemed so strange to him since there were very few pictures of all his siblings together at once. But he had so many siblings, and most of them wouldn't claim him anyway.

It obviously meant a lot to Sam for him to carry that one and only picture around in his wallet.

"I see the resemblance. That was a long time ago."

"It was." Sam smiled. "But that's all of us. The soldier, the teacher, and the cowboy."

"Thanks for showing me that; it's a nice reference for me to have."

He'd been looking for a natural opening in their conversation to bring up work for two days but hadn't found one. He knew if his boy went back to the bar, not only would he see those tired eyes again, but Sam would be working odd hours, full-time, doing freelance work in his spare time, and most of *their* time together would evaporate.

The week was getting short. He was going to have to make an opening.

"Hey, speaking of references." *Good God.* Well, it was awkward, but it might have been subtle enough. "I meant to ask if you've made any headway on the column you were working on."

"The one about the comparisons between commercialism and spirituality in western art? A little, yeah. I'm actually considering—" Sam turned bright pink, the expression one Thomas had never seen before.

He had to grin a little at the blush. "You're considering...?"

"I-I'm considering turning it into a book. Maybe." Sam shrugged, shook his head.

"Hey. That sounds like a worthwhile project." There had to be some way he could work with that. "That's going to take some time, right?"

"Yeah. It's probably a fool's errand, but so is devoting your academic life to western art, and that didn't stop me. There's just something about this idea—southwestern art versus Western art. Pop art and cowboy art. Spirituality and commercialism. There's something here."

"I think you should go for it. Why not? I mean, you have the perfect office for it." He was watching Sam carefully; he could almost see the wheels turning, the ideas popping around in his boy's mind.

The boy just needed the time to write it.

The fact was that Sam didn't need the income from the bar anymore, but he knew better than to say so. He didn't even have to discuss it. Sam would never accept being taken care of that way, and he had to respect that.

But supporting him while he worked on a book? That Thomas could possibly get away with.

"You're not supposed to encourage me, honey. You're supposed to point out that no one needs a book about this and to focus on work that matters." Sam laughed and came to him, kissed him. "I love that you have my back, though."

Thomas returned the kiss and hugged him close. "What do you mean by work that matters?"

"The kind that makes money. I just...I can't seem to contain this idea into an article, you know? I can't make it that small."

"Okay. How much money do you need to make?" Dangerous territory, but he needed Sam to think along certain lines.

"We haven't talked about that, have we? Rent and stuff. I've just been so busy being lost in you." Sam shook his head. "I got a little credit card I pay off every month and my phone and my half of us."

"Mm. Work that matters, you and me, right? And your freelance work, the research and the articles, that's work that matters because you enjoy it. It's what you studied to do. Work that matters isn't actually about money. We can talk about how you contribute to us. I think you should write that book."

"I like that idea—you and me being work that matters."

Sam sighed, hand on his belly. "I don't ever want you to think I'm using you."

He covered Sam's hand with his own. "Sam, if you go back to work at that bar, there won't be time for the work that matters."

"I don't know what to do, Mister. I don't." Sam stayed close to him, resting hard. Trusting in his strength.

"I handled the bills for this place long before you came along and without any trouble, sweetheart. I don't want you to be tired and stressed, I want you to be...productive and inspired. I don't know what James did to make ends meet, but he might well have been miserable when I thought he was happy." He could have helped. He could have, if James had just asked him. "I want you to be as happy as you are right now."

"I'm not a mooch, though. I swear to God. I'm not. You know that, right? I'd do whatever I had to do to stay close to you."

He nodded. "You turned your heat down to forty and washed your clothes in the bathtub. You wouldn't even come use my washing machine when I offered. You wore clothing made for a giant named Daddy Mike. I don't see a mooch here." Hell, Sam had let himself be beaten almost to death. He blinked. *Christ.* Sam had let them beat him without defending himself to stay here. To stay near him.

"You're just jealous I took the sweater back. Don't worry, we can both fit in it. Together."

He laughed. "Can we burn it together instead?" He didn't let Sam answer but kissed him hard. He loved his boy, his lover, this man more than he believed possible. He loved Sam so much, it made his chest ache and his heart race. If Sam had given him a hard time about the bar, he'd have taken those Sundays and nothing more if he'd had to. He'd have taken anything.

"You understand that I love you, right? I mean, I know you hear me, but you believe me, don't you?"

"Yes." Just that. Simple and sure. Yes.

"I'm not going to tell you what to do, Sam. I just won't. I have too much respect for you. I'm not even going to ask, because I don't want your answer to be that you made a decision for me. I want you to make a decision for yourself. Keep the job, leave the job, work out something with Mike... whatever you think is right. Whatever you want. Just keep in mind the work that really matters—that's all I'm asking."

"Yeah. We got to work out the details; then I can make a decision that makes sense. Pros and cons, you know?"

"We'll do that."

But I'd rather you just quit.

Respect, being fair-minded and reasonable and all of that aside, if it were up to him, Sam just wouldn't go back. He took a breath. "We can talk over dinner, perhaps. So we're not on empty stomachs."

"I'd like that. It would be—if we had evenings. Saturdays."

"I would lo—I would be extremely happy with that arrangement." He missed Saturdays at the club. Well, Saturdays at the club with a sub. He'd been going alone, but he spent an awful lot of time sitting at the bar, talking nonsense with Scotty.

"Happy enough for me to be a little tight on cash? I'm making money enough to help right now, but not like I ought."

"Yes. Happy enough for you to help out in other ways. And once your book sells..." He grinned. "Then you'll have money coming in while you write the next one."

"I can spend most of my time on freelance and just give the book a little, but...it's a good idea. Something I could hang a PhD on."

Look at the light in his boy's eyes. The hunger.

"I want that for you. I want what you're feeling right now to be what you spend your time on. Freelance should be enough. When you're actively working in that field, somehow there's always more work."

He mentally checked himself, but he was sure he wasn't handing out wishful thinking or clever bullshit just to keep his lover out of that bar. Sam was inspired. He could write a book; it was in his boy's eyes.

"Yeah. I'm trying not to get all excited and shit, but... yeah." Sam kissed him hard, holding on tight.

Get excited, sweetheart. I'm excited.

Thomas lifted Sam off the ground and gave him a spin. It might be clichéd, but it was fun as hell.

"We can have our time, you and me," Sam whispered against his lips. "Our time."

"Our time. Thank you." He took a kiss.

Now they just had to break it to Mike.

10

Keep your eyes down. Keep your mouth shut. Stand there and admire Thomas's butt and try not to feel naked.

No problem.

He handed Thomas his coat and pulled the brim of his hat as far down as he could. No one could see above his upper lip, so he was safe.

Thomas's excitement was like a lit bulb, and Sam had to admit his lover was beautiful in his western wear. It would be no hardship to watch that fine ass. He wouldn't fuck this up for Thomas for anything.

"This is a lot of shirt. I guess I'll get used to it." Thomas pulled the coat on. "Car's here, right? Are you ready? Are you going to be warm enough?"

A lot of shirt. Good lord. "I reckon you won't let me freeze to death, right?"

"No, sir." Thomas winked. "Come on."

Their Uber was tiny, and he and Thomas sat close as they headed across town, but the ride was so short, they barely had time to think about it.

"Hey." Thomas pulled him close after they'd stepped out

of the car. "I'm proud of you. You're going to be fine. You might even have fun. Remember to breathe."

"I'm on it." *Breathe. Don't look. Don't talk. Watch Thomas's butt. Don't worry about walking around a party in your chaps and no shirt.*

He could totally survive this.

"Midnight is coming." Thomas winked and led him to the door, giving security a nod as they went in. Sound hit them first, the din of conversation over atmospheric music.

He hooked his thumbs in his chaps and followed Thomas in. He had silver medallions right where his fingers could trace them.

As soon as they walked in, people began to greet Thomas, exclaiming over his beautiful lover, and he just stayed back, hiding in his hat. He'd never seen it so full, and there were a ton of biker boots and chaps that had never seen a bull or hit the dirt.

He took the coat Thomas handed him. "Coat check. Leave yours as well." Thomas pointed to a room off to the left, next to the near end of the bar, and gave his hand a squeeze under the coat before letting it go.

He headed over and checked their coats, telling himself that this wasn't weird as all get out and even if it was, it was super important to Thomas, so he'd deal with the weird.

"You look amazing," a voice behind him said. He glanced over his shoulder at another sub with an armful of coats but didn't think he recognized the guy. "It's so cool. The hats. We know just who your Master is. He's handsome too, Master Thomas."

"Yessir, he is. Fine as frog hair." He tipped his hat. "I appreciate it."

"You're with Master Thomas?" The kid at the coat check

was all in black but not leather and had to be just barely twenty-one, looking that young.

"Yessir." He wasn't given a tag; instead the kid hung a card with Thomas's name on it over the hangers.

"Have a good night."

"You too. Don't work too hard." He was grateful to not be on tonight. He'd be busting his hump at the door of Mike's and tossing assholes at an alarming rate.

He caught sight of Thomas and wound his way to the fine son of a bitch, trying hard not to cross his arms over his chest as he went.

"Look who's here."

Shit, he knew that guy. He was introduced at the club that first day with a bunch of other guys. Thomas turned and smiled at him. "Thank you, sweetheart. Do you remember Master Adam? And his boy, Rick."

Adam wore leather well. "You do your Master proud, boy. The two of you are something to see."

"I appreciate it, Sir." Weirdly, this whole thing was a little like going to church when they didn't have youth ministers. You didn't quite know what to do, but you knew you'd better be on your absolute best behavior, or you'd be sitting pretty for a week. He didn't think his momma would approve of his get-up, though. That might make her cross.

Cross? *Shit.* She'd pluck him bald-headed.

"Rick and James were friends, at least here at the club." Adam gave him a nod and left it at that, turning back to Thomas. "The two of you have settled in, it looks like."

"Remarkably well."

"You should know your boy caught a lot of interest when he came looking for Clint the other week."

Thomas laughed. "I don't doubt it. Taking risks to get me

assistance might as well be the definition of loyalty, don't you think?"

"Oh, definitely. But you'll forgive us if we were amused."

"I will. Although there really wasn't anything funny about it."

Rick's eyes got huge for a second, and the sub literally bit his lips together.

"Point taken, friend. Is everything all right now?" Adam glanced between him and Thomas.

"We're safe. Thank you."

"Glad to hear it. Truly."

"Adam, I'm going to head to the bar. We'll catch up, okay?"

"Yes, of course. Get a drink. I'll find you later."

Thomas nodded once, the brim of his hat bobbing, and headed for the bar.

Huh. That was more than vaguely hot.

He followed along, humming under his breath.

"Thirsty, boy?" When it got crowded closer to the bar, Thomas actually steered him around in front, protectively. "We're not playing tonight; you can have a drink if you want one."

"I think I'm okay for now, Mister, but thank you." Thomas was gonna drink, and he didn't like being loose with all the amateurs getting drunk. He wanted to be sure he got his Thomas home safe.

Once they reached the bar, Thomas stepped back in front of him. "Patron Silver on the rocks, Scotty."

Scotty's eyes went wide at the sight of Thomas, and the man paled a little. Sam damn near laughed.

He caught Thomas's grin out of the corner of his eye. "What's the matter, Scotty? You don't like my hat?"

"It's perfect, Master Thomas. Just shocked me."

Shocked, huh? That was funny as shit.

"It's actually not new; James gave it to me a couple of years ago. I've just never worn it to the club. I'm changing things up a little, it feels good. Also, it means I get my boy in chaps."

He kept his hat down, refusing to look up. Thomas had mentioned Scotty specifically—Scotty and Clint.

"He looks amazing. Unique for sure."

That was him. Unique.

"One of a kind, Scotty. Thanks for the drink. Come on, sweetheart, I see Clint. Have you met his boy?"

"I don't think so, Mister. Maybe?"

"You'd remember." They wound through the crowd to a spot with more elbow room. "Evening, Clint."

"Well, look at you, Thomas." Clint's chuckle was warm, fond. "And Mister O'Reilly."

He tipped his hat. "Sir."

Thomas laughed. "*Mister O'Reilly* and I negotiated a bit. Your advice has been invaluable."

"Excellent. I'm pleased to hear it. Would you like to join us? Daniel and I are enjoying our evening, thus far."

Daniel had a gag the size of a Mack truck in his mouth and bright red cheeks. Sam wasn't exactly sure *enjoying* was the right world for Daniel's evening, but far be it from him.

"Thank you." Thomas took a chair. "Oh, sweetheart, run behind the bar, there should be a stool for you there. I made a special request, Clint, I didn't think you'd mind. My boy requires special accommodation due to a rodeo injury."

"Of course not. Their care is our first priority, always."

"I'm on it, Mister." He went to the end of the bar and looked, grabbing the wooden stool. He nodded to Scotty and the barbacks working, then made his way to the table, listening to all the whispers.

That's right, y'all. I look like I belong in these clothes.

Thomas helped him place it, and he took a seat. It was slightly lower than the chairs, but he wasn't kneeling, and he didn't have to stand.

"Will this work?" Thomas asked him, speaking close to his ear.

"Yessir. Thank you. You rock." He inhaled deep, the scent of Stetson and Thomas like magic.

"Good boy." Thomas turned around and took a seat again. "Clint, I'm glad to see Daniel here. He seems as obedient as ever."

"Eminently." Clint ruffled Daniel's hair, mussing it. Daniel looked at Sam, and Sam caught his eye, offering a half smile. The man was here on purpose, after all.

"My boy gave me a lovely crop for Christmas; it's a nice instrument but we didn't have much success with it. Does Chase still run his workshops?"

"He does. We just need enough interest. Three or four couples would be best. A crop, hmm? That's a thoughtful gift."

"Along with my buckle." Thomas stood briefly, showing it off. "Thoughtful and clever. It could be my skill, could be it's not his cup of tea. I just don't know for sure, and I'd hate to give up on it that quickly."

"Chase is the man to help you decide, absolutely. Have you tried tapping gently again and again? I've found it creates a delicious response on a nipple or an inner thigh. Wouldn't you say, boy?"

The urge to point out that Daniel couldn't say dick because there was a rubber ball in his mouth was huge, but Sam managed to not, because well, he wasn't an asshole.

"I have not. I appreciate the suggestion. Perhaps we'll try

that out. I'll drop Chase an email, I believe we would benefit from his assistance. How was your holiday?"

Sam let himself float away, only listening with half an ear. He watched and tapped his toes to the music.

"Little Sammy!" Angel grabbed him up, lifted him right off the stool, and hugged him tight. "Look at you, all collars and cuffs. I approve. I'm going to dance with him, Thomas. I'll bring him back later."

Thomas stood up. "Hey, Angel. Good to see you. You look great." He felt fingers on his arm, and Thomas tugged him gently a few steps away from Angel.

Huh. Okay, so he was going to put that memory in his pocket and pull it out when he needed to feel wanted.

"Thanks. I just came from Mike's."

"You didn't bring a friend?"

"I didn't."

Sam didn't get it. Angel was a teddy bear. A dear, wonderful guy. One hell of a friend. Caring as fuck. And, from all accounts from the whispers in certain corners of Mike's, hung like a bull moose.

"Well, come on then, pull up a chair. You remember Daniel? Doesn't he look stunning?" Thomas gestured to a chair to the left for Angel, then pointed to his stool on Thomas's right. "Have a seat, boy."

Sam chuckled and sat. Apparently Angel hadn't been explained the rules. Maybe Angel gave no shits.

"He's beautiful. Always. No one wears a gag quite like him." Angel grinned over at him, eyes twinkling. "And Sammy did a great job with you. You look amazing. Seriously, man."

Sam nodded and winked. Thomas looked like heaven on earth.

Thomas gave Angel a nod. "Thank you. I feel pretty

amazing, truthfully. Oh. Did you see my boots?" His Sir pushed back from the table and shifted so Angel could see. "Aren't they gorgeous?"

"Damn. Those are something else. Are they comfortable?"

Sam grinned. Poor Thomas had to use the bag trick to get them on, but they were perfect.

"You know, that's the interesting thing. They were a bit of a bear to get on, but they fit like a glove." Thomas shifted in his chair. "So you saw the collar, right? I'm so proud of it. It looks even better than I'd imagined."

Angel looked Sam over before he smiled and nodded. "It suits him to the ground. Honestly. I suppose that means you're not going to let me dance with him tonight, hmm?"

"I was really subtle about that, wasn't I?" Thomas chuckled and patted Angel's knee. "Not on a night like tonight. You understand, I'm sure."

"Well, if you change your mind, let me know." Angel winked at Thomas, teasing terribly.

Sam had seen this over and over at the tavern. Angel would find a little tender spot and exploit it, tease until you wanted to pop him.

"Oh, definitely. I'll move you right to the front of the line, my friend. No one will mind." Thomas picked up his drink and sipped it, smiling over the rim.

Angel's laughter filled the air. "Fair enough. I'm going to get a beer."

He glanced at Thomas, not sure if it was okay to offer to get it or what. Thomas winked and gave him a nod.

"I'll go grab it for you. I know what you like."

"Thanks, Sammy. I appreciate it."

"Anyone else need anything?"

He got an approving look from Thomas. "I'm fine, sweetheart. Clint?"

"Could you bring a bottle of water for my boy, Mister O'Reilly?"

"Absolutely, Sir. I'm on it."

He headed to the bar, whistling a little bit as he waited.

"What do you need, Sam?" Scotty asked.

"Two waters and one Bud Light, please, sir."

"Sure. You having fun?"

"It's a great party." *No talking, no looking.* Was it fun? Being with Thomas was fun, and it wasn't as weird as he'd thought. Maybe a little strange just sitting. He was used to running his butt off.

"You know, James used to love these parties. He and Master Thomas came to all of them. It's strange to see him looking so conservative when he can really rock the leather." Scotty put two bottles of water on the bar and started drawing Angel's beer.

What the fuck did you say to that, exactly? *Dear Mister Bartender, Did I ask you your motherfucking opinion? Kiss my ass. Me. P.S., Darla could hand you your ass on a platter and I survived her.*

He went with grunting. That was one of Daddy's secrets. When in doubt, grunt.

Scotty set the beer down on the bar. "Are you going to be okay carrying all of that? You need some help? Master Thomas said you had a couple of...limitations."

He let one eyebrow lift. "Two waters and a beer?" He worked as a fucking barback in a place that made this club look innocent in a whole lot of ways. "No worries. I got this. Thank you."

Limitations his ass.

There was a very good chance he could shove all his limitations down Scotty's throat and let him gag on them.

Okay. *Damn.* That came from nowhere.

"My pleasure." Scotty tapped the bar, then got called away.

Adam and Rick had joined them by the time he got back, and the table was full. Thomas got Angel's attention. "Ah. Angel. Your beer."

He gave Angel his beer, put one water bottle on the table by Clint, one near Thomas's hand. *Okay. Breathe. Let your butthurt go.* Fuck what Scotty thought. *Look at Thomas.* The man was a fucking wet dream. Was *his* fucking wet dream.

Stare at Thomas's butt and fantasize about...well, how he had beat the fuck out of someone or how it had felt when he'd ridden Thomas into the mattress, wearing Thomas's marks.

Really not a tough decision.

Thomas pointed to the water. "Are you thirsty, boy?"

"Yes, Sir. You want some?" No one had told him the whole etiquette of drinking water after the bartender had been a turd thing.

His Sir opened the bottle and handed it to him. "I'm fine at the moment boy, thank you. Are you all right? Would you like a break?"

A break from sitting? "I'm fair to middlin', Mister. Thanks."

"Very well. Thank you, boy."

He sipped his water and let the music sink in again, only one ear on the conversation at the table as he let his mind float a little. He was rocked back into the room as the bass started thumping and the room went dark, the colored lighting from the dance floor flooding everything.

The group at the table started to break up; it was too loud now for talking.

He looked over at Thomas, trying to gauge what his Sir needed, if anything.

Thomas got up, took his hand, and pulled him to his feet, shouting over the music. "Eleven thirty." He got a big grin. "Dance?"

"Hell, yes." His butt was numb, and he wanted to move. Doing it in Thomas's arms was even better.

Thomas took him by the hand and headed for the busy dance floor, where they were surrounded by men dancing alone, in groups, with partners...it seemed like a much different kind of party all of a sudden.

He pressed right into Thomas, staying close. He needed Thomas's touch now, Thomas's attention. He'd done what he was supposed to.

The arm that hooked around his back tugged him even closer. It didn't seem to matter that the thumping bass and the lighting called for something more energetic, Thomas just held him, and they created their own rhythm. They were good at that.

It was so different, his naked belly against Thomas's clothed one, that buckle. Different and hot as fuck. "Damn, Mister. This is fine."

"Mhmm." He got a deep hum in response that he felt against his skin rather than heard, and the hand on his back traced along what he knew was the edge of his scar.

There were no screens on the dance floor, no Times Square ball drop coverage on the TV over the bar. It could be any night of the year, really, any time of day out there. But it was minutes to his first New Year's kiss in here.

Thomas caught a finger under his chin and turned his

face so he could see those brown eyes, but all his lover—his Sir—did was lick those red lips and wink at him.

"Tease. You're gorgeous, you know that?" He thought it was important that Thomas knew.

Thomas smiled at him with a thoughtful look, and finally just said, "Thank you. You are irresistible, just in case you didn't know."

A sub wearing damn near nothing handed them each noisemakers with mylar fringe on them and little confetti poppers shaped like champagne bottles.

"I'm yours. Balls to bones." He cupped Thomas's jaw, damn near dizzy with it.

"Mine."

Somewhere, someone started counting and everyone joined in, including Thomas, who was looking right into his eyes as they hit three...two...one.

"Happy New Year!" Thomas pulled that black hat off, ducked right underneath his, and kissed him.

He pushed in, reached up, and wrapped his hand around Thomas's nape, holding them together, just about as happy as a man could be.

He sent a prayer winging up, that James was at peace, that his brother understood. Then he let himself have this.

He'd earned it.

11

Monday morning suit and tie. It felt strange to be into his routine again after living in ecstasy for a week with Sam, but it was right. He needed to get back to his work, and he was anxious to discover what their new routine would be like. How they would manage their passions for everything other than each other when they had to function in the real world.

But now that it was Monday *after* work, he was just...anxious.

He'd texted with Sam to wish him a good-night at the bar but had no idea what tomorrow's conversation with his lover would be. In a perfect world, Sam would come home and say he'd quit, Mike was cool about it, and that nightmare would be over. But nothing about the world was perfect and honestly, he wasn't sure it ought to be. He'd just have to wait and see, trust the boy to do what was in his heart.

But that left him facing an evening alone in his apartment. With Sam's rodeo treasures up in the living room and his boy's research all over the desk in the office, it was most definitely their apartment now, and he knew it was going to be a long night.

So, he decided to visit the club instead.

It was nearly empty, only a couple of men relaxing after their day, Scotty at the bar, the lights low and warm.

He took off his overcoat and his suit jacket and found a seat at the bar, glancing at the hockey game that was on TV.

"Master Thomas! Good evening. What can I get you?" Scotty gave him a warm, happy smile.

That was just the kind of welcome he needed. "Hi, Scotty. Just a coffee, please. You look good. Did you survive New Year's all right? That's got to be a crazy night for you." He still felt a little hungover, but it wasn't from drinking.

"It was insane, but Master Clint hired in a number of guys to help, so I wasn't on my own back here. Did your boy enjoy his first New Year's Eve party here?"

"He did, thank you. It was a bit of a trial by fire, but there wasn't much to be done about that. He did beautifully. I loved your face when we walked in." That shocked look was priceless, and about what he'd expected. He hadn't minded the double takes and the curious smiles; he was different. *They* were different.

"No one quite expected it, that's for sure." Scotty handed him his coffee, a carousel of sugar, some cream. "But I've grown used to you in your leathers. No one wears them quite like you."

He snorted. "That's kind, Scotty, but a bit of an overstatement." He added cream to his mug. "Is Clint going to be around tonight, do you know?"

"He is. He called to ask if Bryan was available for a shoulder massage. I'm trying to reach him now."

"Oh, that's a nice idea. Maybe see if he can squeeze me in too?" For all the good it would do him. He wouldn't know what Sam had decided for himself until tomorrow afternoon sometime unless...well, who was he kidding? He wasn't going to sleep.

"Of course, Sir." Scotty gave him a nod and headed toward the back of the bar, texting furiously.

He sipped his coffee, trying to relax. Sam's brother was arriving in a few days, at least in theory, and he had to admit to dreading meeting Bowie. Sam and James's birthday was coming up fast, and that was fraught with complications too.

He hadn't even really talked to Sam about birthday plans, for God's sake. James had never been around for his birthday—the brothers had always spent it together. Vegas or Reno or Austin or Cozumel.

Not New York. Not with him, ever, and definitely not with big brother Bowie. Sam had plenty of reasons to celebrate this birthday, but *he* had just as many to dread it. For Sam's sake he wanted it to be good, and he had to hope at least that Bowie wanted that too in the end.

He didn't even have a birthday present yet. "Scotty, I need to get Sam a birthday gift. What do you think?" When in doubt, consult a bartender.

"Cowhide pajamas? Spurs? Hmm...I have to admit, Sam is the only cowboy I've ever known. He and James are very different. I would say jeweled nipple clamps for James." Scotty offered him a wink.

He laughed. "Right? James was kind of easy like that. Nothing he liked better than being looked at. Sam is more... practical in his thinking. I suppose I could get him a membership. Clint has been very good about allowing him to be my guest."

"That would be a lovely gesture, Sir. Generous."

He nodded. He had a couple of other ideas too. He just

needed to make a decision now. "More coffee, please, Scotty."

"Little help?" Bryan stuck his head through the door and disappeared again.

He glanced at Scotty, then shrugged and slid off his stool. "I got it." He held the door so Bryan could get his massage table through and a heavy-looking backpack. "Thank you. Making the rounds today, so I'm loaded for bear."

"Can I get something for you?"

"Thanks, I'm good. Scotty? Big man's office or am I setting up in one of the rooms?"

"I think Master Clint's office. He seemed to need a deep session."

"Poor guy. I hate to hear that. You need some help too, Sir?" Bryan smiled at him.

"If you have time, but Clint is clearly your priority." Deep session? He wondered what was going on. Everyone was entitled to a bad day, but Clint didn't have many that he'd seen. "Was something up when you talked to him, Scotty? I could chat with him another time."

"He didn't care to say. I'm sorry."

"Well, we'll start with you then, Sir?"

Thomas thought Sam would like Bryan—easygoing, tactile, physical and basically happy, they thought they would make good friends.

"Sure. Sounds good. I'll follow you." He certainly liked Bryan; this was a good idea. He headed for Clint's office, feeling very odd about going in without Clint actually being there.

How many times had he been in here—either on his knees, sitting in that huge leather chair, or pacing as he worked out whatever issue he was having. It was a little like walking into his dad's office at the lumberyard. It felt big even though it wasn't, felt like something he'd never grow into.

"Do you need some help setting up?"

"I'd love that, thank you. Do you like conversation, or would you prefer quiet?" Bryan started unfolding legs.

"Conversation is fine. Quiet seems unnatural to me; people ought to talk." He helped Bryan get the table upright and leaned on it to make sure it was steady.

"Some people don't like it." Bryan began draping the table with sheets. "You need mostly shoulders, Scott said? I can do your feet, whole body, neck release. Whatever you need."

"Hm. Options." He smiled. "How about waist up? Shoulders, neck, back?" Whole body would be lovely, but Clint would be along soon, and he didn't want to make the man wait his turn. He loosened and removed his tie, laying it over the that giant chair, and untucked his shirt.

"Of course. Do you prefer sitting up or lying down?" Bryan lowered the lights a bit and started an oil warmer. "I have a coconut-based oil. You and Master Clint both enjoyed it before."

"Oh, lying down, I think. Might as well really relax, right?" Even as he said that, he was wondering how Sam's night was going. Relaxing was a little bit of a stretch, but he was going to try.

"Absolutely. Lie down when you're ready, and we'll get all the stress of the day away." Bryan's smile was warm, friendly, and he had to admire the man's inner peace. He'd never seen Bryan so much as purse his lips.

"Thank you, I could definitely use that." He tossed his shirt onto the chair and climbed right up. "I'm trying to let some worry go."

"Oh man, that's always the worst, but don't you fret. I can help. Bodies hold worry in so much." Bryan tucked a towel in, all around his waistband. "So much easier with Masters. No collar to work around."

"True, that." He laughed and stretched out on his stomach, then took a deep breath and tried to help things along by willing his shoulders down.

Bryan chattered at him, the sound low and random and not requiring him to respond or listen at all. He wasn't sure he had the ability to fully listen anyway, not with those fingers pressing in and threatening to dig to China to work out the sensitive spots.

Oh, this was a very good idea. Those little hot spots hurt in just the right way, shorting out the capacity to think about much else. He felt himself sink into the table, everything getting comfortably heavy, perfectly warm.

The door opened, a soft chuckle sounding. "Oh, you do look at peace, Thomas."

"Mmm. I stole Bryan. He's magic." He really needed a standing appointment on Bryan's calendar.

"He is. I'm in no hurry. Take your time." Clint sat down in his chair and stretched.

"Good thing. I don't have any rush in me at the moment." He tried to smile, it felt drunk. "Everything okay? Scotty made it sound like you'd had a day."

"Just woke with a bit of a headache that has decided to become a bigger headache. The planning that goes into the party, you know. It's getting bigger every year."

"I noticed, my God. I could barely breathe at the bar. Poor Sam. I'm grateful you asked us to join you at your table." He cracked open an eye. He couldn't help it, he had to ask. "He did well, didn't he?"

"I felt he did, yes. He was polite, obedient, focused for

the most part. Our dear friend is altogether too forward with him, of course."

"Angel is forward with everyone—you know how he is. He and Sam are close from the bar. It was an interesting moment for me, though. Sam had specific concerns about other Doms, so I had to play it so that my boy understood he'd been heard, and also so Angel didn't get his feelings hurt. *Oh. Right there.*" His eyes closed again as Bryan found a spot that needed work.

"Feel all that tension." Bryan actually put one leg up on the table and bore down. "Deep breaths, now. In and out."

He did exactly as he was told, and he groaned as bright fireworks erupted behind his closed eyelids. "Jesus, Bryan."

Clint's soft chuckle made him grin, and Bryan hummed softly.

"You're welcome, Master Thomas."

"My boy went back to his job at the bar tonight." Why did he say that? That's not what he'd come to talk about.

"Oh? Was he ready?"

"I don't know. I wasn't. Last we talked, he'd planned to have a conversation with his boss about...his schedule."

"That's not good, I take it?"

Bryan refused to let the tension climb in again, fingers like magic.

"I think he knows I want him to quit. He also knows I understand he needs to use his own judgment." He sighed, wondering how it was possible to feel so relaxed and so anxious at the same time. "This is just...a crazy time. So much going on."

"He's a special submissive, your Mister O'Reilly. I envy you your process. Not many men get to learn to walk this road twice."

"It's a little more of a maze than a road." He chuckled.

"It's...a puzzle. But we're putting it together. The latest piece is his big brother, Bowie. The Ranger."

"Does he know about your relationship?"

He nodded. "He does. And to answer your next question, I have no idea how he feels about it, or about me. But I'm going to find out. He's coming for Sam and James's birthday. Did I tell you they share a birthday?" He arched. "Ow. Oh, man."

He barely heard Clint's, "Jesus."

"Breathe, please. Keep talking, but breathe." Bryan eased up, added oil, and dug in again.

"Sorry. Breathing." He took a couple of good breaths, trying to relax into Bryan's fingers.

"Are you okay? Is he? Can we help in any way?"

"We've been taking this run of holidays one at a time. We enjoyed the New Year's party. Now we have birthdays. I know he's happy Bowie is coming. I'm not sure what the rest of his emotions about the visit and his birthday are yet."

"I can't imagine. How odd for him, to have his own birthday for the first time in his life."

He gasped, pushing up on his elbows. "Oh, Jesus."

"Master?" He wasn't sure who Bryan was talking to, but Clint was right there, holding his hands.

"I have you, Tommy," Clint muttered. "Breathe. Bryan, keep up your work."

Have his own birthday. "He spent it with James. Every year. You remember? Vegas and...fuck, Clint. I didn't think about it that way."

"Then he'll need you, even if he can't ask. He'll need your attention."

"He had it anyway, but...and with Bowie there I just... Clint, I'm trying but it's frustrating. He needs a break. It's exhausting." He let his forehead fall onto Clint's hands.

"I'm sorry. I had no idea you were so tired." Clint held him, let him rest. "You always have a place here with us. Always. You are my family, hmm?"

"I know. Thank you. I'm fine." He shifted and sat up slowly. "Thank you, Bryan." He sat there for a second, finding his equilibrium. "Bowie will come, and Sam's birthday will come, and we'll just see where we are on the eleventh." The only thing he had any control over was himself, and he knew where he belonged. He didn't have the luxury to be tired.

His boy needed him. Full-time. Not on the weekends. Not when they had time.

"All yours." He slid off the table and went for his shirt. He couldn't head into this in survival mode. He needed to get ahead of it. He and Sam needed to talk.

"Did the massage help, Sir?" Bryan looked worried. "Did I push too far?"

Oh, the boy. He took a breath and gave Bryan a smile, still buttoning his shirt. "You have gifted hands, and it definitely helped. I think Master Clint will agree that you pushed just far enough. Thank you, Bryan."

"Of course. My pleasure."

He checked his phone, surprised to see a trail of texts from Sam.

heading home
quit my job
mike was cool
you hungry
you okay?
see u later

He took a deep breath. "He quit." He turned around and looked at Clint, relief settling into his shoulders along with the massage oil. "He quit the bar."

"Congratulations. That's a huge show of trust."

"It is." He sent Sam a quick reply.

At the club. Just finished getting a massage. Are you home yet?

Lucky man. Go you! Stopped for coffee & pie

I'm relieved about the job. Thank you. Coffee and pie? *Are you alone?*

The answer took a second, an image showing up a single piece of cherry pie, a cup of diner coffee, and a dogeared Nevada Barr novel.

Where the hell was Angel? *I'll meet you there. Text me the address.*

"I need to go." He pulled his wallet out of his pocket and handed Bryan a twenty. "Tell Scotty to put the massage on my bill, okay? Clint. Thank you."

"Of course. Is everything all right?"

Oh cool! You want chocolate cake and a latte?

Carrot cake this time, and yes

"He's alone. They told me they wouldn't let him leave the bar alone." He supposed now that Sam had quit, things had changed. "I need to go. Thanks again." He grabbed his tie and hurried out to the bar to get his coat.

"Are you leaving us, Master Thomas?" Scotty asked.

"Off to meet my boy." He tugged on his jacket and his coat and stuffed his tie into his pocket. "Have a good night, Scotty."

Sam had texted him an address nearer to Mike's tavern than home, and he made his way over, pleased to see a man he'd been introduced to waiting quietly at the door, on his phone, one eye on Sam.

"Little Sammy seemed to want space, man, but Mike said we gotta watch him."

He nodded and offered his hand. "Thank you. Can I buy you a cup of coffee?"

The handshake was firm, strong. "No thanks. I'm going to head back to the bar. I got someone waiting. See ya."

Before Thomas went inside, he pulled out his phone and texted Mike.

Thank you. I owe you one. Maybe two. Don't forget to let me know when you want to visit the club.

He didn't hand them out often, but he was happy to owe Mike a favor. He ducked through the breezeway doors and into the diner, smiling as the smell of baking bread and coffee warmed him, and made his way over to Sam's table. "This seat taken?"

"Hey, stranger. I think I can share with you." Sam looked a little stressed-out maybe, but happy too. "How was your massage? Did my texts bother you?"

"I didn't hear them, I'm sorry. If I had, I'd have answered you sooner. How are you feeling?"

"Okay. A little weird, but okay. Mike was nice, didn't ask for two weeks or anything." Sam shrugged, and he knew that careful motion, knew it hid hours of worry and what-ifs. "It's all done."

He reached over the table and took one of Sam's hands. "I'm right here." He waited until he saw his touch and his words start to register with his boy. "It's hard to quit. But you'll always get respect for doing the right thing. This was the right thing."

"Thank you, Mister. I appreciate that. It was tough. I felt bad, but not bad enough not to do it. Work that matters, right?"

He rewarded his boy with a smile and a squeeze of that hand. "Work that matters. And it's going to matter this week, isn't it?"

"It is. How are you? Good day? Here comes your cake."

"Saved by the cake." He watched Sam as the server set down an enormous slice of carrot cake and a mug of coffee. "Thank you," he said to her, but his eyes stayed on his boy. "I had a long day. I was worried about you and how things would go tonight. I'm relieved that you chose to leave entirely, though I wouldn't have asked you outright to do it. I am going to ask you not to deflect, though, Sam. When does your brother arrive?"

Direct. The more Sam tried to tangent, the more he had to be direct.

"It depends—he's due on the sixth, but it could be the seventh or the eighth. Military transport, you know? And it could be canceled altogether. His current plan is the sixth through the tenth. You have to be flexible when it comes to Bowie." Sam moved his pie around his plate, the motion almost lazy.

"All right, that's fine. Are you going to be happy to have him here?"

Sam blinked up at him, obviously surprised to have been asked that question. "Oh, honey. I got ninety answers for that. Maybe ninety-five. He's my brother."

He snorted. "I know what you're saying; I've got five. I can ask the question differently, but you won't like it as much. What worries you the most about his visit?" That would have half a dozen answers too; he had four or five himself. But he was curious which one Sam would choose.

"That he'll get hurt. That whoever it is that killed James will hurt him somehow."

Fuck. Really? Blindsided twice in one afternoon? Of everything Sam could have said, that was the last thing he was expecting. He didn't care for that feeling at all.

"Sam. Your brother is a Ranger. God help the guy if he

turns up." He needed Sam to stop worrying about everyone and focus on something healthier.

"I know. I didn't say it was reasonable, but it's the worst worry." Sam stole a bite of his cake.

"Okay. Well, if that's the worst worry, then this should be a nice, smooth week for us, right? How's the cake?"

He sat back and sipped his coffee, not really sure about sweets at the moment and even less clear on why he thought sarcasm was a good idea. It really had been a long day.

Sam recoiled like he'd been stung, eyes going wide for a second. "Sorry, man. I didn't mean no offense."

He took a breath and another sip of his coffee to make sure nothing came out of his mouth this time that he didn't actually mean. "No, I'm sorry, Sam. I'm...not at my best today. You haven't told me anything about what I should expect from Bowie, and it's got me a little off-center. More than I realized I guess. I apologize."

"I don't know. The last time we were together in person, we beat the shit out of each other, got really drunk, and blew up a boat." Sam chuckled softly, shook his head. "He's big. Really big. And he thinks I'm a baby. He sent me an original Jack Wells for my graduation. You know how cool that was? That he looked to see what I might want? I mean, maybe he asked James. I don't know. But he did it. Also, if you need to know how to blow something up? He's amazing."

He lifted an eyebrow and stared at Sam. He was fairly sure the last time the brothers were together had been at James's funeral, and he let that fact sink in for a second while he figured out how to deal with his boy's likely deliberate misinterpretation of what he needed to know about Sam's pyrotechnic brother.

"He's big, thoughtful, scary, and you left out closeted. I

know all of that. What I don't know is whether he's likely to throw a punch or a party when he meets me."

"Mister, if he so much as whispers anything against you, I will hand him his ass on a plate. You are mine, and I won't have you disrespected. Not by anyone. I've told him so. He can be decent, or he can go fuck himself. You don't have to worry. I have your back. Always."

Ah.

He crossed his arms on the table and leaned forward. "I love you. I so appreciate how you step up when I need you. I'm sure everything will be just fine, but I have to ask you a favor." He smiled, reaching for Sam's hand again. "When it comes to your brother, I need you to let me work things out with him, my way. Bowie is family, and he's a soldier, and he won't respect me otherwise."

Sam searched his eyes; then that scarred corner of his mouth lifted in a half grin. "Can I give you a baseball bat to use on him? Just for fun?"

He laughed and picked up his fork, dipping it into the cream cheese frosting on his carrot cake. "I'm a little concerned that he'd get one look at it and use it on me."

"Remember, he's a soldier. He's a hero, like for real. I give him a ton of flack, but he's really a good man. I'm the only rodeo trash in our family." Sam smiled at the waitress when she refilled his coffee. "Thank you, ma'am."

"Sam, he's your brother. That's enough for me; I'd have respected him in any case. I just wanted to make sure he didn't have an ax to grind—in my skull." He winked and went for a bite of cake.

The cake was really good. He enjoyed that bite while he thought about what he needed to say next. They'd put the Bowie thing to bed; this would be the harder part. "Hey. Had you and James made plans yet to go anywhere for your birthdays?"

"Yeah. Vegas." Sam shrugged. "We always decided the end of the year before. This would have been..." Sam waved one hand, dismissing.

"Would have been...?" He was careful to keep his tone kind but firm enough that Sam would understand he wanted an answer. "Tell me."

"The eighth trip."

He raised a hand and called the waitress over. "Could we get the check, please?"

She smiled, pulled it right out of her apron, and set it facedown on the table. "There you go."

"Thank you." He pulled out his wallet.

"Started before you were legal to drink, hm?" He watched Sam, putting cash down, making sure they were ready if Sam decided to bolt.

"Yeah. You ready?" Sam stood up, pulled his cap out of his back pocket, and replaced it with his book.

That was quick; he was getting better at anticipating his boy. "Yes." He did take one more sip of his coffee—he felt like he might need it—then set it down and followed Sam out. He might have longer legs, but Sam had more steam.

Sam let him follow for about two minutes. He finally slowed down and rolled his shoulders hard enough that Thomas could see it through the coat. When Thomas caught up, Sam smiled at him. "Sorry. It's been a day, and I'm not ready to think about that."

His heart broke a little for Sam, that the boy felt like he needed to find him a smile when there wasn't really one in there. "It has been a day, that's for sure. But in the end, I'm happy with the outcome. Are you?"

"I'm scared some, but that's never once stopped me before. I'm looking forward to seeing you more. You?"

"I'm not the least bit worried. I'm confident this is what we need. It will give us time to explore everything we are together. Time to enjoy it. I'm looking forward to a little more routine. Knowing what tomorrow looks like will give us room to breathe, room to plan." He took Sam's hand. "It's perfect."

Sam squeezed his fingers. "From your lips to God's ears, Mister. I think I need a long shower when I get home, wash the bugaboos off."

He glanced at Sam, pushing again. Testing. "So we'll get some rest tonight, and talk about your birthday tomorrow night, then."

"What do you want to talk about, honey?"

"The reason you just ran from that diner."

"I needed to move. Sometimes I have to just do something. You know that about me. I know you do."

He did. He'd preemptively paid the bill, hadn't he? "Of course. You needed to move because it had been a long day. And because I was asking you about James, and you don't want to talk about it."

Sam nodded, squeezed his hand. "True that."

"You know, I never once saw James on his birthday. He was always with you."

"Yeah. You want me to apologize, it would be a lie. I'm not sorry. I loved those trips."

"What? I don't...are you serious? I just meant you're bound to miss his company more than I on the tenth."

James loved those trips too. He wouldn't say much about them, but he loved them.

"I don't know. I hate whining. I know you miss him bad. I just..." Sam shook his head. "Jesus, I need a drink."

"That can be arranged." He keyed into their building and held the door.

"Okay. I swear to God, honey, if we find a razor on the door handle I'm going to hurt something. Just saying."

He tried not to roll his eyes. Was it a legitimate worry? Sure. Did it need this much preoccupation? Fuck...maybe. Who knew? He just wasn't going to let the asshole make him live scared.

"You know you're doing exactly what he wants, right? This guy wants you to be paranoid. He wants in your head."

"They made me identify James's body. They sent me a picture of his face. The guy's been in my head for months." Sam chuffed out a harsh laugh. "I hear you, though."

"I'd have done it for you if they'd have let me." He leaned back against the elevator wall and sighed. He didn't get to see James at all. Just a few hours earlier, they'd been having dinner. The next morning, James was a chalk outline, yellow police tape and a dark bloodstain on the sidewalk.

Now he needed a drink.

"I love you. I wouldn't have made you. I didn't make anyone else." There was a moment of pure horror in Sam's eyes, something sick and hurt and raw. "We would have had you come to the funeral. We didn't know. James said he had a boyfriend that he wanted to talk to me about. None of us are evil enough to deny you your place."

He gave Sam a half smile and nodded as the elevator doors opened, the image of that chalk still making his stomach churn. "This is us."

"Home home home." Sam headed straight to the door, unlocked it, and held it open for him. "You mind terribly if I jump in the shower? I'm like frozen rope."

"Of course not, it's your shower too." He caught his lover by the arm, leaned in, and kissed his temple. "Go ahead."

Sam grabbed him, holding him tight for a second, hugging him close.

"I've got you. I'm right here." He tucked his arms around his boy, keeping him longer. This was so difficult. He knew Sam wasn't a talker, but they had to air some of these things, or they'd be no better off next year. Sam's muscles trembled as they tried to remember how to relax, to let go. Sam stayed right there, both of them holding on.

He rubbed his lover's back, breathed him in. "I don't ask hard questions to torture you—torture us. I hope you know that."

"I know. I wish I had answers. I don't. I loved him. He was my bubba. I miss him. One day, we'll be all together again, which is weird as fuck, when I think about that. He'll probably knock out my teeth, then want to swap stories." Sam started to chuckle, the sound just a little wild.

"Good thing you won't really need teeth in Heaven." The whole idea of religion sat uncomfortably with Thomas, but Sam's faith was important to him. That was fine; they didn't need to share that between them. "I don't need a lot of answers. I just need to know you're not burying things."

"I don't even know what that means to you."

"It means deliberately not talking about things. There's a difference between not having an answer and having an answer but not sharing it with me." A big difference. "There's a difference between not knowing what's bothering you and knowing but not telling me about it."

Sam chuckled softly and gave him this look that seemed to say, "Poor, foolish man." "There is. Absolutely."

"Brat." He shook his head. *More the fool, I. Hm?* "Go take your shower."

"Yessir." Sam kissed his cheek. "Don't stress. I always come out the other side improved."

Then Sam disappeared, the increasingly familiar thump of boots sounding on the bedroom floor.

Sure, no stress. Glad you can manage without me. It didn't take a genius to know he'd let something slip through his fingers there. Come out the other side of what?

He'll need your attention, even if he can't ask.

His conversation with Clint was fresh in his mind, and he headed for the wine, trying to let his mentor's words sink in, make sense.

Not if he *won't* ask. If he *can't*.

And Sam couldn't. That was clear.

He started to uncork the wine, then decided better of it and put it back. This integrated lifestyle made it difficult to know when alcohol was okay. He never knew when or how he'd be needed, and he wouldn't touch a flogger if he'd had a drink.

He sighed and looked around his living room, at a bit of a loss. Maybe he should try standing on his head.

12

Sam turned on the water, waited as it got as hot as he could stand, stepped in, and let himself cry.

He cried for James and for their trips and for the goofy shit that James never did with anyone else. He cried for the sadness in Thomas's eyes, for all the things he'd never be able to say because Thomas didn't want to hear them. He cried because he'd just quit a job that was the only thing here he had that wasn't Thomas, and no one seemed to understand how hard that was but him. Then he cried because the weight of being a man was heavy.

He could hear Momma in his head. "Give it to God."

He'd tried. It didn't work so good. These crosses were his to bear, he guessed.

He didn't know.

The storm passed, because they all did, as the water cooled, and he lifted his face to it, letting it rinse him clean, baptize him in the knowledge that no one was given more than they could bear.

Sam had a headache and a dull hole in the center of his chest when he turned the water off, but by the time he was in a pair of sweats, a heavy sweat shirt, and socks, Sam thought he might live.

It was sure as shit better than the alternative.

He found Thomas in the living room, lying stretched out on the couch, staring at the ceiling. There was a game on TV, but the sound was down low. "All clean?"

"Squeaky. There room for me over there?" He needed to touch, fill up the empty places. He wasn't sure exactly what he'd do if Thomas said no.

Thomas sat up, patting the couch next to him. "Always."

"Cool." He didn't bother leaving space between them. He didn't have the energy to pretend he didn't want to be close. "Oh. Better."

There was something about breathing in Thomas-scented air that eased him at a cellular level, in that space that was deeper than intellect, than even emotion.

"Yes. Much better." He felt Thomas inhale deeply, his lover's exhale sounding relieved. "Still want that drink?"

"Right now I want to be with you." The booze wouldn't ease the ache he had.

They'd been sitting there quietly for a bit, listening to the TV drone on and on in the background, when Thomas finally reached over and slid a hand along his jaw. His lover caught his eyes, head tilted and brow creased.

"Would it...can I...?"

"Yes." *God, yes.* With all his heart. "Please."

He got just the barest hint of a nod before Thomas kissed him. The first touch was tentative, but then those fingers hooked around the nape of his neck, and Thomas's tongue pushed past his lips.

Oh, thank God. He groaned, the sound just a little wild, and moved to the spot he liked best, straddling Thomas's thighs. He belonged right here.

"Yeah," Thomas whispered and snaked hungry fingers up under the hem of his sweat shirt, lifting it up.

He nodded in encouragement. *Yes. Yes, love. Sir. Thomas.* "I need you, huh? So bad."

He got a grunt in reply, and Thomas pushed his sweat shirt off, helped him tug it over his head, those fingers painting heat over his skin as they slid down his chest. "Need you. So beautiful."

Sam arched into the touch, offering every inch of skin, every bit of him that needed to be stroked and licked, bitten and pinched and loved on.

Thomas hummed and he could feel his lover's focus, hands exploring his abs like they held treasure, a hot tongue following to lap it up. He whimpered so soft and reached out, his fingers tangling in Thomas's hair.

"Don't stop..."

He got what he asked for but not a reply. Thomas spent time teasing his nipples until they ached, tasting the expanse of his collarbone, nipping at the soft spots under his chin.

Sam gave Thomas his noises—his low cries, his husky curses, his passion. He touched everywhere he could reach, fingertips dragging over Thomas's back.

Thomas groaned and shoved at him, pushing him to his feet for a second before lifting him right off them again and heading for the bedroom.

"Damn, that's the hottest thing ever..." And he was hard as a rock already, his ballsac tight. He couldn't quite catch his breath.

"No. You are." Thomas set him down at the foot of the bed. "I want you, Sam. I need inside your skin." His lover pulled him in, devouring him with a kiss. He tore at the buttons of Thomas's shirt, trying to get it off, just as hungry as Thomas, maybe more. Hell, they were feeding off each other's need.

Thomas got free of the shirt, and the dress pants were right behind it. His lover's cock curved eagerly away from his body, dark and wanting. Thomas crowded into him, bumping their hips together and shoving his sweat pants down.

He pushed against Thomas, rubbing and rocking, his entire body lit up.

"Sam." Thomas panted out a breath and kissed him again, moving him backward, onto the bed, and climbing right over him.

He could drown in this, and he ran his hands along Thomas's side, smoothing his palms along the skin.

One more kiss, then Thomas was exploring again, mouth roaming over his chest, lower to lick the ridges of his abs, and lower still, over his hip.

He lifted up on his elbows, eyes burning as he stared down. *Damn.* Damn, that was fuel for his fantasies forever.

Thomas looked up at him, those eyes like burnt honey, staring right into him as his lover licked up his length with a flat tongue.

"Oh, sweet Jesus." His legs spread like Thomas had hit a button. So fucking pretty. He thought he forgot how to breathe for a second.

"Mhm." Thomas broke their stare and he watched as that tongue drew a circle around the head of his cock before it disappeared past his lover's lips. "Mmm."

His head fell back between his shoulders, and he stared sightlessly as he felt the heat around his cock grow more and more intense.

The way Thomas taunted him was excruciating, offering him almost enough pressure, almost enough depth, but never enough. Never anywhere near enough. His lover shifted from his prick to his balls, up over his hip, down the opposite thigh, teasing and stroking, touching him everywhere.

All these sounds started escaping from him, just impossible to hold in. "Gonna lose my mind, love."

"So lose it." Thomas pushed him back onto the bed, then was moving, slightly trembling fingers rolling on the rubber and betraying his lover's own impatience. He never even saw a flash of lube, but Thomas's fingers were suddenly there, pressing in, getting him slick, making him mad. "Lose it."

"Thomas." He grabbed ahold of his lover's shoulders, bearing down and taking as much as Thomas was giving.

"Oh, fuck, Sam. Look at you. You're stun...ah. Stunning." Thomas's words were interrupted by a low moan. The fingers slipped away, and Thomas pressed up against his hole, thick cock spreading him.

"Yours." Fuck he loved that burn, that deep ache that turned to pure sensation.

The word set Thomas on fire and his lover groaned, pressing in deep. Their eyes met again. "Yours."

"Yes." Sam sucked in a deep breath. "Every fucking inch."

Then he wrapped his legs around Thomas, putting all those crunches to good use.

He felt Thomas rock into him, try to find a rhythm, grunt and try again. He tried not to look too smug when he saw that jaw set, and his lover pinned his hands over his head. He rolled, his entire body responding to that touch, taking it, his balls so tight that they seemed like to squeak.

Fuck, Thomas was into that, and started pumping into him deep and hard, on a mission, eyes searing into his. He let it happen, let Thomas see all the need, all the hunger and passion and desire. That emptiness was pounded into nothing, heat left in its place.

The grip on his hands eased up, and Thomas reached down between them to give his prick a few long, hard strokes. Thomas let go and arched over him, bracing his arms wide. "You do it, I want to see."

Sam damn near shot, and it was fucking good that he had to wait for his brain and hands to start communicating, because that gave him a breath, a second, a chance to do what Thomas asked for.

Thomas ducked his head, looking down between them, then back up at Sam's face, still rocking deep into him. "Hot, Sam. Come on, show me."

"Yessir." He grabbed his cock, pulling good and hard, base to tip. He knew how to make himself need, and he didn't hide a bit.

That earned him a growl, and Thomas bucked into him, losing rhythm. Sam stopped worrying, stopped thinking—his world was his cock, his ass, Thomas. The rest dissolved.

He seemed to float there in that space until, through his haze, he heard Thomas order, low and quiet in his ear. "Now, my own."

"Now." And just like Thomas had drawn it from him, seed spread over his belly, hot and thick.

Thomas's cry was loud in his ears and long; then Thomas kissed him hard, cutting off his air.

Fuck. He couldn't even think. He didn't want to.

He felt Thomas collapse next to him, breathing hard. "Fuck, Sam."

No shit. "Yes, Sir, and I needed it."

At least he thought that was what he said. He wasn't totally sure.

"We needed it." Thomas rolled up on his side, taking another kiss. "I love you, cowboy."

"Love you." He blinked at Thomas, more than a little stupid. He liked this whole "evenings at home together" thing.

"Mmm. Good." Thomas was drawing patterns on his chest and kissing his shoulder. "Can't make a tough day any better, huh?"

He chuckled softly. "You got my number, swear to God."

"Yep. One-eight-hundred, touch-me-anywhere." Thomas sounded pleased with himself.

"Butthead." He started laughing, tickled pink. "Only you. You got the touch."

"Have I told you that 'only me' is the hottest thing I could ever imagine? Every so often, I get a little distracted by being the only one who's ever...whatever. Kissed you right here." Thomas kissed his ribs. "How lucky am I?"

Sam blinked down, a little stunned. He'd never considered not being ashamed of his lack of experience, of feeling like the guy that couldn't. "Only you. I'm glad you said so, that you like it."

Huh. That made him feel ten feet tall, didn't it?

Thomas sat up on an elbow and looked at him. "I love it. I could go on and on...I mean, talk about *mine*. The list of things, of firsts? I'm so proud of you, it's embarrassing."

His cheeks were going to set on fire, just light up. "I—thank you."

If Thomas noticed, nothing was said. He just got a kiss on one hot cheek and a smile.

"The first reward in celebration of your new day job as a full-time author? We get to stay right here and go to sleep."

"Sounds amazing. I was dreading staying up all night tonight." He was beginning to crave this—sleeping with

Thomas's heartbeat under his ear. "I didn't want to miss this."

"Mm." Thomas pulled him over, curling an arm around his shoulders. "I'm not sure I'd know what to do without it." Thomas's words were sleepy and a little slurred. "Night, stud."

"Night, Mister. Love you." He sighed softly, relaxing right in.

He thought he could dream easy now. Dream about tomorrow.

13

Thomas was tired at work. He'd needed a lot of coffee, he ignored the annoying phone calls, and he relied on Ally to keep him on track. He ignored her knowing little looks and grins too. Mostly.

Waking up with Sam on a workday morning, sore in all the right places, and finding coffee waiting for him on the bathroom counter after his shower, was...incredible. Wondrous. Something. What was the word to describe when someone trudged around, half-awake, wearing nothing but hideous reindeer pajamas and bedhead, and made you coffee just because...oh.

He knew that word. That word was love.

Today he was the right kind of tired, and in love.

He was getting ready to head home, but he took a second to drop Clint a text.

All is well, thank you for yesterday. As usual you said just the right thing. I hope poor Bryan wasn't too upset. How do I get us on his calendar? Also, I'd like to gift Sam with a membership. We'll talk

All right. So he'd dropped Clint a text *bomb*. At least he

got his gratitude in first. His next text was to Sam.

What should I bring home for dinner? Or would you like to go out?

What should he bring home for dinner? The question was so domestic, he had to stare at his phone to make sure it was real.

I was thinking Chinese. You in? I can order online so you don't have to juggle bags

Oh, that was a stellar idea. *Yes, do that. Surprise me. Include vegetables. OMW home*

Speaking of firsts, there was actually someone home to order delivery. Wild. Oh, hadn't that conversation about those firsts made his boy happy? Why hadn't he said something sooner?

"Say hello to your boyfriend for me."

"Will do." *Wait.* "Wait. What?" He glared at Ally.

"Gotcha!" She beamed at him. "Is he hot?"

"You could fry an egg on him."

"Shut. Up!"

He laughed. "Goodnight, Ally."

"Deets at lunch tomorrow!"

"Ha!" He let the office door close behind him and headed for the elevator.

Look at him, at them. How fucking wonderful was this?

Good deal. See you in a bit.

Then Sam sent him a selfie—his lover in headphones, grinning, sitting in the office.

He'd never sent a selfic. Not once. He held up his phone and snapped a picture in the elevator, and sent it off to Sam, followed by a text.

My first selfie

Hot bastard. Come home. :D

I'm trying but someone keeps texting me

There was no subway that went in the direction of his apartment, so he usually just walked it. It was a decent walk home. Cold, but not horrible. On horrible days, he'd catch an Uber. He really needed to find a suit that went with his new boots. He'd love to try that out, and they'd be warmer than his dress shoes for the walk home.

He let himself in and got into the elevator, sighing as the doors closed. He was not going to let a psycho with a fetish for sharp shit ruin his buzz. He was going home to Sam. He was living the dream.

When he stepped off the elevator, he did glance around, but the hall was empty and quiet. He knocked on the door and let himself in, laughing as he locked the door behind him. This wasn't college, and his roommate wasn't going to have a guest.

Sam was singing. Loud. He peeked into the office, chuckling as he saw Sam with his earbuds, doing crunches, reading something on his phone.

He dumped his jacket on a chair, loosened his belt so he could breathe, and got down hip to hip with his boy. He knew he couldn't keep up, but it could be fun to try.

"Mmm. Hey, you." Sam pulled off his headphones and gave him a quick kiss. "I was seeing if I could pump them out before you got home. I'm up to three-fifty now, as a rule."

Oh, that was a sweet greeting. "Hey. I'll be good for a hundred. Maybe two. Why did you raise the bar?"

"Habit. You go up when it gets easy. I'll start doing pull-ups on the doorframe next." Sam winked at him. "Good day?"

"Yes, very. Install a pull-up bar if you want to. I'd use it. How was your day?" Maybe they should turn the playroom, which was now essentially a storage room, into a gym.

"I wrote three blog posts, an article, started the outline

for the book, and answered ten thousand emails. It was good." Sam was a goddamn crunching machine, those abs —worth writing odes about.

He felt completely validated. His boy was motivated, had quiet and was comfortable, and look how productive he was. "That sounds like a great day. I knew you had this."

Sam was fast too, doing two crunches to every one of his own. Maybe he could use being over thirty as an excuse. "Aren't you done yet?"

"Uh. I lost count. I was watching you."

"Oh, come on." He laughed. "Next time I'll take my shirt off, maybe it will slow you down a little." He was about to call it quits, so he had to be up around one-fifty. Sam had to be done. In fact, he was going to make sure Sam was done. He flipped over into a plank, framing his boy and getting in the way.

"Mmm. Are you trying to tell me something?" Happiness looked good on his boy.

"Yes." The intercom chimed and he sighed. "Food is here."

He hopped up, fixed his belt, and headed down the hall to buzz the delivery guy in.

Sam plopped cushions on the floor and grabbed the wine and glasses for the sofa table. Easy. This was easy and domestic and equal parts strange and wonderful.

He went out and waited in the hall for the delivery guy, letting the apartment door lock behind him...just in case. But it was only Chinese food, the guy got a nice tip, and he let himself back in.

So, all right, he wasn't going to give Sam a hard time about being paranoid anymore.

"Smells great. What did you order?" He set the bag down on the coffee table and went for the roll of paper towels.

"Beef and broccoli. Green beans. Kung pao chicken. Egg rolls. Hot and sour soup for lunch all week." Sam winked at him. "It warms up like a dream. I love these weird crunchy noodle deals."

His boy was hungry. That was a good sign. "I wondered why the bag was so heavy." He came back and sat down, glancing at the wine. "You're okay if I have a glass?"

"I brought it over so you could, honey." Sam leaned and bumped their shoulders together. "You a fork or a chopsticks type?"

"Fork? Who eats Chinese with a fork? I'll take a spoon for the soup, though." When he first moved to New York, he had no idea how to use chopsticks, and it took him a long time in college to live down the one and only time he'd asked for a fork. To be fair, he still mostly just faked it well, but he knew better now. He picked up the wine and poured them each a glass.

"I know lots of folks. Especially ropers. Me? I learned how. Momma put Daddy on a diet once where he could only eat with chopsticks. He learned fast."

"You're a New Yorker now, stud. That's a skill you'll be glad you already have. Trust me, I know." He grinned at Sam and winked, then raised his glass. "To...what? Productive workdays?"

"To good days and good nights?" Sam nodded and clinked their glasses together. "A New Yorker, huh? Who'd'a thunk it?"

"Life is interesting, that's for sure." He sipped his wine, enjoying how it slid over his tongue. "Did I tell you I told Mike that he and Darla should be our guests at the club soon?"

"Yeah? Daddy Mike is a good guy. Darla, too, unless you piss her off." Sam organized the food, offering him a smile.

"You know, we're going to have to talk about money soon—what I need to pay for rent, utilities, how much the club membership costs."

"We can talk about it. Can we change that up a little, though? Can I ask you to think about what you can afford first?" The membership would be a birthday gift. That, and a gift he'd ordered online that he had hiding at the office.

"Shouldn't we work that out together, you and me? I mean, two minds working is better than one." Sam didn't seem worried, more...eager to work with him? Was he reading that right?

"Sure. We can be open about money if you're good with that. Make a plan together. I've got a set salary, and I know you have some ramping up you're doing." Money could be such a touchy thing. Sam was probably on to something, wanting to work together from the beginning. "Give me a day or two." By which he meant after Sam's birthday. "I'll get the bills together and show you what's what. I have a mortgage here, not rent, so we'll figure something out."

"I like open. I'm not trying to be nosy, just trying to be straightforward and together."

"No, no. I didn't take it that way, not to worry. I like what you're saying." He served himself more of the Kung Pao. "This was a good idea too."

"I had a wild craving for spicy goodness." Sam snapped up a piece of broccoli.

"So, I was thinking you should take your brother down to Ground Zero one day while he's here. The 9/11 memorial might interest him."

"Sure, we can ask him. I'm never sure if something will be interesting or uncomfortable. He's seen things that are terrible. The last time before James's funeral that we saw him, he slept the entire week. Seriously, he slept and ate. Did he never come to New York? Not even once?"

"Not that I am aware of." He wondered when he'd started answering questions like that with a hint of doubt. He would never consider James a liar, but his late lover did seem to prefer to keep the different pieces of a complicated life from interacting. Part of him thought about asking Bowie that very question, but what was the point? He'd rather not color James in an unfavorable light.

"That's a shame. Well, he's coming now. Eventually Momma and Daddy will want to meet you. You could see where I'm from." Sam chuckled softly, one piece of chicken bobbing in his chopsticks. "We could stay in Dallas. Figure out what to do about my pickup."

Then there was Sam, Thomas mused. *Here, let me invite you into all the parts of my life, let me show you everything except for the thoughts banging around in my head.*

He might even get an invitation to those one day if Sam could get them to be still long enough.

"I would love that. Really. Will you plan it? Maybe for the spring. I'd love to know that part of you." Now that Sam had said it, had put it out there for him to grasp, he knew he needed to go.

"Absolutely. Spring is so beautiful with the bluebonnets. If you have time, we'll run down to Austin. Get some kolaches in West. Go to the stockyards in Fort Worth. Momma will cook, and Daddy will show you around."

He had time. He hadn't used vacation time for anything but the holidays in a couple of years. He had plenty banked. "He'd be cool with that? With me?" It only mattered to him because it mattered to Sam. His boy wouldn't get a tour of his own hometown ever.

But he'd already decided he was going to invite Katie

and William over the summer. His youngest siblings were good people.

"He's not going to want us kissing, but he wouldn't want me kissing on some lady, either. He's talking real slow, but he says he wants us to come, and he wants to bring Momma out here when he's better." Sam's smile was fond, warm. "She'll love it here, I think. I know she'll love you."

That casual confidence surprised him, given how pressured Sam had been, how there seemed to be a war waging between Sam and his mother.

His assumption was that Sam was hoping if she liked him, she'd be more forgiving. More supportive. So, he'd just have to make damn sure she liked him. He could be polite and do the dishes with the best of them.

He also had to wonder if Sam's dad was really going to get better. But there was no reason to ask that question right now. "I can't even imagine kissing you in front of either of your parents. No worries." He shook his head. "No."

"Are you saying I'm not utterly irresistible?" Sam was barely holding the laughter back.

"You know damn well you are, brat." He grinned, adding a bit of a leer. "If you're worried you're losing your appeal, I would be happy to tell your father all about what the collar you'll be wearing means. In your mother's kitchen."

"Oh, lord. Can you imagine just trying to make him understand that I let you put it on me, much less that I wanted you to? That would hurt his head." Sam touched the collar and traced it, drawing Thomas's attention to it. "I will wear it, though. In Momma's kitchen. Everywhere."

He licked his lips, glancing up from Sam's fingers on the collar to his boy's eyes. "You honor me, boy. Thank you." He took a deep sip of his wine and dropped his voice into that lower register he favored for certain scenes. "But I don't know. I think your father would understand obedience; it's really just another sort of vow isn't it?"

"An old one. Love, honor, and obey." Sam reached out for him, fingers trailing down his arm like his boy couldn't resist.

"Sensibly updated by more enlightened and integrated couples engaged in power play to add invent, compromise, and negotiate." He smiled, slyly, over his wine.

"We negotiate a lot, you and me."

"We do. We continue to have success with it. We're better when we both get what we want *and* what we need." Formality had its place, just not in their day-to-day.

"And don't think I don't remember you getting on to me about this being a game when you call it power play." Sam winked at him and grabbed an egg roll. "You want half?"

"Yes, please. And it's not a game. A game is something you play in your spare time. It's a distraction. A pastime. And typically players are disappointed when a game ends in a tie." He liked this banter, and he liked Sam's playful challenge. "It's a lifestyle. It's, well for me at least, a bone-deep necessity. It's woven into the fabric of who I am. It's not that kind of play."

Sam broke the egg roll in half and offered him the bigger side. "Work that matters, right? I get that part, mostly." Sam nibbled his food, watching him, focused on him, their conversation. "How did you ever know this was a thing?"

He took the egg roll with a nod and bit into it, trying to decide as he chewed, how much honesty was really warranted. "I knew a boy back home. Grant. He was quiet, a loner; he had the lightest blue eyes I've ever seen."

Grant had been beautiful and shy. "You remember the first time we kissed, how you just knew I wanted to? Well, I knew he wanted to. I knew for weeks, but he never did it. I finally got so frustrated one afternoon after school that I cornered him and I kissed him. He was angry at me and scared. He gave me a shove; I pinned his hands to the wall. Not one of my finer moments I guess, but as it turned out, he loved it. But we were just fucking around. It wasn't until I moved to New York and I met Clint that I understood it. Clint helped me focus."

"Met Clint" was the understatement of a lifetime. Clint taught him...showed him it was okay to be who he was. Dramatically. The better part of the story was what happened once he hooked up with Clint, but he wasn't sure whether he'd be able to tell it.

"That's a great story, and it suits you to the bone."

"I guess. You mean the bit about me being impatient?" He laughed, shaking free of those blue eyes that still caught him off guard every so often.

"You're just real sure about what you want, huh?" Sam leaned back, licking his fingers clean.

"I am. It's a blessing and a curse." He watched Sam. "So when did you figure out you wanted me?"

"When Momma told me she was cutting me off. I sat there for a second and thought, I want to be here with him, even if he doesn't want me yet."

Nothing like pressure to bring clarity. "That was really, really stupid." He laughed. "If I'd been your mother, I'd have cut you off too. But I'm very glad you did something so rash and reckless." It didn't stop there, he well knew, but there were some truths that didn't need a voice. "While I was still busy trying to give myself permission to want anything. Anyone."

"Stupid, rash, and reckless—story of my life." Sam squeezed his hand. "I would have waited as long as I needed."

"I believe that." He pulled Sam's hand closer and kissed the boy's knuckles. "I do believe that. Personally, I could not have waited a minute longer." Once he knew what he wanted, he made a plan to get it. He would never once, as long as he lived, regret leaving that journal where Sam would find it.

"Thank God for that. That kiss saved me, more than a little."

He huffed softly, knowing the smile he gave Sam was a little...off. He looked down at their hands and stroked his thumb over Sam's wrist, trying to find the words for what that kiss had done to him. Remembering how frozen he'd been and how desperately he'd needed Sam's permission. He gave up, realizing that his lover had said it best, and when he looked into Sam's eyes again, his smile was genuine. "Me too."

"Good." Sam kissed the corner of his mouth, the caress gentle, loving. "So, I have to say, supper in the front room on a weekday isn't bad, Mister."

"This was just perfect. Can we do it again tomorrow?" He picked up his wine in one hand and put his other arm around Sam's shoulders.

"We most certainly can." Sam leaned back and offered him a happy little sigh, just pure peace.

Peaceful was a fairly new state for Sam, and he liked it. His boy had earned some peace. He'd earned it too. He squinted at the clock, giving Sam five, maybe even seven minutes before the boy's mind was on to something else. But it was sweet for now, and he'd take it.

Clint had told him a long time ago that nothing was as exhausting or as rewarding as having a full-time sub. Clint was wise, experienced, clever—and wrong. Clint hadn't met Sam yet.

14

S am wasn't freaking out. He was absolutely, one hundred percent, totally not freaking out.

Bowie was here.

Well, not here-here, but here in a hotel, sleeping off his jet lag.

Christ on a sparkly pink crutch. Bowie'd actually showed up.

Now he was sitting and staring and pretending to work while he waited on Thomas to get home. Then they were suppering all together. *Woo.*

God, he wasn't sure if he was going to survive this.

Thomas texted him. Again. *Where are we going again? You said totally not dressy, right? So I need to change*

Thomas was nervous too. Thomas wasn't supposed to be nervous, was he? He was always the one with the level head, the right answer.

A string of texts on the walk home from work was not the right answer.

Bowie's only got jeans. We'll get burgers. I pressed your jeans for you. Dork.

Pressed my jeans? Oh. I'm a cowboy tonight?

Sam did not understand Thomas's prejudice against pressed jeans. *from the waist down*

I'm always a cowboy from the waist down

Oh, no shit on that. *we're not talking about your below the belt until Bowie goes home*

like hell we're not

The front door opened and closed.

"Are you serious?" Thomas's voice came down the hall.

"Last thing I need is to be springing wood from just looking at you. I should have tugged off ten or twelve times this afternoon." Playing with Thomas made things, if not easier, way more fun.

"Oh. That's a challenge. Just for that, I should wear my hat." Thomas hooked an arm around him and drew him into a kiss.

Sam loved these "home from work" kisses. He leaned into Thomas, loving the touch of that hand on his bare back.

"Mm. All right. Now I can think straight. Stop pressing my jeans." He got a wink. "What time is dinner?"

"We're meeting him at seven thirty in the lobby of his hotel." He grinned up. "You ready to meet the eldest O'Reilly brother?"

"No." Thomas laughed. "But I will be. Are you ready for me to meet him?"

"Yes. I'm ready to have the first weirdness over, for all of us. Then we'll just have to feed the beast." Bowie had two hollow legs.

"Maybe it won't be weird. He loves you; I love you. We'll come to an understanding, I am sure." Thomas headed for the bedroom, fingers lightly curled in his to drag him along.

"I am too." Right. He hoped. God, who knew with Bowie? Sometimes the huge things were just taken like they were nothing, and sometimes the tiniest things became these gigantic issues.

"So I'm wearing jeans...and what else?" Thomas gave him a knowing look. "Do I get to dress myself?"

"You do. I've seen it with my own eyes. You totally know how." He was wearing his green button-down. Thomas liked it.

Thomas went to the closet. "Well then, as much as I appreciate your hard work, I'm wearing these, and my black boots. Are they clean?" Thomas set the leather pants on the bed along with a black Henley. "Not what I'd wear to meet your mother, but we are in New York."

Sam trailed his fingers along the leather. Christ, Thomas was trying to kill him. He was fairly sure they'd had the "no below the waist thoughts" talk. "They're clean. I checked all the boots Monday and polished everybody up."

"Thank you, boy. Can you bring me the comfy ones? The black dress boots, not my chunky club stompers."

"Chunky club stompers. I like that. You know you're going to make me all goofy with your leather." He went to grab the boots for Thomas. All he had to do was put his shirt on. He was already cleaned up and had his smell-good on.

"Well, that's a nice side effect, but the leather is more about my own peculiar psychology." He rolled his eyes, and Thomas sighed. "That translates into 'I feel badass in my leather.' Happy?"

"I am. And I get that. You look badass in your leather. You make me want—" That wasn't anything he wanted to share right now. "What shirt do you want?"

"Good. Want." Thomas watched him, fingers closing up the top button and smoothing the leather down in front.

"You could go without…oh. Did you mean me?" His lover winked at him. "Black Henley on the bed."

"Right. Sorry. Distracted. Remember, no thinking below the belt, and I'm wearing the green shirt." *Butthead man.*

"Oh, I love that green shirt." Thomas gave him a pleased smile and reached for the Henley. "And *you* said no talking about below the belt; you're not the boss of what I'm thinking."

Sam chuckled, just about tickled. "No, Sir. Hell, I'm not the boss of what I'm thinking ninety percent of the time."

"I'll behave, sweetheart. Don't worry. He's family. I think I remember how to be polite. I suppose we'll see." Thomas laughed, sat down on his chair, and pulled on the dress boots he'd found.

"He is that. I'm looking forward to seeing him. Maybe I won't hit him this time." They'd been in total war mode last time, trying to kill each other over James.

"I think that might put a damper on my meal." Thomas sounded so serious.

"You might think it's hot, who knows, but we never fight at the supper table. It's a rule." If he'd had a dime for every time he'd heard Daddy's low voice at the head of the table saying, "Boys, what are the rules?" Christ, he'd be a rich man.

No fighting. No kicking under the table. You have to have your clothes on. Bow your head during grace. No throwing food—including rolls shaped like footballs.

"I recall my brothers having rules. As I rarely broke any, I'm not sure I even recall what they were." Thomas stood up and went to look in the full-length mirror that hung inside the closet door.

"Such a good boy. Me? Not so much with that." He used the fact that he needed his shirt to grab Thomas's butt.

Thomas swatted his hand away. "What? I'm shocked." He felt his lover's fingers trace over his abs for a second; then Thomas moved away. "Am I too stubbly? Should I have shaved?"

He grabbed his shirt before he turned to look. Oh, he thought that little bit of scruff gave Thomas an air of danger, a bit of "Fuck you, I don't care." Also, it would make Bowie and his spit-and-polish self itch. Perfect. "I like it."

"You do? All right, then. I'm ready."

He buttoned up and got his jeans and belt undone to tuck in, make himself presentable. Not bad. Not bad at all.

"I'll grab coats and my hat."

"You look great, sweetheart. That shirt and your eyes... mm. I'm a fan." Thomas followed him down the hall.

"Thank you." He took Thomas's hand and squeezed it. "Let's go see the bear. He'll just want food and to get to bed early tonight, huh? Tomorrow he'll want company and touristing."

"Oh boy, tired bear. All right, let's do it."

Thomas said almost nothing after that, just kept hold of his hand and leaned close on the subway. They came up out of the station directly across from Bowie's hotel, and the wind coming down the street felt sharp as it sliced between them.

"Whoo. Cold. Damn."

"I know, right? My nipples could cut glass."

Bowie was standing in the lobby, staring at the big abstract painting hanging there. He looked good, solid in his jeans, turtleneck, and high and tight.

He stayed back a few steps. "Hey, you."

Bowie turned, and for a second, Sam thought Bowie would salute. "Baby boy."

"Brother."

Bowie grabbed him, hugged him, and for a wild second, Sam felt James, right there, right with them like it was supposed to be; then Bowie stepped away and looked at Thomas.

"You must be the one that's going through O'Reilly men." Bowie's grin was pure evil as he held out one hand. "Too bad you're not my type."

"Oh, I'm everyone's type. But if you're getting in line, there's a very, very long wait." Thomas returned the grin and shook Bowie's hand. "Thomas Ward."

"Bowie O'Reilly. Pleased to meet you, sir. Sam has said a lot of good things about you."

"That's good to know. Sam uses words like 'hero' to describe you. It's my honor. I hear you're the hungry type?"

Well, it had been a full minute, and no one had thrown a punch or growled. Good start.

"Starving. Burgers you said, baby boy?"

"Yessir. Come on, I'll feed your wee bitty body." Sam snorted. Bowie had fifteen inches and more than a hundred pounds on him. Itty-bitty indeed.

Thomas and Bowie flanked him as they hit the sidewalk without any negotiation at all.

"How was your trip up here? Sam didn't tell me where you're coming from."

"Fine. I flew in from Rota, caught a good flight this time."

Sam had learned everything he'd ever needed about non-answer answers from Bowie. Bowie had learned it from Daddy.

"Rota?"

"Spain. Lovely place." Bowie grinned at Thomas, then down at him. "You look good. The way Momma was going on, you were starving to death and selling your soul and blood."

Sam rolled his eyes. "She's...Momma."

"No shit on that."

"To be fair, the last time she saw him was for a funeral. He's gotten a little sleep and a meal or two since then."

"Yeah, I can tell. I appreciate that." Bowie nodded once to Thomas, right over the top of his fucking head. He hated being short.

He elbowed Bowie. "I'm right here."

"I can see that, baby boy. I felt a gnat at my belly button. I have to be honest, Momma wants me to convince you to come back home. She's lonely and totally having empty nest shit." Bowie chuckled, evil in the tone. "There. Are you convinced?"

"Uh. No." Sad for her, sure, but he was home for twenty-five years. He was ready to go.

"Too bad. You resisted. If she asks, I tried hard, okay?"

"Works for me. Twisted my arm and shit."

"Good boy. Jesus, it's cold. I'm not used to this."

"I'm sure it's hot in whatever desert you escaped from to get to Rota. Whoops. Us." Thomas stopped short and opened the door to the restaurant for them.

He breathed in deep. Beef. Bacon. Frying potatoes. Hell, yeah.

"This should satisfy." Thomas let him go first, then Bowie, and the hostess had them seated right away.

"It smells like heaven, man. Good choice." Bowie settled in, creaking and groaning like an old house. "Thank y'all for inviting me to come visit, by the way. I appreciate it."

Thomas glanced at him and looked at Bowie again. "Sam talks about you a lot. I'm glad you could make it, especially right now. I know it can't be an easy thing to work out."

"I told him I had some leave, and I wanted to meet you.

He said he wouldn't shoot me on sight, so we were good."
Bowie picked up the menu, and Sam noticed Bowie's hands
were shaking, just a little. He looked up, meeting Bowie's
eyes, and Bowie shook his head, just a little.

Right.

Not open for discussion.

Thomas opened his menu as well. "What are you
drinking, Bowie?"

"They serve beer here? If so, that's what I want. I'm not
driving."

Thomas nodded, not looking up from the menu. "They
do serve beer. Plenty of it."

Their server arrived then, as if his ears were burning,
and they ordered their drinks.

"Their California burger is excellent if you like avocado."

"I want a triple with jalapenos, I think."

Sam rolled his eyes. "Pig."

"You want the junior burger with applesauce, baby boy?"

They stared at each other; then the laughter started,
hard and loud, both of them just losing it.

Thomas snorted, grinning. "Thank goodness for dinner
table rules," his lover muttered, nose still in the menu.
Thomas played along well and seemed to be relaxed, but it
was hard to tell what was going through that mind. His lover
had plenty of patience with them, if nothing else.

They got their drinks, ordered food, and settled in. Bowie
looked at him after a long draw of suds, shaking his head a little.

"You still working at the bar, man?" Bowie asked.

"I'm not, no. I'm doing my freelance work, writing on a
book."

"Good on you. You were always the smartest of us all. I'm
glad to hear it."

Sam blinked. Him? James was the smart one, right? He was the fuckup.

"He really dug in when he got here and figured the city out, and he's made some great choices. This book he's working on is creative and interesting. I'm proud of him."

Bowie looked at Thomas, so serious and steady. "Good. He deserves someone that believes in him. We'll have our 'I will rip off your head and shit down your neck if you hurt him' talk later this visit, I'm sure."

"What kind of brother would you be otherwise? Bring it on." Thomas held up his wine and clinked Bowie's beer.

"Leave it to you to end up with a wine drinker. I warned you, once you started drinking that shit..." Bowie winked outrageously.

"Hey, I'm damn near classy and shit. Educated."

"Yeah. Yeah, exactly." Bowie turned back to Thomas. "So, Sam tells me you work in a museum? You like it?"

It was only a matter of time before Bowie brought up James.

"I do. I'm in development. I help find sponsors for various exhibitions and museum projects, marketing, that kind of thing." Sam liked the way Thomas sat a little taller talking about work, his lover's smile making those brown eyes shine.

"I don't even have the slightest idea how someone trains for a job like that, but good on you. That sounds tough as hell."

"Doesn't it? I tell him he has to be way more patient than me." Sam wasn't the type to figure that sort of thing.

Thomas laughed. "It's really just a lot of ten-dollar words for begging people for money. One of the things I learned early on was that if you want to ask fancy people with money for something, you have to talk like you're one of them. So I learned."

"So, this is not a second career for me, huh baby boy?"

"No, man. I don't think so. However, you could totally extort rednecks for petty cash. Maybe for the snake museum on 35." Oh, that one was good.

Thomas barked out a laugh loud enough that he wondered if they should apologize to the people eating near them. His lover even took a second to gingerly put the wineglass down before letting the giggles win.

Oh, yeah. He was on fire. Sam grinned into his beer, listening to the sound of laughter, thinking how it hadn't taken long at all for them to find how things worked.

"Hey, everybody needs to make a living." Thomas giggled again, then snorted like a pig. "Oh. Fuck. Excuse me." His lover's eyes went wide.

That set them off again, and Sam had to brace himself on the table as he howled. Bowie was crying by the time they calmed down, eyes sparkling.

Thomas sighed, leaning back and shaking his head. "Jesus Christ. I think I hurt something."

"I haven't laughed that long in forever." Bowie wiped his eyes. "Lord, I've missed you, baby boy. You tickle the living shit out of me."

He grinned at Bowie, stupidly pleased. Some things never changed. Your big brother's approval still felt good.

"Oh." Thomas sat up again as their food arrived, huge plates of burgers and french fries, pickles and coleslaw. "I am very ready for this."

"Hell, yeah. Looks perfect, ma'am. Thank you."

Sam stared at Bowie's burger. "My mouth's not that big."

"Poor Thomas."

Thomas's head snapped around to gape at him. "It wasn't me! I didn't say it."

Sam rolled his eyes. "My classy-assed big brother. We're *so* proud."

Thomas looked at Bowie, hands folding neatly. "I was expressly told certain subjects were off-limits. How's your burger?"

"Oh? What are we not talking about—your dick, Sam's mouth, or blowjobs?" Bowie grinned at Thomas like butter wouldn't melt in his mouth.

"All of the above, asshat. This is the supper table." Sam kicked Bowie under the table.

"Hey." Thomas calmly met Bowie's gaze, not challenging, just getting his brother's attention. "I think we should respect his wishes on this one, okay?"

Bowie arched an eyebrow, and Sam got ready for a growl, but Bowie just nodded. "Fair enough. Pass the ketchup?"

"You got it. You want another beer?" Thomas handed off the ketchup and waved the server over.

"Yeah, I think I will. Thanks, man."

He worked on his burger, careful not to let the juicy thing drip on his shirt.

Thomas ordered them two more beers and went back to eating, the table going quiet for a couple of minutes.

"You got any idea what you want to do tomorrow and Sunday, brother?" Sam asked. There were a thousand options.

Bowie looked at him, grinned a little sheepishly. "I want to make chili and watch football Sunday. Tomorrow I'm at your disposal. I mostly want to be relaxed and see where y'all live."

"Oh…" Chili. *Oh, God.* "Can you show me how? I'm desperate."

"Sure. Absolutely. Don't tell Momma that Daddy taught me."

"Your secrets are all safe with me."

Bowie stared at him, then at his collar. "Ditto."

Oh. Oh, God. What did that mean? *What the fuck. Whoa.* Also, breathe and focus on onion rings. *Mmm. Crispy onions.* No thinking about anything.

He felt Thomas's eyes on him for a second before his lover spoke up. "Well, I had a couple of ideas for tomorrow. Have you been to New York before?"

"A few times, yeah. I've been with buddies for a day here and there on a layover, and I helped James move here. He was freaked as fuck." Bowie shot him a look. "I didn't worry about you, even with the situation. I knew you could deal. You're like me."

"I ran this idea by Sam and he said he wasn't sure, but the new 9/11 memorial and museum is really beautiful if you're up for it. If not, I haven't taken Sam out on the ferry to the Statue of Liberty yet, and there's also the Intrepid."

"Sounds good to me. I'd love to see the memorial. By tomorrow I'll be back in real time, huh?"

"Yeah, you must have crazy jet lag." Sam shook his head. He couldn't quite imagine Bowie's life.

"Also, I hear those Spaniards know how to party." Thomas winked at Bowie and pushed his plate away. "You're going to have to roll me out of here."

"Yeah, this was a good idea. Are y'all breakfast people or should I decimate the hotel's offerings in the morning after my PT?"

Thomas looked at him. "What do you think, stud?"

"We'll meet you at ten with decent coffee. I know you;

you'll be up at five pumping iron and wanting breakfast by seven. Fair?" No way was he going to get up to meet Bowie that early. He loved waking up naturally with Thomas.

"Totally."

Thomas waved the server over again and tapped Bowie's empty glass of beer. "I assume you're not going for three?"

"Not unless y'all want to carry my ass. I'm wiped. Y'all want to head to the hotel and sit a minute?"

Sam looked to Thomas. He was easy.

Thomas handed the server a credit card. "We'll walk you back, but then I think we should say goodnight. This has been a great evening, but you should get your rest."

"Thank you, sir. I appreciate it. I'll get supper tomorrow."

Sam nodded. "Yes. Thank you for supper, Mister. Very much."

Thomas smiled at him, that pleased, warm look he got when he'd done something good. "You're welcome, sweetheart." Thomas looked at Bowie. "It was my pleasure. We appreciate that you came all this way. Are we ready?"

"I am. I have an appointment with a long hot shower and a soft mattress." Bowie stood and stretched before pulling on his coat.

This time, when they left the restaurant, Thomas put an arm around his shoulders as they walked, keeping him close and warm. "It's supposed to be warmer tomorrow. Thank God. This cold snap has been something else."

"It has. Sunday it's supposed to snow. Perfect for chili."

Bowie grunted, and Sam thought the sound was pleased.

"Snowed in with chili and football? Sounds like a winner to me. Oh, hey." Thomas stopped outside Bowie's hotel. "Let me give you my cell number."

"Hell, yeah. Please."

They exchanged numbers, and Sam got a hug. "Good to see you, baby boy. Real good. Ten o'clock tomorrow."

"I'll be here."

"I might even be with him." Thomas offered a hand to shake. "Goodnight. Rest well."

"You too."

"Love you, Bowie." He wouldn't ever let Bowie go without saying that again.

"I love you. Go. I'll see you in the morning."

And Bowie headed off.

Okay.

Okay, that went well.

Thomas steered him across the street to the subway, and they went down underground where it was warmer. It wasn't until they were on the platform, waiting in the quiet for a train, that his lover finally said something.

"I like him."

"Yeah?" *Thank God.* "He liked you too, I can tell. He teased you, talked. If he doesn't like someone, he just growls."

"I think I made a pretty good impression. I'm relieved." Thomas ducked under his hat and kissed him. "I've been dying to do that all night, though."

Oh. Thomas did know how to make him buzzed. "You make me ache when you do stuff like that, in the best way."

"I'm glad." Thomas chuckled and took his hand as their train arrived.

15

Thomas hung up his armful of coats in the hall closet, shaking his head at Bowie's and adding a second hanger when the first one drooped under the weight. Sam wasn't kidding about Bowie's size; the man had to be six five or six six, easy. Easy. Apart from maybe Angel, he wasn't used to looking up at people.

So far so good on that score. Bowie was more rested, relaxed, and seemed impressed by what they'd done down at Ground Zero, so it was a good day, and everyone had gotten along just fine. Now to get some food into the bear, as Sam would say, before Bowie got growly.

"Find your brother the menus, stud. Do you like Chinese, Bowie?"

"I do. I love me some pork fried rice. You remember that weird old place in Greenville, baby boy? The one with the crazy buffet."

"Oh, God. It smelled like a swimming pool, and the walls were peeling!" Sam brought the Chinese menu over and handed it to Bowie. "We used to eat those cinnamon fried biscuits by the dozen."

"Their pork fried rice is really good. And Sam and I can't resist the egg rolls." He sank into the couch with a groan. "Oh, that feels good."

"I'll order for us. Y'all just stay sat." Sam's gaze dragged along his body. "You decide what you want to drink."

"Take my card, Sam. I promised to get supper tonight." Bowie pulled his wallet out.

He didn't argue; he wouldn't have in any case, but he also got distracted by Sam. "Thank you, Bowie. Would you like a beer? Your brother's got something in the fridge."

"I would, thank you."

"Give me two shakes and I'll grab it. What do you want, Mister?" The honorific sounded good on Sam's lips.

He stretched his arms up over his head and sighed. "Wine, please, boy—friend." *Oh, fuck. Really, Thomas?* "Are you sure you don't need some help?" Because he needed to go get his foot out of his mouth.

"I got this. One beer, two glasses of wine, pork fried rice, our normal order, and a thousand egg rolls." Sam winked at him.

"You'd think he'd worked in a bar or something." He grinned at Bowie, utterly unable to read the expression on the eldest O'Reilly brother's face. "We usually just eat Chinese out here on the floor, is that weird for you? There's a table over there if you'd rather, but three would be tight."

"That's cool with me, man." Bowie leaned back, carefully not looking at him. Once Sam was in the office placing their order, he said, "Does Sam know what that necklace means?"

Oh. Well, not saying anything was one thing, but he wasn't going to lie outright. "Yes. He knows exactly what my collar means."

"And you're experienced, because I know full well he's not, and I want him well taken care of." Bowie spoke low, but there wasn't a bit of hesitation. "And I know the difference between abuse and consent."

Fair question, carefully phrased. Interesting. "I am. I've got ten or so years of experience and formal training. We belong to a private club. And I appreciate that question." He looked squarely at Bowie, even though Sam's brother didn't seem ready to meet his eyes yet. "I am glad he has someone supportive in the family that is looking after him without judgment."

"That's my job. Was with James too, and I failed him. I won't with Sam."

He let that statement breathe because he couldn't say one way or the other what was true. As far as he'd known, James wasn't out to the family. That didn't turn out to be true, of course, and in fairness might have been more of an omission than a lie, but regardless he'd only known "Bowie" as "Jim."

"I may have as well, as it turns out. James created a complicated system to protect himself. I'm sure he knew you wanted to be supportive. If you're concerned about Sam, why don't you ask him about me?"

"I will. I have some questions, but mostly about the fact that you were James's man first."

Also fair. Impossible to explain, but fair. "I was. Love is complicated, and I did a lot of soul-searching. I don't have whatever you're looking for. Answers, reasons. Sam is...special."

"Hey, I told Sam. It happens all the time. I see it a lot in the service. There's something about them—genes, smell, mannerisms, whatever. It happens. There's no shame there."

He shook his head. "No. This isn't...that. I mean, yes, I was struck by how much Sam's eyes reminded me of James's at first, but they're not the same. Sam isn't anything like

James at all, actually. Not a bit. What Sam and I have doesn't even feel like what I had with James."

"Good. I just want Sam happy and safe. So far, so good."

"You have my word, Bowie. I will keep him that way." He'd swear on anything Bowie asked him to. On his honor. On his life.

"Good." And that, was apparently that.

It must run in the family. The genes were strong with the O'Reilly boys.

He decided he'd better change the subject before Bowie disappeared any farther into his couch—which was quite a trick for a man Bowie's size.

He leaned back again and put his feet up on the coffee table, grinning. "Where's my wine?" He almost added the "boy," now that things were open, but decided that he and Sam should talk first.

"I was having the devil's own time with the website, so I had to call. I'm getting it, Mister. Two shakes." Sam handed Bowie his beer and card, then gave him his wine. "Technology is great until it sucks, right?"

"Oh, not to worry, sweetheart. I was only playing with you. Get your wine and come sit with me."

Bowie looked pointedly at Sam's wineglass when his boy wandered in, the neatly pressed shirt traded for a soft, old long-sleeved tee. Sam looked right back and arched an eyebrow before both brothers chuckled.

Thomas smiled, enjoying the brothers' joke. "At least you can't blame the wine on me. He was drinking that before I met him."

"I know. Weirdo."

Sam shrugged. "I like it. I like beer too. I'm an equal opportunity drinker."

"But not the hard liquor much, huh, baby boy?" Bowie muttered.

"Shut. Up."

He looked at Sam, curious. "Oh, you haven't had any with me. Is there history?"

"Yeah. A little."

Bowie opened his mouth, and Sam pointed at him.

"I'll tell it. Asshole. I don't have the best luck with hard liquor. From the time we found Granddaddy's hootch when I was seven to the times James and I explored how stupid two men could get on the Strip to a certain remarkable night in a drunk tank after a fight with, what was it Bowie, the entire bravo company of the 313th at Fort Bragg?"

Bowie howled with laughter. "That one was the best! Like banty rooster man kicking ass."

Thomas offered them a wry smile and shook his head. He didn't put his foot down with Sam—he knew better— but as far as he was concerned, his boy's banty rooster days were over. "I can't even imagine. Sam can get himself into enough of a fight completely sober. I know firsthand."

"Whiskey makes Sam a little mean."

"A little stupid, more like."

"I'm inclined to agree. Watch your wine." He pulled Sam down next to him, settling his boy close. "No pressure if you and Bowie just want a quiet day together, but I was thinking it might be fun to make a little party out of the game tomorrow. We could invite Angel, he loves football, and he and Bowie would have something to talk about. Maybe Bryan too, have you met him yet? He's Clint's massage therapist. I've been thinking about trying to set them up; he doesn't seem to be spoken for."

"You know it. Bowie's cooking, and we can make queso

and grab something sweet." Sam leaned hard. "You'll like Angel, Bowie. He's a good guy. EMT. One hell of a medic."

"You know me, I like meeting folks. I live in a world filled with new faces."

"Perfect. I'm on it." He pulled out his phone and started texting. "I'll have Angel bring beer." He looked at Bowie. "Angel knows his beer."

He decided to invite Clint and sent a quick text, just because it was nice to get an invitation, but at this late date he had to assume his mentor would probably have made other plans.

Angel! Football tomorrow at my place, the Texans are making chili. Will you bring some beer?

Then to Bryan, a much more formal invitation, with a mention that his boy needed to get to know some other subs and make some friends, and could he help a Dom out? He wasn't one to push a setup, but he could put the men in the same place at the same time and let them take it from there.

Beer. Chips? Time? Sammy cooks?

Angel made him chuckle, and he showed Sam the text.

"Tell him to kiss my butt."

He laughed. "You know he'd be all too happy to, sweetheart."

Chips yes. My boy's big (BIG) brother the Army Ranger cooks. Oh. Sam says you can kiss his butt. I say over my dead body. Game's at 4, come early

On it. U could tell Sammy to bend over but I can't reach that far down

He laughed and glanced at Sam, then put his phone on the coffee table facedown. "Angel is coming."

"Good deal." Sam grinned at Bowie. "I can't wait for you to meet him."

"Yeah? Where'd y'all meet?"

"First at Thomas's club, then at the bar I worked at, Mike's. He's a regular there."

He noted that Sam left out the details of why they'd met at the club, and he let the boy have his privacy. "I think Gabe was released from the service after an injury but that's about all I can tell you, I've known him seven or eight years, and he hasn't offered details. He's a dear friend. He knew James well too."

"Is it weird, baby boy? Knowing that you're in James's shadow forever?"

Did Bowie just say that?

"I've been in y'all's shadow my whole life. It's no big thing." Sam chuckled softly. "There's worse things to be."

"It's the plight of younger brothers. My brothers had very big shadows as well. It took a while to get into the sun." Possibly the very best description of his childhood.

"Yeah, I guess so." Bowie looked at Sam again. "How are you gonna celebrate your birthday?"

"I haven't thought about it. It's a Monday. I'm sure Momma and Daddy will call and sing."

"I took the day off and I have some ideas." Something similar to their Christmas Day plans, but with cake, and singing. He hoped the no kissing in front of Dad rule didn't extend to Bowie, because he'd felt Sam tense up and decided the boy needed one. He kept it sweet and light, though, just in case. "We'll celebrate you."

Sam took a deep breath; then he got one of those smiles that offered him the entire world. "Yeah?"

"Yes, sweetheart. We'll make some good memories. Like we did at Christmas."

The blush Thomas saw proved that Sam knew exactly what he was referring to, that his boy understood his intentions, welcomed them.

He nodded to his boy and glanced at Bowie. "He'll be well occupied. And we'll have some cake."

"Good. No moping, huh?" Bowie had a knowing look in his eyes.

"No moping," Sam agreed.

"I don't mope. I brood. But I'll endeavor not to." He chuckled, but he knew what he was doing. Keeping Sam occupied that day meant that his mind would be occupied as well. His intentions were far from selfless.

"You'll be traveling, Bowie?"

"I will. I'm going home to Texas for a couple days; then I'm back to work."

"We're talking about heading down in the late spring." Sam sounded so pleased.

"Oh, bluebonnet season. Good idea. You taking him on a road trip, baby boy?"

Sam nodded. "The ranch, then Fort Worth, down 35 to Austin at least. Maybe to Galveston if we can."

"Can we see the snake museum?" He gave Sam a toothy grin.

"Absolutely. I love it there. We can ask about getting Bowie his post-retirement job."

He laughed and sipped his wine. So much for Big Bad Bowie. Maybe he lucked out, but he found respect important, he loved Sam, and since they had those two attributes in common, they were getting on just fine.

God help him if he really fucked up somehow, but he couldn't even begin to imagine what that would take. He and his boy had trust.

The intercom chimed and when Sam started to get up to answer it, he put a hand on the boy's shoulder. "No. I've got it." He didn't allow Sam to open the door to strangers right now. He buzzed the delivery guy in, grabbed his keys, and went out in the hall to wait for the food.

"This smells fantastic," he said, hauling the takeout bags inside. He made sure the door locked and took the food into the living room.

"...haven't seen any of them since the bad cut."

"Jesus, Sam! Stitches?"

"Angel fixed it up. I pulled them out."

"Such a cowboy." He'd been hoping this wouldn't come up, but he supposed he ought to have known better. The police would have contacted Sam's parents, but he didn't know how much Bowie knew. It sounded like very little. "Not to worry. We have security cameras up."

That answer would sound far too cavalier to Bowie and he knew it. "Sam? Can you see if you can find some soy sauce in the kitchen? I don't think they sent any."

"Dammit. I asked special. Sure. You want some sweet chili sauce, Mister? Bowie, another beer?" As soon as they both nodded, Sam stood and wandered off.

Thomas watched Sam go, then sat down, speaking quietly and quickly in case the boy came back. "You should know that Sam is never alone. I have arranged for someone to watch the building and tail him if need be when I am at work, and otherwise he is with me. He doesn't know."

"The police think it's you. You know that, right?" Bowie managed to ask the question without accusing him of anything.

"Of course. We were lovers, I'm kinky, and I'm the only lead they have. We were also seen leaving a restaurant together three hours before his murder and I have no alibi." He shrugged, but he made sure to look Bowie in the eyes. "I loved James. I miss him."

Bowie nodded to him, the look just like his Sam's.

Understanding and silent, somehow managing to convey pain and sympathy and his loss all at the same time.

"I know." He patted Bowie on the knee, relieved that he at least knew how to process that look now, even if it still hurt. "Sam, too."

Sam walked in, those quick eyes reading them both. "It's almost like he's here, isn't it? Like he's playing a shitty joke on us."

"I think the three of us, here together, is the closest we can to get to him. I think he'd like this." He slid over on the couch and tapped the seat for Sam to come sit and be with Bowie. The man needed something, a hug, some contact, and he wasn't the right person for that.

Sam sat next to Bowie and sighed. "I'd offer to go outside and beat the fuck out of you, but it's damn cold."

"You little shit." Bowie grabbed Sam in a headlock, giving Sam a noogie until Sam pinched his thigh and Bowie let him go. "I love you too, baby boy."

He caught himself smiling and wondered what James would have thought about that exchange. How nice it would have been to have this while James was still...

"I'm starting in on the egg rolls. I suggest you catch up quickly." He reached for the bags and finished unpacking them.

"Save two for me, Mister!" Sam leaned toward him, laughing at him. "The pork's for Captain Caveman."

He handed off the container of rice to Bowie, letting the food distract him, curious that he didn't seem to feel as well adjusted about James at the moment as he thought he was. It was just all the talk. And in the end it probably wasn't James actually, but all his questions that would never have answers.

"Do you have a craving for any stupid television, Bowie? Jeopardy, maybe?" He grinned at the big man.

"Works for me. That man doesn't age, does he? He's been the same age my whole life."

"He's got a portrait somewhere. Or how about a movie? Sam? What do you guys watch?" He handed Sam the remote. "Let me guess. Chick flicks?"

"Bowie's a Food Network guy. And he loves thrillers, right?"

"How about something old school. Jurassic Park? I saw that in the theater with Uncle Teddy. I remember thinking that they'd brought them back to life for real." Bowie chuckled. "Momma was pregnant with you, I think."

Thomas laughed. "Damn, Bowie. You're old. I bet you have a year or two on me at least."

"Thirty-three on the fifteenth."

"Ancient old man," Sam teased. "Although I remember when you were eighteen and I was eleven, it seemed like I'd never be as big as you."

"Sam, you're never ever going to be as big as me, shrimp."

"Doesn't seem to stop him from trying." He winked at Sam. "Does it?"

"I will beat you both. At the same time." Sam laughed, handing Thomas chopsticks and food. "One hand tied behind my back and everything."

"Mm. I like that image." He took a bite, thoroughly enjoying his mental picture of Sam all pissed off and tied up. Possibilities abounded.

At least once Bowie was gone.

16

"How much meat goes into this, man?" Sam sat on the counter, watching Bowie do his thing and taking notes. Onions. Garlic. Hamburger. Tomatoes. A metric fuckton of chili powder.

"Lots. We're feeding a mess today, and I want you to have enough for tomorrow. Happy Birthday."

"Thanks. It's weird, huh?" It was sort of like it was just James's birthday now, like he was the ghost instead of James.

"What's weird?" Thomas came in with a couple of grocery bags and set them next to him on the counter, then planted a kiss on his cheek. "Hi."

"Hey, stranger. You need help?" He hopped down, sliding along Thomas's body all the way.

"Whoa, stud. What kind of help are you offering?" He got a wink. "I just picked up the last-minute stuff Bowie had on his list and some iced tea for Bryan. He doesn't drink."

Thomas walked around Bowie on one side, around to the other, trying to see into the pot on the stove. "That smells so good already."

"It does. It'll just get better as it simmers. We have queso and chips for snacks."

"Thomas will be your friend for life for queso."

"Sam, how many times have you made it in the microwave? You telling me you haven't made it for your man?"

"We haven't had a chance!" And Thomas seemed classy for nuker queso, to be honest.

"Mm. queso. I would sell my soul for queso. You can make it in the microwave?" Thomas was salivating.

"Yeah. I can make it on the stove, but it's better in the microwave, right, baby boy?"

"Yeah. I mean, I've only ever done it in the microwave."

"And you haven't shared this magic with me until now? I wonder if James used to make it in the microwave? He could cook."

Sam looked at Bowie, who shrugged at him. He didn't remember James ever liking to cook, but what did that mean? What he knew of James was sitting by the pool and reading thrillers in the sunshine, and drinking. A lot.

Thomas looked between them and started unpacking the groceries and putting them away. "Well, he made good queso, however he did it. I'm looking forward to having some."

"The O'Reillys won't disappoint. Sam and I are on this."

Sam nodded. This part wasn't hard. "You want sausage in it?"

"Or I can put a scoop of hamburger meat in?" Bowie asked.

"Surprise me." Thomas put the empty bags away. "Hey, Bowie, do you mind if I steal your brother for five minutes?"

"Of course not. He belongs to you, after all."

Sam rolled his eyes at Bowie but followed Thomas out of the kitchen. "What's up, honey?"

"I just wanted to make sure...you know he knows, right?" Thomas touched warm fingers to his collar.

"I'd guessed, yeah." He leaned in, letting the touch ease some of the raw spots. "I'm not sure what's weirder—that he knows or that he can possibly know, you know?"

Whoa, that was the convoluted sentence of doom.

Thomas shook his head and smiled at him. "Listen to you. You are well overdue for a session. Tomorrow, boy."

"Tomorrow." Okay, was that wonderful or awful? Was he worried? Excited? Itching? He didn't know. Maybe all of it at once.

"But until then, I wanted to ask your permission to... speak to you the way I normally would in our home. Especially with our guests coming over. If it makes you uncomfortable, I won't."

He gave that a thought. Everybody called him something different, and this was their place. They shouldn't have to lie here, right?

"It's going to be worse if you feel awkward, especially if Bowie knows. I'm doing okay, right?" Because he hadn't been worrying about it.

"You're just fine, sweetheart. It's just that in this company I know the word 'boy' will come out of my mouth by mistake, and I'd rather just own it than make a thing of it; does that make sense? I'd rather know I'm not going to upset you."

"Thanks for asking me. That means a ton." He kissed the corner of Thomas's mouth. "Seriously. Our house."

"Thank you, love." The intercom chimed. "Guests! I've got it. Go back and learn how to make that chili." Thomas grabbed his ass and headed for the door.

"Lord have mercy." Thomas was cute as all get out, so excited to have folks over. That boded well. He liked to see people too—he didn't cook, but he could make a drink.

He heard quiet voices in the hall, so he knew it had to be the sub Thomas had invited. Sweet that his lover had been thinking about someone for Angel.

"There's chili happening in the kitchen," he heard Thomas say, the voices getting closer.

"It smells amazing."

Thomas led a tall guy in a round-collared button-down into the kitchen. "Bryan, this is Sam, and Sam's big brother, Bowie."

"Pleased to meet you." He walked up and held out a hand, offering Bryan a smile. "Can I get you something to drink?"

Bryan smiled right back. "Yes, please. Water would be fine, or maybe iced tea if you have it?"

Thomas winked at him over Bryan's shoulder.

"I'm on it. I do love me a glass of iced tea."

Bowie gave Bryan a nod, a smile. "Hey, there. Pleased. I'd shake, but I'm a mess."

Sam poured iced tea, handed Bryan the glass, then stirred the queso. *Go, multi-tasking O'Reillys!*

"No problem, I got you." Bryan bumped elbows with Bowie and smiled. "Can I help?"

"I don't know, can you?" Bowie's smile was teasing and warm.

Bryan laughed, "Well, gosh. I guess I can't." The guy made a face at Bowie and stuck out his tongue.

Bowie laughed, the sound filling up the kitchen. "Brat. I'll put you to work if you're not careful."

Bryan turned to him and held pumped up arms out dramatically. "Is it me? Didn't I just offer?"

Sam chuckled and handed Bryan a bag of tortillas and a huge bowl. "If you'll take those to the front room, please? I need hot pads for the queso."

"Yeah, sure." Bryan took the chips and the bowl and smiled at Bowie on the way out of the kitchen. "Happy to help."

Lord have mercy. Were they flirting? Because Bowie was... no flirting.

"He's so friendly, Bowie. Am I right?" Thomas teased. The intercom chimed again. "That will be Angel."

"Friendly. Bowie. Totally. Like a Rottweiler." He winked at Bryan. "Queso."

"Queso!" Thomas echoed as he headed for the door.

Bryan laughed. "Rottweilers are very sweet and loyal if they like you."

"Hello, Angel. Come on in."

"They also drool and fart so bad you can't hardly bear it." He looked over and winked.

Bryan broke into a fit of giggles. "Noted."

"Look out, Sam. Look who's here." Thomas gave him a smug grin.

"Little Sammy! You look great! We miss you at Mike's, man. Well, most of us do. Darla says she misses your eyeliner most of all." Angel laughed and scooped him into a bear hug.

He squeezed Angel hard; the big man gave the best hugs. "I miss y'all too. The eyeliner was an aberration."

"Oh, no. The eyeliner was hot." Thomas's voice was low but somehow it cut right through to him.

Bryan whistled softly.

"I didn't hear anything but compliments myself." Angel chuckled.

"If you don't know how to apply it, I can totally help." Bryan grinned. "I can see where it would suit you."

Sam's cheeks heated and he grinned. "I don't know. Maybe?"

"Yes. Thank you, Bryan." Thomas smiled at him. "Do you think your brother can get away from the kitchen for a bit, Sam?"

"Sure. Angel? Mister? Y'all want a beer?" Sam could stir for Bowie if he needed.

Angel nodded. "Thank you, Sammy, I do."

"It's football, right? I'll have a beer, too, sweetheart. Oh. Sam, I left Angel's beer and chips by the door."

"Hi. I'm Bryan."

"Oh. Goodness, I'm sorry. Bryan, have you two not met at the club?"

"I think I would have remembered." Bryan smiled and held out his hand.

Angel shook Bryan's hand, and oh, Bryan liked big guys. Good to know. Bryan was sparkling.

He grabbed the chips and the beer and headed into the kitchen. "Thomas wants to introduce you around. Do I need to do anything with the chili?"

"It'll sit. Beer me?"

"You got it." Three beers and a bowl for the chips. They managed to get out into the front room with beer and food, and somehow they were having a party.

"There he is. Angel, this is Sam's brother, Bowie. He's visiting for Sam's birthday."

"Bowie. I like it. Good to meet you. Your brother is one of my favorite people."

"Mine too." Bowie held out his hand. "Pleased."

Angel shook, then pulled him into a quick man-hug. "The chili smells good."

"He's been cooking it all day. It's the most use that kitchen has had since I moved in here." Thomas sipped his beer.

Bryan stepped clear of the men and looked at him. "Everyone in this room is taller than I am except you. Do you know how weird that is for me? It's like giants live here. Super hot giants."

Sam's lips quirked. Bryan was damn near Thomas's height, which still made Sam the shrimp. Good thing he was tough as shit. "Welcome to my world, man."

"I kind of love it. Do you know how hard it is to find a Dom that's bigger than I am? And I'm standing in a room full of them." Bryan wasn't a toothpick. The sub was broad-shouldered and in great shape, which he guessed the guy had to be to give massages all day long.

"Well, enjoy it. Bowie's heading out in the morning, but Angel's a local and a good man. I love him dearly."

"I plan to. Bowie's leaving so soon? Such a flirt, the way he gave me shit right after saying hello. I thought he was into me. I should have known. Dammit." Bryan sighed but the man's eyes shifted just that quickly from Bowie to Angel.

"He's a soldier. He's just here on leave." A flirt? Bowie? He didn't know about that. Of course, he didn't think he'd ever get used to men just looking at another guy and talking about flirting or interest or sex. Ever.

He was way more used to measuring whether he was going to kick ass or get his handed to him. He reckoned Bowie was about the same there, just with seven years more practice and the ability to build a bomb out of steel wool and laundry detergent.

"You lucked out with Master Thomas. You have no idea how many of us were trying to walk that line between being respectful and giving him our cell numbers." Bryan laughed. "No hard feelings."

"None taken." He wasn't sure exactly what magic they'd made. Adrenaline and loss and something special, possibly James not wanting them to be unhappy. More unhappy. Something. Whatever it was, it was. "You a football fan?"

"I wouldn't say I'm a fan—I don't follow any teams or anything, but I don't hate football. I do like chili, though."

"Well, Bowie's tastes like my momma's, so you're in for a treat." He'd loved the whole taste-test part of watching Bowie in the kitchen.

"Sounds great. So I heard you're a bartender or something?"

How to answer that? He didn't know how because no one wanted to hear about freelance work and "I'm writing a book" was basically code for being kept, which he wasn't. He was going to contribute, and his research brought in some and was going to grow. "More like a bouncer."

"Whoa. I'd like to see that, you must be pretty scrappy. I mean, you're obviously built solid enough but big and drunk, or even worse, big and sober must be a challenge."

"Folks don't expect a little guy to be an issue. I surprise them, every time." He chuckled, then shook his head. "I haven't been there in a few weeks."

He didn't think he missed it. He missed some of the people, but not the work.

"Well, holidays and all. Oh! You two looked amazing at the New Year's party! I wasn't there long because I was working, but I stopped in to say hello to some people. I only saw you across the room, but you made such an impression."

"Thank you. Thomas can cowboy up with the best of them. He made my mouth dry, sure as shit." His heart beat a little fast, and didn't he feel daring as all get out? "This is all real new to me, but I'm trying."

Bryan's head tilted. "Like new, new? Or new to the whole club scene?"

"Like new, new." His cheeks were on fire. God, he had to learn to stop that.

Bryan smiled at him. "Oh, that's awesome! Don't blush, silly boy, we were all new once, right?"

Okay, that was one hell of a point. "Right. It's easy to feel like the only one."

"It is, especially when it looks like everyone else knows what they're doing. The reality is some do and some don't, and it's hard to tell who is who when everyone is on their best behavior at a party. You two need to come to the club more. Then you won't feel so out of touch. Are you a member yet? There's a sub loop."

"No." They were going to talk finances after Bowie left and they'd had his birthday. He wasn't sure if he could afford it. He found himself looking for Thomas, and when their eyes met, he smiled and relaxed a little. "Not yet."

"Well, when you join you'll get all the info. It's helpful. People ask questions, ask for advice, offer help. It's a great group. In the meantime, you can talk to me whenever, too. Everybody always has something to learn, you know?" Bryan sipped his tea. "I hear the Dom loop is heavy. We're pretty laid-back, but I can see the Dom loop getting intense."

"I can't imagine." But he was curious, and he could research like a fiend.

"We should have lunch sometime. I have a weird schedule, but I work more early mornings and late afternoons than anything else. And I'm at the club a bunch in the evenings. I'm kind of unattached right now.

In every sense." Bryan's eyes found Angel and looked the man over.

"He's a good man. Kind." He smiled at Bryan. "You should go say hi."

"Yeah? I don't know, he's with friends." Bryan caught a lip between very white teeth and looked at him. "Will you go with?"

"Well sure, honey. Come on." Sam winked and waded in, pushing Bowie out of the way to make room. "Y'all are hogging the queso. Let this man in to eat, would you?"

"You better hurry up before Thomas eats it all."

Thomas laughed. "I'd protest, except that Angel is absolutely correct."

"I only came for the queso. And the chili. Also, I didn't have any better plans." Bryan glanced at Angel. "You either, apparently."

"I came to meet the third O'Reilly. You have to admit, they're like Mutt and Jeff."

Sam pinched Angel's arm. "Butthead. Any of y'all need another beer?"

Thomas gave him a smile and he could feel that pull, like his lover wanted him closer. "I'm fine sweetheart, thank you."

Bryan went for the queso. "They are, although I was just telling Sam that I'm not used to being on the short end of a crowd. You people are unnatural."

He shifted, moving closer to Thomas, his gaze caught.

Thomas put an arm out to draw him in, and Angel's boisterous laugh faded into the background. "Having a good time?"

"I am. Bryan's a nice guy." He inhaled, breathing in the scent of Thomas and letting it fill him.

"I don't know him that well, but he gives one hell of a

massage. I'm going to talk with him about getting on his calendar, are you interested?"

"Sure. I gave them up once I got here." Cal had been working on his shoulder, on unfreezing it.

"Good. I'll get us in, then." Thomas tucked a hand into the waistband of his jeans. "Your brother seems really relaxed today."

"I think he misses cooking, huh? And just being a guy."

"It's a shame he can't stay longer; it would do him some good. His job is no joke, right? And he's been doing it a long time."

"He deals with bombs. Every day. I can't imagine." He had ridden bulls, but not every day, and he got hurt, but he didn't have to think about killing other people.

"I can't either, to be honest." Thomas gave him a squeeze. "He's saving lives, though. You're right to call him a hero."

"Where's your remote, Thomas? It's game time!" Angel was nosing around the television, trying to find it.

"Probably between the couch cushions where my boy leaves it when he falls asleep in front of the TV." Thomas laughed. "Go help the man out, sweetheart."

"Hold up. I'll get it." He dug around until he found it, then dialed up the game. They all settled in, Bryan between Angel and Bowie on the sofa and Thomas in his chair. Sam perched on the arm of the couch, leaning on the padded back.

Thomas watched kickoff like it was the most important moment of the game, and he stretched out long. "So, how long before this famous O'Reilly chili is ready?"

"It's just simmering. Y'all can have some whenever you want." Bowie sounded satisfied, happy.

Christ, it was weird.

"Bring me some while you're up, Tommy." Angel's eyes were glued to the TV.

Thomas snorted. "Well, I guess I'm getting up. Anyone else?"

"I got it, Mister. I'm up anyway." Sam made his way to the kitchen, grabbing a beer and throwing it back while he pulled down bowls.

He listened to the voices from the other room as he served up the chili, Bowie and Angel shouting something at the TV, Bryan laughing, Thomas's playful disapproval.

Sam slipped out, snapped a photo, and sent it to Momma. Bowie was laughing hard, there was queso, you could see the Cowboys on the TV—it should tickle her.

He started bringing bowls—Thomas and Bowie, then Angel and Bryan. He made his bowl and grabbed a kitchen chair to sit where he could see. Momma texted back with a heart and a Go Cowboys sticker.

Lord have mercy.

"Oh." That was all Angel got out before taking another bite. After that it was just yummy noises. "Mm. Mhm."

Thomas was nodding as he chewed. "Outstanding, Bowie."

It did taste just like Momma's, didn't it? *Damn.* He had this weird moment where his old life and his new one crashed together and meshed. Was this what James was trying to avoid? Was it that bad? Weird, sure, maybe even a little hard, but Sam wasn't sure it was bad.

Thomas caught his eye. "Are you all right?"

"Hmm? Yeah. Yeah, I was just..." *Lost in my head. Thinking. Navel gazing.* "...eating."

"Mm. Food takes you home sometimes, hm?"

"It does. You need anything?"

Thomas gave him an indulgent look and didn't say

anything more about home. "Just you where I can reach you."

"Angel, how long have you been a member at the club?" Bryan bumped shoulders with the big man and grinned at him.

"Hm. I think it will be nine years this summer. You?"

"Just two."

"Baby." Angel teased.

"We can't all be as old as you are."

"Hey!"

Sam shook his head and started laughing. "Good lord and butter."

"So tell me about this club, y'all." Butter wouldn't melt in Bowie's mouth.

Thomas stared until he stood and brought the chair with him to sit next to Thomas's recliner.

"It's a gentlemen's club—"

"For men who aren't gentle." Angel laughed loud.

Thomas sighed, but he was grinning.

"Well, I'd fit right in, except for the gentleman part. There ain't a gentle bit of me." Bowie was getting blustery.

"Damn. Are you sure you have to leave tomorrow?" Bryan smiled at Bowie, but he was leaning just a little on Angel.

"I'd take you over there if you had time," Thomas offered. "It's a respectful place, a safe space to be who we are, explore."

"I'll be back. This was just a flyby to check on my baby brother, make sure he was being good."

"Shut up, asshat." He flipped Bowie off playfully.

"No, no, no, get him. Get him!" Angel sat up and leaned toward the TV, almost knocking Bryan off the couch.

Bowie caught Bryan handily against his chest. "I got you, honey."

"My hero." Brian smiled at Bowie and leaned right into him. "And you, Angel, are such a brute."

Angel laughed. "You look okay to me, little one."

Sam caught Thomas shaking his head.

"Lord have mercy." Football. Chili. Queso. Focus on anything not his brother sitting on the sofa with two guys.

Angel pinned Bowie with a stare. "You're looking pretty good over there yourself, Bowie. Leave looks good on you."

"That's me. I'm a stud." Bowie flexed, and Sam rolled his eyes.

It wasn't the size of the muscle; it was the body fat percentage and stamina.

Angel chuckled. "Don't worry, we're happy to stroke your ego as long as you're saving lives."

"You know what? I need more tea." Bryan hopped up off the couch like he'd been bit and took off for the kitchen.

What the hell was that? Had he missed something?

Sam blinked over at Thomas, eyes wide.

Thomas leaned close. "I'm guessing all that testosterone is making it a little hot on the couch."

"Hmm." Sam met Thomas's eyes. He didn't see it. Both Bowie and Angel were stacked, but they weren't Thomas.

Thomas held his gaze for a long moment, the hint of a grin fading, changing his lover's expression to something more bewildered. Then Thomas leaned just that much closer and took a kiss, the gesture infused with affection, and the barest hint of need.

He held Thomas's arm, sighing softly as all the sound faded. Better. He hadn't even known he was ramped up. *Lord.*

"Will you two stop it?" Bowie growled, and he flipped his brother off without looking.

"If you're jealous, I'm right here."

Did he actually hear Angel say that?

"Don't make me beat you, man."

"This is totally weird, Mister," he muttered.

"I bet." Thomas chuckled and leaned a bit. "Do I have to take a hose to the pair of you?"

"Just having some fun, Tommy." Angel shifted his stare to the TV again. "Slow game."

Bryan came back with a glass of iced tea, looking totally composed, set it down on the coffee table, and started cleaning up bowls. "Anyone need another beer?"

"I'm gonna switch to coffee, I think. You need anything, Mister?" He'd had two in short order; he was done.

"Coffee sounds perfect, sweetheart. Thank you."

"I'll go one more." Angel handed an empty to Bryan. "How about you, Mister Stud?"

"I'll take another, sure. I'll be taking a cab back to the hotel."

He went to make a couple of coffees as Bryan dealt with the beers. "Do you need anything else, Bryan?"

"I'm good. Those guys had me going for a minute, though." Bryan laughed at himself easily, no shame at all, and shot Sam a view of those white teeth. "Poor Angel. I think he just needs to get laid."

"I wouldn't know. Good luck, though, to both of you." He doctored Thomas's coffee, started his own. "I think everyone ought to get a chance to be happy."

Bryan snorted. "I wasn't suggesting tonight! I'm not that easy. God."

Oh. Right. *Dammit.* He went for the tried and true grunt of agreement.

What did people here do without a backyard to go out to smoke or pretend to smoke? Normally his happy ass would be out there, getting air and taking a break.

"I have a beer to deliver," Bryan sang cheerfully and left him alone in the kitchen.

Everyone shouted at the TV. Cowboys must have scored.

He leaned against the fridge and waited for his coffee to make, closing his eyes, and just chilling.

"That game is just about over. Whether it's actually over or not. They can't catch up." Thomas had the empty queso bowl and stuck it in the sink to soak. "I can't believe I was so worried about this visit. Your brother is great company. He hasn't threatened to break my neck for me once."

"He's a good guy. A bit of an ass, but basically decent." Unless they were beating the fuck out of each other. Then he was a turd. "Your coffee's ready."

"Thank you. I haven't had beer in a long while. Remind me next time that it sits heavy in my stomach." Thomas leaned a shoulder against the fridge and looked at him. "What kind of cake do you like?"

"Pineapple upside-down cake is my favorite." It always had been. It was Daddy's favorite too, and it had been his grandaddy's, too.

"Ooh. Complicated. All right." He got a quick kiss. "Come on, let's go finish out the game."

"Sounds good." He grabbed his mug. "Let's go be social."

Bryan was in Thomas's chair when they got back, so he sat next to Angel, and Thomas sat on the floor, leaning against his knees. The game got better in the third quarter, with a couple of good plays and a couple of bad calls that got everyone fired up.

Halfway through the fourth, it was a real game. With the

score tied up, it was so tense that even Thomas was shouting.

Bowie popped Angel in the shoulder. "Look at that! Goddamn! Fumble the goddamn ball!"

Sam had one hand on Thomas's shoulder as he leaned forward. "Come on. Come on, y'all."

"Shit, I'd've sworn this game was over an hour ago." Thomas leaned hard into his knees, one hand wrapped around his ankle.

"Are they gonna score?" Bryan set his tea down. "Wait. Is he gonna...?"

"Fuck, yeah. He is!" Angel popped right up off the couch. "Yes!"

Bowie hooted. "Fuckin' A!"

Sam cradled Thomas in his legs, making sure that the bouncing and celebrating didn't end up knocking his Sir out.

"Game over, boys. They're just running the clock down now." Thomas sounded pleased. He didn't even know Mister was a football fan. Probably because they'd had to move their club days to Sundays for a while.

From now on, Sundays would be for queso, football, and snuggling on the couch.

Maybe even Li'l Smokies in barbecue sauce. It was amazing what you could do with a microwave.

17

Thomas sipped his coffee and looked out the windows in the living room at the busy Monday morning street below. It felt so odd not to be at work when the rest of the world was out there rushing. It was a lovely morning; there was sunshine for his boy's birthday and blue sky for James, who liked to complain that New York was too gray.

They'd never spent James's birthday together; that was what he was sticking to with Sam because the boy didn't need his baggage today. But they'd texted every year, no matter what boondoggle James and Sam were on.

Happy Birthday, pet. I love you.

I love you, Master. You're the best gift I'll ever get.

He pressed his forehead against the cold window glass and made himself breathe. He knew it was normal, the guilt and the helplessness. Someday he would get over feeling like he should have done more, like James's death was somehow his fault. Just not today.

Today was about Sam, not James. Today would be about Sam from now on. Missing James was understandable and allowed, focusing on the man was not.

He took one more deep breath, then pushed off the window and went to get Sam's presents from where they were hiding in the playroom.

The office door was closed. Sam had been up and moving well before dawn, on his phone texting Bowie, Thomas was sure.

Angel had promised to get Bowie to his hotel last night, the eldest brother having had at least one or two too many, and the good-byes had been short and gruff.

He understood the closed door. Apart from being polite and not wanting to wake him up—which was ironic because he really hadn't been sleeping—he understood the desire to hibernate, to hide, to just not deal with the day. If it was just his grief or just Sam's in a vacuum he might even allow it. But he was anticipating many birthdays with his boy, so they had to deal with the day, and themselves, before the grief took on a life of its own.

He knocked on the door, giving Sam that much privacy at least, and allowing himself to slowly build up to his plans for the day.

Sam opened the door, offering him a half grin that didn't quite meet his eyes, his boy already jittering a bit. "Morning, honey. How goes?"

"That's not a real question, is it?" He reached for Sam, pulling the boy into his arms. "We need a lot of this today. This is how we're going to make it better, together. Enough of this and it won't just be better, it will be good."

"I'll be fine. I'm just checking emails." Sam pushed close, though, and stayed there, soaking him up.

"Did Bowie get off okay?" The boy could say anything at all. Thomas knew Sam would say all sorts of things today— looking out for himself, protecting his Master—it wasn't what the boy said that needed attention; the truth about how Sam was feeling was in his body.

Sam felt...stiff. Tight. They would have good work to do in a bit.

"He did. His plane left half an hour ago. It was good to see him." One finger drew on his belly, the touch soft, restless, just hard enough not to tickle.

"It was good to meet him. I enjoyed his company. I think the visit did him some good too." He caught his boy's fingers up in one hand and kissed them. "Would you like some breakfast? Coffee? Presents?"

He didn't offer Sam a real kiss; those would be rewards today.

"I'm not hungry, and I'm on my fifth cup. Presents?" Sam traced his lips with the same light touch.

Jesus. "No more coffee for you, boy." He'd have gotten himself out of bed sooner to supervise Sam more closely, but he'd been going over the day in his mind and needed the quiet. "Have you done your crunches yet?"

"I did. I was up early. I wanted to say good-bye to Bowie. Did I say that already?" Sam chuckled and shook his head. "He liked you a lot, you know. He wants to come back."

"Best possible outcome, right? Come on, sweetheart. Come open your presents." That seemed like the best thing to do while Sam was this wound up. The boy needed to settle a little before he'd be able to find focus. He pulled Sam out of the office and down the hall to where he'd left them in the living room, just two wrapped gifts, sitting on the coffee table.

"You even wrapped them!" Oh, now that was a pleased smile. Sam's eyes lit up. "Thank you."

"Of course I wrapped them, they're presents." Did people not wrap birthday presents? Well, he was glad it made Sam happy anyway, Sam deserved that. "I told you we were going to celebrate you."

"You did." Sam's hand shook slightly, and he pursed his lips. "Can I open them now?"

He led Sam to the couch and sat with him, staying close and keeping a hand on the boy's back. He knew he was going to have to lead his boy through this day, dig deep for patience and clarity. But that didn't mean it had to be a bad day at all.

Work that matters.

"Start with the small one." The club membership might be the more expensive gift, but he felt like the bigger box was more personal and might actually mean more to his boy.

"Yes, Sir." Sam leaned hard and opened the gift, eyes going wide as he opened the folio and read. "Thomas? This is...really?"

"Yes, my own. Really. Clint feels you've earned it, and I know luxuries are a bit of a stretch for you right now. It seemed like just the right gift." Clint hadn't hesitated at all when he asked, just told Scotty to charge him and handed him the welcome folio.

Sam looked at him, grabbed him, and hugged him hard. "Thank you. You're good to me. Seriously. Thank you."

He held his boy, returning the hug. "You are most welcome. I love you, sweetheart. Being good to you isn't difficult. It makes me happy." Sam needed to understand what their relationship, every aspect of it, did for him. It wasn't the tangible gifts that brought him the most joy. He decided he would remind Sam about that later.

"I love you, Mister." Sam didn't hurry to open the second gift, going over the information from the club, giving it attention while snuggled into his side. Finally, Sam reached for the second gift—a hand-tooled saddlebag made into a satchel. "Oh."

Score.

That was a good sound.

"Seems like an author should have a good bag to carry his research in."

"Thomas. Wow." Suddenly he had a lapful of pocket cowboy.

"Happy birthday, Sam." It was questionable whether his boy had actually earned a kiss, but he wanted one, dammit, and wasn't he entitled? He pulled Sam down by the chin and pressed their lips together. Sam kissed him happily, the connection sure, steady. Confident.

"It's perfect, Mister. Perfect."

That felt good. It felt good that he'd picked something Sam liked, it felt good that his lover appreciated the gift, and he was relieved that his boy was more focused on the positive now and on them.

He smiled at Sam. "I can't wait to see you use it."

"It's amazing. Honestly. Suits me to the bone." Sam grabbed it, holding it between them. "Look at that tooling. Someone took some real care."

"You'd love the place I bought it. I'll take you over there sometime. They have all kinds of neat things." He rubbed Sam's back, noting the boy's still-tight shoulders.

Sam leaned into his hands a bit, muscles trembling the barest amount. "I'd like that. Thank you again. This was amazing."

"Good. We're off to a good start then." He touched Sam's collar, drew a finger around the little ring. "What do I need to know today, sweetheart? What do you think you need?"

Sam closed his eyes and took a deep breath. "What do you need to know? Everything feels weird. Not horrible, but...brittle. Like that first ride after an injury—you know you're fixin' to face-plant, you know you're not going to make the eight, but you know you got to ride or you'll never do it again."

He nodded slowly, thinking about that. "That's a marvelous analogy, sweetheart. Quite helpful, thank you." Next weekend he would take Sam to the club for something intense, something demanding of his sub. It was time to push, time to learn something new. Today he might poke and prod a little, but he needed to get Sam solid again.

He shifted, coaxing his boy off his lap, and stood up. "Come on, love. There's more of you to celebrate." He tangled his fingers with Sam and led him down the hall.

"I appreciate it, you know, the idea of you celebrating me."

"I don't want you to appreciate it, boy." He led Sam into the bedroom. "Get your chair." He let that statement float out there for Sam to worry over, giving the boy a puzzle, something else to think about.

Sam shot him a surprised look and let out a silent breath and went to grab the chair without comment.

"Usual spot, please, and bring me your blindfold and cuffs." He pulled his T-shirt off and tossed it away. He thought about changing out of his jeans, but the boy wouldn't be able to see him, and he was comfortable.

Sam didn't respond, but he didn't hesitate either, just moved to do as Thomas asked.

"Good boy." He took what the boy brought him and set them on the chair. "Strip for me, please. Just right there. Slowly." He gave Sam a hint of a grin, something wicked pulling at the corner of his mouth.

Sam saw it, though, responded to it. It didn't take much for his boy to see him.

Sam pulled off his T-shirt, showing him the tight belly, and eased off his pajama pants and folded them. Mmm. Whoever had done that ink had done it lovingly, had paid attention to how it climbed Sam's body.

"Good boy." He stepped closer, fingers drawn to the ink and he moved around Sam, finding that knot on his boy's lower back and tracing the barbed wire over Sam's hip.

Sam's eyelids went heavy, and he licked his lips as his entire body leaned toward Thomas.

"I do love your ink, boy." He moved away again, but noting how his boy swayed just a little without him, he came back quickly, blindfold in his fingers. "Give me your words, please."

"Yellow and revolver."

Thomas could tell this was familiar now. Comfortable. Part of Sam.

"Thank you. I remind you that I expect you to use them. It's never a sign of anything other than respect and trust to need a break, and it's not a failure to need a hard stop. You and I have only begun to touch on your limits, I don't know yet where they all are, and I wouldn't expect you to either. Remember we're building something; it's not a test. It's never, ever a test. Do you understand?"

It was more than important. He'd repeat this often, even if he knew his boy trusted it.

"I do. It's hard to not get into that 'grit your teeth' mode, but I hear you."

"Yes, that's just it. Excellent. And I will stay aware as well. Close your eyes, boy." He waited for Sam's eyes to close, then tied the blindfold in place. "Now you have my voice, and my touch, and your ears." He led his boy to the wall, placed Sam's hands flat against it, and retrieved the cuffs.

Sam tilted his head, following Thomas's footsteps as he moved, that tongue flicking out to wet his lips.

He made sure to let the heavy links of the short chain rattle in his fingers so his boy could hear as he made his way back. He stepped up behind Sam, hips against the boy's ass, and reached out to put the cuffs on.

Sam gasped, the sound making him smile. The way his boy craved contact, soaked up his touch, would never get old.

"Test the cuffs for me; then settle your hands wherever they are comfortable." By now, Sam knew that meant to make sure they didn't pinch or rub and to make sure they were solid. He didn't move, letting Sam bump and lean into him as the boy followed orders.

Once settled, he hooked an arm around Sam's waist, flattening his hand across those delicious abs. "I said I didn't want you to appreciate the idea of being celebrated. I don't." He leaned close to his boy's ear, hard enough that Sam was nearly flat against the wall and whispered, "I want you to love it."

He felt the reaction that rocked Sam—the full-body shiver, the way Sam flushed hot against him, the quick inhalation.

Electricity shot through him and he let the sound out, a low hum just for Sam. "There's my boy."

"Yours." Sam sucked in another breath; then he stretched out his fingers before he let them relax against the wall.

"Such a very good boy." He pushed away, giving Sam plenty of room to breathe and leaving lots of hot, bare skin to cool in his absence.

Sam tried to follow, managing to stop himself from leaving the wall with a husky little chuckle.

"If we were following conventional rules, you'd have earned yourself a couple of strokes for that, boy." He kept his tone even. "One for moving without permission, and at least one for the laugh." There was a piece of him that craved that ritual—the morning discipline, the evening punishment—the things that reminded them daily of their status and their responsibility to one another. But not enough to impose it on a boy that didn't understand those things yet. Perhaps that would come.

"You're not allowed to be happy?" The question honestly surprised, even shocked.

He laughed, genuinely touched by that response. "You, my boy, most certainly are. I was commenting on how different we are. How remarkable." He headed for his boy, the new flogger in one hand and a toothy pinwheel in the other. "You think you would have made it in that blindfold?"

"Made it where, Sir? I wasn't trying to move. It just happened. You're like a magnet." Sam's lips quirked. "I guess that makes me a nail."

He snorted. Right now Sam was more like a pile of iron filings. A little splintered and disjointed. "Not yet." He didn't explain. "Pinpricks," he warned and drew the pinwheel lightly over one of his boy's shoulders.

Sam stilled as he focused, chin lifting. Thomas was more than a little addicted to the way Sam responded, the little movements, the way his physical reactions were offered over.

He angled the pinwheel down along one side of his boy's spine and up the other, drawing similar patterns on both left and right, covering as much skin as possible and watching as it first went white, then filled in just slightly pink. He moved from shoulder to elbow on each arm, and down over the perfect curves of Sam's ass, opting for silence, letting his boy just feel.

Goose bumps began to pop up on Sam's skin, Sam's muscles tightening, rippling as he drew the Wartenberg wheel in one pattern after another.

"How does that feel, boy?" He asked the question, but he pressed the wheel harder into the skin on the top of his boy's shoulder and followed it with his tongue, knowing it would make it difficult for Sam to answer.

Sam went up on tiptoe, gasping out garbled syllables that could have been tingles or stings or both. But the boy didn't say "yellow," so whichever it was, it seemed like Sam was into it.

"Beautiful, my boy. This birthday celebration was an excellent idea." And it was only going to get better.

He rolled the wheel down Sam's back again, taking it low, lightly tracing what he could reach of the barbed wire tattoo, then kneeling next to his boy so he could reach the rest.

"That feels so weird."

God, look at Sam's leg muscles jump and tighten like he was dancing.

"Weird because it's on your scar? Or weird everywhere?"

"The scar. I can feel it, but I can't. I can feel it inside me."

"How odd. Was getting the tattoo like that?"

"Some of it. Most of it was just riding the waves."

He nodded. He didn't have anywhere near as much ink, but he knew that feeling. "Nice." He drove the pinwheel off the scar and around behind Sam's thigh.

"Can you comfortably spread your legs just a bit wider, sweetheart?" The question wasn't innocent, so he made sure it sounded appropriately suggestive, and slid a hand along the inside of one thigh.

Sam offered him a sweet little sound, even as he spread, giving Thomas more access. "Sensitive there, Mister."

His laugh was low. "Are you reminding me or warning me, boy?"

Sam's chuckle answered his. "Six of one, half dozen of the other, Sir."

"Well, I better see just how sensitive then, hm?" He leaned in to taste, gliding his tongue from the back of Sam's knee as far up the inside of one thigh as he could manage.

If Sam could have crawled up the wall, Thomas thought he might have. Best of all was the arch, the way Sam rocked and cried out. So pretty.

"Boy." He stuck the handle of the pinwheel into his pocket to get it out of his way and repeated the attention on Sam's other side, this time spreading his boy with both hands, going farther, tasting the hot, salty skin behind Sam's balls.

"Oh, sweet fuck!" The strangled words tore from Sam's throat, and he seemed caught for a long, few seconds between pulling away and pushing toward, body rocking in his hands.

"Mm." Sam's height made it difficult for him to get too enthusiastic in this position, but he dragged his tongue slowly across Sam's tight hole, giving the boy something to think about, before ducking out from underneath the boy and grabbing for his flogger.

Sam panted, back just beginning to lose its needy, desperate arch, calves still bunched as he rocked on tiptoe.

He stood up and stretched, then tried out the flogger a few times on the chair to see how his arm felt, knowing it would do double service because Sam would hear it too.

"My arm feels good, boy. Strong, loose." He moved close,

tucking the handle between Sam's thighs and stroking it against his ass. "How do you feel?"

"E-excited." Sam was flushed, focused on him, fingers splayed on the wall.

He adjusted himself in his jeans, the tension in Sam's voice making his cock take more interest. "Oh, that's a good word. This is your flogger I'm holding; would you like me to use it?"

"Yes, Sir." Sam moaned for him, rolling his shoulders. "You said you feel strong. I want to wear your marks. Please."

"Coming, boy." His boy's words stretched his spine a few inches and made him growl. He stepped away, carefully measuring the distance. "Breathe, count these first few. I'm listening for your words."

He took a breath himself, intending to give Sam a warm-up, but not much of one. He'd judge how sensitive the boy's skin was after that wheel; then he'd get to the real work. "Four to start." He rolled his shoulder, reached back, and brought Sam's flogger down four times, two high on the boy's shoulders, two lower around the rib cage.

The counts started rough but smoothed out by the fourth; Sam's body reacted like it knew his arm, his will.

"Good boy." Oh, very good. Sam dropped into this zone so easily now, it was possible the boy didn't even realize it. Headspace was still tricky, not because the boy couldn't get there, but because the place where Sam was the most at peace and receptive wasn't the kind of subspace most people talked about. Getting there wasn't tricky for his boy at all; it was just tricky for him to recognize.

"Breathe. Count if you like, speak as you please. I'm listening." He was going to push, challenging himself to pull up before Sam needed that yellow. "My boy."

He took a breath and a pause to focus, then used his full arm and the precision of his boy's flogger the way it was intended, the way they both wanted.

Sam locked into his rhythm, body dancing under the blows. There wasn't a bit of stillness to his boy now, no silence, just a steady fall of moans and whispers. Sam's hands slowly moved up the wall as he stretched taller.

Thomas relaxed into it, letting the rhythm soothe his rough bits, letting the sounds his boy was making sink in and fill the spots that ached. He loved watching Sam move. He wondered if his boy understood how much his soul needed to be appreciated, craved that kind of validation. Sometimes he only just barely understood it himself.

"Mine, boy. Just perfect."

"Sir." Sam stretched tall, back popping. "Oh God, love you."

"I love you...sweetheart." The words sounded rough to his ears, and he'd had to enunciate carefully to be understood. He was sweating now, and he knew he'd need a break, but Sam wasn't quite there, so he poured himself into a half a dozen more strokes before the handle of the flogger slipped in his grip, throwing off his aim. It didn't land badly, just not where he'd intended and he pulled his next swing, the falls barely grazing his boy's skin.

Sam shivered, his head falling forward toward the wall, breaths sounding like sobs. His boy was decorated with his will, with his arm, and they burned together.

He took another second to catch his breath and went to Sam, leaned his back against the wall, and rested a hand on Sam's trembling abs. "I'm here, my love. My own."

"Yours." Sam pressed in toward his hand, face resting on his bound hands. "Damn."

He smiled. "Indeed. How are you on your feet, boy, do

you need to sit?" His own adrenaline was flowing, but he needed to make sure Sam was safe before he'd let himself enjoy it.

"I got this, Sir. Thank you." Sam's breath began to slow, gasps deepening.

He nodded even though he knew Sam couldn't see it. "All right." He pushed off the wall and stood where he could get a good long look at his boy's skin. He'd managed to touch nearly every inch, some spots pink and some spots an angry red. The long stripes everywhere raised and burning. "Oh, boy. You're just...on fire. Gorgeous."

He reached out and touched a bit of red skin, feeling the heat under his fingers.

Sam sucked in a deep breath, held it, then released it. "On fire is about right. I can feel you everywhere."

It was remarkable how articulate Sam still was, a good indication of the boy's depth. Or rather, a good indication that he hadn't seen it yet. The things they could explore at the club....

His fingers traveled down Sam's side to rest on the boy's hip and he stepped closer, his chest brushing against his boy as he leaned in and kissed the base of Sam's neck.

Sam groaned for him, the chain on the cuffs rattling with a short little song.

He reached up and took hold of the chain with one hand, pinning it, and Sam's wrists, to the wall as he placed more kisses carefully across the boy's shoulders.

"Oh, fuck." Sam pushed toward him, hands slapping the wall. "Hot."

He grinned. "Mhm." He dropped the flogger and slid that hand over Sam's side, letting it rest low on the boy's belly. Sam was pure heat; it was radiating off the boy's skin and reflecting in the way Sam was moving against him.

Thomas tried to judge whether Sam had more in him, or if he should wrap things up. There were rewards coming to Sam for this work when it was time.

The restless motions began to ease, became more slinky, as Sam rubbed against him. Thomas smiled at his boy, at how Sam let the burn, the ache, the pain, send him soaring.

Slowly, he raised his arm and removed Sam's cuffs, fingers working gently and in no hurry, but he wanted Sam to be able to move, and he didn't want the boy's hands to fall asleep. When that was done, he dropped the cuffs alongside Sam's flogger and removed the boy's blindfold.

"You and I have more celebrating to do, don't we?" He reached around Sam, running both hands from waist to chest, leaning close to the boy's back.

Sam pressed closer, holding nothing of himself away. "Yes, Sir."

Thomas wasn't sure Sam was actually hearing him, was anything more than pure sensation. He took Sam by the shoulders and turned him, taking a deep kiss, giving the boy his tongue and a heavy groan. Sam grabbed him, sucking his tongue, the sudden flash of passion surprising and blistering.

He supposed he shouldn't be shocked, given that he'd held his boy off last night and made them save that sexual tension for today, but even so, the way Sam wanted him was always stunning. He let their kiss burn hot, let it ease some of the urgency and be an outlet for some of their pent-up energy.

Sam never let him doubt, never let him question their connection, even when their lips separated and they rested, foreheads together as they breathed.

It was moments like this that Sam was so simple and still so complicated at the same time. His desires were obvious;

they were written in every twitch of muscle, carried on every breath. But Thomas had to carefully listen and watch for the boy's needs.

For now, though, Thomas would give the boy the reward he'd earned, and the gift he was asking for. He steered Sam toward the bed, bumping gently into the boy and urging him on, step by step, until they'd reached their bed. "Mine." He dropped a hand down between them and curled his fingers behind Sam's sac.

"Every inch." The answer was immediate, sure, as Sam went up on tiptoe.

The first time they were in this moment, he'd wondered if he ought to look after the welts on Sam's back before they got lost in each other. He didn't worry about that anymore; he considered this part of the scene as well as part of the aftercare and, provided Sam wasn't injured, there would be time to look after his boy properly.

"I know, sweetheart. Such a gift to me." He tilted his head toward the bed for Sam and slid his jeans and briefs off, leaving them on the floor where they fell.

Sam sat, then shot him a hungry, happy look. "Let me suck you, Mister? You smell so good."

The only thing better than giving his boy an order was...*fuck*. That. *Jesus Christ*, his balls pulled up so hard that for a second he couldn't speak; all he could do was nod. There was no way Sam hadn't noticed the slip in his control. When he finally got a breath, he willed everything to relax. "Good boy."

"You're good to me." Sam reached for him, tongue dragging over the slit of Thomas's cock, the sensation almost too much, as Sam tasted him. A callused hand cupped his sac as Sam opened up to take him in.

"God...sweetheart." Fuck, Sam's mouth became

everything. The damp heat, the way the head of his cock rubbed and bumped against his boy's palate, made him moan, made him need. Added to that was the sight of his boy's back, covered with his marks, curled over as Sam took more—his teeth sank into his bottom lip, digging in.

He made himself breathe, but he was fighting for the reins a bit. His hips rocked toward Sam, and he stroked his fingers through his boy's hair, caught for a moment in all the sensation, lost in a haze of hormonal indecision.

Sam looked up at him, staring at him as that suction kept on. The look was happy, focused, hungry, and he could see himself reflected there.

A content, relaxed sub that took joy in serving exactly what he wanted for his boy, and to be perfectly honest, for himself too. That thought settled him—the idea that a sub's joy and duty was to serve. It didn't matter that their dynamic didn't fit into anyone's mold; the gift was the same no matter how it was wrapped. Sam was beautiful in his brand of submission, and he accepted his boy's love as it was given and took what was offered.

"Mm. So good, my own." He enjoyed his boy, more fully in control, and watched Sam, encouraging him, praising him.

Sam hummed and began to bob his head, taking him in slow waves, bit by bit, hot hands exploring his belly, his thighs, his balls.

The heat built in him, drew his focus. He gripped the back of Sam's head and slowly pushed in deep, then pulled away and did it again, watching his boy do his very best to relax and let him have what he wanted.

He pulled out one more time, tugging free of Sam's mouth and firmly placed his hands, fingers spread, on the tender skin of his boy's shoulders. Sam looked up at him with a dazed expression, lips swollen, slick.

He cupped Sam's chin in his fingers. "Beautiful boy." He gave Sam a smile. "Up for me, sweetheart. Tummy or back, your choice." If Sam could manage to make a choice, he'd let the boy have it. He moved around to the bedside table and the rational part of his mind dealt with protection before he even got into bed, tossing the lube up by the pillows. He wanted to have a conversation about doing away with that barrier soon, but he wasn't sure of the etiquette. He'd have to look into it.

That was enough of being rational. His eyes turned to Sam, the only thing he had any interest in focusing on now.

Sam was settled on his back, watching him, gaze sliding over his body like a starving man's. His boy was hard, cock curving over his belly, adrenaline still high enough that he was rolling his shoulders against the sheets, riding the burn.

God, so gorgeous. Those sheets were going to sting like hell before long, and he shook his head, but he had to grin a little too. He'd just see how that went for his boy. He didn't waste time, slicked his fingers quickly and slipped them right inside, his boy's willing heat making him lick his lips and swallow.

"I won't break, Mister." Sam grinned at him, eyes twinkling with mischief. Sam reached for him, hands sliding over his chest, abs just tensing.

His laugh came out dark and rough. "I'm learning this about you, boy." But there was nothing like that look in Sam's eyes to make him want to try.

He pushed in steadily and slowly despite his boy's insistence, but once their bodies settled together, his patience was through. He hauled his knees up to Sam's hips and folded Sam's legs back, going for a steep angle and a lot of sweet leverage, and started in hard and deep, making sure the boy felt it all the way up that rounded spine.

"Fuck!" Sam arched his neck, throat bared as he took every inch, muscles fighting for a little control and not finding it.

Yeah, fuck. Sam's mouth was lovely, but this was his own personal heaven, and the way his boy felt made him burn. He held on to Sam's legs for balance and lost himself in rhythm and pressure. He could feel Sam trying to move, to participate, fighting strength and gravity, but he didn't give the boy an inch or a second to latch on to.

One low groan followed another, this submission so much harder for Sam to find, so new.

"Mine," he reminded Sam through gritted teeth, shifting his knees and changing the angle just as his boy found a way to buck against him.

"Yours. Please. I fucking need you!" Sam didn't understand what Thomas wanted—that was written on his boy like a book.

"Boy." He barked out the word, voice deep, and with great effort that he managed to find only for his boy's sake, he slowed his thrusts, breathing through it as he backed off, and tried not to lose his own damn mind for the sake of a lesson.

Sam blinked up at him, stopped, and stared right into him. "Sorry. Making me lose my damn mind wanting you."

"Sorry, *Sir.*" He corrected. He knew that feeling. If Sam didn't catch on soon, he was going to have to start visualizing icebergs. "Wanting is wonderful. But if you're *mine*, if we're in that space, then...?"

"Sorry, Sir." Sam closed his eyes, took a deep breath that Thomas felt all around his cock. Sweet fucking Christ, this boy was going to kill him. "If I'm yours, then I'm all yours like this. You got this. Me. Now."

He nodded, hoping that what he was hearing and what Sam was telling him were the same thing, even if they were both too worked up to be truly coherent. "Work that matters, boy. All mine."

He stretched out over his boy and gave Sam a kiss, then gave his boy a wink and rocked back on his knees as he was before.

"All yours..." Sam stretched and groaned, but he didn't push, even as he shivered around Thomas.

"Good boy." He closed his eyes just long enough to move into his own space, regain his focus. When he opened them again he wrapped a tight hand around Sam's stiff prick and stroked him several times, fast enough to make his boy breathless.

Sam's ass clenched tight, his boy gasping, shoulders trying to leave the mattress.

"Jesus, fuck." He hauled on Sam's hips, pressed up on his knees and thrust deep, searching for his rhythm and keeping Sam off guard.

Sam keened, his entire body flushed, cock dripping and dark with need. Sam had his elbows tucked under him, abs like a washboard.

That pause, that necessary lesson, was rewarded by the way his boy looked right now. He drank Sam in, every trembling muscle, every damp inch of skin, the hungry look on his boy's face. All of it working against his resolve, and he grunted and let it have him.

"That's the way, boy." He reached for Sam again, curling his fingers carefully around his boy's aching cock. "Ask me."

"Please. Touch me, Sir. I need *you*."

Perfect. Oh God, his boy was stunning. "Yes." That was

all the lucidity he had left. He tightened his grip and leaned back a bit, giving Sam room to move. And move Sam did, letting that core strength drive up into Thomas's hand and down onto his cock.

He dug deep for enough focus to stay with his boy, make sure Sam got the relief he'd promised—the release, his boy's reward.

Sam gasped, body jerking hard around Thomas as those bright eyes went wide, desperate. Then Sam gave him what he demanded.

He curled over Sam, shoving those knees up and took his boy hard and fast, grateful that the boy could handle it. He couldn't hold back, couldn't think about anything but his blinding need. He was gulping air and far from any kind of control when he finally shot, sobbing out Sam's name with the powerful surge of heat and seed.

Sam panted under him, silent except for those rough gasps, body arched and trembling beneath him.

He rested on his heels and lowered Sam's hips down to the mattress so the boy could relax, then watched Sam with his hands braced on his thighs as he took in huge breaths. He had to settle. Sam could potentially need anything as the boy came back to himself, but there was aftercare at the very least.

Sam had his eyes hidden with one arm, and Thomas wasn't sure if the wetness on Sam's cheeks was sweating or crying. He climbed up alongside his boy, sliding a hand over Sam's chest. "I'm right here, sweetheart."

Sam nodded, swallowing convulsively for a few long seconds before he leaned close.

All right. He had his answer. He gingerly tucked an arm under his boy and pulled Sam into his chest. "It's all right, my love. I've got you." Sam needed this, and he hoped the boy would just let it out, let it be. "You're safe with me."

"Shh." Sam sucked in one breath, then another. "Just big."

Yes, but Sam was hidden in his chest, holding him tight.

"It is." That was all he said, respecting Sam's request for quiet. He had plenty of patience, they had nothing but time today, and it felt good to hold his boy this way. He stroked his fingers through Sam's hair and kissed the top of the boy's head. He'd stay here with his boy as long as Sam wanted him there.

When the shivers started, he knew he had to take care of his boy's back, do some aftercare. He tried to pull away, and Sam held on.

"I need to take care of you, sweetheart. Just roll onto your stomach, I'm not going anywhere." He coaxed his boy's fingers free but kept hold of one hand. He could reach his kit in the nightstand without going far. "Go on, right onto your stomach. Good boy."

Sam held his hand but moved for him, settled on his belly. "Sorry. Just...you know."

"I do. No apologies for your needs, remember." It happened that for the moment he felt strong, he was still in the mindset of looking after his boy, but he knew all those emotions were real for them both. "I'm here."

He climbed into bed again, a little awkwardly with Sam's fingers tangled with his, but he managed. He studied Sam as he got out what he needed. The boy's skin was angry and red, irritated by rubbing in the sheets and from all of Sam's movement. He followed the length of every stripe and welt with his eyes, admiring as much as he was taking note of trouble spots.

He took the hand that he'd been holding and placed it

flat on the pillows by Sam's head. "I'll need both hands on your back, boy. Breathe, remember."

"Breathe. Yes, Sir. I remember." Sam took a deep, deep inhalation and blew it out.

Breathing was easier to forget than one might imagine. He often had to remind himself as well. He pulled out his preferred ointment, one with a topical anesthetic in it to help Sam rest, and got to work on the bits of broken skin. He took his time, channeling his love and his assurances into his fingers as he worked.

Sam groaned a couple of times, stiffened once, and Thomas gentled his touch, doubling up on the ointment so it didn't drag. Soon Sam began to relax for him, ease into his hands.

The trust made his mouth dry.

Later, once the ointment set in, he'd follow up with an arnica cream. But for the moment, having finished with the more urgent bits, he smoothed the ointment anywhere the skin was dark, anywhere there was a hint that his flogger had touched.

"Boy, you are stunning. I can't wait until you are able to get a look for yourself. Such a good boy."

They needed water next, both of them, and rest.

"Wearing your marks. Nothing like it. Nothing."

Wearing his marks.

When Sam had used those words earlier, he'd heard them in the moment, and in another context. Now that his mind was more relaxed and focused solely on his boy, he recognized the significant leap that Sam had made in the last week. Most of Sam's growth so far had been fairly subtle —a little shift in vocabulary or a new habit—but this time the boy's words represented a complete change of mindset.

Wearing my marks.

Sam had gone from simply embracing what Thomas's flogger could do for him personally to recognizing what it all meant. He'd grown beyond thinking simply about the way the marks looked on his skin and had made a new connection. He understood the constant reminder, how those stripes felt and how they looked, was *for* him, but were not his. They belonged, as he did, to Thomas.

It was moments like this one that validated Thomas's efforts—helped him set aside his worries and fears for Sam and the moments of doubting himself. They'd celebrated several milestones together on their journey, times of high emotion that his boy could see and feel and be proud of. But these moments of quiet triumph, the ones he could silently acknowledge and keep as his own, made him the most proud.

"Nothing like it."

18

S am floated, thoughts sliding around in his head like mist. He thought he might be asleep, or at least dozing, or maybe not.

Maybe he was more awake than he normally was.

He didn't care, not really, because there were a couple of thoughts that he wasn't sure how to process. Not about James, weirdly enough.

Sam missed him, and it was weird but...

He let that thought go, and the sadness faded with it.

Then he explored the buzz in his back, the heat dancing on his skin, making his ass feel cold, his legs. Respect and love left on him.

That was a thought he could live with for a little while.

He didn't want to think about how he'd been near to out of his mind when Thomas was taking him, and he absolutely didn't want to think about crying.

Cowboys didn't cry. Ever.

Sam pushed that away and let himself feel the spark of lightning across his skin.

"Water, love." Sir's voice seemed far away but more

present than ever. He felt the water bottle tap his shoulder, the weight and the cold plastic startling him.

He jumped, eyes flying open. "Water. I was..." Away. He'd been deep inside where time stopped. "...dozing."

"I know where you were, boy. I know where you are. But you also need to drink." Thomas was sitting up, leaning against the headboard and watching him, eyes warm and focused.

He took the water, not wanting it at all until the first drops hit his throat. *Oh, God yes.* That was good.

"Drink it down, I have another for you." Sir was drinking too, throat working with the big, long swallows. "Did you know that tears shed due to pain or the release of strong emotion contain a natural painkiller? It's one of the reasons our eyes feel puffy and numb after a good cry."

"What?" For a second he was convinced that Thomas had been listening in; then he shook his head at his own flights of fancy. "No shit?"

"Absolutely true. One of the subs at the club, who also happens to be a doctor, explained it to me one night when I was sitting at the bar feeling sorry for myself. I believe you were working that night. His name is Merlin; isn't that a wonderful name for a doctor?"

"Merlin? That rocks. I bet he caught some shit. At least Momma named us after men with reasonable names. I'm still surprised she didn't name us Dallas, Austin, and Houston."

"She named two of you James. Or Jim. Whichever. Technically it's the same name." Sir smiled at him and stroked a finger along his jaw.

"Yeah." Oh, that touch felt good. Less than electric, more than warm. "She's a history nut. It runs in the family."

"Merlin also said that crying, even that sort of ugliness

that may or may not have happened to me shortly after I learned about James, is good for you. It releases the pressure you can't find any other way to deal with."

"Bowie and I beat the fuck out of each other and blew up a boat, so I get that." That was way less scary than crying. Crying meant you were broke, somewhere deep. He'd done it, sure, but it was something that was...no one needed to know all that shit. That part was private. Bowie knew it. So did he.

Hell, James knew it. How many times had James pinched him, given him an Indian burn, popped him, waiting to see if he'd break down and bawl?

"That sounds about Bowie's speed." Fingers brushed through his hair, traced around behind his ear. "Point being, I guess, that crying isn't something that concerns me at all. Every sub I've worked with has cried at some point. Things, as you say, get too big. What worries me are the things you don't let out. More water?"

"Please." He drank deep, and he swore he could feel the water splash in his belly. "It worries me too, but..."

There was nothing to be done about it, was there? He had all these things bouncing around, and there was nowhere for them to go.

And what if they did? What if they started to spill out and he couldn't stop? Then he'd just vomit up all the bullshit in his brain, and then what?

Are you quite done? That little thought was clear as a bell.

"But?" Thomas's fingers paused, like the man was actually expecting an answer.

"I guess it's just me?" He didn't know what to say.

"All right." Sir's fingers slid across his scalp again. "We'll just have to see."

Oh, that felt good. "Love how you feel, Mister. All the way down."

"I'm proud of you, boy. You have settled so naturally..." Sir's head tilted a little. "Into your skin. You're relaxed, you're asking for what you need, things that are important but new for you."

"Thank you, Sir." He wasn't sure he had done anything. He closed his eyes because he didn't think he had more to say. Of course, that was when words slipped out. "Earlier, that was harder."

"I know. I hold that trust close, sweetheart." His Sir set an empty bottle of water down on the nightstand and settled into the pillows with him. "I'm still celebrating you, you know. I want you to think about what you're proud of, about yourself, and about this journey. The things you know were hard and aren't as much anymore, the things that may have been scary at one point but you've overcome. That sort of thing."

He didn't know how to unravel that, but he didn't have to, not really. He got on the beast and rode it—even the unridable ones. He didn't know if he was too dumb to stress the fall or if he just knew it was inevitable. It wasn't if you got hurt bad, it was when.

Hell, he even knew about the hits that broke you and left the big scars. Sam had gone through two so far—his leg and James.

One was covered in ink and the other one was still in that "just past stitches" stage. You were back to wearing old jeans, but sometimes it pulled, so hard that you were right there again.

Sam slid his thumb over the scar on his palm, feeling the puffy edges.

"Have you told me about that one?" Thomas drew a finger along the scar, following his thumb.

"Blood brothers." It hadn't mattered when Bowie had left for the service, but losing James had been terrifying for a fourteen-year-old kid that didn't know what he was going to do. It had been a ridiculous worry—he'd played softball and done junior rodeo, Daddy had bought him a bunch of calves to take care of, and he'd helped rebuild a four-wheeler that year. He'd been busy as hell, but that night before James had driven off to college? Jesus, he'd been lost and scared that he was just going to disappear into the tall grass.

James had pulled out his pocketknife and sliced them both, holding their hands together.

We share a fucking birthday, baby boy. I'm just going to school. We'll always have our birthdays.

James had so lied.

"I wonder—uh." Thomas took a breath, coughed lightly. "I...wondered. But we were talking about you."

"We can talk about him. It's James's day too." It always had been. It always would be. That wasn't bad. It was just the truth. "Did you know he loved chocolate cake, and in the middle of the night after our birthday, he would go to the kitchen and fix a huge bowl and pour milk over it and eat it with a spoon?" Sam snorted. "So fucking gross."

"That's disgusting. But why are you avoiding my question, sweetheart? Surely there is something you're proud of since you met me." Thomas chuckled.

"That we figured out how to eat a meal together without having a snarl." That was the tiniest part of the best thing, which was that he thought they heard each other more, that they were starting to speak a mutual language.

"Ha!" Thomas laughed, rolling onto his back. "Indeed.

That is quite a thing. That has saved us a great deal of indigestion."

"I'm proud that I stayed. There were lots of reasons to go home and just one to stay." And maybe that was silly, but it was what it was.

Thomas turned his head to look at him, then rolled to face him again. "I'm grateful. Bewildered, confused, and stunned, but grateful. I'm hoping you've got more than one now, but if one is all you need, it's solid."

"It is what it is." The fact that he loved Thomas was weirdly not between him and Thomas. That belonged to his soul. Being in love, sure. That was different. He hadn't understood about that when Daddy had tried to explain it, how in love and love were two things. Being in love came and went, but love just sat with you.

"Yes. True." Thomas leaned closer and kissed him. "I suppose all the reasons I want you to stay are really one reason too."

"Mmm." That kiss was luscious, soft. "I was pretty damn proud of us at New Year's. We were fine."

"I was so proud of you. Clint said he thought you did well. That's high praise because if he thought you hadn't, I'd be in the Domhouse. We were hot, cowboy. I should show you the emails."

"The Domhouse?" Sam began to laugh, the hilarity just bubbling up out of him. Oh, sweet Jesus, what a thought.

Thomas snickered. "Yeah, that's an old one. That what we used to call it when I was training with Clint, and he was not pleased with one of us. Me, Aggie, Fredo, David, Ross...it was a great group. I spent so much time in the Domhouse. God."

"I think it's probably quicker to just get a bloody nose,

huh? I worked with a trainer for bull riding, you know, but not long."

"I don't think you'd want me striping your back with that flogger without knowing how. Quicker isn't an option with Clint. It's right, or you're not a member. Angel doesn't visit the club wearing his EMT hat often. Clint is proud of that, and rightly so."

"I wasn't making fun. You forget, I started at a bar that needs an EMT weekly." He'd had to get a little help every now and again.

"Oh, no. I forget nothing, trust me." Thomas's tone wasn't quite as harsh as his words seemed, but his lover certainly did have a hang-up about him working at Mike's. "In any case, I will show you the pictures from the party; maybe your mother would like one." That suggestion came along with a sideways grin.

"Oh, totally. She's seen my naked ass, more than I'd like to admit. She would look at the pictures and say, 'You've lost weight, baby boy.' " He leaned in a little closer. "I have to say, I felt more naked without the shirt than I thought I would, but I got over it."

"Well, there wasn't a man in the club that wasn't checking out your moguls." Thomas drew a finger across his belly. "And knowing they couldn't touch them." Thomas looked about as smug as he'd ever seen.

"No. That's not for public consumption." He flexed, grabbing Thomas's finger with his abs. "So the whole thing with Angel at the club—that was...awkward. Are there rules I ought to know?" Beyond the "no looking, no talking" part which he'd been good about.

"You did just fine. That situation was mine to handle, sweetheart. Angel overstepped. He knew he had but he's... you have to make allowances sometimes for friends and personalities. He obviously meant no harm." Thomas's hand spread out flat. "The rule is, a Dom doesn't touch any sub, including unattached ones, without permission. If you find yourself in a position like that again, hopefully any Dom that sees it will step in. But if not, well, you are free to get creative. You only need to be respectful to the extent that they are, if you follow me."

"Sure. I promise not to redneck up on anyone." He wasn't worried. No one was going to mess with him. "And Angel's just used to hugging."

"I know, I wasn't upset with him. If he'd asked permission, it would have been different. But since he didn't, and it was Clint's table...Clint wasn't pleased with him, and I had to handle it appropriately. Angel understood, I think."

He had to admit, he didn't get it. He told himself it was a little like eating at his Granny's house. She believed that children should be seen and not heard and, if you wanted to have Mamaw's cooking, you were quiet. And if you weren't quiet, it reflected bad on Momma. It was Clint's house, Clint's rules.

"He didn't seem pissed at all."

"He really wanted to dance with you." Thomas grinned. "I thought at first he was joking around—he wasn't. He's a good Dom, but...he hasn't had a sub in a few years. Clint tried to set him up for a while and eventually let that idea go."

"He's like a teddy bear and one hell of a friend, but..." Not his type. "He's not you."

"No." Thomas kissed him again, slow and easy, and didn't pull away for a bit.

He could do this for days. Stay close and breathe, talk with Thomas, learn a little more and a little more.

"It's getting dark. We've been in bed a while." Thomas smiled. "Are you hungry?"

His belly snarled, just loud as all get out. "Nope. Not at all." He rolled his eyes, laughter in the air. Had he even eaten today? *Lord have mercy.*

Thomas laughed too. "Right on cue. Impressive." His lover sat up and turned on the lamp by the bed. "I'll come around and help you up."

He thought about arguing, but he was tender as hell, and he wanted the touches, and it was his goddamn birthday, so he could nod and mutter, "Yes, Sir."

"Good boy." Thomas helped him sit up, got an arm under him, and got him on his feet. None of that was as easy as it seemed—he'd been lying down, keeping still too long. His skin pulled and burned, his hips were stiff, and his balance was off enough that he leaned on his Sir for a second to keep from falling.

"All right?"

"Yeah. I stiffened up big-time." He shivered, a cold chill hitting him for a second, and he shook it off.

Thomas touched his reddened skin lightly in a couple of places. "I can't put anything more on this yet. Sweat pants, boy. I'll turn the heat up a bit. I don't want you cold."

"Yes, Sir. You need a pair?" He braced himself on the chest of drawers, finding his fuzziest sweats and a pair of good socks.

"Can you manage? Be honest, boy."

"I'm stiff, Sir." And just a touch dizzy.

"I've got you." He felt Thomas's hand on his lower back, and the other hand reached around to pull out sweats as well. They dressed and moved out to the kitchen, where Thomas sat him in one of the chairs at the little dining table.

"I make a mean grilled cheese if you're interested. I am also very adept at peanut butter and jelly, and eggs."

"Grilled cheese sounds delicious. Seriously." He leaned from side to side, trying to test himself out. "You want coffee? Tea? Water?"

"I want you to sit until you've eaten something. You refused breakfast, remember, and we worked through lunch." Thomas brought him a banana and another bottle of water. "Start with that. I'm making a pot of coffee."

"Yes, Sir." He drank the water, swallowing deep. God, he couldn't get enough in him.

He watched Thomas make sandwiches in the kitchen. It was pretty ironic that a man with such skill in other aspects of life couldn't even butter bread without looking awkward. "Back to real life tomorrow morning." Thomas sounded wistful.

"Yeah. I haven't found that rhythm yet, but it'll happen fast, I bet." They'd gone from one thing to another, so quickly, that the idea of "real" was fuzzy. "At least real life isn't stealing time on Sundays, right?"

That was the right thing to say. Thomas looked up and gave him a happy smile. "It's wonderful, isn't it?"

"More than. I get to sleep with you. Have suppers. Weekends. All the good stuff."

"Saturdays at the club. I miss that. And I love when that alarm clock goes off and you're there, waking up next to me. I love that you bring me coffee." Thomas flipped the sandwiches over in the pan and they sizzled as Sir chuckled. "I love that I don't have to iron anymore."

"Your ironing skills are not vast." He arched an eyebrow. "And you'll get used to pressed jeans."

Thomas laughed. "No. No, I don't think so. I can't see getting used to pressed Levis. Levis are supposed to scrunch and hug, be soft and comfortable. They're supposed to look like you slept in them. Stiff Levis are weird."

A grilled cheese sandwich landed on the table in front of him along with a mug of coffee.

"You like me in my Wranglers just fine." He groaned in pleasure. "Smells so good. Thank you."

"I love your ass—I mean you in your Wranglers. Eat. You need calories." Thomas went into the kitchen.

"You showed your love for my ass just fine, Mister. I damn near lost my mind." He took a big bite.

"That was definitely one to commit to memory. You looked...you were just flying. Gorgeous." Thomas came back to the table again, set a big slice of apple pie with a candle in it down in front of him, and started singing "Happy Birthday," Sir's voice a respectable baritone.

"Well, thank you." He blew out his candle, then stood up for a kiss. "Thank you ever so."

Thomas caught his hips. "You're welcome, my love." He got the kiss he wanted, strong and affectionate, with more than a hint of that hunger that seemed to simmer under them every time their lips met.

He wrapped one hand around Thomas's neck, leaning into the connection. Melting into them.

19

K nowing Sam was working from home, just walking distance from his office, was more distracting than Thomas could have imagined. It took a great deal of self-control not to simply go home for lunch every day.

It wasn't that he thought he wouldn't be welcome—he knew very well he would. But apart from the fact that it would be torture to have to tear himself away to go to work again, it wasn't a habit he wanted to get into. He and Sam were together every evening now and all weekend long. Their unorthodox, integrated lifestyle was rewarding, but it nevertheless took concentration and patience.

They needed some time apart, not to shut that off, but to remember who they were as individuals. Sam had research and writing and was excited and motivated by that. His boy also, potentially, had some time to make friends, possibly meeting someone else for lunch, a walk in the park, or even just a movie. Thomas had his job, which was demanding, and he liked it that way. He also had his work friends who were an entirely different focus. Using that piece of his brain was a little like fresh air. It fed him and energized him in another way and sent him home to Sam more complete.

He pushed back from his desk, shaking his head and laughing softly to himself. This was also good work, his work, to make sure his sub's needs were met, and the boy was healthy and whole. Was he overthinking things? Of course he was, but it was part of his idiom as a Dom and he wore his foibles comfortably.

Somehow he doubted Sam was thinking about all this, and if he was, he knew how his boy was dealing with it. His family had sent running shoes and a pull-up bar, so his boy had added long runs and upper body work to his core workouts.

Expending energy, Sam called it.

He knew better and had different names for it, like denial, avoidance, and internalizing. He'd figured out a great deal about Sam and what made his boy tick, but he hadn't yet figured out how to make Sam talk if the boy didn't want to. He could ask questions from any angle, ask them outright, give an order....If his boy didn't want to share, there was very little hope of getting answers.

He knew Sam was nervous about having enough work. He knew not bringing in half of the house costs made his boy anxious. It didn't matter how he spun it—except, God forbid he imply he was taking care of Sam, that hadn't gone over well—no matter how many times he explained that it made him happy, that it was a gesture of love, there was a piece of Sam that found it unacceptable and always would.

He supposed he would have that stress to thank for Sam's soon-to-be pumped-up biceps. There were worse things to look at.

Don't forget to eat lunch

That text wasn't intrusive, right? He'd found a bunch of

frozen things that Sam could throw in the microwave to make sure his boy would have something easy to eat. He knew about going down a research rabbit hole; hours could go by without notice.

Got a phone interview with Jack Wells O.o Met him in Cheyenne. Bet he doesn't remember

He assumed that Wells was an artist, and he quickly typed the name into his browser. *I'm googling him but this sounds like a big deal? Congrats! Eat.*

Big deal to me and I have a couple articles for it. Will grab a sandwich in a bit. Too buzzed now. Love you

He smiled. Sam could have said anything before that "love you," and he would have been happy.

Excited for you! Want to hear more later. Love you, sweetheart

He was excited for Sam. Some success, and time to enjoy it, was exactly what his boy needed. Probably more than the boy needed lunch, so he let it go.

He read all about Jack Wells, the artist's work and role in creating the Professional Rodeo-Cowboy Artists Association and decided that, yes, this was a pretty damn big deal, especially to someone like Sam. He was impressed.

He saw a new email from one of his donors and opened it, realizing he'd better stop daydreaming about his boy and get to work, and when he came up for air two hours later, he realized he hadn't eaten lunch either. He pulled his phone out and made a recurring reminder for himself. He wouldn't manage to take care of Sam if he didn't take care of himself.

At least he'd gone to the gym that morning. It felt good to get that into his regular schedule again. He didn't need to tell Sam he'd added more crunches to his routine; with any luck his boy would notice on his own in a month or so.

It was getting close to five, and he didn't work late if he could help it. He dropped Sam another text about dinner.

Dinner in or out? Something, anything, other than Chinese ;-)

Whoa. Where'd the day go? Sounded like Sam had lost time too.

Right? Me too.

Out. Pizza?

Pizza. Home soon

He'd grab Sam, and they'd take the short walk over to Two Boots. It was light out until close to six these days, but it was decidedly still winter.

"Leaving early?"

"Only ten minutes."

"You're in such a hurry to get home this week, Thomas. Everything okay with Sam?" Ally gave him a big, knowing smile.

"Just fine, thank you." He didn't have to play that game.

"I knew he was young, but I thought at least he'd be potty trained."

He stopped, scarf halfway around his neck, and looked at her. "I'm young too, thank you."

"Sorry." Ally pretended to go back to her work, but she made sure he heard her. "Not that young."

"Good night!"

"Night, Junior!"

He laughed. There was no winning with her. He bundled up and headed out.

Music filled the apartment when he opened the door, the smell of steam, shaving cream, and Irish Spring proving that his cowboy had showered and shaved for him. Sam was singing, and when he walked into the bedroom, Thomas found him mostly dressed, trying to pick out a shirt.

"Damn, cowboy." His fingers itched to touch and he

went over, stepped right into Sam's space, and slid a hand up his boy's side. "Now I'm hungry for more than pizza."

Sam arched, so fucking pretty. "Cold out there, is it?"

Then Sam kissed him, a slow and lazy greeting that made his eyes close. God, he really liked the way his boy could linger over the slow ones. It was like he'd been holding his breath all day long, and Sam found him some oxygen. Squeaky clean cowboy-scented air. "Mm."

Sam went up on tiptoe, sliding them together. It would have been so easy to throw his boy on the bed and devour him, but just as the temptation hit, Sam's belly rumbled at him.

He smirked against Sam's lips. "Saved by the stomach."

"I ain't gonna starve." Sam winked, but then that sound came again, louder.

"True, and the sound of your growling guts is really, really hot." He waggled his eyebrows at Sam.

"Butthead." Sam swatted his ass and hugged him hard. "Good day, honey?"

He returned the hug, happily. "Busy day. After all that talk about how you should eat, I forgot. I spent the afternoon puzzling out how we're going to pay for a touring exhibit coming through at the end of the summer. You?"

"Good. Good interview. Jack gave me some more names. Talked to a buddy from Austin who's on staff at UT, got some more names to hunt up here."

"Wow. Productive day. Get your shirt on and let's go eat. I want to hear about the interview. I looked him up; I see why he's a big deal now. "

"He's amazing. Bowie got me an original when I got my master's. I think I told you. It's hanging at Momma's. I'll get it when we go home to visit." Sam started chattering a million miles a minute as he grabbed his shirt and tucked in.

He did remember now that Sam mentioned it, but he wasn't going to try to get a word in right now. He loved how excited Sam was; he could see how much this meant to his boy. He listened to Sam talk as they got their coats. He was still listening as they left the building. All he could manage to do was smile and nod. When Sam actually wanted to talk, there was no interrupting him.

Sam stopped long enough for a breath as they got to Two Boots, and he opened the door for his boy. He took advantage of the moment. "You have three articles out of this, you think?"

"God, yes. At least. I'm going to shoot for one of the bigger magazines. Why not? All they can say is no, right? Jack's a legend and he swears he remembers me. I think he lied, but that's cool." Sam looked over at him with bright eyes. "Damn, it smells good in here."

Look at those eyes. He couldn't imagine how it would be possible for him to fall more in love with Sam, but he just did. He took his boy's hand and pulled him up to the counter. "What good would it possibly do him to lie? What are you having?"

"Can I have one of everything? Maybe two pepperonis and a giant Coke? I swear to God, I burned it off today."

"You got it. What did you do today that you burned it off?" He ordered for Sam, got a slice of the Buckminster and a bottle of water for himself, and they went and grabbed a table.

"Jogged for a while, then two sets of crunches with pull-ups between. Did some leg stuff too, but I had work." Sam grinned at him. "I ran into Scotty on my run, from the club."

"Really? I don't think I've ever seen him outside of the

club." He wasn't even sure he'd recognize Scotty not in his sub-gear. "What was he up to?"

"Getting coffee, I think. He wants to go running with me sometime. We'll see. I sort of like to just focus and push hard."

"Sometimes it's nice to have running partner; they can push you too. Maybe you should try it and see how you match up." Wasn't he just today thinking his boy needed friends? Scotty knew everything and everyone at the club, and he'd be a good resource for Sam. "I'll run with you sometime if you want. I run at the gym every morning."

"Sure. You just got to remember that I have little legs. Running for me and running for you are probably two different things." Sam grinned sheepishly. "I have to admit, jogging like that, on the bad leg? It's like pull-ups with the bad shoulder. I'm gonna have to figure it out."

Ah, yes. When Sam talked about pushing, he assumed Sam meant all-out hard. He hadn't thought about the leg. "Hey, I do it for the cardio; I'm not training for a marathon. But, it's up to you. I'm up for trying it sometime to see what happens."

"Sure. I'd love to. Just think, one day it'll get warmer, huh?" Sam leaned back and grinned at him. "So, I've talked your ears off."

He nodded as their pizza slices arrived. "I love how passionate you are about it, Sam. I like to listen. I'm knowledgeable about art, different artists and disciplines, but your niche is one I know almost nothing about, and it's so rare I get to learn something about the art world that I don't know. I promise I'm not bored."

He wasn't at all. Although it was possible that his boy could read the phone book with that same enthusiasm, and he'd be just as enthralled. Sam's energy was intoxicating.

"It's fascinating, and it's everything about me, in a weird sort of way, you know? I wanted to be a cowboy on the range, but that world is gone, and I wanted to be an artist, but I don't have talent—so this way I get to be involved in both."

"That's brilliant. I have no talent either." He loved the pizza here; the sauce was spicy and the crust super thin. It had seemed so strange to him that Sam would give up his way of life in Texas, but when the boy explained it that way, most of what he loved about it he could do from a desk just about anywhere. He felt a little better about his boy being so uprooted.

"Eh, if we could all do it, it wouldn't be art, right? So, the buddy of mine in Austin? He's introducing me to some people here with private collections, which rocks. I'd love to see if I can make some connections with work that isn't easily available." Sam grinned at him. "Rodeo art compared to western art. Commercial art compared to pop art. It's all so rich. I mean, rodeo is the commercialism of ranch work, but it started out as a celebration of it. Just a competition, and…"

And there Sam went again, and Thomas got to listen to the wonder that was his boy's mind, to be honored by the fact that Sam was offering him more words than he'd heard from Sam in, well, ever.

This was talk about the book, and it was an exciting idea. All the talking made him wonder how many people at home listened to this. Sam's parents, maybe? Did Sam have friends he could share his passions with? Bowie didn't seem the type, and he wasn't available much anyway.

James. He must have shared it with James.

James used to listen to Thomas babble about some new exhibit at the museum; he had to have listened to Sam too.

Jesus, it seemed as if every time he turned around, he learned about something else Sam lost when he lost his brother.

"You know, if you run into a sizable private collection you think should be seen, that the owner might like to have seen, let me know. It could be something the museum might be interested in."

"Totally. How cool would that be? If I could help you out. I'd love that." Sam gave him this smile that heated him, top to bottom. "Got a text from Bowie, did I tell you? He flew out early. Said he was losing his mind at the house. Momma was hovering, asking him to come home and take over the ranch. Bowie. Can you imagine?"

"Doesn't seem like his speed, no." He suspected that was her not so subtle way of saying that if Bowie didn't want to do it, a good son would convince Sam to come home. He had a hard time imagining that for Sam now, though. Or maybe he just wished that was true. "Do they need help? Perhaps you should send them what you're making and let me—"

He shut his mouth abruptly. He really ought to have filtered that thought.

"Oh, you are a good, good man. It ain't money, honey. It's time and manpower. I don't know what to tell them—part of them had to know once I quit rodeoing and put my head to school, right? I'm good at this. I can manage a ranch, sure, but..." Sam frowned deeply and tapped his fingers against the table. "Listen, I'm never going to make a bunch of babies and run the ranch like they want. I got given that expectation because Bowie didn't do it, and James didn't do it. Everybody thought I would because I'm easy, but..."

Sam stopped, blinked, and pressed his lips together. "Right. Diarrhea of the mouth."

"I'm just as interested in this, sweetheart. Keep talking. Please." *Please.* Finally, Sam was giving something, working through something and trusting him to hear it.

Sam looked at him for a long, long minute. "It's just that I'm not copying my brothers. I tried to be what all my folks wanted, but I can't. Not only that, but I don't want to. I miss home, but in that way that you get nostalgic for something familiar and easy. That can't be a fault, not if we all needed out. It has to be something inside us."

Say something. Anything. Don't just stare at him. Reward that.

"You're right, of course. It's interesting how doing what you need to do, no matter how right, can feel selfish." That wasn't too bad.

He felt like he was talking to his little sister, Katie. Their parents had taken her to doctors and specialists because at age three and a half, she wasn't talking. They all said she was hearing fine, understanding fine, and they couldn't figure it out. Then one day he was doing his homework at the kitchen table and Katie walked in, said she was hungry, and asked him to please make her a peanut butter and jelly sandwich.

Katie had been perfectly capable of speaking all along. She just didn't want to do it until she knew she'd be understood.

"Their inability, or refusal, to accept what you need isn't a reflection on you; it's entirely about them."

Sam wasn't looking at the pizza, at the table. No, his boy was talking to him, looking him in the eye. "I tried to be what they needed, but I knew it wasn't ever going to happen. I gave them warning—rodeo, school, even running away and hitchhiking to the beach for a month. They had to know I was...me."

He nodded, holding those eyes, staying right with his boy. "I suspect they did. But you kept going back, right? This time they're probably shocked that you didn't. When your mother told you to come home, she expected you would say yes. You went to the beach and came home. You took off for the rodeo, and you came home. You were supposed to go back."

"I was; then I fell in love with my brother's lover, and that was a reason not to go." Sam shook his head. "There was probably going to be a reason someday no matter what, but you are the one that I chose."

He reached over and took Sam's hand, curling his fingers tight. "I wasn't your brother's lover when you met me. I was just a man in need of a friend. I chose you too."

"Yeah, thank God for that." Sam grinned at him, squeezed his fingers tight, and winked. "Lord have mercy, I'm not sure I tasted that pizza, but my belly sure feels better."

"I'm not sure how you found time to chew with all that talking. I think you just kind of sucked it down." He smirked and returned the wink and leaned back in his chair. "Thank you for sharing that with me."

"Thank you for hearing me out." Sam finished his Coke, licked his lips, and smiled. "It was a big day."

"Always." He looked at Sam seriously for a second to make sure that sunk in, then smiled as he pushed his chair back and stood. "It was a huge day. I'm really thrilled for you."

"Yeah. Yeah, thanks. Can I buy you dessert and coffee?"

He smiled, touched by the offer. "I accept." Their last dessert and coffee hadn't gone so well. But their first dinner had been a disaster too, so there was hope. They made their way out into the cold, and he offered Sam his arm.

"Thank you, Sir." Sam laughed for him. "Lead on, Macduff. Whipped cream on something, ho!"

"I'm more interested in the coffee. I don't have time for a thousand sit-ups and two hundred pull-ups after a twenty-mile run."

"Yeah, yeah, yeah. I have to work off this energy somehow. We can split it."

"Deal. And afterward we'll go home, and I'll help you work off some of that energy." He glanced over at Sam. "Get a head start on tomorrow's workout."

"At least I'll sleep good after, right?"

"I guarantee it, boy."

20

8 *54. 853. 852.*

Sam counted down from a thousand, trying to focus on being quiet and still while Thomas did his thing. It wasn't usually a challenge, but he had a hitch, right under his left shoulder blade, that made him want to stop breathing or twist or just dig in and rip the muscle out. It wasn't scary or anything. A pulled muscle from too many pull-ups, too fast.

An irritation.

Still, this was Saturday, and Thomas was so damn excited to be at the club, and he wasn't fucking this up for love or money.

Monday? He was finding a chiropractor, but today, he was the king of still and silent and not fucking this up.

765. 764. 763.

All Yessirs, all the time.

At some point, he'd have this whole thing down to a fine art, right?

God, he hoped so.

At least he was dressed, and Thomas let him keep his

hat. For now. His Sir said they'd have to talk about it for next time, something about working on his posture and his eyes that made him a little nervous, but he'd have to worry on that later.

Thomas was sitting at the bar, and that was awkward because he was standing kind of out in the middle of things behind Mister's barstool, with people walking by right behind him. Seemed better than kneeling, though, like some of the guys were doing. How did they not get stepped on? He was pretty sure some of the boots he'd seen walking by would hurt.

Eh. Obviously that was a thing. Do not step on anyone's calves, or you'd lose a ball. That would prevent the problem, right? If he was on his knees and someone stepped on his calf, they'd lose something.

He'd had a bull do that—more than once. That shit hurt.

Now if Thomas was a rodeo guy, he wouldn't be a roughstock guy. Possibly a roper, although you'd be in a shit-ton of trouble if he was heading and you were the damn heeler. Shit, you talk about disappointed? *Whoa.*

No. Not roping.

Announcing.

Thomas had a solid voice, and the man could talk for hours. It wasn't hard to listen to, but it could flow over you like water too, which was important, because if you got too caught up, then you couldn't ride.

Wait. Voice. Had he heard Thomas's voice?

"I think so. Don't you, boy?"

"I'm sorry, Sir. I missed what you said." He'd been quiet and still and all.

And thinking about populating a rodeo with these yahoos. God, Angel would be a fucking killer bulldogger.

Thomas's sigh was subtle, but he recognized it. "Master

Adam was just saying how healthy you look, remembering the first time he met you."

"Thank you, Sir. I'm fat and sassy, happy as a pig in shit." He really was happy with Thomas, with work, in general. He was thinking about talking to Angel about where to go here to get more ink, even.

Adam laughed and socked Thomas in the shoulder. "You've got a live one, don't you?"

Thomas snorted. "You could say that. He's a good one, though."

Adam's voice got softer. "Does he always hide in that hat, or just here?"

"Rome wasn't built in a day, hm?"

"To each, his own?"

"Something like that. Are we going to keep trading clichés? I have a million of them; I'll win."

Oh, he didn't know about that. Sam hadn't even started pulling his out. He had been on his very best non-redneck behavior with Thomas from the start. Now, some of his very best wasn't very good, but still...

Also, folks were obsessed with his damn hat. He was a cowboy. This was his hat. This was how he dealt, and he wasn't giving it up. *Dammit.*

"Well, you both look fantastic. He's good for you. It nice to see you back on your feet."

"Thanks, Adam. He is. I've really never been happier. How's Rick? In fact, where is Rick?"

"My boy has the flu. He's in bed. I'm just here while he's sleeping because I needed out of the house for a while."

"Poor thing. Tell him I'm thinking about him."

"Will do. Excuse me, will you? I need to catch Clint while he's free. Nice to see you both."

"Of course. Take care."

Thomas turned on his barstool to face him. "Are you all right, boy?"

"Yes, Sir." He offered Thomas a warm smile, taking the opportunity to roll his shoulder in its socket as he admired Thomas's pretty belly.

"I'm concerned because you weren't following the conversation. A Master doesn't like to have to repeat himself. But you look fine. Try to stay present, boy." Thomas pulled him a step closer and ran a hand down his arm.

No one had said he was supposed to be listening. Seriously, all these guys were kneeling there, just listening to small talk and waiting for someone to ask them a question?

Was there going to be a quiz later?

No one was here to have a deep discussion about the price of tea in China, for chrissake, although he'd bet Thomas could talk about it like he knew the answer, whether or not it was true.

Thomas could bullshit with the best of them. He couldn't wait to get him and Daddy in the same room, wind them both up, and let them go.

"Yes, Sir?" Thomas looked at him.

"Yes, Sir. I'm never going to get this right, am I?" He had to chuckle at himself.

"Not if you keep telling yourself that, you won't. Why do you do that, boy? There hasn't been a single thing I've asked of you that you couldn't manage." Thomas turned on his stool and waved Scotty over. "Scotty, a bottle of water for my boy, please. And I'll have a coffee."

"Yes, Master Thomas."

Sam reminded himself to keep it to "Yessir" and "Nosir." Thomas wasn't in a rhetorical question place.

Thomas handed him the water and turned back

around on his stool to pick up the coffee. Sir talked to a handful of people about the hockey game on the TV behind the bar, about the weather, and almost all of them asked how work was going—honestly, how many times did he need to pay attention to the same answer? He tried. He really did, but he was starting to feel like Bill Murray in Groundhog Day.

That movie was as old as he was, but he still thought it was pretty damn funny. He'd watched it with James in a hotel in Cozumel when he was like nineteen. They'd been a little stoned. Just made it funnier.

James had to have been good at this. James was the one that would sit in class, sit in church, and be good. Him? *Christ.*

Sammy, pay attention.

Sammy, sit still.

Sammy, where are you?

"Sam."

"Yessir." That was Thomas, right? *Shit.* Goddammit, he did it again.

"Our room is ready." Thomas slipped off his stool and walked toward the back of the club. He moved stiffly to follow.

Lord, he needed to watch the running. He could feel it in his knees, his hips today.

Thomas led them down the hall slowly, taking time to look into the public rooms they passed on the way. The room with all the cuffs and chains was busy, with subs bound in various positions over benches, against walls, some to each other, while their Masters milled around talking or playing cards, or playing...with them.

There was the crack of that whip again, more than one this time, along with cries and deep moans, and Thomas lingered in the doorway for a bit, watching before moving on.

Eventually they made it to their room, and Thomas let them in with a key, then hung the key on a hook by the door and locked it once he was inside.

"I have to ask you again, boy. Are you sure you're all right?" Thomas's tone was even, not upset, didn't seem overly worried either.

"What do you mean? I'm okay—couple three aches and pains from getting old." He winked at Thomas, trying to dissipate the weird almost-not-quite tension.

"Nothing, never mind. Come here." Thomas pulled him in, tucked an arm around him, and gave him a kiss. Not the slow, patient kind—the I'm about to pull out my flogger kind.

Oh. Hello.

Sam hummed softly, the world seeming to tighten for a second, go a little bright and sparkly.

Thomas kissed him until he couldn't breathe, then let him go to look into him, copper eyes shining. "Undress," his Sir said and paced away, heavy boots thudding on the floor. "And up on the table."

He hadn't actually noticed which room they were in until now, but it was the one with the big platform in the middle and the cabinet at one end.

"Yes, Sir." He shivered, shaking off his kiss-stupid. He'd stand and be quiet for hours for those kisses.

"Good boy." Thomas pulled things out of the cabinet and waited for him at the end of the platform.

He got undressed, careful to fold his shirt so he wasn't wrinkly on the way out. He didn't dawdle, but he didn't rush. His lover liked to watch some.

Sure enough, Thomas gave him a smile as he made his

way to the table. He used the little step stool there to climb up and sit, legs dangling over the edge.

"Eyes low, boy. You're free to talk all you like, about anything you like, but your eyes stay low." Thomas showed him a heavy-looking collar as wide as his thumb was long, with a big, D-shaped metal ring on it. Then, without a word, it was placed around his neck, ring in the front, and Thomas adjusted it. "Too tight?"

He rolled his shoulders, trying to make the odd sensation less distressing, but it was unavoidable. Stiff. Weird. Oh, now. He didn't like that. Not one bit. His nostrils flared, his jaw clenched, and he tossed his head, feeling like a fractious horse. "Yes. Take it off."

Thomas looked at him calmly, then reached up to the side of the collar and he heard a click. "That is not how you speak to me, boy."

A flash of pure, fear-fueled rage threatened to flood him, and the urge to lash out and hit Thomas right in the jaw was damn near unavoidable. But this wasn't Bowie. Or Angel. Or James. Right? Right. No hitting the man you loved. "I'm trying real hard not to lose my shit, here," he bit out. "Take the fucking thing off me."

"I see that, sweetheart. I can tell you're panicking. I'd like to try to work you through why it bothers you so much. You know you're safe with me. I find it hard to believe you can't figure out how to handle this with my help. However, if you're shutting me down, use your safe word. I won't take orders from you. You have words for a reason."

"I can't breathe." Which was fucking stupid. He could. Obviously he could. He could talk. If you could talk, you could breathe.

But he couldn't breathe.

"Because this scares you for some reason, and you're

panicked." Thomas took his hands, held them tight. "Look at me, right in my eyes. You're fine, you can breathe. Let's figure out what's going on."

He grabbed on, trying to suck air, and he stared into those fucking pretty eyes, trying to will his jaw to unclench before he broke a tooth.

"Let's break this down." Thomas was still and steady, rooted in place. "It's a stiff piece of leather. It can't get any tighter than it is. It has no meaning of any kind that I don't give it. Right now, as you sit here, it's completely ornamental. It could as easily be around your wrist or your ankle, right?"

"It's not, though." That wouldn't bother him at all. It was touching his neck, trapping him, changing how it felt to hold his head, and he couldn't fucking move like this. His hands began to shake when he swallowed, and he felt the leather against his throat.

"Yellow and revolver. I'm listening, sweetheart." Thomas leaned closer and breathed with him. Calm and quiet and breathing. "Talk, Sam. Tell me what it feels like."

"It's stiff. It's on me." He moved his shoulders, trying to give his neck more room. "I don't like it. I need it off so I can..." A thousand thoughts slammed into his brain, and his abs tightened so fast and hard they cramped. "...breathe."

"Do you trust me?" Thomas was watching him again. Watching.

"Yes, Sir." More than he trusted anyone.

"Good boy. Thank you, sweetheart. All right. I want to minimize the input, I want to simplify this for you. First, try lying down on your back, or even your side, and tell me if it feels better or worse."

He tried, but he couldn't figure out how to move. His abs

wouldn't unclench. He couldn't figure his balance. What the fuck? "I need help. I'm froze."

"Good boy, asking for help. Excellent, Sam. Come on, then." Thomas lifted Sam's legs and set them on the platform, then moved around behind him, hand pressing between his shoulder blades. "Lean into my hands, boy. Lean right back, I've got you."

Come on, you asshole! Cowboy up and do this shit. He slapped himself on the thigh hard, the sharp sting letting him lean, gritting his teeth against the wave of tension coiled in him.

"Easy, boy. That's it. I've got you. You're safe, I promise you." Thomas lowered him down, cradling his head and neck on long arms, setting him down flat on the platform. "Breathe. Tell me if this feels better or worse."

He stretched as hard as he could, trying to make room for the front of his throat, the stiff edge digging into the back of his neck. "Better on the front."

Lord help him, he felt like he was fixin' to shake apart.

"Let's go with that for now. I see how difficult this is, sweetheart, I see how hard you are trying." Thomas held a familiar blindfold in front of him. "I think fewer distractions might help. I know it seems counterintuitive, but I think if you try to relax into the sound of my voice and the things that are familiar, it could help. I'm going to put it on you now."

"I don't like this." He could just reach up, though, and take it off. He could just get up and put his clothes on and leave. He could just say "revolver" and Thomas would stop, and they could go home, and he could have coffee and a shower.

"Understood. Use your words if you need them. I'm listening." Thomas's fingers moved quickly, putting the blindfold in place; then those strong hands landed on the tops of his shoulders, pushing down slightly. "I'm right here."

"What do you want?" He felt like a fucking horse with blinders on, and it pissed him off that his heartbeat slowed some.

"I want to understand, Sam. I want to know why this is so difficult for you. And I want you to find the place inside yourself that wants to wear that collar simply because I want you to wear it. Not the part that will tolerate it, the part that wants this."

He didn't even know what that meant. How the hell was he supposed to do that? He needed this thing off. He reached up and got his fingers underneath, got some air on his skin.

"No, sweetheart." Thomas gently moved his fingers away. "You might hurt yourself."

"I'm trying to understand," he bit out. "I'm trying not to lose my shit."

"You won't. You trust me. You will use your safe word because you know I will see to everything you need." Thomas moved alongside him; he heard it, felt it. "Tell me why you haven't yet. Let me help you understand."

"I don't know! I'm trying to fucking figure this shit out!" Goddamn it, he was trying to breathe, to calm down, but there was this thing around his neck, and he hadn't expected it to be so fucked.

"Shhh." Thomas hushed him like he was a hysterical child, then suddenly was on the platform with him, straddling his hips. He felt Thomas's hands land near his shoulders. "You're doing beautifully, boy. You've done everything I've asked. I know this is hard, but I'm proud of you. Breathe. Think."

He sucked in air, the pressure of Thomas a welcome weight, something familiar, right. He searched for something that made sense, to himself if not to Thomas. "I'm so frustrated."

"I understand that. You're processing so much at once. But look at the foundation you have, Sam. Look what you're falling back on. Trust in me, trust in our process, believe in yourself. You're fine. You can figure this out."

"I'm not even sure what I'm figuring out." He was starting to relax, though, the leather around his neck bearable if he didn't move, didn't think about it.

Thomas's kiss surprised him, the gesture sudden and out of nowhere. It was brief but intense, focused on him, the electricity between them so real it left him tingling. A question came next, Thomas's voice steady. "Why are you still wearing that collar?"

"Because I trust you, and I'm trying to understand what you're trying to tell me." Because he hadn't hit Thomas, when by all accounts he should have. Because that was natural for him, but he hadn't.

"I'm trying to tell you that you already have the answer. It's all right that you don't see it yet. It's not something I know how to explain, and you know very well that even if I did, it still might not make sense to you. You're fine. I'm still so proud of you."

Proud of him for what? Still not figuring shit out? Fucking go him. He was so ready to just give up. Scream. Something.

"How does the collar feel?"

"Hot and heavy. I'm trying not to move my head, in case."

"In case?" Thomas ran fingers along one edge, drawing a hot line across his neck.

He grabbed Thomas's wrists, more holding than pulling. He didn't want to feel that panic again. "I'm trying not to be a psycho."

But it was right there under the surface. Pure overload.

"You're controlling the emotion, but you're still fighting it. This isn't getting easier?" Thomas was carefully freeing one wrist and then the other from his grip. "Then the other question you need to answer is why the collar frightens you. First thing we need to rule out, even if it sounds silly...are you claustrophobic? Are there other small, tight spaces that make you feel panicked?"

"Not that I know of. I been in MRIs, up under the house, locked in a toolbox." Even the toolbox had more pissed him off than anything.

"Toolbox." He heard Thomas snort. "The other thing to think about is past experience. Choking, suffocating, neck injuries, that sort of thing. Anything that might have made you feel afraid or helpless. Can you think of anything like that?"

"Anything?" Shit, look at his life. Look at what they did. All the bullshit that they'd done to feel alive, knowing that one step, one bull, one hit, one accident, one fight would be the one too far.

The sudden image of Bowie's trembling hands floated in his mind, the scars. The way Bowie just shook his head. One too far.

He shook his head to clear it, that fucking thing around his neck right there and he went still.

Thomas rubbed a hand in wide circles on his chest. "Tell me what you're thinking. What just came to mind?"

"Bowie and his damn hands. How they shake all the time, and someone's gonna notice and get rid of him."

"You mean discharge him? He's got a lot of years in. Help me understand how that relates to this?"

"I don't. It doesn't. You asked and I told you the truth. Who knows what the hell is wrong with my brain?" Thomas should just be grateful he wasn't trapped in here, right?

Thomas's hand halted for a second; then that weight was gone as he felt Sir climb off the platform. "I always appreciate the truth, boy." Thomas touched his thighs, smoothing fingers over the muscles and scars, lower over his knees, under his calves. "Why do Bowie's hands shake?"

"Because he's pushing it too far. That feels good, Sir." His muscles started trembling under the touch. "Feels good."

Can you feel your feet?

"You're worried about him. More than your normal 'he's off saving the world' worry." Sir worked fingers into his heels, under his instep, over the tops of his toes to his ankles.

"I can't afford to lose any more brothers." Sam groaned softly. "I can feel you."

"Good boy. And no. No, you don't want to lose Bowie. But Bowie will make his choices. That's scary, but he's living the way he wants to." He felt something soft, like velvet or fur, slip around one ankle, but it wasn't until Sir put the second cuff on that he realized what was happening. Thomas had restrained his legs, secured them to the table.

He sat up in a single rush, hands searching for Thomas, eyes moving behind the blindfold. This time the flood of weird emotions was less like a tsunami, less raw.

"Right here." Thomas caught his hands. "I've got you. Lie down, sweetheart."

"Right here. This is hard, Mister. I'm not good at this." He held Thomas tight, refusing to relinquish the contact.

"It is hard. You don't need to be good at it, I'm only

asking you to try." Thomas slowly helped him settle back down, keeping hold of his hands. "Breathe. You're still safe. You're still with me. You still have your words, and I'm listening. We're figuring this out together, right? You'll let me know if it's not working for you."

"Yeah. Yes, Sir." He rubbed his thumbs on Thomas's palms like they were his own personal worry stones. The collar shifted and he tried to make his neck longer, give his head more room to move.

"Your anxiety binds you sometimes, making it impossible to free your mind. No one can think that way; it's paralyzing." Thomas placed one of his hands carefully on his chest and left it there, then stretched the other out along his side and smoothly slipped another cuff around his wrist.

Sam panted softly, trying to parse things out, but he couldn't. He didn't know how to figure this out, and he felt it like a weight on his neck, stepping on him. "I need to get up and move."

He heard Mister moving around the table in slow, measured steps, and his Sir's answer was silent and simple. Thomas took hold of his free hand and cuffed it, anchoring it down.

Everything in Sam stiffened, stilled, and he could hear the panicked fluttering of his heart in his ears.

You let him do this. You're letting him do this. What the actual fuck is wrong with you? You're letting him do this. Get up and tell him you're leaving. Going home. Going for a run. Going anywhere not right here. You know how.

He wasn't even sure he was breathing.

"I'm right here." Thomas kept touching, slowly sliding warm fingers over his hip, across his abs, up the center of his chest. They traveled farther, grazing a nipple as Thomas reached across his body. "Breathe, sweetheart. I've got you."

Something soft and fairly wide settled high on his chest. The touch was light at first but quickly pressed into his skin from one side of his body all the way to the other. "That's the last one for now, sweetheart. Don't try to sit up, just breathe."

"Let me up. This isn't good." His voice sounded weird, thin. Off. Like it didn't belong to him. He took a deep breath, trying to figure out what to do next. "This isn't cool."

He felt Thomas's fingers comb through his hair, a soft kiss on his forehead. "Do I need to remind you of your words, boy? I'm listening."

"I don't know what to do." The words just slid from him. He was stressed out and confused, anxious and desperate to understand, and every time he couldn't cope and his Sir offered him a way out; he found he didn't have to take it, which made no sense.

"Then just breathe." His Sir kept contact, kept touching him, still slow but more random now—fingers on his collarbone, dragging up his thigh, a hot palm on his shoulder, pressure on his abs. "You breathe, and I will tell you how beautiful you are, the way these dark cuffs stand out on your skin, a little bit of sweat making your six-pack shine."

He took one deep breath after another, tied into the touches, into Sir's low voice—not the words, just the tones of it.

Every so often he would jerk, pull hard at a cuff, and that touch would be right there, gentling him.

He wasn't asleep, far from it. He was caught in that place right before he nodded his head, right before he jumped off the barn roof.

"...and this." The grip around his cock was firm, a hot palm searing into his flesh. "This is also very pretty."

He gasped, the touch shocking, huge, and his eyes went wide behind the blindfold as his ass cheeks clenched.

The touch didn't linger long; it slid down his shaft, around and under his sac, and continued slowly down the inside of his thigh.

His leg tried to draw up, but it wouldn't go, and he huffed out a sigh.

"You're still wearing that collar, sweetheart. You hadn't forgotten about it, surely."

Forgotten? No, but he was focused on those touches, caught in that and his Sir's voice.

"Are you able to tell me why you are wearing it?" Sir's fingers started that slow, deliberate tracing of his ink.

"For us. Because it's our work."

"Very true. Neither of us could have known keeping it on would be so difficult for you, but that discovery has taught us both a great deal. And look where you are now. You're relaxed. You're beautiful. Tell me how you feel."

"Like I'm right here for you." It was the best he had. Hopefully that was enough.

"Thank you. That's just perfect." He got a kiss for that, a nice one. Sir's tongue slid along his own, curious and hungry. He opened, his jaw bumping the collar, and he whimpered into the kiss.

"Mm." Sir ended the kiss, touched his hair again; then he heard those boots take a few steps away before the room went silent.

Sam held his breath, listening hard for sounds—any sounds.

It was quiet for another long moment but finally, Sir gave him something to focus on. "Breathe."

Oh.

He gasped, realizing suddenly that he was lightheaded. *Damn.* Okay. Right. Listen and breathe.

———

THOMAS LEANED AGAINST THE WALL, watching his boy, finding himself in the unusual position of having to reconcile a host of conflicting emotions.

He'd had a moment of panic almost as intense as Sam's had been, when his boy demanded to be let out of that collar. He hadn't been completely sure Sam wouldn't hit him for one thing—strange things happened when Sam was emotional. But beyond that, he simply hadn't expected a reaction so violent. Discomfort, he'd been ready for. Perhaps even an argument. But that? That had caught him completely off guard.

He made sure Sam was still deliberate about breathing, then crossed his arms over his chest as he thought things through.

He was elated, of course, by the journey his boy had taken from pure panic over a collar to quiet acceptance of multiple restraints in such a short time. The trust Sam placed in him took his breath away, validated his approach.

But he wondered if he'd smoothed the way too well, made it too easy for Sam to let go of his anxiety. Despite Sam's huge steps forward, they were no closer to understanding why the boy reacted to the collar the way he had.

It would do Sam a disservice not to get to the bottom of something that was so emotionally unsettling.

The collar, the cuffs, the chest restraint...Sam had adjusted to each one in turn. So, if increasing the stressors wasn't getting him results, it was time to start decreasing the comforts. He planned to go big and start with taking away the thing that Sam relied on most—contact. He'd wait his boy out a bit, play into the tension, and force his boy to rely on his words alone.

Eventually he'd ask the question again. Maybe they'd find an answer.

Sam started wiggling, restlessly at first, then with intention, the calm beginning to fray at the edges.

There it was. That was what he'd been looking for.

"You're safe. I'm listening."

"I—what do you want?"

Oh. Poor Sam. He could almost hear the boy's thoughts starting to spin out. "What do you mean, sweetheart?"

"What do you want me to *do*, Sir?" Sam tugged hard at his wrist cuffs, testing them now.

He took a reflexive step toward his boy and stopped himself, hands itching to touch. To soothe. "Relax." The answer was as much for himself as it was for his boy.

"Relax." Sam pursed his lips and stretched his neck long and lean.

"Yes. And stay focused." He watched Sam stretch, admired the way just that small movement made the boy's shoulders ripple. Sam was so strong, he knew there was no way this aspect of their relationship would be possible if the boy decided not to allow it.

It honored him, knowing Sam's trust in him was so deep.

Sam's toes started curling, the motion reflexive as Sam fought the need to move. He recognized that from their early days working together.

"Toes, boy. Be deliberate about your movements. Don't let them be reflex. Relax, and breathe."

He knew Sam would need to sit up before too much longer, have some water, but he was going to have to push it as far as his boy would tolerate. The boy was like a pull-back car, patience diminishing with every click.

"I need to get up and move. I can't just stay here like this."

"I think you can. Didn't you say you were right here for me?" Sam had thrown the need to move at him a handful of times already, and he had given the same answer every time, but he was having to get creative to maintain its impact. "If you have needs that you are concerned I am unaware of, you should use the appropriate safe word."

Sam groaned softly but set his jaw and settled. Question was—was his boy counting or singing?

He had to smile at how seriously Sam took the use of his safe words. He believed his boy would use them when needed, but he also knew Sam wasn't going to cry wolf. He wouldn't hear those words, not even the yellow, unless his boy truly needed his help.

"Eight hundred forty-two, eight hundred seventeen, nine hundred fifty-one, seven hundred sixty-six..." If Sam was counting, that ought to piss the boy off.

"What is going on? What are you playing at? I'm trying, goddamn it!" Sam slammed one hand on the table. "I'm trying so fucking hard."

Sam tried to turn his head and look for him, the growl when the collar stopped him pure frustration.

It really was dazzling the way his boy could go from launchpad to ozone in nothing flat. Worrisome and slightly intimidating but dazzling.

"Boy." His tone was a warning. But he stepped closer to the table, careful to keep out of reach. "Sam. I have asked you two separate questions. You have been unable to offer me an answer to either, and yet you lie here as bored and restless as a preschool child. If you wish to please me, turn your mind to the things you have not been able to accomplish today. Tell me why that collar worries you so."

"I'm not bored. I'm uncomfortable. I'm hot. My shoulder aches. I'm thirsty and I can't move my head. Don't you fucking call me a child—how many fucking men have you seen carried off on a backboard? How many good men have you been in an ambulance with, them begging you to not tell anyone they can't feel their feet? Have them beg you to shoot them because they're trapped in a piece of shit body that don't work no more? Don't you ever tell me you think I'm acting like a child, you motherfucker. Revolver. You let me up *right now*."

Safe word.

"I'm here, boy." He went immediately into motion, unlocking the chest strap first, Sam's wrists, then feet. He let the boy tear the blindfold off but stopped Sam after that. "Stop. Breathe. Let me take the collar off." He reached for the lock and turned it, loosened the clasps, and carefully lifted it away.

Sam moved off the table and toward his clothes, dragging on his jeans in jerky motions, bright red, heartbeat visible in his throat.

He'd heard every word Sam had said, but he hadn't had one second to think about it. He'd heard a safe word. A full stop. His heart was pounding, adrenaline was making his hands shake, and his boy was not okay.

He knew he had to stay calm. The more emotional a sub became, the steadier he needed to be. But he'd only been to this point a few times and never once with James, so it had been a while. He gave Sam space for a minute, watching him struggle with his clothing, but he knew he couldn't let his boy leave like this. Not in this state, and not alone.

"Sweetheart." He took a couple of steps closer, making sure they were confident and not tentative.

"What? I ain't ready to apologize to you for cussing you yet." Sam managed to get his shirt mostly buttoned, those fingers shaking violently.

He reached out and took Sam's shaking fingers, forgetting until it was too late that his weren't terribly steady either. "I don't expect an apology, and I will give you space to work this through if you want it, but first I need you to look me in the eyes, so I know you're going to be all right."

It took longer than he liked, but Sam met his eyes, the hazel gone a bright, almost shocking green. "Don't you worry on me. I ain't broke. I promise."

"I will worry. I love you. You really can't tell me not to." He tried a half smile, cupping a hand under Sam's jaw. "When you're ready, I want you to talk. I want to listen."

Sam nodded for him, kissed his palm. "I think I need to go home. I need a shower. I don't know how it works, but I can't go out there."

"I would never have asked, sweetheart. We're both done." He reached down and fixed the rest of the buttons on Sam's shirt. "Tuck in, grab your hat." He'd take Sam out through the back.

Sam made himself ready, grabbed his hat, and the only skin he could see was that chiseled jaw.

He pulled out his phone and sent Scotty a quick text that he was leaving the key in the room, that he and Sam were tired and didn't have the energy to be social. "Follow me, we'll get a cab home."

He headed out, feeling Sam right at his heels, and went left instead of right, taking a long narrow corridor to a heavy fire door. An alarm sounded but turned off instantly. *Thank you, Scotty.*

They were in a cab, and out of the cold, in minutes.

Sam sat still and quiet. Thomas didn't read anger in Sam's body or the silence, just emptiness.

He replayed Sam's words on the drive, finally getting a chance to think about what his boy had actually said, instead of obsessing over that safe word. He thought he understood what Sam was telling him, but he needed to think about what to do next. He reached out and slid a hand over Sam's thigh, curling his fingers around the back of Sam's hand.

Sam took a deep breath and turned his hand over, letting their fingers join.

"Better." He let that be enough for the rest of the ride home.

The apartment was still and dark, and he turned on the hall lights as soon as they got inside. "You go ahead start your shower. I'll bring you some water."

Do you want company?

He thought it, but he didn't ask. He didn't want to put Sam in a position to feel awkward saying no. He'd hold his boy later, in the quiet of their bed.

Sam disappeared into the bathroom, the sound of music starting up almost immediately, the water falling right after.

He pulled a couple of bottles of water out of the little fridge next to the dresser. He'd had Sam take it out of the playroom and bring it in here when it became clear that room wasn't something they were going to use. He sucked down one bottle himself in a second and got out another, taking both of those to the bathroom for Sam.

Sam was sitting in the tub, head on his knees, the water slamming down on the back of his neck.

"Sam." He set the bottles down, tugged his T-shirt off

over his head, and knelt by the tub, resting his hands on his lover's shoulders. "I'm here."

"My head's fixin' to explode, Mister."

"Hang on." He stood again, grabbed a bottle of Ibuprofen out of the cabinet and a bottle of water, then handed three pills and the water to Sam. He hit the knob and flipped the water off.

"Take those and let's get you out of there." It was hard to know just looking at his boy whether this was a rebound headache or if it was his neck, but either way, the meds would help some, and rest wouldn't hurt. He'd call Bryan in the morning if it wasn't better.

"Thank you." Sam took the pills and sucked down the water in huge gulps. "I don't know what happens next."

"Don't worry, sweetheart. I've got you." He pulled a towel out, offered Sam a hand up, and wrapped his boy in it.

Sam stepped close to him, eyes searching his face. The hug he got was unexpected, but welcome.

He sighed, relieved, and pulled Sam in tight. "I'm so sorry about your friend." Sam was right; he'd never been in that position, and he couldn't imagine how horrific it must have been. But he saw just how traumatic it was for his boy, with fear and memories that carried into their scene. He was glad at least to have the connection, but hurting and sad for Sam.

"I haven't thought about JP in a long time. Didn't know..." Sam sighed softly and shook his head.

"How would you know? These things just happen." He loosened his grip enough to get Sam into the bedroom and help him into some briefs. He grabbed Sam another bottle, then ran his fingers over the back of Sam's neck where the collar had left pressure marks. "Does your neck hurt?"

"No, my shoulder's bothering me some." Sam leaned back into his touch. "That feels good."

"Come sit." He pulled Sam over to sit on the end of the bed and climbed up behind his boy where he could use both hands and dig into Sam's neck and shoulders. This was good, it would help with the headache, and Sam would also get the touch he craved.

And who was he kidding? He needed this too. He'd forced Sam into that outburst, goaded him into the emotional and justifiable use of the safe word. He'd done it knowingly, but that didn't make him feel any better about making his boy hurt so badly, and it would be a bit before he completely rid himself of his own worry and emotion.

"Uhn." That sound was emotional release, pure and simple, and Sam shook with a cold chill. "You're good at that."

"I've had a little practice. I've never met anyone with shoulders tighter than your brother's." He found a knot low in Sam's shoulder and worked it carefully, unsure what he should and shouldn't mess with, considering the injury and surgeries.

"Oh. Right there. Harder. It's been driving me crazy for days."

"For days? Why haven't you told me?" He dug in hard, working the knot under his thumb, feeling it slowly start to let go. "I need to know these things, sweetheart, before I do crazy things like restrain you."

"Oh, God." Sam groaned as goose bumps covered his skin. "I did say, sorta. Just a little...oh. Thank you."

" 'Sorta' isn't clear enough for me to make a good decision. But you're right, I did hear it." He just kept at it until the knot was barely noticeable. "How's your head feeling?"

"Better. Less like I'm fixin' to stroke out."

"Well, good." He laughed softly. "That would be disappointing." He pulled his hands away slowly. "Are you hungry? Or just ready to rest?"

"I couldn't eat right now. Maybe later." Sam stayed where he was, facing away from Thomas. "I wasn't lying to you. I didn't know what was wrong until I told you."

"Oh, sweetheart. I never once thought you were lying. I could see how frustrated you were. I'm sorry I had to push you that hard. But you needed that connection, or it would eat at you until you figured it out. I'm not really an asshole." He leaned in and kissed the side of Sam's neck. "Really, I apologize. But I think it was the right call."

"I'm not a kid. That's important to me. I don't do still so well, and I may not be the brightest motherfucker on earth, but I'm solid. I deserve that respect from you." The words weren't angry, but they were calm and firm.

He started to protest. He had nothing but respect for Sam, and that comment was meant to be flip and meaningless, but he realized it didn't matter what he meant; what mattered was that Sam knew respect was important to him too.

"You're certainly not a kid, and you're one of the smartest people I have ever met. You're right to demand respect from me; you deserve it. I hope you'll accept my apology."

"I will. Thank you." Every time Sam did that— demanded his apology, then accepted it and trusted that he meant it—his estimation of his lover grew higher.

"Come lie down and let me hold you for a while. We could both use some rest, and clearer heads. That was hard work, sweetheart, one of the most difficult evenings I've ever had at the club." He knew it proved to be one of the most rewarding too.

"Yeah. I just want to be quiet with you a minute." Sam stood up and moved to the edge of the bed, pulled down the covers, and slid in.

He did the same, holding his arms open for Sam to come to him. Once again, nothing had gone as he'd planned at the club. Was it the energy of the place? Was it Sam? He just didn't know. It was good work, though. It was. He was proud knowing he'd made sure his boy had his needs met each time despite the sudden twists in his plans.

He couldn't say he always got everything he needed or even wanted; the things he planned were typically designed to be more balanced. But he didn't need as much as Sam did. He was fine.

21

S am woke up at the crack of dawn, slipped on his clothes, and left a note that simply said, "Running."

Then he headed out into the bitter cold and started going. Thomas had to think he was an idiot. Just a pure fresh off the turnip truck moron.

Jesus fuck.

He hadn't been thinking of JP at all. Hadn't for years, really, which was a damn shame. The guy had been his best friend for a long time.

Still, it had been, what? Six years? Seven, now? Seven this fall, he guessed.

Shit.

He needed to stop this shit. What would Bowie say to him? Hell, what would James say?

Well, he didn't want to know what James would say, because obviously James was—had been?—better at all this.

He still felt a little like he was in a TV show. *Redneck in the City* or something.

Sam had to wonder what Thomas felt like, whether he wished that James was there to be with him instead. Sam wouldn't blame Thomas for that. He'd read James's diary that once. James was...James got it. James was good.

Then Thomas got the ADHD redneck miniaturized version of the O'Reilly.

Shit Marthy.

Sam ran harder, turned the music up louder, pushed himself to pure muscle failure, then turned around to walk home on trembling legs.

Coffee. Velveeta and Ro-Tel. He needed to go to the club and get their coats.

Bench. He needed a bench. *Whoa.*

He found one and plopped down before he puked.

Huh. Faboo.

"Sam? Sam, that you?"

Sam looked up. Scotty. Yay. He didn't need this shit right now. He was tired. "Howdy. How goes?"

"I'm great. Looks like you had a rough night, though." Scotty didn't sit, just stood over him like some haughty, metrosexual crane.

"Does it? Just a long run." If I hit you, motherfucker, you would never recover. Never.

"I meant last night. Sneaking out the back door, didn't even want to send you up front for your coats. Thomas really wrung you out, huh?"

"I'm a lucky motherfucker, right?" Sam started counting backward from one hundred.

"Right. I mean, after Master Thomas discussed finding another sub and finding you another Dom with Master Clint, I was worried."

Jesus save him from assholes.

"You been saving that one for a while, have you?" He'd say he was surprised that Thomas wanted someone else, but he'd just been thinking it. Stung a little that Thomas would talk to someone else about him, but maybe that was a thing here. God knew, back home you never said dick to anyone about this sort of shit. "You are a piece of work, honey."

He let the honey drawl out, let his upper lip curl. He knew how infuriating that was.

Scotty's eyes narrowed and one way too perfect eyebrow arched at him. "Master Thomas is hard to please. Your big brother wasn't enough, and he was conscientious." Scotty straightened his jacket, tossed his head like a prize pony and started to walk away. "I wish you luck, *honey*."

"I'll make sure to look that ten-cent word up." Catty little bitch. He stood up without sparing Scotty another glance. Thomas wouldn't thank him for fighting with the guy who could spit in your drink.

Note to self. Don't drink anything from the bar.

He really was going to have to make himself a cheat sheet for this.

Assuming that Thomas wasn't already...

Stop it. Just stop.

It wasn't like he didn't already know that he sucked at being "good"—and God, he hated that term, because he wasn't a bad guy. He was a white hat. Still, he wasn't like the others. He'd figured that out. He wasn't stupid.

Hell, Sam secretly thought it would be a little easier if he was, if he could just stop thinking and...but he couldn't.

Okay. Obviously, he hadn't run far enough. He picked up from walk to jog.

Coffee. Coffee. Coffee.

The house was silent when he got home, and he thought at first that Thomas was still asleep, but he caught his lover sitting on the couch, reading the newspaper, coffee in hand.

"I brought you a caramel coffee deal. Morning." He went over to give caffeine and a kiss. "How's you this morning?"

"Fine. Have a good run?"

"Hard. It was a hard one today. I'll go get cleaned up. I probably stink to high heaven."

"You're overdoing it. The Ibuprofen is in the cabinet on the left." Thomas sipped his coffee and went back to his paper.

"Thanks." He finished his coffee and jumped in the shower, telling himself he couldn't be in the doghouse already. He hadn't even been home, he'd brought coffee, and he'd left a note. Maybe Thomas just needed some quiet time, and he was ramped up and nervy, so he just needed to chill out and breathe.

He bundled up and padded into the kitchen to fix him another cup and grab a banana.

It looked like Thomas hadn't so much as twitched since he'd left the room, except that the coffee he'd brought home was in his lover's hand now. "You want some eggs? You need protein."

"Sure, if you don't mind. I could make toast." He was so tired already. Maybe he could just go take a nap. "You sleep okay?"

Thomas pulled out the eggs and a pan. "I slept very well. You must have as well to be up and ready to run so early."

So, he was in the doghouse. He wasn't sure what for, but he was absolutely sure he didn't have the heart to deal with it. If this was what "normal" weekends were going to be, he was going back to work at Mike's on Saturday nights. The week had been so good.

"I woke up to pee; then I was wide awake. Thought I'd run off the…" Jitters? Nerves? Bullshit? "…excess energy."

He pulled out bread and butter.

"Yes, I woke up with a little excess energy myself. I

missed you." Thomas poured his eggs into the hot pan and they sizzled.

"I haven't ever learned that 'sleep in on the weekends' thing. Guess it's being a ranch kid? I have a clock that goes off in my head." He dared to walk over, wrap one hand around Thomas's waist and give him a hug from behind. "You were on my mind too."

Thomas turned in his arm and hugged him back, sighing, and he felt the tension in his lover ease. "Wake me up. I need you more than sleep, especially the morning after a scene like..." Thomas sighed again, but it was different this time, and those strong shoulders drooped a little with it. "I'm...God, I'm going to burn your eggs."

Thomas turned to the eggs and stirred them.

"I can eat burned eggs." He grabbed Thomas's shoulders and started rubbing. "I'm sorry about last night."

Thomas shut off the stove but leaned into his hands. "I don't want you to be sorry. It was good, Sam. I'm stunned by the strength of what we have between us. It was so good. It was just...so *hard*."

"Yeah." He imagined dealing with a crazy-assed Texan was exhausting. He was tired and he was used to being him. He kept rubbing, kept working those shoulders, and trying to ease Thomas.

"It was hard watching you go through that. I had to make hard choices for you, to help you find that place where..." Thomas shook his head. "Sorry. You're supposed to think that I can do this in my sleep."

"Why? I'm supposed to be your lover, your friend, your partner. That's not very sensible." He found another sore spot and rubbed.

Thomas's head dropped forward and he moaned. "Not *supposed to be*. You *are*. You are all of those things. And also my sub. I guess I just need to think about how that all works." Another sigh and Thomas turned around. "What happened to JP? After that ambulance ride?"

Master Thomas discussed finding another sub and finding you another Dom with Master Clint.

"He died in the hospital twelve days later."

"Oh, sweetheart." Thomas's hands went to his face, thumbs dragging over his cheeks. "I'm so sorry. I hope working through that trauma and that fear will help you. If it hadn't come out last night, it could have at some other awful moment."

"I hadn't thought about him in a while. He was my best friend out of high school. He was eighteen."

Thomas's eyes widened for a second. "So young. How do you keep riding after...witnessing that?"

"Keeping on was never a question. I was on a bull the day after he got broke and the Friday the day after he died. You get back on and ride." JP had asked him to do it, to kill him, but he hadn't had to. No one was sure who had—could have been JP's momma, could have been a number of people. What mattered was that JP's wishes were carried out.

Thomas nodded. "I guess I understand that, but it couldn't have been easy." Thomas kissed his cheek. "You better eat those eggs, they're getting cold."

"Let me grab our toast. Hold up. You got plans for today?" *I promise not to have a breakdown of any sort today.*

"Yes. Whatever your plans are." Thomas divvied up the eggs onto plates.

"Good deal." He'd work some on Thomas's shoulders, then go get stuff for queso and make it. "You want queso for the game?"

That got him a smile. "I will never turn down queso.

Which game are we watching? I don't even know who's playing today." Thomas handed him a plate and a fork.

"Cowboys have a bye this week, so what does it matter?" he teased. He made himself an egg sandwich and sat down to eat.

"Seriously, why even watch?" Thomas sat with him after stopping by the coffee table and picking up the cup of coffee he'd brought home. "We can just have it on as background noise while we make out and eat queso."

"Sounds perfect to me. Making out with you is one of my favorite things." He reached over and rubbed his hand over Thomas's shoulder.

Thomas leaned slightly toward his hand. "I guess I need to head down to the club later and pick up our coats, or it's going to be a very cold walk to work in the morning."

"Yeah. You'd freeze your nipples off. You want me to come with, or you want to split errands?"

"Oh, I don't care. I wasn't planning on staying there long. Do you feel like going to the club with me? I can go on my own. I guess we'd get home faster if we split up."

"Whatever turns you on. I want to love on your back a little bit. You're like frozen rope."

"Like you last night." Thomas nodded. "Okay, so we'll split up so we...oh. It's Sunday. We'll stick together."

"What's special about Sunday?"

"Oh. We split up during the week, sweetheart. We should just be together on the weekends. Don't you think? It'll be just as fast, there's a little grocery near the club." Thomas took a big bite of the eggs and followed it with a bit of toast.

"I'm all over that." Wandering around, being with Thomas? Those were good things.

They finished up and Thomas took their plates into the

kitchen. "Let me just deal with these dishes, and we can get going so we're back for kickoff."

"Yes, Sir. I'll put on jeans and all. Two shakes." He rolled his shoulders and told himself that his feet weren't too sore to fit in his boots. Running was a bitch to learn. They'd do their thing, get coats and groceries and something yummy and sweet, then come home and make each other feel good.

Thomas got them an Uber because it was too windy and cold to deal with walking the few blocks to the subway, and Sir hunched around him so he'd stay warm as they hurried into the club.

"My very own personal heater," he teased. "Thank you."

"No problem. I hear Texans get frostbite chewing on ice cubes." Thomas laughed and hustled him through the door. "I'll just duck into the coatroom."

"Don't tell all my secrets now!"

"Little Sammy? Is that you?"

Sam looked up to see Angel and his big smile. "Nope. It's another bull rider."

Angel laughed and waved him over but didn't go for the hug like the night of the party. "I heard you two were here last night; I didn't expect to see you today."

"We came to get our coats. How you doing? Staying busy?"

"Super busy. Mike called me three times this week. You two were too high to remember your coats?" Angel's grin lit up blue eyes.

"We were warm." Thomas bumped shoulders with him and handed him his coat.

"Can I give your boy a hug, Master Thomas?" Angel sounded like an excited kid, and that grin grew even wider.

Thomas gave Angel a nod. "It's fine with me, but you have to ask him."

Angel arched his eyebrow and looked to Sam, and he just opened his arms. "Hey, you."

Angel scooped him up and hugged him tight. "I swear to God, Sammy, you get lighter every time I see you."

"Butthead."

"It's good to see you, Angel. What are you doing with yourself now that you don't have Sam to fix up every weekend?"

"Ha!" Angel's laugh rang out through the room. "My best customer!"

"Yeah, yeah. I'll need you for something soon, no doubt. I can't stay out of trouble for long." He could tease right back.

Thomas offered a hand and Angel shook. "We're not hanging out, we've got plans, but it's good to see you. Let's get together for dinner or something this week."

"Sounds good. Send me a text and we'll meet for something spicy and wonderful."

Sam took another hug. "Good one, man. Talk at you later."

"Be a good boy, Sammy." Angel was still chuckling as they left.

"Coat," Thomas said, turning the collar up against the wind. "Would you like my gloves, or do you have some in your pockets?"

"Coat." He snuggled into his jacket and searched for his gloves that Thomas had given him, cheering when he found them.

They had to walk a couple of blocks to the store, but they bought everything they needed for the queso. "I still can't believe James let me think all that time that he was working so hard to make queso, and he was really just throwing it in the microwave." Thomas laughed. "I am such a sucker."

"He could be a shit that way. He told me that an elf came in and taught him how to read, and if he never showed up, I'd never be able to read."

Thomas snorted, still laughing. "I swear, I never saw him pull a practical joke or a fast one on anyone. He was just straight as an arrow. He must have played me."

"That doesn't surprise me at all." At Thomas's shocked look, Sam shrugged. "James was always the good one—at school, at church, at Scouts. But he could fight like a bastard when no one in authority was around. You know how many times I got my butt beat because James said he didn't do something? Lord have mercy."

"And I was authority." Thomas shook his head and led him down into the subway for the trip home. "I was his lover, but I was authority. God, he was complicated."

"He was. Me, not so much. He had lots of faces." And there had been something about those faces that Thomas had loved.

Thomas laughed. "No. No, you're not complicated at all. Completely straightforward. I had you figured out the second I met you. Sure."

"That's me. Just a simple man. Easy as pie." He winked over. Really, he wasn't like James, with different boxes for different places. He was just one guy with a lot of shit in the same box.

"Sure. A bronc-riding, art historian turned submissive New York City author. Easy as pie."

"Riding you's way more fun," he muttered softly.

"And you don't need body armor. Definitely my favorite sport to watch." Thomas tangled their fingers as the doors opened at their station. "Almost home."

"Queso, football, necking promised, with riding on the possible list. I'm ready."

Thomas leaned close to his ear. "Can we ride first, then watch football and eat queso naked?"

Heat flooded Sam in a rush, and his shiver was pure happy pleasure. "God, yes. Please."

Thomas followed him into their building, hustled him into the elevator, and didn't wait for the doors to close to kiss him. "I love you. You're just too much fun."

"Mmm. I love you. All the parts." He begged one more kiss.

Thomas gave it to him and didn't rush him off the elevator as the door opened; his lover just stuck his foot in the door until the alarm rang, making them both jump and laugh. "Oops. I'm telling mom that was your fault."

"I swear to God, I end up taking licks and I'm coming after..." Sam stopped, the sight of the apartment door with a huge X gouged in it, a razor blade still dug into the wood, making his belly go taut. "Get back."

"Like hell." Thomas shouldered past him, face darker than he'd ever seen it, and unlocked the door, shoving it open wide.

"Goddamn it!" He pushed in, determined to protect his Thomas at all costs.

"It was locked, Sam." Thomas looked the door over, shaking his head. "We need to call Colletti." Sam jumped when Thomas slammed the door closed and turned the locks. "Fucking coward!"

"Still. Stay here." Sam looked in every room, every closet, everywhere, just in case. Just in case.

Just in case.

"We weren't gone that long; he had to know....What?... This asshole doesn't know Colletti's schedule is nine-to-five, find the detective and have him call me. Now." Thomas was pacing the hall, exactly where Sam had told him to stay, on the phone.

Sam opened the door and took a photo of the damage, closed it, and locked it before he picked up the groceries and put them away.

Then he started making himself a cup of coffee.

Thomas hung up the phone. "Can I move now?"

"Yes. No one's here. I had to make sure. Coffee?"

"Yes, please." Thomas joined him in the kitchen, but he was fidgeting and looking pissed off. "Fucker. I've had enough now."

"Yeah. Me too." His kidneys screamed at him, the sudden rush of adrenaline like a little shock after yesterday.

Question was, what should they do?

It wasn't like he'd been the king of figuring that out already.

Thomas took two deep breaths and reached for him, pulling him in close. "I'm sorry, Sam. I don't know what the hell to do anymore."

"Shit, honey. I haven't known what the hell to do from the start. This is fucked up." Sam held on to Thomas with all he had. "I don't need you to be this perfect man. I need *you*. And also, I might need to beat this crazy motherfucker to death with his own arm."

"I trusted the cops, you know? I thought they'd get on it and find the guy. I really believed that. But somehow, he's getting into what I thought was a fairly secure building and getting away with this still. *Still*. And I'm being told not to worry, that the detective will call me when he gets in tomorrow. It's no kind of priority for them at all."

"I don't know what to do, either, but...someone has to."

Maybe he'd go talk to Daddy Mike and get some advice, maybe a firearm. He'd text Bowie too and just say "Help."

Thomas held him quietly for a little longer, then let him go, catching his eyes. "We're not idiots, you and I. We'll figure it out."

"We're not, and we will. Let me go pull that razor out so no one hurts themselves on it."

He got a quick kiss. "Be careful, and don't touch it. Wear gloves."

"Get me a bag or something?"

"Yes. Right here." Thomas pulled a Ziploc out of a drawer. "You should be impressed. Not only do I have one, but I know where it is."

"Man, I am duly impressed." He pulled his multitool out of the little drawer of shit that had nowhere else to go and used the plier to grab the razor blade.

Thomas had followed him partway and was hovering just in view. "Got it?"

"Got it. Open the bag." He plopped the razor in, nice and careful. "Okay. Put that somewhere safe, and I'll make sure we're all locked up. I took pictures."

"Right. Good idea, I should have thought of that since they're not even sending cops 'just for vandalism' until tomorrow."

Thomas took the bag into the kitchen. "I'll leave it on the counter. Hopefully someone will pick it up in the morning."

"I'll make sure. If they don't, I'll go down and deal with it at the precinct myself."

Thomas pinned him with a hard look. "You don't leave this apartment alone. I'll stay home tomorrow. I don't want you going anywhere alone anymore, Sam. Not until they catch him."

"You know I can't do that. Neither one of us can." He got

it, though, the fear that something would happen to Thomas. "That's not how life works."

"You can. You work from home. I don't know why James went out that night after I left him. I shouldn't have left him alone. I'm not letting it happen to you. You have to stay home."

"Breathe." He wasn't going to argue about this. Not now. This wasn't about reason. This was about being scared. They'd lost James to this fucker, but they weren't going to be surprised. They were going to be ready. "Can we go to the sofa? You promised to let me rub your back. God knows we both need that now."

Thomas sighed and went to the couch without a word, sitting heavily.

Okay, that was cute.

Pouting Thomas.

Oh God, don't laugh. Don't you dare laugh. No laughing.

"I'll grab the oil and a towel. I just want to love on you a minute."

He got a nod, and that was all.

Poor guy. It wasn't that he was less upset; he just...shit, he'd been scared so often he thought his panic button was loose and after yesterday? Shit, he was panickless. Depanicked?

Too fucking worn out to care.

Pick one.

He stripped down to his skivvies, pulled on his sweat pants, and grabbed his supplies.

Thomas was opening a bottle of wine when he got back. "You want some?"

"Mmm. Please." He got the towel spread out on the sofa.

Thomas moved to the couch and set two glasses down

on the coffee table, and the T-shirt his lover had been wearing landed on the floor by his feet.

"Come stretch out, honey. Let me make it better."

Thomas nodded and took two huge gulps of wine before getting comfortable. "I wish I knew why. I don't know why it matters to me, but it does."

"Yeah, if there was a why, maybe we could stop it. James never said anything..." *Stop it, Sam. He's stressed out enough.*

He watched the muscles in Thomas's shoulders tighten up. "Nothing. Never. If anything like this was happening to him, I knew nothing about it. I never saw anything like this myself. The cops asked me the same question that morning, and again when they called me in for questioning the first time. I've been over this a hundred times in my head. I still can't think of a goddamn thing."

"Me either." He poured some oil in his hands and started rubbing, nice and easy. Think of something else to talk about. "Did you meet Angel at the club?"

"What?" The sudden change of subject seemed to freeze Thomas up for a second, but then he relaxed. "Yes. He was experienced and imposing, and Clint started matching him with subs almost right away. He caused a bit of a stir."

"Imposing? Angel? He's a teddy bear."

"Not if you didn't know him and he had on several cows' worth of leather."

"Fair enough." No way. Not a chance. Angel was...dear and caring and funny. Not imposing.

"He was different then. He's changed some since...since I first met him."

"Yeah? I supposed he'd say the same about you. Everyone changes." He rubbed in lazy circles, encouraging Thomas to relax. He loved the lines of muscles, the inked lines of the word "integrity" on Thomas's shoulder.

"Mhm." He knew he was getting somewhere when Thomas's eyes slid closed. "You have talented fingers, sweetheart."

"Thank you, Mister. They love touching you." And there was the simple part.

"Angel would say that. Everyone who knew me as Tommy would say I've changed dramatically since they met me. I think you're changing me back a little, and I'm enjoying that."

"I like you, you know?" He traced a long line up along Thomas's spine, thumbs digging in. "We have a good time together."

"We do. We're good at finding fun, making our own fun. I didn't know how much I missed that, honestly. I've been very focused and serious. And that's good too, I guess. I wasn't unhappy; I just haven't laughed like I do with you in a long time."

Oh, didn't that feel good. "Thank you."

He leaned down and kissed Thomas's shoulder.

Thomas hummed happily. "This feels so decadent. I'll return the favor when I can move again."

"No worries. Just let me love on you a little while. I'm happy where I am." In this, he felt like he wasn't trying to learn a new language. He could touch and love and help them both relax.

"I'm happy too." Happy enough that it wasn't long before he had Thomas dozing.

Sam covered Thomas with a blanket, grabbed his wine, and curled up in the recliner with his phone.

He sent Bowie the picture of the front door, then sent one text.

Brother, I need help. How do I find this guy and stop him

22

Thomas sat down on a bench in the sun, half a block from his building and looked at it—tall and formal, his home since he moved out of Clint's place—and wondered how long they'd stay there.

"All good?" he asked.

The guy at the other end of the bench nodded.

Mike's added surveillance was costing him a pretty penny, but it was worth it. Apart from running, because that kind of tail was difficult to engineer, Sam had eyes on him, or at least on the building, all day, every day.

Colletti, in the couple of weeks since Sam pulled that razor out of their door, had continued to be worse than useless. They had no leads.

"Did he go out?"

"Run. Bodega on the corner. Library."

"Thanks. Have a good night." He got up and headed home.

He could hear the music when he opened the door, hard and driving. Sam was in the middle of the floor, surrounded by books and papers, scribbling furiously.

The whole picture made him smile. Even the music, which wasn't entirely to his taste. He walked over and reached down to ruffle Sam's hair.

The music immediately lowered and changed to something less frenetic. "Man, I lost track of time. Sorry."

Sam made a few more notes, then closed all the books and bundled them off.

He understood, and he wished Sam wouldn't apologize for things like that. He appreciated the change of music, though. "It's fine, you're working. Good day?"

"Not bad. Went to the library. Ran. Worked. Got a bagel. You?"

"Hit the gym, had an unsatisfying salad for lunch with a coworker who wants to meet you, and worked. I still can't find a sponsor for this one show that's coming in. I get that photography can be controversial, but it's getting old now."

"Gym is good. Salad is...salad. There's half a bagel in there if you want it. And someone will decide that it's worth it." Sam grinned at him, "Good to see you, Mister."

"Good to see you too, sweetheart. I do love seeing you working when I get home. You shouldn't apologize for being occupied." Sam's smile warmed him, and he put his arms around his boy. Lately he needed that moment of comfort almost as much as he knew Sam did. "Can I take you out for something not-salad? We've been sitting in this apartment too much."

"Sounds good to me. What all is your tongue set on?" Sam leaned into him with a soft sound.

"Mexican. Tacos. Or a big, fat burrito. Super hot salsa." All week. He'd wanted spicy salsa all week. "And it's not freezing out. We can walk."

"I'm always up for Mexican. Note that I didn't comment on your big, fat burrito." Sam went to tug on his boots.

"Really?" He snorted. "Note that I didn't comment on how like a twelve-year-old you are. Oh, wait. I did."

"Yeah, yeah, yeah. No one ever accused me of class."

He knew a thing or two about class. It was overrated. He'd take real over class any day. He grabbed Sam's coat for him. "I wouldn't dare."

Sam laughed and kissed him—good and deep, just enough to make him need to catch his breath—before taking his coat.

He grinned at Sam. "You know just what you're doing when you do that, don't you?"

"Saying hello in the best way." Sam grabbed a gimme cap. "You ready to *hasta*?"

"*Vamonos*." He hooked an arm behind Sam's back and steered his boy out the door. "What did you do at the library?"

"Looked at books." Sam shot him a wicked grin.

He locked the door, then double-checked that it was locked. It was routine now, normal. "Oh, you can read?"

"I mostly just looked at the pictures." Sam's chuckle filled the hallway. "Don't worry, the librarian made sure I wasn't in over my head."

"Oh, good. It's all about building confidence." He laughed. "Brat. Oh, it's so nice out here."

"It is." Sam inhaled deeply, stretching up tall. "Good to shake out your cobwebs, hmm?"

"Exactly. So, seriously, are you finding what you need at the library?" He tangled his fingers with Sam's and settled into their walk. It was a little stretch of the legs, but this was as much about getting some air as it was about dinner.

"I'm mostly working on general information for the book, making sure I know what I'm basing my theories on.

I'm working on some weird costuming questions a client had. And I have a couple of personal projects too."

"Academic ADD." He laughed. "Because why have one project when you can have five?" It suited Sam, though. One project wasn't enough for that busy mind.

"Absolutely. When you find something in one that makes you hiccup, you go to another and come back later."

"Makes sense. I'm more of a 'push through it' type myself, but I completely understand how that would work for you." He really believed that their different approaches to just about everything was part of their strength as a couple. It had taken some patience to figure out how they fit together, but they were better for it.

It was so much easier now, the give and take much more natural.

"I would never have guessed that about you." Oh, his boy was in a fine mood today, playful and warm, happy.

"It's all right. You'll get to know me eventually." He shook his head. He was fairly sure Sam knew him better than anyone ever had, maybe even better than Clint. Oh. "Hey, Clint texted me, he's found some other couples that are interested in a seminar on bats and crops, what do you think?"

"Bats? I'm relatively sure I'm not going to let you whack me with a bat." That was a wide-eyed look. "When you say seminar, what does that mean, exactly?"

"A bat is basically just a very short crop, dork. And the seminar isn't a lecture, if that's what you're thinking. It's three or four couples and an instructor, learning different ways to use the instrument safely, correctly, and creatively." He thought he knew what Sam was worried about. "Using them, for real."

Sam tilted his head. "I have a few questions, then, before I can answer yours, I guess."

Well. All right, let the negotiations begin. He smiled. "Go ahead."

"Well, I guess the big question is what you'll expect from me, huh? Because if I can't manage it, I'm not going to waste your time."

Christ. How many times had he told Sam that his only expectation was that the boy try? Was Sam ever going to believe him? "Are you used to going into classes already knowing all the answers?"

"Of course not. But this...this is different. This is like... almost like taking a class in Portuguese when you speak Spanish—you're getting it, but you really have to work at it. You say all the time that there aren't expectations, but that's not true, not exactly. I'm not sure you even see that sometimes because it's so much of who you are. Or maybe we're saying different things, but at the club, you have expectations. And in a class situation? I know you do." Sam's tone was easy, conversational—not devoid of emotion, but open and trying to communicate.

He listened, then quietly tried to sort through what Sam was saying. One thing he knew was, if Sam took the time to form that specific an observation and found the words to actually say it so coherently, it was important. He heard what Sam was telling him about his expectations when it was just the two of them and his expectations at the club.

"You're right. I do have expectations at the club. The club...has expectations of me." That was it, wasn't it? Sam's behavior at the club reflected on him.

"Exactly, yes!" Sam grinned at him, squeezed his hand. "And I'm not super clear on how to do this whole thing. To go back to the foreign language analogy—I'm trying to learn, but I'm still having to translate at the club, all the time. At home, when it's just us, I feel like, even if I don't know what to do, I know that with you, I'll figure it out.... Does this make sense? It sort of makes sense in my brain."

He nodded, eyes on the sidewalk as he tried to process that. "At home..." He was thinking out loud, he knew, but hopefully Sam would follow. "All the rules are mine. I can give you as much room as you need, as much space and time to figure something out as I have patience for." Right, that made sense but at the club... "At the club everyone has the same rules—customary rules—but for you, they're not the same at all, are they?" It was like taking Sam's little Wrangler-clad butt and sticking it in an English saddle. Still riding, different posture.

"Right? And I don't want to embarrass you for all the world." Sam bumped their shoulders together. "Like, for instance, I don't know how to be in that situation—learning about the crop with you, answering questions, not just taking it because I'm with other people. I mean..." Sam blinked, looked up. "We're here, huh?"

"Good catch. I wasn't paying attention; I'd have walked right by it." He took Sam's arm and pulled him to the side, away from the door to the restaurant. "We'll go in, just...I want to clear something up first." He hooked a finger under Sam's chin and made sure he had the boy's eyes. "If I have anything in my hand—a crop, a flogger, anything—then my focus is on you. My expectations no matter where we are will be the same as they are at home because that is for us, not for the club. Not for show, not for anyone's approval. I really don't care what those other couples think. I would hope they would be just as focused on themselves. I want to learn how to make that crop work for us—if it can work for us. And finding out that it doesn't or it can't is a completely valid outcome. We're not there to make it work, we're there to learn something."

"That's what I needed to know. This is...so far outside the realm of anything I've ever done, you know? But I want to learn something new with you, something new to you."

He smiled, then gave Sam a light kiss. "You understand that if I'm going to take a crop to you, you'll probably be naked." At least for some of the time. Part of the class would be him and a practice dummy.

"Yeah. I have some worries about that, but it's not a deal-breaker. Just things to talk...work out." Sam opened the door and held it for him. "After you, Mister Burrito."

"Thank you, I think." He laughed and stepped through the door. "Just remember you have your words. Always, everywhere."

He said that; and he wondered if it was as obvious to Sam as it was to him. As far as he was concerned, those words were sacred anytime. Their immersive lifestyle required that.

"Hell, I'm just happy that we can talk to each other about this now. It took a while to get a shared language."

"You mean it took you a while to talk. Period?" He winked. "I'm kidding. I'm proud of that. It took real work and trust in each other's intentions. And it's solid now."

They got a table, menus, and a great big bowl of chips and salsa.

"Oh, man. I want one of everything." Sam grinned at him. "Combination plate for me, I'm thinking."

"I'd get that big, fat burrito, but I already have one. Fish tacos, maybe?" And half his weight in salsa. He dug in, feeling the heat on his tongue.

"Fish tacos. God help me, it's a good thing I love you."

"Oh? What would you recommend, boy?" He liked fish tacos.

"You had a salad for lunch, Mister. Get something hysterically wonderful. Oh...fajita chicken chimichanga. Fried tube of cheese and chicken." Someone was begging for a beating.

"So, fish tacos then." He grinned. "I'm already spending an hour at the gym in the morning. Let's not make it three." Truthfully, it was more like an hour and a half since he added the extra core work.

"Stud." There was a wealth of admiration in that single word.

"Careful. I'm starting to believe that a little." A little. Maybe. He certainly felt it more and more. Sam's kind of love was good for him, body and soul.

He smiled at his boy. "Margaritas?"

23

Standing in the club right now was the last place Sam wanted to be. He was tired, like bone-deep weirdly tired, like he'd been awake for days. At the same time, his brain wouldn't shut off, not even for a second.

James. The killer. The book. Costumes. Bondage. Submission. Bowie. The folks. Running. Planning their trip to Texas. His jeans didn't fit. There was nothing to fix in this place when he needed to do something, which led to "he really was useless" thoughts, which led to more working, more running, more...

And he wanted to ask Thomas for a second of ease, just a minute of quiet, but...

Thomas was having work shit and was wound tighter than a coiled snake, and that wasn't fair. And what if he asked and Thomas just said no?

And he felt like Chatty Cathy when Thomas came home at night, just jabbering like an idiot, but he was so wound up with ideas and shit that...right.

He finally kind of got the idea Thursday when Thomas

just sort of stared at him until he'd shut up and gone back to the office. Thomas had fallen asleep on the sofa, and he'd chatted on some weird message board all night about nothing at all while mainlining hours of Homicide Hunter on ID GO.

Friday he'd had supper ordered when Thomas got home, and he'd kept his fool mouth shut to give Thomas time to work through his mad.

Seemed like Thomas had, too. He was laughing and talking with his buddies, talking about work and shit, relaxing enough that the lines around his mouth had eased.

Maybe he should call Angel and go have coffee. Just talk to a friend for an hour. Bullshit. Ask if he was ever going to get this. Ask if it was true that Thomas was in the market for someone here at the club or if it was just that asshole trying to get a rise out of him.

Ask about James, maybe.

He didn't know.

"Boy, go get Master Adam a Perrier with lime and a bottle of water for his boy."

Boy, not sweetheart. Maybe Thomas wasn't as relaxed as he looked after all.

And at what point was *please* not appropriate, for fuck's sake?

"Yessir. You want anything?"

Thomas glanced at him. "No, thank you. But you may get a water for yourself if you're thirsty."

Wasn't he a good dog? Fetching and all *and* he could have a drink of water. *Fucking A.*

Thank God for his hat, or he'd be caught planning chaos.

Oh goodie, Scotty the Ass was bartending. Okay. Simple.

Polite. Do not hit the man in the face. These Yankees got a little weird about that.

Well, not all of them. Daddy Mike's people were pretty good at it.

"What can I do for you, *honey*?" Scotty leaned on the bar, getting a little close for comfort.

"A Perrier with lime and a bottle of water, if you don't mind." The *motherfucker* was implied.

Scotty pushed off the bar and got what he needed and set them down. "Ice for the Perrier?"

"Can you please give me a glass of ice? That way he's covered either way." See him say please and not dickhead? He deserved a cookie. Or a shot of Patron. A shot of Patron with a churro. That worked. Hell, he survived this week, and he was buying himself a bottle.

"One glass of ice." Scotty set it in front of him. "When are you going to stop hiding under that hat?"

He lifted his chin and met Scotty's eyes, staring the man down. He had stared down bulls, bikers, and broncs; he'd be damned if he was going to let this little fuck give him shit.

Scotty gave it a try but didn't last. The bartender dropped his eyes to the glass of ice and pushed it across the bar to Sam. "Better run that over before Master Thomas gets impatient."

That's what he thought.

Sam took the drinks over, thanking God he'd had all that practice serving drinks at the bar because the last thing he needed was to spill. Not that he hadn't done it on purpose once or twice, but this wasn't the place.

"Thank you, Sam." Master Adam gave him a smile and a nod, then opened the bottle of water and handed it to Rick. Rick was quiet—and shirtless because his back had recently been striped bright red. The sub took Adam's hand and kissed it after taking the water, and Adam whispered something in return.

"Good boy, have a seat." Thomas pointed to his stool.

Jesus Christ, the temptation to point out that he knew the stool was sitting was damn near unavoidable, but he let it go. Settle in. Shoulders down. Unclench the teeth. He knew this. Namaste and all that bullshit.

Somewhere in the back of his head, Bowie was laughing his ass off at the thought of him being all peace and light. Just having a total mess of kittens.

"Looks like Clint brought in a little posse of new subs, did you see?"

"I wondered what that was about. Is that Matt talking with them?"

Adam nodded and laughed. "It's like a little freshman class. I guess it's good to have some free agents floating around. There's a handful of unattached Doms. You never know who's looking."

"Mm." Thomas nodded, looking at the group of men sitting around a table with Matt. Or was he watching?

Stop it. Don't let that evil asshole get to you. If Thomas wanted someone else, Thomas could say so.

Sam thought he would probably respond in spectacular fashion, but Thomas could totally say so.

They all looked alike. Was there a sub uniform? Little tight T-shirt, skinny jeans, clean-cut and all.

He was totally growing his beard back out. Long hair was just stupid on him—it was all curly and shit and made his hat fit weird.

Thomas's head tilted slightly; then Mister started laughing. "It's like a little hipster sub club. They all look exactly alike." He felt Thomas's hand land on his knee and give it a squeeze. "Not my style."

He grinned, stroked the inside of Thomas's wrist. It didn't take much, did it, to make him feel good?

"Guys like the newbies; they can mold them into just what they want."

Thomas shrugged, that hand still sitting solid on his thigh. "I tried that, it was a bad call."

Adam laughed. "Indeed. You've gone rogue, Thomas."

"You should try it sometime. It's enlightening."

Sam wasn't sure, one hundred percent, if he was supposed to be worried or pleased that Adam thought Thomas was so far afield. Wasn't being unique a good thing? He thought so. He thought Thomas thought so too. Jesus, Dom peer pressure was a thing.

This whole Mary Poppins mindset could be taken too far. Perfect was impossible. There were no hundred-point rides.

"Well, it's a topic of conversation for sure. I think you've rattled a few nerves. People are starting to worry you don't care what they think."

He could feel Thomas's grin without having to look in the set of those shoulders. "Good."

Adam laughed. "I'm staying on the side of right here."

"What side is that?"

"The side that sees that Clint hasn't thrown you out yet."

Now, hold up. He hadn't done anything worth getting them thrown out. Not one goddamn thing. He was polite, quiet, decent.

"Clint has been supportive, in fact. Sam is a full member now."

"I saw that! Congratulations, Sam. And welcome."

"Thank you, Sir. I appreciate it." He offered Adam a warm smile, a nod.

"You two know you have friends in us. No worries. But I don't think you'll need it; people just take time to come around to something new."

"I'm not worried. I've been a member as long or longer than most of them."

"Truth, old man."

"Wise. I'm wise."

"Wiser than I am." Adam laughed.

Thomas gave his thigh a pat. "Are you ready to work, boy? Our room should be ready."

"Yes, Sir." Maybe he could get rid of some of this tangle of shit and be better for it.

Thomas stood. "Take your stool; we'll drop it off behind the bar. Adam. Your boy looks marvelous, so well-mannered as always." Thomas shook hands with Adam.

"Thank you. He's not in a state to speak at the moment, so I will thank you on his behalf."

"Have a good night." Thomas didn't give him any further instructions, just took off toward the long back corridor.

He grabbed his stool and took it back to the bar, making sure to put it where it wouldn't foul anyone working.

"Scotty, key please?"

"Yes, Sir." Scotty brought him the key to their room. "Your boy looks wonderful tonight."

"Thank you, Scotty." Thomas took the key, but hesitated, looking Scotty over. "Did you get a haircut?"

"I did. Yes, Sir."

"It looks great. Have a good night."

"You too, Sir."

Sam figured Scotty could jack off over that compliment until his dick was raw.

Thomas took him down the hall and let him into the room. They hadn't been in this one before. The room had heavy burgundy curtains, floor-to-ceiling, over all four walls, and a wide padded bench in the center.

"Strip, boy. Put your things by the door."

He hung his hat up and worked his boots off. He had to wonder if the curtains had a purpose besides looking rich. They would be a stone-cold bitch to hang right, he'd bet.

He didn't have to wonder long. Just as he was turning around, Thomas pulled a cord at the opposite end of the room and the curtains on that wall parted, tucking into the corners neatly.

It was hard to tell what was going on with that wall at first—there were so many chains and cuffs and other strange pieces of hardware hanging everywhere. He stared at it, trying to figure the maze out, until the sound of a small motor distracted him, and a set of chains came down from the ceiling, directly over the bench.

"Jesus, would you look at that." He knew he had to be gaping, but while part of his brain was shocked, another bigger part was going, *How the fuck did all that work?* because he loved shit with moving parts.

Thomas's low chuckle was a little disconcerting, though. His Sir went to the wall and pulled down a long, metal bar and placed it near the bench, then pulled down a pair of cuffs, which he attached to the chains that hung from overhead. "Sit, boy."

Man, he totally needed this in the office. Think of the ab work he could do. The back extensions. Just hanging upside down until he got dizzy. The options were endless.

He wandered over and sat.

He understood quickly what the metal bar was for as Thomas crouched by his feet. One thick cuff was wrapped around his ankle and Thomas closed the buckle, then reached for the other side, and his other foot.

Huh.

That was a little weird, but not bad. He had to roll forward a little so that he wasn't sitting back on his tailbone, but he could handle it.

Thomas ran soothing fingers over his calves, just a light, reassuring touch, before standing up. "Are you all right, boy?"

"I think so. It's strange, but I think so, yes, Sir."

"Good boy, thank you." Next Mister put his wrists into those cuffs he'd taken off the wall and set them in his lap, only a little slack in the chains. "Interlock your fingers and place your hands on top of your head. Let me know if that's too hard on your shoulder."

Thomas walked over to the wall again.

"It's not bad." He'd been working the fuck out of the shoulder on the pull-up bar. He wouldn't be surprised if he got it stretched out someday.

"Good boy. I expect it to get tired, but if it hurts or is too uncomfortable, I want to hear a safe word." Mister reached for the wall and touched a plate, and the chains shortened up until they just barely lifted the weight of his hands and the cuffs off the top of his head. "Still all right?"

"Yes, Sir." Weird. Like he was on a practice barrel, kinda, but all right.

"Now you get to make a decision boy. Sight, hearing, or speech. Pick one to keep. And don't worry about safe words, we'll discuss that. Take a minute and think about which one you want to keep."

Except for the first wild rush of panic, that was actually pretty straightforward. He didn't mind the blindfold—hell, he found that easier sometimes—and he knew how to keep his mouth closed, but he'd be damned if he got trapped in his brain with only his thoughts to hear. That might kill him.

"Boy?" Sir stood there in front of him, arms crossed. "Do you have a decision?"

"Hearing." God, he sort of already wanted to go home.

Relax. Remember, no freaking out. No psycho bullshit. Just chill and remember that Thomas is in this with you.

"I'd guessed that, but I wanted to be sure." Thomas dug around behind one of the other curtains and came back, shaking a little ball in one hand. A little bell inside it jingled. "This will be both of your safe words. Shake it for yellow; drop it for revolver." Thomas tucked it into his left hand. "Try both, make sure you trust it. Let me know if you don't."

"Yes, Sir." Sam shook the little thing, dropped it, and when Thomas put it in his hand again he knew—he knew without a shadow of a doubt—that he would screw this up. He would roll it because it was in his hand and that was what you did with shit in your fingers or jerk his hand or something. "So, I have to really make a definite shake for yellow, right?"

Thomas laughed. "Shake it like you mean it for yellow. If you're able to keep that thing completely silent, I'm not doing my job." Thomas checked it, made sure he had a good grip. "Let me hear it."

He shook, letting Thomas's laughter make things better, letting it ease him, straightaway. It amazed him, how that sound made him feel that much lighter.

"Very good. And if you drop it, throw it, or even if it just rolls out of your fingers, that will mean the same thing as revolver. You have my word, boy. Now," Thomas gave him a good look at another contraption. "Do you know what this is?"

He nodded. Yeah. He'd done some research and seen pictures, and no. He didn't need a gag. "I'll keep my mouth shut, I swear."

Thomas chuckled, giving him an indulgent look. "It's a very gentle one, I promise. Open your mouth, please."

Sam was caught between the urge to just demand that Thomas let him go home and the promise that he'd made himself not to act like a kid and just suck it up and quit acting like this was some big deal.

Right, because this was so utterly fucking normal. To let your lover, who may or may not be pissed at you because y'all sure as shit haven't been on point for the last week, tie you up and gag you—with something you have no idea how many mouths it's been in, thank you very much—and blindfold you when you aren't sure what is fixin' to happen and you are in a place that is, at best, totally not on your side. Totally frigging normal, Sam.

And what kind of psycho did this make him? That he was going to let Thomas do it because he didn't want to deal with another week of walking on eggshells? That he was trying desperately to give Thomas something that he was becoming more and more frightened he was not going to be able to do? He didn't understand what Thomas was trying to get out of him.

Maybe it was just the visual.

He was going to have to ask Angel.

"I really can keep my mouth shut." *No hysteria, Sam. You're a fucking cowboy. Act like it.* He stared at Thomas and let his lips part.

"The point isn't what you can do, sweetheart, it's what you can't. Wider, please." He felt the weird ball squeak against his front teeth.

His entire body stiffened, and he informed himself that

he would not barf or threaten to bite Thomas or anything. *Breathe, Sam.*

He opened up and started counting to himself, forcing himself to relax.

"Good boy. That's it, just breathe now, sweetheart. Don't push with your tongue, that's tempting but it won't seat right. Just breathe." Thomas set the ball in his mouth and tightened the strap, forcing his mouth open a bit wider.

"Breathe. Make sure you toss that ball if you start to gag or choke on it. It takes some getting used to. I'm right here." Thomas's hands rested on his shoulders, kneading and rubbing. "Right here, boy. You're safe."

His entire body felt like granite, and he kept sucking air like a mad thing.

"Sweetheart, there's plenty of room to get air; try to relax. I wouldn't suffocate you, would I? Trust me and breathe normally." Thomas's fingers dug deeper into his shoulders, fighting with the tension. "Close your eyes. Breathe."

He let his eyes close, let himself listen to Thomas's voice.

"That's it, boy. Don't fight, just accept it. Just relax. You're safe." Thomas's fingers lifted off his shoulders long enough to fit the blindfold on him, then went right back to their work. "I'm right here."

Please God, please let me do this right for us. Please let me understand.

Thomas's hands moved lower and lower until they were gone and all he heard was Thomas's footsteps, pacing the room.

He counted the steps, comparing how many there were to how many he did on a short run, starting at the apartment door. Thomas was already down to the third floor of the stairs.

"You're making progress with the bondage, boy. You look

good, though not as relaxed as I wish you could be. Do you remember the little feather teaser that I used on you a while ago? Just nod if yes."

Thomas's footsteps moved around him, stopping at his back.

He nodded. He remembered. It had stung like nettles.

"Good boy. I'm glad. So that is what you're feeling now." Thomas ran the soft feathers over his shoulders. "I suspect it won't feel quite the same as it did then. Not yet anyway."

He didn't understand how something so soft could become so sharp. He just didn't.

"Just like the blindfold alone, the fewer things you are able to do, the less you have to think about, and the more you can concentrate on letting things go. The more you give control to me, the less you have to worry about. If I have control, you don't have responsibility. I'm responsible. You're just...existing, relaxing, serving me." The feathers glided across his skin, over and over in the same places, slightly more intense in one spot, lighter in another, drawing his attention. "You can't speak, so there's no need to answer questions or to be coherent. You can't see, you're well-bound, so you can really only experience."

He listened to Thomas's voice, following the cadence, following the ebb and flow, the rise and fall of it and he caught himself breathing with Thomas, looking for that connection.

"That's it, boy. You're mine. I've got you. You just feel." His skin started to heat under the feathers. "I'm switching now. This one is stiffer." Thomas touched him, sweeping the larger feather over one shoulder blade.

He tensed, his shoulder jerking hard as he anticipated that sting. "Shh...relax, boy. Be still." The feather moved to his other side.

Relax. Be still. Breathe. Right. God, he was bad at still. For Thomas he'd try.

The feather was slow, strange torture. It wasn't stinging yet, but it wasn't comfortable either. It was like a continual burn with random pinpricks, like a bad sunburn rubbing on a rough shirt. Like ink without the actual ink.

Ink. He could totally sit for some ink. Something intricate and slow, something he could melt into.

"Lovely, boy." Thomas pulled the feather away and everything went still for a second; then Mister blew cold air across his shoulders.

His arms tightened, and his ass left the bench, the chains' rattle so sudden and loud.

Thomas took him by the shoulders and guided him down again. "Good boy. Pinwheel now, stay as still as you can." Sir touched the pinwheel to the base of his neck, and rolled it lightly down along his spine first, but on the way back up traced it along the curve of his shoulder and through sensitive skin.

His toes curled, and he grunted, the sound huge inside his head.

After that first pass, Thomas didn't let up, driving the pinwheel in random patterns everywhere—down his sides, over his chest, along his abs, and especially across that already sensitive skin.

His muscles jerked and rolled, and there was nothing he could do about it, no way to stop it, control it.

Suddenly the pinwheel was gone, and the room went quiet except for his own breathing and Thomas's. Then he felt hands on his shoulders, pushing him down. It wasn't until he sat on the bench that he realized he'd pulled up again. Thomas unsnapped his gag and removed it.

"Breathe, boy."

He sucked in a deep breath, licking his lips. Had he not been? He wasn't sure.

"Are you all right? What do you need? Is it your shoulder?" Thomas felt close and had a warm hand on his face.

He shook his head, confused as all get out. "My muscles just jerked like crazy. They wouldn't stop."

"I'll get you some water. Do you need me to let your hands down? Take the blindfold off?" Thomas sounded concerned. Not upset or panicking but definitely concerned.

"No. No, I think you must have set off some nerves that I can't even feel anymore."

"Well, you did the right thing, ringing that bell. I'm sure that was disconcerting."

He'd rung the bell? Seriously? "I couldn't stop it. I had no control over it."

"How does everything feel right now? Hang on, water first." Thomas held the bottle to his lips and very carefully let him drink.

Oh. Oh, God, that tasted good—cold and fresh and perfect. "Tingly. Hold the ball, please Sir? Just to stretch my fingers."

And to make sure they'd wake up.

Thomas took the ball and massaged his hands. "If they're numb, I want to know."

"More tingly than numb. I was holding them tight."

"I'm going to let them down." He heard Thomas move away; then his arms grew heavy as they lowered into his lap. "Water is on your left on the bench." A second later, Thomas was taking off his blindfold too.

The urge to ask if he'd messed up was huge, but he knew that frustrated Thomas, so he drank his water and breathed and prayed that he hadn't.

"You're sure you're all right?" Thomas bent and kissed his forehead. "I'm sorry. I should have...sorry." Thomas loosened the clasps on his wrists and pulled the cuffs off.

"It was a muscle spasm. Those nerves are a little wonky, that's all." He offered Thomas a grin. "You got a slightly imperfect model, but they say that former professional athletes have good resale value."

Thomas bent and started freeing his feet. "Not for sale, I'm keeping this one until it's an antique. I just have to...stop playing with it for a while before I break it." What he thought was concern was starting to look more like real worry. Thomas was distracted, not meeting his eyes.

Sam sighed softly. "I didn't mean to."

He hadn't, and now he'd made it worse, not better.

"It's not you. It's not you, sweetheart, you're fine. I'm...off. You did just fine." Thomas took the bar away and set it on the floor along the wall, piling everything else they'd used there with it except his blindfold, which Thomas stuffed into a pocket. "Do you need more water?"

"No, Sir. I'm okay." What was he supposed to do next? His instinct was to give Thomas a hug, but he wasn't sure it would be welcome.

His clothing landed on the bench next to him and his boots on the floor near his feet. "Go ahead and get dressed. We'll head home."

He dressed quickly, biting back the gasp that wanted out when he tugged his shirt on.

Somehow he didn't feel any less tired and, worse, he bet he'd be up all night again.

He grabbed his hat, put it on. "All dressed."

"Great. Good work, sweetheart. Let's go." Thomas may have meant that, but Sir was preoccupied, and it didn't sound all that sincere. They walked down the hall toward the club and out past the bar, Thomas moving at a good clip while he followed. "Will you...no, that's okay. I'll get our coats." Thomas left him standing by the door.

Stand still, eyes down, be quiet.

God, he wanted to go home.

24

S am didn't sleep again.

Thomas woke up alone for the second time that week, and the second Sunday in a row. Granted, Thursday night he'd crashed on the couch, but Sam hadn't made it to bed that night either.

He'd thought trying something new with Sam last night at the club would help them both, and it was possible it might have helped his boy if he'd been able to push through what wasn't working for him. The boy had been trying, he knew that. But it wasn't a safe or sane approach to try to make something work that didn't, and the effort wasn't paying off for him.

Twice in one week. That was wrong.

He'd had a bad run, no question. He'd been handed his ass by one of the higher-ups because he hadn't yet found money for the photography exhibit. He would, he always did, he just wasn't used to the pressure. Add to that the constant underlying worry of coming home to razor blades....

He couldn't say for sure what was going on with Sam,

other than the boy wasn't sleeping. Stress, obviously, but what exactly he couldn't say. That was an issue for sure, wasn't it? He ought to know.

One thing he could say for James's approach—he always knew where to start repairing things when something went wrong. It was either work, their personal life, or their Dom/sub relationship. These things didn't bleed. One could affect another, but he could always find the root neatly separated from other things.

This morning he felt like he'd tossed all his balls up in the air, and not a single one was coming down where he could reach it.

He and Sam weren't communicating. It wasn't the first time they'd had that issue, but the problem now was that he couldn't figure out where the disconnect was happening, and worse, it was possible it was just...everything.

He couldn't fathom a way to untangle something that had been so deliberately entwined. Sam was many things at once in his mind. His lover, his friend, his partner in life, his partner in grief, his boy, his submissive, his reality check.

Yes, he was wishing for James's well-ordered boxes right now.

He made a cup of strong, black coffee and sipped it while he tried to sort through what had gone wrong the night before.

Sam came in from his run, two coffees and a bag of doughnuts in his hands. "Morning."

His boy had huge dark circles under his eyes from sleepless nights, cheeks still flushed after his workout.

"Morning."

Why run when you can come to bed with me?

He didn't understand. Hadn't he just told Sam to wake him up last Sunday? And, frankly, he was surprised that

Sam could run at all. At this point, one had to wonder where the energy was coming from.

He put his coffee cup in the sink and accepted the one that his boy brought him instead, but he wasn't hungry for the doughnuts.

"How're you today? You have want lines."

He put his coffee down with a sigh. "Is it too much to ask for you to spend Sunday morning in bed with me? Is it wrong of me to want that?"

Fuck. That wasn't the way to start this conversation. *You couldn't just say, I'm fine?*

Sam looked at him for a long second, then shook his head. "No. Of course not."

So what the fuck? It was too much to ask this morning, obviously. "All right. So...just on Sundays that you decide not to come to bed, then?"

"I was just ramped up last night. So were you."

He nodded. So, it was his own fault? *Fine.* He picked up his coffee and headed for the couch and his newspaper. At least that was consistently there on Sundays.

Sam disappeared into the bathroom. Thomas heard the shower turn on and off again before Sam reappeared in jeans and a heavy sweater and came to settle next to him.

He glanced over, then back at his paper. "Looks like rain late tonight, and it's going to be strangely warm." There. Weather. Completely noncontroversial except for the fact that it was going to be nearly seventy degrees in February. That fact was most certainly a controversy.

"Yeah? I thought it felt like home a little."

"If home feels humid and warm, you're dead on." He turned the page on his newspaper, already sick of one depressing headline after another. Maybe he'd just skip to the crossword puzzle.

Sitting next to Sam shouldn't feel awkward. He didn't know what to say, and he wasn't sure he could count on Sam to say anything either. He could apologize. Maybe he should, but he didn't know what for yet. Whatever it was that had him "ramped up" had him equally confused.

"Yeah, a little bit. I'm looking forward to showing you around."

"I'm looking forward to the trip." That was the truth, for a lot of reasons. Traveling with Sam, meeting his parents, soaking up everything that made Sam...Sam. "Did you pick dates?"

"I figured April, but I know you have to clear it with your work and all. My people are easy." Sam traced a line on his leg with one finger.

"I'll get you dates. Whoa." His thigh twitched away from the touch and a zing went up his back. He grabbed Sam's hand so the boy didn't get the wrong idea. "Sorry, you gave me chills."

"Magic fingers!" Sam waggled his finger at him. "That's what happened to me last night. A cascade of them."

Last night. He'd rather stick to the weather. "You were twitchy, all right. Muscles jumping all over the place. Pretty wild to watch." He'd never seen that before.

"I bet it looked like rehab. They stick deals all over you and light you up."

"It looked like nothing I'd ever seen. It didn't feel safe to me." He needed to get some advice before that happened again. Or something else like it. Beyond Sam's control was one thing. Involuntary was something else.

"Yeah. I would say I could call my guy, but I don't think he'd quite understand all this."

Sam had a guy? "What guy? A therapist? Can we find you one up here?"

"Yeah. His name's Charlie Watson. Good friend of James. I haven't had to go in a while, so I...I'm sorry it scared you so bad." Sam petted his arm. "Seriously."

"It worried me. But I was also...I don't know. My head wasn't right. Something wasn't working for me." He should have suggested they stay home last night. If he'd really gotten a look at Sam before they went to the club, he might have.

"Yeah, you seemed almost pissed off." That hand kept sliding, up and down, up and down.

"Frustrated. And I should have known...we shouldn't have been there." They could have stayed home, worked where his boy was more comfortable. He had no business pushing. "You did well, though. You wouldn't have been the first sub to choke on that thing."

"I didn't even know I had. I was trying to make my arms stop shaking."

That was exactly what had alarmed him. It seemed like Sam hadn't been aware of a lot of what had been going on. He wasn't even sure Sam realized that bell had rung. By all rights, the boy should have tossed it across the room.

He hadn't ever considered all the challenges of working with someone like Sam—someone with a wild pain tolerance, scars and surgeries, someone who was so new to the scene that he squeaked.

Someone who had a couple of genuine physical limitations but preferred to pretend they didn't exist. Someone willing to push further than he was and seemed to have no idea why.

He really did need some advice.

"Should I worry that you're not sleeping?" That was a ridiculous question; of course he should worry. But he wanted to worry about the problem, not the symptoms.

"I'm just having a little insomnia. I think I'm too tired to sleep. There's a lot to figure out right now."

"Oh, I see. Good to know." He was fairly sure he was still worth consulting, but Sam apparently had decided not to.

"Are you pissed at me?"

He shifted on the couch to look at Sam. "You have so many things to figure out that it's giving you insomnia, but you'd rather just not sleep than discuss any of it with me. Should I be pissed or hurt?"

"Hold up now. You've been giving hard core 'don't talk to me' signals. I was trying to respect your space."

He frowned. "I had a bad week. I rarely have a bad week." He couldn't say he wasn't giving off vibes; maybe he was. He felt like a walking disaster right now. "I need to get dressed." He started to stand up, then sat right back down again. "Oh."

"What's wrong? Are you okay?" Sam reached for him to steady him.

He snorted. "I'm fine. I just realized I was giving off more of those 'hard core don't talk to me signals' by getting up."

"It's okay that you don't want to talk. I know you're having a shit week at work. I tried to be helpful."

He couldn't really fault Sam for not talking when he wasn't either. "I'm just not sure I...I mean, there's not a damn thing you can do. I still can't fund that exhibit is all, and it's caught the attention of some people that think they're in a position to give me shit about it. It's made going in a little tense. You have to demand my time when you need it, sweetheart."

"I know I can't help except to offer to knock heads together, but I want to ease your burden where I can."

Ease his burden? What burden? He'd had a bad week. Otherwise he was the luckiest man alive. "You're good to me." He leaned over and dropped a promise on Sam's lips. He'd get dressed, call Clint up and make an appointment, then take Sam for a walk in the park. Get the boy to talk a little. "Do you mind if I go get out of my PJs? Then we can go enjoy the weather. What do you think?"

Sam chuckled softly, one hand dragging over his ass. "Well, I suppose...I do love how your butt looks in these."

"Good. I'll put them on for you when you actually come to bed with me tonight. Hm?" He winked at Sam.

"If I'm lucky, you won't have to."

"That works for me. I'll be right back." Blue jeans. Maybe he'd wear his hat for Sam. He pulled his cell phone off the dresser as he went into the bedroom and called Clint while he dressed.

"Good morning." Clint sounded...just like Clint.

"Good morning." He looked at his watch. It wasn't that early. "Did I wake you?"

"You didn't. I was reading. How are you this morning?"

Clint was a reader. What the heck did he read? "I'm improving. I had an off night at the club with Sam."

"Did you?" He heard the book settle on the table and the clink of Clint's coffee cup.

He smiled at the visual. All Clint needed was a sign that read *The Doctor is In*.

"Yes. Sam had an involuntary physical reaction that neither of us was prepared for. Muscle spasms like I've never seen. I came very close to hitting that panic button."

"Does he need medical attention? Was it a seizure?"

"No, I'm fairly sure it wasn't a seizure, but it was extreme. He had a bell he was using as a safe word and rang it without realizing he'd done it. He was floating a little at the time; I think he just wasn't entirely aware of what was going on. But yes, I think I should find him a PT. He's been overdoing it lately."

"Overdoing it?" He loved these leading questions.

"He's added in running and upper body. He looks exhausted and a little drawn. I'm not sure he's eating when I'm at work, really."

"Hrm. Are you two in a twenty-four seven relationship? Are you prepared for that?"

"Definitely twenty-four seven." He sighed. "And I'm starting to wonder." Prepared? Not at all. "We've been figuring things out as we go along. It was good at first, but the longer we're together, the more obstacles I'm running into."

"Tell me about what you're facing, then? What aren't you getting?"

Right, because once he could verbalize it to Clint, he could begin to communicate to Sam. Sam wanted to give him what he needed, just like Thomas ached to give to Sam.

"He tries so hard." He shook his head while he pulled on his jeans. "Honestly, Clint. He trusts me without question; he tries everything I ask."

"But what about you? What are you facing?"

"Facing? He's a challenge. He makes me nervous. I worry about my choices. Every single scene we do is something new, and I don't...there's a leap he's not making, and I don't know how to get him there." One mistake could be all it took for something catastrophic to happen. Yesterday was the perfect warning flag.

"Why are you nervous? Why are you questioning?"

"I don't want to make a mistake." He couldn't afford a mistake at this point. "He's more fragile than he lets on. And that trust is so important. It carries over from the scenes to the bedroom to...everything. He trusts me to get it right."

"That's a huge amount of constant pressure, going from sharing keys with James to live in sub with Sam."

He could suddenly hear Sam in his head going, "No shit on that."

"I love living with Sam. That's the best part of this whole thing." All right, why did that come out sounding defensive? "Right. So, it complicates things, but it's worth it. There is some pressure, but I think I put it on myself. Sam is always saying he wants to help." *Ease your burden.* Those words suddenly meant much more than they had ten minutes ago.

"Do you let him?"

"What?"

"Do you let Sam help? Do you let him do the things for you that come naturally to him?"

He thought about that. "Well. He likes to clean my tools and he keeps my boots polished. He brings me coffee in the morning and sometimes he'll arrange dinner. He gives a really nice massage…is that what you mean?"

"So, your Mister O'Reilly understands the value of service." Clint chuckled softly. "Does that help the pressure you're feeling? The tension?"

"It makes me smile. It makes me proud. So, yes, I think it helps. I do wish…" All right. He was talking to Clint, not Sam. He really didn't have to worry about being understood, right? "I wish that when he was enjoying cleaning my flogger, that he wasn't just enjoying it, that he was enjoying doing it *for me*." Submission was a study in context. There was a difference between polishing boots, and polishing *his* boots.

"That is a challenging thing to explain, to understand. You've set him to a project he doesn't love to do and praised him, made the connection that way?"

"No. When I find something he doesn't do with a smile,

I'll let you know." He laughed. "I guess I haven't deliberately tried that yet either. He does things, though. Things he's clearly uncomfortable with, he'll do them because I ask him. He did that yesterday with the ball gag. God, he didn't want me to use that. He tried to convince me he'd just keep his mouth shut."

Clint chuckled. "I can only imagine that would...chafe his pride a bit."

"His pride, his dignity, his...cowboy. Whatever you want to call it. You know, we had this conversation when he had so much trouble kneeling for me. In fact, this whole integrated thing is really your fault." He grinned. Clint's idea was brilliant. It just made him have to, as Adam had said, go a bit rogue.

"It's a process, is it not? If you wanted someone that could act perfectly, you'd hire a professional."

"It is. And I'm enjoying the process mostly. Yesterday was just...I'd had a bad week, he hasn't been sleeping. We probably shouldn't have been at the club. Or not doing a scene there anyway. That was a bad call on my part. Those scenes aren't as balanced as I'd like them to be, I ought to have known I wasn't up for it. Then to have him...well, it left my nerves a little frayed."

"You need to listen to yourself, and maybe...did Mister O'Reilly know you were having a bad week? Did he give you signs?"

"Yes, he knew. We talked about it this morning. And I'm not proud of it but..." Honest with Clint, always as honest as he could be. "I slept on the couch, and he didn't come to bed Thursday night at all. Or last night either. I guess I made it fairly obvious."

He'd meant to make an appointment to have this conversation, not to hash it all out on the phone. Sam would be waiting for him, probably wondering what was taking him so long.

"Well, you two do have an enormous amount of stress. You've both lost someone close to you, he's moved from a Texas ranch to here, there's a stalker threatening you both, he's changed jobs, you've both changed how you live. All in a matter of months. You're bound to have rough patches."

He nodded even though Clint couldn't see. "We're doing well. We've figured out so much already, we'll figure this out too." Of that, at least, he was confident. As long as he could stay patient and Sam could find words, they'd figure it out. "Listen, I promised him a walk in the park. Can we have lunch later this week? Maybe Tuesday?"

"I'd love that. I'll pencil you in and check with you Monday evening."

"Excellent. Thank you, Sir. As ever. Enjoy your Sunday."

"Enjoy your walk."

He hung up the phone. "Sorry!" He called out as he pulled on his sneakers. "I called Clint, I thought that would be a quick conversation." He half-heartedly combed his hair in the mirror and pulled on a hoodie, then hurried out to the living room. "I'm trying to decide where we should go. Do you run over there? You probably know your way around better than I do."

He was met with silence, and he frowned. "Sam?"

There was a note on the table in Sam's so neat handwriting.

Mister, if you're going to tell somebody all about the things I do wrong, at least let me know to go out so I can pretend that I'm not totally fucking this up.

Going for a walk. I'll bring home lunch.

Also, I thought I was doing this for you.

25

T homas looked at his phone. Again. He had it plugged in and sitting on the coffee table because he didn't want it to be dead if Sam tried to call.

When Sam tried...when he called, and he'd call soon. He'd get an Uber home. He was mad, that was fine, they'd work it out. It was just a misunderstanding.

He'd be home soon.

Thomas smoothed his fingers over Sam's note. His boy just forgot to bring home lunch. Maybe went to the movies and turned off that ancient cell phone or got lost in the stacks at the library. Sam lost track of time reading constantly.

Still, a phone call would be nice. They'd talk about that when Sam got home. It was just good manners, so people didn't worry. There were a lot of crazy people in this city, right?

One of them had left a big X on their front door.

Sam was okay, he knew that. Now if he could just get his heart to stop pounding and his hands to stop shaking, that would be good.

Thomas stood up and went to the window. Again. It was too dark to see anything but traffic lights and cars. Still. Same as an hour ago. He couldn't really make out people.

He heard a thump and his eyes snapped up. "Was that the door?"

"No, Tommy. That was just some asshole walking by." Angel's thumbs moved like a blur on that phone of his.

"I'll check." Clint stood up and looked through the peephole. "There's no one there."

"I'm sure he's in an Uber. If he wasn't all right, Angel would know by now." Angel was checking with everyone he knew and couldn't find any sign of Sam. That was good, right?

Right?

He walked over and sat down again, checked his phone, ran his fingers through his hair, pushed Sam's note around on the table.

"He's not fucking anything up, I wish he'd stop thinking that. I'm proud of him; he tries so hard."

This time when he looked up there was someone at the door. Mike was coming back from having a look around the building, Thomas's keys in one hand.

"Hey, Mike," he said. "All good?"

Mike looked at him strangely but nodded and went to say something quietly to Clint.

Clint pursed his lips and shook his head.

Angel glanced up at them, then kept on texting.

"Are you guys hungry? You want to order a pizza or something?" He wasn't hungry. He felt sick to his stomach. But Angel and Mike were big guys. They needed calories.

Clint came to him, sat close. "We'll figure it out. We'll find him. He's just...we'll find him."

Clint needed to move farther away. He could make

himself believe anything, pretend he had it together with Clint across the room, but with his mentor sitting this close...he knew he could be honest with Clint; he wouldn't be judged for being the wreck that he was, he just didn't want to go there.

He was afraid if he let himself lose control, he wouldn't be able to get it back.

"He is fine." He forced the words out like they didn't want to be said, like some part of him knew it was a lie.

"Goddamn it." Angel stood up in a rush and punched at the screen of his phone before putting it to his ear. "Mark. You the one with the John Doe? Ink? Okay, I need a status and a location."

Angel started waving to them, motioning them toward the door.

"I'll get us a car. No problem. Meet me downstairs." Mike was out the door.

John fucking Doe? Oh, God. "How bad is it? Is he alive?" He needed answers. Now. "Clint what did he say about John Doe? Angel..."

"Get your phone and your charger, your wallet. Move, Tommy."

Phone. Charger. All right. Wallet. "Wallet." Coat? His coat. He hurried to the closet, stuffed his phone and his charger into the other pockets of his jacket, and tugged it out of the closet. "It's Sam. Tell him it's not John Doe, it's Sam O'Reilly. Tell him to tell Sam I'm coming."

Angel gave him a thumbs-up. "Sam Houston O'Reilly. Thigh surgery, shoulder surgery...Thomas? What else? Allergies? Birth date?"

"January tenth, he's twenty-six, and...he's allergic to feathers. Real ones. Like from birds."

Angel blinked at him.

"What? Tell him."

Angel relayed the information and they all headed to the elevator. "Looks like he was robbed. No wallet. No phone. Someone found him in an alley around five and called it in. He hasn't regained consciousness, he's lost some blood, and he's been beaten pretty badly, but we all know he bounces back from that."

He listened intently, taking in what all of that meant, what the possible issues could be. Angel hadn't mentioned any specific head or neck injuries thank God. "He's alive. Is he stable? Did they break anything?" After he saw Sam he'd be able to breathe, right? "Where are we going?"

Mike waved them over to a car and they piled in.

"Bellevue ER."

"God, I hate Bellevue." The place was always packed. "Please don't anybody mention his parents in Texas. I made that mistake with James."

"No. No, you're his partner. We have it this time." Clint shook his head. "This is ridiculous."

"This isn't all that unusual," Mike pointed out.

"This is bullshit. So, sitrep. As far as my people know, he's in having a CAT scan, checking for brain bleeds. He is unresponsive, but he was out for a while and he lost blood. Looks like he has a beat-up wrist from defending himself and took a couple hard hits to his head."

Thomas didn't know what to say to that, so he just didn't say anything. A couple of hard hits sounded bad, it sounded really bad. Unresponsive sounded bad. Fuck, it was all devastating.

When the car pulled up he got out and followed close behind Angel who was storming into the ER like he knew where he was going.

He was going to have to call Sam's parents. Text Bowie.

Jesus. Bowie was going to put him through a wall the next time they were in the same room. He'd promised to keep Sam safe. Promised.

Thomas learned quickly that having a certain EMT around was very much like having an angel for real. Before he could think, he was being whisked back to a bay where Sam was on a bed, gray and still.

"You sit here. I'm going to talk to his nurse. He's not in surgery, right? That's good."

"Thank you, Angel." It was difficult, looking at Sam, to think anything was good. He reached out and touched Sam's arm, indescribably relieved when his boy's skin was warm under his fingers. "I'm here, sweetheart, I'm right here."

Breathe. Breathe. Breathe.

He was dealing with so many emotions at once. The last thing he needed to do now was pass out.

Sam sighed, the sound deep, rough, and Sam's fingers twitched.

He looked at Clint. "Did he hear me? Do you think he can?" He slid his hand down and curled his fingers around Sam's. "It's all right, Sam. Just rest. You're safe now. I'm here."

If there was the tiniest possibility Sam could hear him, he was going to make sure the boy heard his voice, knew he was there. Just like in a scene. "I'm here, you're safe. I won't leave you."

Clint pointed at the heart rate monitor, which had spiked. "He's hearing you. He may not even know it, but he is."

He nodded. He could help, then. If Sam could hear him, there was something he could do.

"Fuck, Clint. They really beat the crap out of him." Sam's head was bandaged, his wrist, there were various smaller bandages here and there and the bruises...it was hard to tell where one ended and another began.

A couple hard hits to the head... "They could have killed him." Maybe they were trying to.

"But they didn't." Angel came in, eyes looking at monitors, the big man's presence undeniable. "Because our Little Sammy is a scrapper. Not the most street-savvy kid on earth, but a cowboy through and through. Good news. Bad news. Which do you want first?"

"Jesus." His heart almost stopped. "Don't do that. Just tell me."

"Bad news—his attackers drugged him like he's a bull moose when he's hummingbird-sized. That's basically the good news, too. There's some bruising to his brain, but nothing they think won't heal, but they won't know for sure until he's conscious. The doctor wanted to know how many car accidents he'd been in, and I explained he was a rodeo rider." Angel shook his head. "Someone drugged him to the gills, and he still fought back. They didn't pick an easy target."

"Drugged him with what? Was it the same thing as...as before?" Someone took the time to drug him and beat him up?

"Rohypnol. Different drug, same basic MO. He would have been confused as hell. There's no sign of sexual assault —this was a robbery, man."

"A robbery. He probably had five dollars on him, and his phone is a hundred years old. Sam." He shook his head. "You idiot. Next time just give the asshole your wallet."

Not his Sam. If they hadn't drugged him, he'd have torn them to pieces in that alley.

He stroked Sam's hand with his thumb and smiled. His cowboy. *Christ.*

He wished someone would use all those words that were meant to make loved ones feel better like "stable" and "out of the woods." But with a head injury, he knew until Sam woke up, no one would. Still, Sam was drugged to high heaven and heard him anyway. If anyone on earth could get there, it was Sam.

He just needed patience, and he had plenty.

26

Thirsty.

God, he was thirsty.

Sam flailed for his bottle of water that was always on the bedside table.

He tried to open his eyes when he couldn't find it, but damn. *Damn.* He wasn't sure what he was hung over from, but he wasn't drinking that again.

Shit Marthy.

He felt like he'd had his bell rung but good.

He felt hands on him, one on his arm, another a warm weight on his chest, and he heard a weird, echoing, familiar voice.

What the hell? Okay. *Whoa.* Breathing. He had that down. *Jesus.*

He needed his water bottle and he couldn't find it. Maybe he knocked it off.

"Sweetheart."

Okay, yeah. He knew that voice. That was...uh. He tried to swallow to clear his clogged ears.

"I'm right here."

Water, please. Did that come out? God, his tongue felt six inches thick.

Okay, this wasn't hungover. He knew from hungover.

Sick? Wreck? Come on, man. Think. Where are you?

He was in a bed. Okay. That meant hotel, home, or hospital.

Look at that. Three H's. That was funny.

Except hospital wouldn't be so funny, and this didn't smell like home.

"Sam, you have to lie still. Your handsome Nurse Brady says if you keep flailing around, he's going to have to strap you in, and we both know how much you love that. Just relax, sweetheart."

There was a pause and then, "I think he's thirsty. Can he drink anything yet?" Thomas was talking to that nurse.

"I need to know he can swallow, but yes."

"Do you think you can swallow without choking, sweetheart? Don't nod. Just lift a finger."

Okay. So. Head injury. He knew about this.

He focused and lifted his index finger, curled his toes. All his parts had feeling. Cool.

"I'll get out of the way." The warmth on his chest was suddenly gone, but a straw brushed over his lips.

"Try a sip, Mister O'Reilly."

My name's Sam. He sucked, the water splashing on his tongue, and fuck, his head hurt.

He reached up to hold his brains in, hands finding all these bandages. *Whoa.* Also, *ow.* And *shit.*

And...

Thomas.

His eyes flew open, and he yelled for Thomas to run. *Go. Hurry. Now!*

"Okay, man. You want water, it's probably best not to knock it out of my hands."

"Sorry. I've got him. Shh. Sweetheart. I'm right here." Thomas caught his eyes and he saw that deep brown that went on forever as Thomas tugged lightly on his arms, pulled them away from his head, settled them down again, squeezed his fingers. "Hey. You're safe."

Oh. Oh, damn. Hey. Hey, Mister. You scared me. I thought you were hurt. Lord, my head is killing me. You look tired as all get out.

"Hi." Thomas touched a finger to his lips and smiled. Mister looked a little better smiling. "Shhh. I know you're trying to speak, but we can't understand you yet. Can Brady give you some more water? You have to be still."

Still. Okay. He could be still. He was so thirsty.

"All right, Mister O'Reilly—"

"Call him Sam."

"Right on. *Sam*. Let's get you hydrated."

Sam held his Sir's gaze, letting it ground him, because God knew he needed it. The water hit his belly, and he swore he could hear it splashing inside him.

"You were admitted to Bellevue Hospital last night, sweetheart, and you're pretty beat up. You have a head injury, they're sure you're concussed, but they don't know how badly yet. You didn't need surgery, I was relieved by that, but you still have to take it very easy. All right? It's fine if you can't get words out, it's all fine. It's not a worry. What you need most right now is rest. Just know you're safe, and I'm not going anywhere."

But there wasn't an event here this weekend, was there?

He frowned at Thomas, trying to understand. *What happened?* He'd been...something...waiting? Walking?

"Probably enough water until we see if you can keep it down, Sam." The nurse stepped away.

Thomas cupped his cheek. "The docs expect you to be a little confused, Sam. Don't worry."

Don't worry. Okay. He could work on don't worry. At least he thought he could. He tried sitting up a little, but his head felt gigantic, and his heart slammed, rattling his rib cage. Sure. Maybe staying down was better...

"No, no. Stay down." That nurse was back, hands on his shoulders. "Your partner promised me you'd behave, but if you can't stay still—"

"He'll stay still, Brady. He probably just keeps forgetting. I've got this." Thomas put a hand on his chest again, just a little weight.

"Behave. No sitting up." Brady looked at him seriously before disappearing again.

"I've been worried about you." Thomas gave him a smile. "It's good to see you awake. But you rest when you need to so you can get out of here sooner."

Sorry. He wasn't sure what had happened, honestly, but he knew enough to get that he'd lost time, and that was always a challenge.

"The docs won't let me tell you what happened; they want to know what you remember first, I'm sure now that Brady knows you're awake someone will be in—"

"Promptly."

Thomas looked at whoever had just walked in.

"Promptly. I'm Thomas, this is Sam."

"Nice to meet you both, I'm Doctor Collins." He watched the doctor checking things out. "Sam, I hear you've had some water." The doctor took his hand. "You can try speaking but if that's still difficult, one squeeze for yes, two for no. Do you think that water is going to stay down?"

Yes. Lord, yes. When can I go home?

"You're a little bit scrambled. Breathe and squeeze. One squeeze for yes."

He squeezed.

"Good. Do you know where you are?"

"Oh...I told him a few minutes ago, sorry."

"Okay. Do you remember what Thomas told you? One squeeze for yes, two for no."

He squeezed again.

"Do you remember what happened?"

He pondered lying—because that always got you in trouble, not remembering shit—but he didn't have the foggiest.

He squeezed twice.

The doctor nodded. "Okay. Not to worry, as I'm sure you know with your history, that's quite common. That was a no. He doesn't ride anymore, does he?"

"No." He watched Thomas shake his head; then the doc shined a light in his eyes.

"Good. No more hits to the head, Sam. You've pushed that needle about as far as it can go. Got me? Not even with a helmet. You've had enough."

"Got it." Thomas answered for him.

"Keep the water down today, maybe tomorrow you can eat something. Get some rest, Sam, and I'll see you tomorrow." The doc stepped away.

"That's it?"

"For now. There's not much we can do to help. He needs rest, we need to wait and see about his speech, but he's tracking with his eyes, tracking the conversation. He lucked out."

Thomas snorted. "Lucked out. Can I talk to him now?"

"Yeah. You can if you don't upset him. He needs to stay

calm. He'll get more pain meds and a sedative soon if he needs it."

"Thanks."

Thank you. He just needed to chill out a minute, focus. Figure shit out.

"Hey. I'm going to give you a kiss. Kiss me back for yes." Thomas leaned in and did just that, nice and gentle.

He reached up, blinking as he found a cast on his wrist. Huh.

Thomas caught his fingers and put his hand back down. "Broken in the...would you like me to tell you what happened?"

God, yes. I hate not knowing what I've done. What's been done. The last thing I remember is...we were going to walk? We were walking? Something?

"You do. I know you do. I would." Thomas shifted and took his hand. "So, the answer is, we're not entirely sure. You were...out for a walk and someone drugged you and robbed you, and apparently that didn't sit well with you because you fought them despite the drugs. They think that's how you broke your wrist. You were found in an alley unconscious, you'd lost some blood, thankfully it wasn't freezing out."

Out...whoa. Drugs? What kind of drugs? Did you find me? Lord, he couldn't quite believe it.

"You have questions, I know. I see. Let me think...you... oh. Angel said the drug was a lot like the one on the razor blade but not the same thing. Rohy...Rohypnol, maybe? He'll be able to tell you. They took your wallet and your phone. They didn't take your collar, but the docs don't want you wearing anything that close-fitting, so I have it safe for you."

Thomas stroked his hand, over his wrist, and up his

forearm while talking, keeping contact. "It was a random alley close to Midtown, so you'd walked a good way to get there. There are a couple of bars in the area, but no indication whether you'd been to any of them. Angel made a bunch of calls before he found you. One of his buddies had brought you here to the ER."

He held Thomas's gaze, trying to force his brain to make sense of what he was being told. It wasn't his first concussion, but he never forgot more than a minute or two. This seemed like he was missing a few hours.

Thomas looked right at him, steadily. "Maybe it will come back in a few days. It won't be the end of the world if it doesn't. You're safe, now. You had everyone pretty worried. I've never had so many Doms in the apartment before. Angel, Clint, Mike...they were there for us."

He wasn't sure what it all meant, but he wanted to comfort Thomas, tell him everything was fine. Would be fine.

I want to go home, Mister. Please. Let's just go, okay? You and me—we'll just leave.

"I'm just babbling now. I'm sorry. You should close your eyes and get some rest. I love you, sweetheart. You know that, right? I know you do. It's good to see those eyes. Get some rest, I'm not going anywhere. I promise."

"Love." The sound of his voice shocked him. "Love."

Please stay. I want to go home. Now.

"Oh, I know, Sam. I know. Sleep. I'm right here." Thomas sat in a chair next to the bed and kept hold of his hand.

Okay. He watched, his eyes falling closed, over and over as he fought to keep them open.

Eventually though, Thomas outwaited him, and his eyes closed and stayed there.

27

Thomas couldn't remember the last time he was on a motorcycle. He knew for sure, though, that he hadn't been the one riding bitch. There was something ironic and amusing about him riding as Angel's second that he thought Sam would love, and he filed the experience away to share the next time his boy woke up.

He didn't like leaving Sam in the hospital; he had promised he wouldn't go anywhere. But Angel and Mike weren't taking no for an answer and they did have a fair point—he hadn't left Sam's side for three days, and he needed a shower. It was Angel that had finally convinced him, and the man was right. He needed to take care of himself so he could take care of Sam when he brought his boy home.

Mike was there. He was a friend to Sam, and he would make the boy understand. Hopefully.

Part of him was shocked not to find razor blades everywhere when he got home. With days to fuck around, he thought for sure their stalker would manage something spectacular, but no, everything was fine. How wrong was it that he'd been simply expecting something instead of dreading it? He'd disconnected the emotions—somehow that didn't seem healthy.

Everything was fine, though, and it didn't seem like Sam's mugging was at all related. Just another day in New York.

He shaved and finished his shower, feeling fairly refreshed, then put on clean jeans and a long-sleeved T-shirt. It was amazing how much better he felt for just those few simple things. He packed up a bag for Sam with T-shirts and sweat pants in it, the iPod that Sam ran with since the boy's phone was gone, and added the collar that had been in his pocket for days to the bag as well.

He'd get Angel to take him back to the hospital. Maybe Sam hadn't even woken up and he'd luck out.

"Thanks, Angel. That shower felt fantastic. I'm ready to go."

"Great. Where do you want to eat?" Angel hauled off the couch and stretched. Jesus, it made the man look massive.

"Oh, I'll just get something at the—"

"Fuck that. I'm taking you for real food and a beer."

"Angel. I have to get back to Sam; he needs me."

"He did just fine for months in the other apartment. He managed by himself for years. He can handle the hospital for a few hours with Mike."

He stared at Angel. "You're really not going to let me go back there yet? Did you and Mike plan this out?"

"Would we do that? I'm hungry. You're hungry." Angel stood there, arms over his chest. "He's sleeping. He's starting to talk easier. Mike is there."

"Fine." He sighed. He was hungry, that was true, and the longer they stood there and he thought about real food, the hungrier he got. "Burgers? Italian? Just not more pizza and salad bar."

"Burgers and beer, bay-bee." Angel grinned at him. "Your bag will fit in the saddlebags. Are Sam's folks coming out?"

He shook his head. "She said so long as I had him, it wouldn't do anyone any good."

She'd talked to Sam, he'd chuckled, and she'd just said that she was needed there at the ranch.

Bowie'd had more to say.

"Go ahead. I'll lock up." He locked the door, checking it twice, as usual. "I just don't understand, Gabe. Why Sam? What the hell could he possibly have been doing that someone...what? Roofied his drink at a bar? They don't even know how he...he wouldn't have gone looking for a fight, would he?"

"If he wanted one, he knew how to find one, I think. Could have been the hat. Could have been the 'y'all.' Hell, it could have been anything." Angel shrugged. "Shit, maybe he's just fucking unlucky."

"Shit, his hat. They took his hat." That was somehow worse in his mind than the wallet and the phone. He waited for Angel to open up one of the saddlebags, and he put Sam's things inside.

"We'll find him another one. You'll have to buy him a new pair of jeans too. The boots are intact, if in need of a cleaning." Angel didn't seem to understand how important this was.

He shook his head as he climbed onto the bike behind Angel. "But that was *his* hat. That hat was..." He wasn't even sure he could to explain it. Sam had other hats. But that was the one he wore every day. That was the one he wore to the club.

That was...Sam's hat. There was a little piece of him that was just intuitive enough, or maybe even cowboy enough, to get that much at least. The way that Sam understood that he wanted to keep James's hat.

Maybe it was hard to explain because there just weren't words for it.

He got comfortable and gave Angel a thump to let the man know he was ready.

At least Sam was starting to make sense. That first day there had been nothing comprehensible; then more and more words started to come together.

Now they were mostly "I love you" and "Take me home." Both of which made his heart ache a little, for different reasons.

The burger place was busy, lots of people enjoying food and company, and just the vibe made him feel a little better. Maybe this was a good idea after all. Maybe it was all right for him to unplug from that damn hospital and feel human for an hour.

He dropped his jacket over the back of his chair and took a seat. "All right, you win. I'm hungry."

"Of course you are. Man cannot live on hospital shit alone. You can't do your job like this, and it's going to get harder in some ways when he's home and restless."

"Yeah, no kidding. He's a challenge when he's keeping busy. His brain just...never stops." Restless. He wondered if Angel understood how restless Sam could be already. It would be a little while before he could bring his flogger into play again, which was the most effective way to bring them both some peace. He'd have to get creative. *More* creative. God. "Well, he's been laid up before. Maybe he's got coping skills. I can hope, right?"

"Shit, he's been torn up a bunch. I imagine you'll just

have to tell him no long runs for a couple days." Angel grinned at him, the look wicked.

"Oh. Good idea. He listens to everything I tell him." He rolled his eyes.

He let Angel order him a beer, and they both ordered burgers. He was reminded of the last time he had a burger with Bowie. He wasn't entirely sure where they stood at the moment, but he didn't think Bowie was too pleased...well, with either of them, frankly.

But then, he'd been more honest with Bowie than he had been with Sam, hadn't he? He'd told Bowie everything. He hadn't gone through the story of why Sam left the house alone with his boy yet.

His coat slid off the back of his chair and when he caught it, Sam's note fell out of the pocket. He snatched it up like it was precious and spread it out on the table, reading it again.

...pretend that I'm not totally fucking this up.

...thought I was doing this for you.

He sighed. "I guess we have a lot to work on when he's well enough."

"Isn't there always stuff to work on?" Angel looked over at him, one eyebrow lifting. "I mean, isn't that part of the fun?"

He squinted. Fun.

Sitting in Sam's hospital room, with his sleep patterns regulated by when his lover decided to be awake and when the nurses decided it was time to check vitals, he'd had a lot of time to think. Too much. Enough to realize that things with Sam were amazing, to understand more fully all the ways that Sam had filled holes in his life, in his heart, that needed it. And enough to know that something was off.

"Something is missing." That was how it felt, the

thought that had occurred to him just that morning, "We're out of balance."

"Yeah? I can see that. Sam's a different bird than James was, for sure." Angel just laid it out there, didn't he?

That made him smile. No stress, just the facts, hm? "He's a whole different species. There's virtually nothing even similar between them. James essentially begged me to accept his submission, relinquished himself to me. It was beautiful. Sam is also beautiful. He's trusting, his needs are deep and complicated. He submits physically, but he doesn't..." He shook his head. "Something is missing. A connection. Here." He tapped his forehead with one finger.

"Have you ever watched him fight?" Now that question came from left field.

"Watched him...? No." He didn't think that was something he ever wanted to do, either.

"I have. A few times. He starts slow, Little Sammy, letting himself test the waters, try out a new guy, see how it works. Then he starts fighting back, kicking ass some. A couple times, though, he lost it. Like just let himself open up and lose his shit. Thought it was interesting, me and Mike did, how you know once Sammy lost it, it would be a long time before he'd be looking for a fight again."

He thought about that, he knew Angel was trying to tell him something, but he just wasn't sure what it was. The first part was fairly obvious as analogies went—testing him out, fine. Fighting back a little, sure, he could make that connection. But what about... "You're telling me you think he needs to lose it? I don't understand."

"I'm telling you that he needs to believe you can take it —his submission. He doesn't know how to give it yet." Angel shook his head, smiled at him. "Forgive the comparison, but Sammy's a little like having a wolf living with you. He can take you, you both know it, but you have to be the alpha so he can find where he fits."

The server brought their beer, but he didn't even look at it, he just stared at Angel. "He thinks I'm not tough enough. I...I'm not demanding enough. Is that it?"

Angel sipped his beer, put it down. "I think that it's impossible to submit when you're spending all your energy holding on to your control with both hands, so you don't let your Dom down."

He sighed, exasperated, and picked up his beer. "I don't get it, Angel. Let me down? How the hell could he possibly think...he trusts me. We've spent a lot of time figuring out how things work for us and learning how to communicate. We've put a lot of energy into...wait." Hold on. He took another sip of his beer.

"We've done a lot of negotiating, but we haven't...I haven't set any rules. He doesn't know where the boundaries are." He looked up at Angel again. "He doesn't respond well to rules."

"No, but they're there for reasons." Angel said that like he'd said it a thousand times.

He nodded, feeling that he was starting to see what Angel was getting at. "They are. But it's hard when we live together. I don't know if he'll accept them full-time."

Their burgers arrived and he picked up a french fry and chewed on it thoughtfully. "You know he won't kneel for me. I mean, he will but he doesn't like it. It makes him very uncomfortable. I think he thinks it's humiliating."

"Have you spoken to him about it? Honestly, I watched him work, Tommy. The kid never chafed at the rules."

"He needed that job; it's not the same thing. Unless..." Unless it was. Sam followed the rules to get the paycheck he needed. Would the boy follow rules to get other things he needed?

"I really want us both to get what we need, every time. It's not like it never happens, it's just..." Would Sam follow his rules just so that Thomas could get what *he* needed? That was the real question. "He needs me to take his submission. I suppose I've got something to think about, Angel."

He took a bite of his burger and ended up sucking half of it down in four bites. He hadn't realized just how hungry he was. Talk about out of balance.

Angel ordered them more onion rings and shakes. When he opened his mouth to argue, Angel popped a french fry into his mouth.

"Okay, so let me ask you this. Do you think you'll be able to patch me up after Bowie gets his hands on me?" He grinned at Angel and picked up his shake.

"If he shows up, bring him to me." That was an evil twinkle in Angel's eyes.

He laughed. That would be something to see. "Yeah, sure. If I live that long." Of course, he thought Bowie was actually equal parts annoyed with him and exasperated with Sam. "This shake is really good." He was going to crash in a food coma when he got to the hospital. Sam had better not have convinced Mike to get released while he was at dinner.

For a second, Thomas genuinely panicked. Just the thought of Sam walking out of the hospital overwhelmed him a little, and Angel nudged his leg.

"Breathe, Tommy."

"Sorry. Shit." He blinked and took a deep breath. "Will you please take me back to the hospital now?" He needed to be with Sam.

"I will. You think Sam would like a milkshake to go?"

He smiled at Angel. The man was such a good friend. "He might take a few sips. We've been babying his stomach a little, but he's doing fairly well." It would be fun carrying that on Angel's bike.

Soon they were off again, heading for the hospital, for Sam. It was good, letting the wind blow out the food coma cobwebs, letting himself breathe for a second.

He climbed off the bike and grabbed Sam's things, then followed Angel inside through some super-secret EMT lounge and up a private elevator. It really was nice to know people. "It's like being a VIP."

"It makes things easier. I'm going to talk with the nurses and find out how today went, when they're chatting about releasing him." Angel knew how to get the information they needed, and for the thousandth time today, he gave thanks for his friends.

"Thanks so much." He ducked into Sam's room and found Mike sitting in one of the chairs. "Hey. All good? Thank you for this."

"Not a problem. He got up once for the bathroom, but that was it. He made it fine, but I'm not sure he even saw me. He turned on the TV and immediately fell back asleep." Mike chuckled softly, shook his head. "I'm going to get home, hmm? You holler if you need me."

It sounded like Sam didn't actually wake up for that bathroom trip. He stuck out his hand. "We will. Thanks so much, Mike. I needed some air more than I realized."

"It's tough, having your boy hurt." Mike enveloped his hand in a shake. "His stitches are itching. He keeps reaching for the bandages."

"Yeah. Thanks." That had been going on since last night.

Maybe he could ask someone about it. "He's a trooper. I bet I get him home soon."

"Yeah. I bet day after tomorrow. He's ready, huh? To get back to his life, his bed?"

"Mister? That you?" His boy had radar.

"He is. And that's me. Thanks again, Mike." He gave Mike's shoulder a squeeze and went to Sam. "Right here, sweetheart. Everything all right?"

"I want to go home." Sam was trying to get at his bandages. "I'm hot. I need a shower and a drink and to be home with you, huh?"

"I'll ask again, boy. But I think it will be another day or two." Sam asked to go home constantly, completely undaunted by how many times they said no. He gently took his boy's hands in his and lowered them into Sam's lap, then started folding the blankets. He was fairly sure the best his boy was going to do was a sponge bath until they got home. "I brought some things for you. Sweats and your music."

"Oh, you rock. Thank you." Sam watched him like a hawk, like he might disappear. "I just need to go home and rest. I'll be okay. I don't like the soft cast. It's hot. Everything here is."

"Soon enough. Breathe, boy." He went right to the bag he'd brought and pulled out the iPod and the boy's collar. Sam was getting itchy, anxious, and he wasn't going to be flogging a boy with a concussion, so they needed to work on some coping skills quickly.

"I think you're upright enough that you can have this." He put the iPod down on the bed, then reached for Sam and put the leather collar around his boy's neck where it belonged. "Stop touching your head when you're uncomfortable and touch this instead. Right here." He took his boy's fingers and placed them on the metal ring.

Sam's face visibly relaxed, and Thomas wanted to cheer, but he settled for a soft kiss on his boy's lips.

"Better. Good boy." Next he helped Sam out of his hospital gown and into some underwear and soft sweat pants. He didn't really care whether the nurses liked it or not, his boy had limited patience, and little comforts would help keep him calm.

"All right. I suspect they will yell at me for giving you this. Just keep the volume down very low. The cops didn't recover your phone, so I hope there's enough on this iPod to keep you happy for a day or two." He helped Sam with the earpods. "Volume very low, boy. Actually low, not just low for you." He grinned. He knew his boy liked the music loud.

He had a feeling they might try to take the iPod away, but if Sam could find a volume that was low and comfortable, he'd argue with the nurses. He knew his boy better than they did; the distraction was imperative. Sam was about to lose his mind with all this sitting still.

"Oh. That's perfect. What do I do about my phone?" Sam stroked his arm, petting him, touching him.

"We'll have to get you a new one. I contacted the carrier to let them know it was stolen. Don't you worry. I'm on it. I can't help with your wallet, though, I don't know what was in it. You can deal with that when we get you home."

"My picture was in there. The one with the three of us." Sam looked at him in a panic. "Mister! That's the last time we were together."

Goddamnit. How much more did the Universe think his boy could stand to lose? He took Sam's hands in his. "I'm so sorry, sweetheart." He'd text Bowie. Maybe someone else had a copy of that same picture, or one like it.

He didn't want Sam to dwell on the emotions

surrounding that picture, not right now. "Hey, I just took a ride on Angel's motorcycle. He drives like a fiend."

"He does. I've been for a bunch of rides." Sam sighed softly. "I need to go home, get back to work. I...I'm going to tell them in the morning. They can't make me stay here."

"You'll do no such thing, boy. Angel is talking to them now, and he's getting your status. You'll stay put as long as they say. And when you do get home, you'll adhere strictly to your restrictions, and you will not push. I want you home too, but I plan to enforce doctor's orders. I presume that's clear enough for you."

Sam stared at him, wide-eyed; then he just slumped back on the bed. "You're supposed to be on my side, you know."

"I believe we're all on the same side, aren't we? I'm looking after my sub, and my own best interests. I can't take a flogger to a boy that hasn't healed properly." He let himself smile, having gotten his point across. "There's also the little matter of being in love with you. I want to see you back doing the things you want to do as soon as possible."

"Tomorrow. I know it." Sam opened his eyes, gaze dragging over Thomas's face. Thomas could almost feel the touch, the way Sam drank him in. "Miss our bed and waking up next to you."

He appreciated that look and let Sam enjoy it, but he didn't let it sway him. He didn't think it would be tomorrow. Probably the next day, like Mike had suggested. He was interested in what Angel could find out. "I miss you in it and...I hate waking up alone." He *hated* it. Once Sam came home, he'd make sure it didn't happen again.

"I know. I remember..." Sam frowned suddenly, brows lowering. "You...are you still mad at me? Were you mad? Is that right?"

"No. It's not important. We can talk about it another time." Or not at all, that would be just fine with him.

"I keep trying to remember things, but there's a hole. I remember I brought home coffee. I remember a shower and...then it just goes black. I don't know. I can't remember what happened."

He lifted one leg and perched on the edge of Sam's bed. "We had a rough night at the club the night before; do you remember that? I'd used a ball gag on you. You had an involuntary reaction...?"

He really didn't want to rehash this right now, but what was he going to do? Deny Sam his memories? Pretend like it didn't happen?

"Muscle spasms. Yeah. All those nerves that you tickled that I couldn't feel because of the scars." Sam nodded, the motion careful, slow. "I shook the ball and didn't know it."

"That's right, and it worried me. It had already been such a difficult week. You weren't sleeping, so much on your mind, and I was irritable about work and keeping to myself....We hardly spoke when we got home from the club. I went to bed, and you never joined me."

"I'm sorry." Sam squeezed his hand, and Thomas hated the little tremor in the touch. "I don't think I wanted to fight with you."

He covered his boy's hand and held on. "No. No, you didn't, neither of us did. We weren't fighting, I think we were both just out of gas and not coping well. I wasn't mad. I know you weren't."

"I want to come home and just sleep for a day or two. Just rest." Sam shifted, then moved to sit up. "Going to see if I can't use the restroom. I'll be back."

"Hang on, sweetheart." He pulled the earpods out of Sam's ears and set the iPod on the nightstand. Mike said the boy had done this on his own while he was gone, but it made him nervous to let Sam walk alone. "Let me help."

"Okay. I do okay. I want the bandage off." Sam grabbed his IV pole with his uncasted hand and started to stand. "I want the IV out too. At least the catheter is gone, right?"

"Hey, they trust you to get up and pee. That's a step." He spotted Sam to standing and took a few steps with him, but Mike was right, his boy seemed to be fairly steady considering. He backed off and just followed along in case. "You're looking good, boy."

"I'm a stud." Sam looked at himself in the bathroom mirror, lifting the medical tape to peek under the bandages.

"We'll talk to the nurse about those, but I assume they are still there to keep you from scratching. You were even doing it in your sleep."

"The stitches itch. I'm gonna look like Frankenstein's monster. Grr. Rar."

Thomas laughed. "Terrifying. Go do your business, Franky. I'll wait out here."

Sam was sounding more like himself by the day. In some respects, by the hour. It was a relief, but in some ways it was also a warning. Sam's cheerful personality was returning, and along with it the boy's persistent anxiety, which needed managing and wasn't going to resolve in a hurry given this incident. Sooner or later they'd have to get around to talking about the reason Sam left the apartment that day, and perhaps even something of what happened after the boy left home if Sam could remember. They had work ahead of them.

In fairness, not giving in to his boy's impatience was a bit of a trial. He wanted Sam home too—tomorrow would be perfect, even right now would work. It was astounding to him how quickly and naturally his apartment had become theirs. Their home. Their little bit of peace. He'd get his boy home, tuck him into their bed, and let Sam rest as long as the boy needed.

Possibly longer.

That thought brought his smile back.

28

"I want to go home." Sam stared at the neurologist, willing the man to hear him. "Now. I swear I won't whack myself in the head. Just let me go home."

He was tired and hurting and ready to get back to real life. Emails and pizza and snuggling and crunches and long showers. He wasn't going to take no for an answer.

"Mister O'Reilly, you have a bruised brain."

"Is it getting less bruised in here?" He hadn't had to have a piece of skull removed, so he was okay, for the most part, right? "I can walk, I can talk, I can pee."

If his patience wasn't where it normally was? Fucking sue him. He couldn't afford this.

Mister's long, heavy sigh was obviously disapproving. That was frustrating; he knew Thomas wanted him home too. What was the problem?

"Doctor Marsh, what are the reasons you'd want to keep him here?"

Obviously to make him insane. Wasn't that clear?

"The danger zone for a brain bleed is four to six days."

"It's Friday!"

"Calm down, sweetheart." Mister put a hand on his arm as if to say, "Let me handle this."

"I understand. And what's your experience with patients with no sign of trouble developing a bleed on that sixth day?"

"It's highly unlikely, but you have had a serious injury. You need to be incredibly careful, if I agree to release you."

"I promise not to bash my head against the floor, Doc." At least not hard.

"He won't be alone for a minute." Thomas looked at Sam and grinned. "Except to pee."

"Mister Ward—"

"Sorry. I will keep a close eye on him. I'd prefer he not end up back here, and I'm sure he feels the same way. He needs rest and he needs to relax, and that's just not happening here. I think he'd be better off in his own bed."

Hey, maybe Mister was on his side after all.

"You'll need to watch the stitches, watch for confusion, dizziness…"

The doctor kept talking, but Sam stopped listening. He was going home. He needed to get dressed.

He grunted at Thomas, not once, but twice, when his lover pressed him back down into bed. Was that doc still talking?

"I very much appreciate your understanding, Doctor. I think Sam would have caused some trouble if you made him stay another day."

"I think that Mister O'Reilly needs to consider taking care of himself a bit better. You have a number of major injuries for a twenty-six-year-old."

"I'm a cowboy." What else was there to say about that?

"Rodeo. Clear as mud, right? We know, no more concussions."

The doc shook his head. "Good luck, then. Both of you."

Thomas turned to him as the doctor left the room and smiled.

"Thank you. Time to get the IV out. Now." He could do it. He knew how.

"Patience, boy." Mister's voice was stern, and those brown eyes narrowed.

"I have been patient. I've been good. I've done all the things. I want a real shower and a real night in our bed. I want to sleep with you. I want a not-shitty cup of coffee." *Whoa.* Was he whining? He might be whining.

Thomas sighed dramatically. "I think I might have made a mistake. How the hell am I going to rein all of *that* in?"

"I just need to get home. Back to normal. Real life. Not this. This is hell." He needed to deal with his bank, his phone, his emails. Hell, he needed to be able to breathe and be naked and smell like himself again.

"I know, sweetheart. Just another hour or so, right? Let the nurses do their thing, we'll get your discharge papers, and I'll take you home."

"Hey! Mister I Want to Go Home is going home!"

"Brady." Thomas nodded.

"Okay, Sam. Tell me what you want." Brady grinned at him.

"Take out the IV, give me whatever meds you have to, and sign my ass out. Please. Now." *Home. God. Home.*

"Can do, cowboy." Brady laughed. "Damn, I am so glad to see you go. And I mean that in the nicest of ways." And just like that, the IV was out and Brady was putting a Band-Aid with some gauze under it in its place. "Get dressed. I'll get your meds and your chart."

"Right on." Okay. Clothes. Sweats? Jeans? Were his boots here? What about his hat? *Christ.*

Thomas offered an arm. "Now, you can get up. I've got sweats and T-shirts. Uh...your running sneakers."

"Okay. Thank you." *Please God, don't let me pass out or puke when I bend over. Thank you. Amen.*

It was like Mister was listening in, because he got no help at all. Thomas just stayed close by and watched him, in that way his Sir always did, eyes busy and thoughtful.

He managed his pants and shoes, panting openmouthed as he sat up, willing the nausea to pass; then he looked at his T-shirt. *Fuck.* Was that going to fit over all his bandages?

"Hm. Be right back." Thomas left the room and when Mister reappeared, he was following on Brady's heels.

"Happens to everyone. Your partner wouldn't be the first to forget a button-down."

Thomas coughed. "In my defense, I didn't think he was going home until tomorrow."

Brady handed paperwork and a bag that seemed to be from the pharmacy to Thomas and held up a pair of scissors. "Can I sacrifice this one, cowboy?"

"Yeah. Yeah, I'll need one until they release my noggin." He hadn't even bothered to look at the scars. He knew they ran all over the left side of his head, but his hat would cover them, most of the time, even if his hair grew in weird.

Brady cut a slit down the front of his T-shirt, then helped him get it over his head. "Your man has your paperwork, your meds, and all your discharge instructions. All you have to do is listen to him."

"Not to worry."

Oh. He wasn't sure he liked that tone.

He held out one hand to Brady, willing it not to shake. "Thanks for all your work, man. Seriously. You rock."

Thomas did the same. "Thank you, Brady."

"Take care of each other. No hitting your head."

"I'll do my best." He made no promises.

"You ready to go, stud? I got us a car; it should be downstairs in a minute." Mister pointed to the wheelchair sitting outside in the hall.

"I can walk it." He could. Seriously.

"Hospital rules, man. Don't get my ass in trouble."

"Sit, sweetheart."

Mister said "sweetheart," but he heard "boy."

"Okay. Okay, sure. Lord have mercy." He sat, his eyelids a little heavy, the world feeling a little out of his control, a little too big, a little too loud.

The wheelchair moved and it was so damn weird, sitting like this, moving and being low. He remembered this from when he'd busted his leg. The world looked different from a wheelchair.

"That's probably our car," Thomas told Brady once they got outside. He got up, but a bunch of hands kind of placed him in the back seat. He didn't really feel like he'd walked it. Then the car was moving. He tried to keep his eyes closed, but he was fighting the queasy, so he went for open.

"Y-you ready to get home, Mister?" *Talk to me, man. I'm feeling off-center.*

Thomas rubbed his thigh with a firm hand. "I am. You're clearly still unsteady, so I'm a little nervous about getting you home to be honest, but I'd rather have you there than anxious and unhappy in the hospital."

"You'll be amazed at how good it'll be, to get a real night's sleep." All he wanted in all the world was for Thomas to hold him for a while. Just to hold on and let the constant itch ease. To hear normal sounds. He just needed for things to go back to real.

Thomas found his fingers and tangled them together. "I

don't give a shit about sleep; I just need to get my arms around you."

"God yes. Please." The words sounded shattered, cracked plumb in half, and Sam found himself scared to say anything else. The hospital had been...weirdly safe, different enough that he could ignore the part of him that whispered about how he'd been drugged. Beaten. Damn near killed. And he didn't remember.

"Hang on, boy. We're almost home." Thomas squeezed his fingers. "I'm right here."

"I know. I'm okay. Just ready." He found Thomas a smile because he didn't want anyone to believe this was a bad idea. Not for one second.

"Mm. You and I both know you're not, but I agree this is better for now in any case." The car pulled up outside their building and Thomas helped him out, letting him lean as much as he liked. "Just a few more steps, right?"

"Yeah. We need my bag of stuff, huh?" He focused on the door, focused on one step after another. Just need to get to the elevator. Get upstairs. Get inside. Get sat down.

"Right. I've got it." Thomas dragged the bag off the seat and looped it over one shoulder. "Just take it slow, I've got you."

They made their way inside, but once through the breezeway doors, Thomas lifted him right off his feet.

"Mister!" He sucked in a breath of air, his eyes rolling back in his head. "You're going to hurt yourself!"

Sir snorted and managed to hit the elevator button with his elbow. "You know, I'm not the delicate flower you seem to believe I am, boy."

They got on, but Sir still didn't put him down. "I've obviously given you the wrong impression."

"What?" He wasn't following along. Sam loved Thomas,

didn't want to hurt him, stress him out. That was good, right?

He didn't get an answer until they were off the elevator and Sir had to put him down to fish a key out and open the door. "I'm not going to hurt myself by picking you up, boy. And I'm not going to...*hm*. A conversation for another day. We're home."

"Oh." He couldn't have stopped his smile for all the money on earth. "Thank God."

They managed to make it inside and lock up, both of them leaning together for a moment.

"Let's get you comfortable and off your feet." Thomas got an arm around his shoulders, got him down the hall, and sat him down on the bed.

"Oh..." He toed off his shoes and curled up on his right side, his head cradled on his pillow. *No crying. None. Just close your eyes.*

Thomas slid into bed, tucking in tight behind him, and wrapped an arm over his chest. "Is this all right, sweetheart?"

He tried to nod, but it didn't want to work, so he croaked out, "Perfect. Oh, God. I-I missed home."

"I missed holding you. It's all I've wanted to do since you went missing." Thomas's fingers balled into a fist against his sternum, and the last couple of words sounded thick in his lover's throat.

Sam took Thomas's hand in his, catching it against his cast and bringing it to his lips. He kissed each knuckle, trying to decide whether he should be sorry for getting hurt or just grateful to be home.

The sigh behind him was heavy. "Go to sleep, sweetheart. Everything from here is going to be slow-going; we have plenty of time."

"Mmm. Stay with me, please." He let himself lean, let himself breathe and believe. He didn't need Thomas to answer out loud; he knew better. Thomas wanted this as bad as he did. They just held on like children in a stampede, trusting they'd see it through to the end.

29

The first thing Thomas did when he woke up and untangled himself from his lover, was get out his phone. Their bedroom was still dark, the blueish dawn just beginning to sneak through the blinds. It looked as if Sam had barely moved overnight. His boy was still curled up, but he could see even in the low light how much Sam had relaxed.

He'd already texted Bowie, asking about that damn photograph. He wasn't hopeful, but it couldn't hurt to ask since he had no hope at all that they'd recover Sam's wallet. He needed to let everyone know that he'd brought Sam home, but no one in their right mind was awake at this hour but him. He'd wait at least until the sun was up.

So that left him with work email that he had no interest in focusing on and watching his boy sleep. He'd had a lot of practice at that this week, but Sam hadn't been in their bed, and the boy hadn't really been sleeping. This, he was fairly convinced, was the real deal.

Sam began to shift and move, pushing closer, searching for where he had been. His sensitive boy.

He smiled and put a hand on Sam's side, gliding it down to the boy's hip and back, and whispered, letting his boy know he was there and trying to help Sam settle again.

He looked at the time, realizing that it was probably time for more meds. Neither of them had eaten anything since yesterday afternoon, either. It was no wonder Sam was waking up restless.

"Oh, Mister. We're home." The utter satisfaction in Sam's still-asleep voice hit him in the pit of his gut.

"We are." Home, safe, and mostly sound. His smile grew and he bent and kissed his boy's shoulder. He finally felt right for the first time in days.

"Mmm." Sam leaned harder, almost turning over. He pressed close, keeping Sam where he was. The stitches went near the back of Sam's head, and they'd already discovered how jarring rocking onto those were.

He realized that he'd been so focused on Sam's recovery and just getting the boy home, that he had no agenda whatsoever for the day. Or even the next few. He supposed that was best, considering he had no idea what they would bring. He knew Sam would have questions, frustrations, and would just need a lot of physical help.

His only plan was to stay close and look after his boy, enjoy their little sanctuary, just keep the world out. And keep Sam from doing anything crazy.

Because that was going to be a full-time job.

"Mmm. I need to get up at some point and use the restroom, but it's good here."

"When you do get up, I'm putting you right into the tub." No point in wasting the boy's energy walking back and forth. "You need a bath." He grinned. "Oh, and good morning."

"Good morning. I love you. I could totally use a shower. I

smell like the hospital. Shower. Coffee. I'll even share my Cocoa Puffs."

He laughed. "I love you, sweetheart, and that's kind, but no thank you." Bath. Not a shower. This was going to be an argument, he could tell. "Hey, I have a nice long day of doing absolutely nothing planned for you."

Sam chuckled softly, fingers tracing his hand. "I may actually have the energy for that. Maybe."

"Let's call it a goal." He tucked his arm over his boy. "It's dawn. We slept forever."

"We both needed it, hmm? No one woke us up all night."

He felt better and better the longer he lay there chatting with his boy. Uninterrupted sleep mattered more than he'd realized. "Nothing was beeping, no lights going on and off, no ambulance sirens right out the window....I think your room was just a couple of floors above the ER." After a while, one noise was as bad as another.

"I know, right? I felt like I was losing my mind. Now I feel like I can think enough to make some decisions. You know, the big ones like, do I want some milk in my coffee and do I ever want to see anything on the Food Network ever again?"

"Ha. I'm still stuck on do I really have to get out of bed? You feel good." He rolled onto his back and stretched out long, his shoulders and hips popping. That felt really good too. "Oh, yeah."

"Mmm." Sam sat up, hand sliding over his belly. "You need me to rub your shoulders?"

"Whoa." He sat up as well, surprised by how quickly his boy had done that and watched Sam for a second. "How's your head?"

"It hurts." That was clear and sure, wasn't it?

"You sat up too fast, sweetheart. You need to take it easy. Stay put—I'll get your meds." He climbed out of bed and brought the bag Brady had handed him at the hospital back along with the discharge instructions, which he skimmed through, quickly finding doses. "I probably should read these, hm?"

"Eh. Do I still need them?" Sam stood up, slowly moving his head, side-to-side.

He watched Sam move and got up, standing close just in case. "Well? Maybe not. You want to just try some Tylenol?"

"For now, yeah. If it gets bad, I'll tell you. I have to eat with the antibiotics." Sam moved pretty well, pretty stable. Excellent.

Just as well, the heavier pain meds made Sam sleepy and glassy-eyed. He followed his boy toward the bathroom. "Yes, I set those aside for after your bath. Unless you want to eat first. That's up to you."

"I'll have them after my shower. No problem."

"I'd really prefer if you sat in the tub today, Sam. Just humor me? I don't want to be trying to catch you if you lose your balance when you're slippery."

Sam gave him the strangest look; then, to his surprise, he got a wide, silly grin. "Wow. I haven't had a real bath since I was five. You sure you want to risk me not being able to stand up, once I get down there? Hell, are you sure you want to risk me moving into the hot water permanently?"

He tried to imagine a wee five-year-old Sam taking a bath, but it seemed easier to imagine six-year-old Sam stubbornly deciding he was done with them. "I can get you up more easily than I can keep you from going down. And the soak might do you some good."

He reached over and started the water, grinning. "I'm all out of bubbles, sorry."

"Damn. No boats either?" Sam grabbed a couple of towels and put them along the edge of the tub.

"Nope. And I can't even give you a cup because you're not allowed to dump water over your head." He laughed and pulled the bottle of Tylenol out, placing a couple on the counter. "Take those."

Sam slammed them back dry, then started pulling at the edges of the bandages, trying to peel them off.

"Hang on, I'll do it." He gently moved Sam's fingers away and pulled the tape up carefully, exposing the stitches, dried blood, and deep purple contusions. "Oh. That's pretty." He did his best to keep his expression neutral, but the look of his boy's injuries was more than a little shocking.

"Yeah. My hats will cover them for the most part, at least until my hair grows in." Sam sighed and looked in the mirror, lips tight for a second. "I hope that I hurt them back."

God, Sam's hat. Was there a right time to tell Sam it was gone? "Me too. That wrist makes me believe you did." He turned the tap off and tested the water. "If you like it hot, you're good to go."

"Yeah. I like it hot." Sam looked at his head again and sighed softly. "Man. I don't know...I got this. I'll be careful to wash and dry like they told me."

I got this meant...Sam wanted him to go? "You don't need help? Can you get in on your own?"

Sam looked at him, lips tight. Then Sam reached for him, holding on. "Tell me you don't think it's nasty looking?"

What was he supposed to say to that? It didn't look good. "Sweetheart, it looks like you survived something pretty scary. I'd rather look at that than the alternative."

Sam scoffed softly and stepped into the tub, squatting down into the water to grab the edges of the bath and sit without looking down. "Okay. That's my coping skill of the day. I'll crawl out tomorrow."

He sighed and sat on the edge of the tub. "That was a decent skill. I'd give it about a nine." He took Sam's hand. "Would you like some coffee? I can make some while you scrub. I'll come and help you with the noggin."

"Please. That sounds great." Sam squeezed his fingers. "Can I have a splash of milk?"

"I think I can manage that." Sam seemed like he needed a breath alone. He understood; they were going to be in one another's space for days, and however honest they wanted to be, there was still that face you put on even for a loved one. He leaned over, kissed his boy on the forehead, and stood. "I'll be right back."

Thomas made two cups of coffee, added cream, listening for sounds of splashing, of distress.

What he heard was nothing but silence.

He headed back in with coffee, finding Sam washing himself with his right hand, trying to clean the medicine and dried blood off that poor head.

Somehow it looked even worse now. Sam needed help, whether or not he would ask for it.

"Coffee." He took a quick sip of his and set both mugs down, grabbed a towel for Sam, and dried that wet right hand so it could hold a mug, then held out Sam's coffee. "My turn, you sip."

"I know it's gross." Sam drank deep, throat working hard, holding the mug carefully between hand and cast.

He sat on the edge of the tub and picked up the washcloth his boy had been using. "It is a bit. I've dealt with worse. Overflowing septic? Now, that's gross." He worked carefully, trying not to pull the stitches, cleaning all the goo off Sam's skin.

"Yeah. I hear you." Sam pulled the plug, letting the water out along with the detritus, and filled it up again.

He kept working, and by the time he was done, it looked better. Still purple, still stitches, but the blood and the ointment were all gone, and that actually did make a difference. It had to hurt, though, all his poking and messing with the skin.

He moved Sam's coffee to the counter, surprised the boy had actually finished it, and let the water out of the tub. "You think you can stand up and just get a quick rinse in the shower? I'll help."

There was some ointment and some gauze in the bag from the hospital. They could just cover it lightly; the boy probably didn't need a giant padded bandage anymore.

"Yeah. I can do it." Sam reached for him, balancing on the cast.

"You're going to break that, you know," he pointed out.

"I know. I'm not worried about it."

He sighed, helping Sam to his feet. Fine. As injuries went, what was a broken wrist to a rodeo cowboy? He'd let it go and fight the bigger battle, keeping Sam from overdoing it, making the boy rest, looking after that concussion.

"Yeah. If it gets irritating, you can just tear it off with your teeth." He winked at his boy, smiling, trying to lighten things up a little. "Super studly."

"You do get me, don't you?" Sam chuckled softly, reaching for him, balancing. "My brain feels like...I don't know. I don't quite feel like me yet. This is the worst one I've had."

He nodded. They said this needed to be the last one too. They'd discuss that soon. "Give it some time." He turned on the shower. "Want it warmer?"

"Please. Just a little." Sam was starting to wear out, to shake in his hands.

He let it get nice and hot, let it rain down on Sam's back,

careful to keep the boy's head and wrist out of the spray. He knew he needed to get Sam back to bed, but his boy was relaxing so nicely in the water.

When it seemed like enough, he got Sam out, dry, and took his boy to bed despite the weak protests.

"I'm so done with being in bed." Sam settled though, curling up under their blankets. "I want to go take you to breakfast. I want to love on you. I want to be better."

He understood Sam's frustration. "I promise you, sweetheart, I want those things too. We'll have it all back in time. You need to rest up so we can enjoy the energy you do have, right?" He propped some pillows behind Sam so he couldn't roll over; then he leaned in and kissed his boy's temple. "I love you. Rest. I'm here."

God, that was all his boy had the energy for? A bath? Sam didn't even get to eat anything. Well, that would be for the next time his boy woke up. He'd have something made and ready. He needed to fill his own time, anyway.

"I'm sorry. I don't remember what happened, but I should have been more careful." The words were whispered, so soft. "I'm not real good at careful."

Maybe it was time to fill Sam in on why he'd left the apartment that day in the first place. The boy didn't need guilt on top of everything else. "Sweetheart. Don't be sorry. I'm fine and I'm just happy you're home. We'll talk when you wake up again, all right?"

"Yeah. All right." Sam blinked at him, watching him for a few long breaths before he crashed, sound asleep.

He looked around the room. The curtains were still drawn, but he could see the daylight coming in now, and he was still in the clothing he'd been in the day before. He needed a shower, some food, and he wanted to text Mike, Angel, and Clint so everyone knew he and Sam were home.

There was laundry, and he had work phone calls to make. Lunch for Sam.

And he needed to figure out how and when to give his boy the rest of the details. He had plenty to keep him busy.

Assuming he didn't just crawl back in bed to hold his boy.

30

C hrist, his head hurt.

Sam stared at his computer, trying to make the shapes make sense to him. He knew he could read. He'd done it in the hospital, but it was dark and the screen was bright and the words were moving, totally without his permission.

He needed to order a phone. He needed to order a bunch of knit caps and a new Stetson. He needed to check his emails. He needed to get Momma to send him his birth certificate. He had his passport, so he was good there. He was pretty sure it was late, late Saturday night, early Sunday morning. Whatever it was, Thomas was sleeping, and the sun wasn't up.

"Come on, Sam," he whispered. "Come on. You know how to do this. You got this."

He needed to be a functional adult, dammit. He was already proving to be a worthless son of a bitch everywhere else. Soon Thomas wouldn't have any reason to keep him.

Sam frowned, the thought coming out of nowhere. What the fuck?

The office door opened slowly, and Thomas stuck his head in. "There you are." Suddenly there were arms around him, Thomas sighing against his neck. "Our bed is lonely, come back."

"Yes." He knew he had things to do, but nothing made sense. He turned in his chair and wrapped his arms around Thomas's shoulders. Thomas made sense.

Thomas pulled him right to his feet like he weighed nothing and led him to bed. "You shouldn't be looking at screens yet, Sam. They said at least a full week. You'll just give yourself a headache. Or...a bigger headache." He felt Thomas's chest vibrate with a soft laugh.

"Yeah. It's hard." He inhaled deep and let Thomas walk him as he focused on the soap and musk scent of his Sir.

"What were you trying to do?" Thomas sat him in bed and climbed up under the blanket. He moved right into the curve of Thomas's body, resting hard.

"I wanted to buy some knit caps, a phone. Get hold of Momma for my birth certificate. Buy a new Stetson for when I can wear it."

"Sure. We can do all of that in the morning. But I got you a phone; it's actually in the living room charging."

"Oh." He kissed Thomas's jaw. "You're good to me."

You're a worthless motherfucker.

He frowned and stiffened. What the hell? He was not. He knew better. Fuck a doodle doo, if he was going to start hearing voices because his brain was broken, he wanted good messages all in Ewan McGregor's accent, dammit.

"I knew you'd want to call your mom and get in touch with Bowie. It's bad enough you're stuck on your ass, you should at least be able to be in touch with people." Thomas ran a hand over him. "Are you all right? Do you need some more Tylenol?"

"I will, yeah, but I need this more." He wasn't sleepy, but he was exhausted to his marrow. "How are you doing?"

"Well, it's the middle of the night, but otherwise I'm fine." He felt Thomas smile against his forehead. "I got a surprising amount done yesterday. This working from home thing has its advantages. People don't interrupt me as often, and I can watch the History channel while I'm in a meeting."

"Oh, that sounds good. I go through a lot of music during the day. If I can't sleep, I stream weird MTV shows. They're like drugs."

"You're very used to living alone, hm?"

"Not at all, but I'm used to living in one room—my bedroom. The front room was Momma and Daddy's, so...I just stayed in my space, you know?" Did that make sense?

"Sure. I get it. What I meant was that you're not used to having someone you can wake up when you can't sleep. I'm a much better drug than MTV." Thomas laughed again, that chest jumping. Mister was in a good mood.

"That's true. I worry about waking you up. A lot. You should see me, sliding out of the bed so I don't bother you."

"You shouldn't worry at all. I bet you anything I'll figure out a way to get you back to sleep. Eventually. When I'm done with you."

Oh, wasn't that a fine idea? "Yeah? Because...that sounds way more fun than...shit, anything."

"Mhm. See what you've been missing?" Thomas tucked him in a little closer.

"Just trying to take care of you, honey." He snuggled in, the sound of Thomas's heartbeat strong and steady.

"I'm not used to that, not the way you do it. I like it. Thank you." Well, that felt good. To be appreciated. See that? Not so worthless after all.

Stupid brain.

"You're welcome. It matters to me, you know, that you have what you need, that you have someone that can take care."

Mister's chest lifted and lowered with a deep breath, the exhale sounding satisfied, or maybe...relieved. "I needed to hear you say that, boy. Thank you."

"I thought you knew. I tried to show you, swear to God."

"Oh, I'm sure you did. I did see it, I just didn't understand completely what was in your mind, and I wasn't sure how to ask you. I can be a little...obtuse. Anyway, it was good to hear it that way, from you."

"Good deal." Every time they figured something out, he felt that tension that held him ease a little more. "You're so warm."

"You feel relaxed; that makes me happy. In fact, at this moment, I feel pretty damn good, boy. And far too awake for middle of the night." Thomas kissed his forehead. "I think the hospital threw off my sleeping pattern. Maybe we should watch a movie."

"Hospitals are hard. We can do anything, if I can stay like this with you for a while." Just a while longer because this was perfect. Even with the stitches.

"Of course." Thomas's fingers traveled over his shoulder and down his spine. "How about forever?"

"Yes, please." He was all about forever. Possibly forever and a day.

READ the thrilling finale of the Cowboy and Dom series!

Interested in learning more about BA's cowboys and Jodi's gentlemen? Want free fiction and news? Join our newsletters!

What's Up with Jodi
https://readerlinks.com/l/2317334

Spurs and Shifters
https://lp.constantcontact.com/su/A9CRUzp/baandjulia

Hey, y'all!

We want to thank you for giving Razor's Edge a try. We hope you enjoyed the story and are looking forward to the next book in the series, No Ghosts.

If you can spare a few minutes to post a review at the retail website where you made your purchase, we'd very much appreciate it!

Don't forget to "like" our Facebook pages and groups to keep up with all the news--new releases, sales announcements, giveaways, sneak peeks-- and of course the rodeo pictures, coffee memes and just general fun. We'd love to have all y'all!

Yeehaw and thanks for reading!

BA & Jodi

THE COWBOY AND THE DOM

Book Three: No Ghosts

Months after his murder, it's time to give James his final sendoff. Sam takes Thomas, his Dom and lover, away from New York City on a vacation that includes a stop at Sam's family's home in Texas to meet his parents, and a visit the peaceful cemetery where James is buried.

Thomas is finally able to get some closure, but their time together is also an opportunity for Thomas and Sam to move beyond the past, let go of their baggage, and finally solidify their tumultuous relationship.

How will they get past the last roadblock to their happily ever after? Thinking he is doing what's best for his sub, Thomas has been keeping something from Sam, and Sam is sick and tired of everyone in his life knowing what's going on but him. It's the worst time for their trust to break down, because their final confrontation with James's killer looms, and if they want to walk away, they have to do it together.

Read No Ghosts now!

ABOUT JODI

JODI takes herself way too seriously and has been known to randomly break out in song. Her MCs are imperfect but genuine, stubborn but likable, often kinky, and frequently their own worst enemies. They are characters you can't help but fall in love with while they stumble along the path to their happily ever after. For those looking to get on her good side, Jodi's addictions include nonfat lattes, Malbec and tequila any way you pour it.

Website: jodipayne.net
Newsletter: https://readerlinks.com/l/2317334
All Jodi's Social Links: linktr.ee/jodipayne

ABOUT BA

Texan to the bone and an unrepentant Daddy's Girl, BA Tortuga spends her days with her basset hounds, getting tattooed, texting her grandbabies, and eating Mexican food. When she's not doing that, she's writing. She spends her days off watching rodeo, knitting and surfing Pinterest in the name of research. BA's personal saviors include her wife, Julia Talbot, her best friends, and coffee. Lots of coffee. Really good coffee.

Having written everything from fist-fighting rednecks to hard-core cowboys to werewolves, BA does her damnedest to tell the stories of her heart, which was raised in Northeast Texas, but has heard the call of the high desert and lives in the Sandias. With books ranging from hard-hitting GLBT romance, to fiery ménages, to the most traditional of love stories, BA refuses to be pigeon-holed by anyone but the voices in her head.

BA loves to talk to her readers and can be found at http://batortuga.com/ and her newsletter signup link is http://bit.ly/BAJulianews

AVAILABLE FROM JODI & BA

The Cowboy and the Dom Trilogy

First Rodeo, Book One

Razor's Edge, Book Two

No Ghosts, Book Three

The Soldier and the Angel, a Cowboy and Dom Novel

Sin Deep, a Cowboy and Dom Novel

East Meets Westerns

(single titles)

Wrecked

Flying Blind

Special Delivery, A Wrecked Holiday Novel

Temptation Ranch

The Merry Everything Series

Window Dressing

Cowboy Protection

The Higher Elevation Series

Heart of a Cowboy

Land of Enchantment

Keeping Promises

Bigger Than Us

The Triskelion Series